AN AGNES TAYLOR MYSTERY DUO

Absent Beauty & Silent Sands

EVA BERNHARD

EB PRESS

Books by Eva Bernhard

Agnes Taylor Mystery Series

Absent Beauty - Short Read Prequel

Silent Sands – Book 1

Writer's Death – Book 2

Snowbound – *A Holiday Mystery* – Book 3

Stormy Night – Book 4

Louise Penfold Mystery Series

Death at Rosewood Manor – Book 1

Death at Eagle Roost – Book 2

AN AGNES TAYLOR MYSTERY DUO

ISBN 978-1-0690966-9-2 (Large Print Paperback)

ISBN 978-1-7777877-6-9 (EBook)

ISBN 978-1-7777877-7-6 (Standard Print Paperback)

Cover Design by EB Press

Images under license from Stock.adobe.com (Cottage by the sea watercolor painting By Thye Aun Ngo) under license from Pixabay.com.

Copyright

Absent Beauty – Agnes Taylor Mystery - Short Read - Prequel © 2021 by Eva Bernhard

Silent Sands – Agnes Taylor Mystery - Book 1 © 2021 by Eva Bernhard

Interior Illustrations by EB 2025, AI generated in Nightcafé.

Editorial Services for both books by Pam Clinton (pam@pccProofreading.com)

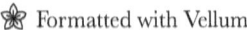 Formatted with Vellum

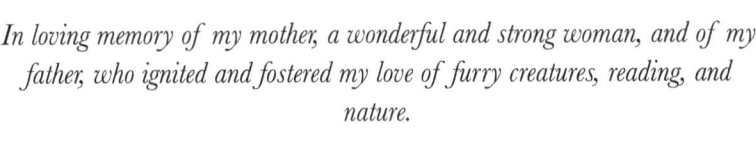

In loving memory of my mother, a wonderful and strong woman, and of my father, who ignited and fostered my love of furry creatures, reading, and nature.

AGNES TAYLOR MYSTERY

- SHORT READ - PREQUEL -

Absent Beauty

EVA BERNHARD

Absent Beauty

AN AGNES TAYLOR MYSTERY NOVELLA

By Eva Bernhard

Chapter 1

AGNES

No sight of her. Foggy mist wafted in from the sea. Or maybe from all those lakes and wetlands. Leaning further out, Agnes raised the binoculars again to scan the deserted street in both directions.

Frustrated, she lowered the vintage field glasses. A muffled thud caught her ears. A young woman hurried down the front steps of the crummy low-rise apartment building across the street. Masses of long, black corkscrew curls in disarray and baggy sweater askew spoke of a hasty departure.

Something about the woman did not seem right. As she reached the sidewalk, Agnes brought up the glasses in reflex. The unexpected close-up of a panicked expression stunned her. Dark eyes extended wide appeared huge—their whites contrasting with the velvety mocha of flawless skin. A hauntingly beautiful face—in evident agony.

Shocked by her own voyeurism, Agnes dropped the heavy binoculars. The girl, no more than early twenties, ran out into the road, skidding on the damp asphalt. Skinny legs in black leggings stuck in turquoise trainers virtually flew along the pavement.

About to retreat, Agnes hesitated. A movement straight

across caught her attention. To her dismay, someone else was watching. Then she realized the guy in a grubby undershirt paid no heed to her but stared after the girl, now almost out of sight. As he leaned out, his tousled dark hair fell onto an unusually high forehead. He pulled back, wiping his mustached mouth with his naked forearm. A lovers' quarrel then?

The sliding window banged shut just as the front door opened again. Still rooted to her spot, Agnes watched a skinny male in preppy clothes come down the steps. One hand hung on to the rickety wrought iron railing. Now on the sidewalk, he pulled off his glasses. Maybe they fogged up in the mist. Without stopping, he wiped them with his fingers and hastened after the girl. Or, at least, in the same direction.

Quite the morning entertainment, Agnes thought while shutting out the damp air. After only a brief exposure, her long, black-brown hair felt stringy as she reached up to twist it into a bun. Might as well have another coffee.

She went over to the minuscule kitchenette of the Airbnb hosted in a dilapidated, great-dame Victorian. Inexpensive—relatively speaking—and close to both downtown Halifax and the university area, it was okay for a few nights' stay. As she stirred powdered coffee creamer into her mug, the door burst open.

"Sorry, Angel! Am I late?" A panting Rachel crashed into the only easy chair. Lanky legs in skin-tight joggers stretched out wide, she grinned pleadingly.

"You've got exactly fifteen minutes, Ray. What with driving to campus and parking—If you make me late, I'll kill you."

"Whoa, Agnes. Keep your pants on. Hey, it's your own fault. If we were staying at your mom's, we'd be minutes from the college. And I could jog in Point Pleasant Park instead of this dreary neighborhood."

"Don't knock it. This area is perfectly decent and much closer to downtown," said Agnes. Hope the girl from across is okay, she added to herself. "Besides—you know Mom and I hardly ever see each other. Staying with her is more than I can cope with."

"C'mon, Angel. Aunt Sera is an awesome person. Isn't it time to let go of your old grudge?" With a noisy gurgle, Rachel swilled water from her bottle.

"So, I'm at fault, am I? You forget, Sera abandoned me—not the other way around."

"When you use her first name, I know it's serious," Rachel grinned. "But Agnes, don't be ridiculous now. Back in the day, she just had to accept that awesome professorship down here. You were what? Sixteen? Why didn't you move with her to Nova Scotia? I'm sure she wanted you to." One hand reaching up, she pulled the elastic at the nape of her neck to shake out shoulder-length blond locks now matted with sweat. "Hey, of course, I'm glad you remained in Toronto with my family instead."

Resentment built up like acid at Rachel's lack of empathy. They'd known each other from when they were in diapers. Okay, she'd already been potty trained when Ray was born. An involuntary smile twitched the corners of her mouth.

"Well, speaking of jobs. Just get ready, Ray. My colleague went out of his way to arrange for me to meet this Department Head from Saskatchewan. Don't want to blow it by being late." In further enticement to speed, she said, "Didn't you want to catch a paper this morning at your society's meeting?"

"Which one?"

"Whichever tickles your fancy today."

They both laughed. Eternal student, Rachel had finished a Master in anthropology and now pursued another one in art history. Both learned societies, just like Agnes's own philosophical one, were meeting at the Congress hosted by Halifax's Dalhousie University. Some of the attending scholarly societies chose the smaller colleges around town as venues.

"Are you meeting Aunt Sera for lunch today?"

"No. Mom texted to meet her tomorrow at the office and go to a bistro."

"Sorry that I can't join you. But hey, you'll both come to our keynote address tomorrow night, won't you? You'll love it. Professor Potter is a totally charismatic speaker. Tons of his talks are on YouTube. To meet him in person is like a dream come true."

"Yeah, sure, I can hardly wait." Curious, yet apprehensive, about his talk on ancient Greek vase paintings, she grumbled, "As long as he doesn't embarrass his audience with ancient porn… The things those satyrs got up to are not fit for public viewing."

"Oh, Agnes. You old prude. It's art."

Chapter 2

AGNES

"So, you're arguing it's okay to evade punishment and fight arrest?"

"Hold on. Not *I*," said Agnes with calm emphasis, "but Thomas Hobbes argues—"

"You're splitting hairs." The belligerent voice rose a notch. No longer sprawled back as he'd sat for the past half hour, the guy thrust his chin forward. "It's your paper."

"Before I respond, may I ask your name? Kind of awkward—"

"Call me Rex," he cut in.

"Okay, Rex, my paper discusses the implications of Hobbes's argument," Agnes explained patiently. "The philosopher claims that the natural right to self-preservation is inalienable. In other words, it can't be taken away from you," she added automatically. "Whether in a state of nature or in a civil society, trying to preserve our freedom and our life is our top priority. Hence, resisting imprisonment and execution stems from this natural desire for self-preservation. According to Hobbes—not *me*."

A burst of laughter penetrated the thin walls and diverted

her attention. The well-known presenter in the room next door —a philosopher from the States—drew a crowd.

Her own audience consisted of the obnoxious questioner and a silent young female. At least that one nodded and smiled encouragingly to everything Agnes said. One couldn't count the Chair of her session, who paid little or no attention and fiddled restlessly with the conference program. Nor the commentator Jamie who remained equally uninvolved. To give him credit, Agnes admitted to herself, he paid heed, judging by his alert expression.

"C'mon. You were the one to say that even jail-breaking is okay," insisted Rex. His arm brushed over his mouth as if to wipe away his sneer.

The gesture gave Agnes a sense of déjà vu.

Her eyes swerved to Jamie, who had read a bland commentary on her paper. Him, she'd recognized right away. The prep school dark-blue blazer over a spiffy white shirt and narrow burgundy tie—reminiscent of the outfit from yesterday morning —had given him away. That and the habit of cleaning his horn-rimmed glasses with his fingers.

Confirming her suspicion, the gadfly Rex swiped back his longish black hair to reveal a prominent forehead.

"Again, Rex, the paper is not about my personal opinion. All I did was to cite an example from Germany," and stupidly believe it funny, she groaned to herself. "They have no law against escaping from jail. So, you can't be punished for scampering. But they punish you for any damage caused in the process. Say, to property if you tunnel through the wall. Or for assault if you punch the guard's nose on the way out."

The girl giggled. Agnes smiled her thanks. At least someone appreciated her. Of course, attacking wardens wasn't a laughing matter.

"Well, if there are no other questions…" Bored, the Chair aimed to end their misery.

"Not so fast. I'm not done yet," said Rex. "Tell me. If I

commit a crime, no one can force me to admit to it. Isn't that what you claim?"

To prevent herself from committing one right then and there by strangling her tormentor, Agnes tugged her hands under her armpits. Who cares if it signals defensiveness, she thought.

"Hobbes, indeed, says that self-accusation under duress is null and void. Any confession obtained by force or torture is worthless. A threat of punishment counts as use of force. So, yes, only a voluntary confession counts."

"Thank you very much, Dr. Taylor," broke in the Chair. "A most illuminating talk. Please join me," his palms clapped listlessly, "in expressing…" The rest never came.

Tired and discouraged, Agnes shuffled her papers. Another waste of time, she sighed. This morning she'd woken up full of hope. Driving over from the Airbnb, she pictured a full house. Donned her one and only power-suit—a tailored outfit in anthracite gray with a light-blue linen shirt—for the occasion. Darling Ray had styled her hair into a neat French braid.

An audience hanging at her lips in rapt attention, Agnes fantasized as she marched into the building, ready to conquer. Yeah, right, the cynic in her jeered. Not after yesterday's fiasco.

As she stuffed loose pages, plus Hobbes's *Leviathan*, into her backpack, Agnes cursed her colleague, Austin. The meeting with the Department Head of a small university in Saskatchewan was a total write-off. Trust Austin to exaggerate their interest in her research. Within five minutes over coffee, it was clear that man had zero clue who she was. Nor did he care to find out. When Agnes introduced herself, his face looked blank. So much for making a good first impression. It certainly would not give her an edge when they finally posted the position in the history of philosophy, her area of expertise.

Not even Sera had shown up for her paper today. Well, thanks for small mercies. One less witness to her humiliation, she supposed. Glancing up, she saw Rex jabbering at a mute, red-faced Jamie in the hallway. Thunderous applause rose from next door. Her own room sat silent and empty.

Time to catch Sera and head for lunch. As if on cue, her phone vibrated.

An SMS from Sera.

S >Gwen's office in 204<

Change of plans then.

Chapter 3

RACHEL

"Got time for a coffee with us?"

With a smile, Rachel turned to Terry beside her and asked, "Who's us?"

"Me and two or three other girls were going to meet up in the Concourse at Timmies."

"Count me in," said Rachel as they left the room with another few stragglers who'd stayed to chat with the speaker after a talk on 'Women in Pompeian Art.' Happy to have been able to introduce herself and to ask a couple of questions, Rachel didn't mind leaving. The poor woman, a very kindly professor from a university on the Canadian West Coast, was still beleaguered by some other graduate students eager to network.

She knew Terry from a conference they'd both attended the year before. Though unlikely to become real friends, they'd kept in loose contact. Back when she and Agnes decided to attend the Congress in Halifax, she'd texted Terry to meet up. After all, this was Terry's home turf, and she was bound to be helpful in meeting people.

It took them only a few minutes to cross the green space surrounded by old buildings to reach the Concourse, a newer glass-and-steel addition. Inside, the usual fast-food outlets took up the inner space while tables and counters with barstools faced the window walls. Timmies—an endearment for the ubiquitous Tim Hortons, whose coffee and donuts no Canadian town or campus can do without—was hard to miss. At eleven in the morning, it had the longest lineup.

Finally, they were armed with paper cups of fresh brew, a blueberry muffin for Rachel, and a chocolate glazed donut for Terry. In no doubt where to find her friends, Terry led the way to the far end facing the Green. One of the girls caught sight of them and hollered to come over.

"Where've you been? We've been waiting for ages," a plump girl in tight leggings and an oversized orange-green sweatshirt said. In front of her sat a half-empty carton of Timbits, tiny bite-size donuts in various flavors and colors.

"Hey, I'm Rachel." Since Terry just plonked herself down without making any effort to introduce her, Rachel figured it best to do so herself. "I'm an art history MA from Toronto, here for the Congress."

"I'm Megan. Pleased to meet you," said a skinny girl in jeans and pink t-shirt with super-short hair dyed deep black. "And this," waving her cup in the direction of the chubby girl, "is Sam and," pointing to her other side, "this is Kathy."

"Nice meeting you all." Rachel smiled at each in turn. The last girl nodded at her and pushed up her glasses that promptly slid back down her narrow, freckled nose. Dressed in black slacks and an ironed white shirt with tiny blue flowers, her mousy-brown hair severely pulled back into a low ponytail, she advertised conservative propriety.

"So, what's up?" asked Terry while chewing her donut, chocolate coating both sides of her mouth.

"Didn't you hear what happened last night?"

Why Megan's question should make Sam break out in giggles, spewing a few bits of sprinkle topping, beat Rachel. By contrast, Kathy frowned in obvious disapproval.

"Do tell," drawled Terry and leaned back in her chair.

"After all the fuss she made, she didn't show up," said Megan with meaningful eye-rolling.

"What do you mean?" Lazy interest glittered for a moment in Terry's glance.

"Left him standing at the airport," chipped in the giggler, her cheeks red with merriment. Somehow, Rachel assumed it was a nervous habit rather than mirth. The small pale-blue eyes did not share the amusement but looked anxious.

"How do you know?"

"Tell her, Kath," ordered Megan.

Fingers busy rightening her glasses yet again, Kathy sat up straight as if readying to lecture the newcomers. "Dr. Martin called me early this morning to ask if any of us had heard anything from Tania." Then, with an almost imperceptible sideways nod at Rachel, she pursed her lips primly. "Perhaps we can talk later?"

As the other three shifted uneasily and avoided looking at her, Rachel became uncomfortably aware of being an outsider. With no clue who and what they were talking about but sensing some underlying excitement and even malicious glee, she thought it was time to part company.

Casually, she slid the rest of her muffin back into the brown paper bag and closed the tab on the lid of her coffee. "Sorry, guys," she said to their obvious relief. "There's another session I want to catch before lunch. Good to meet you all."

To Terry, who'd made no move to detain her, she added, "Catch you tonight at the keynote address."

For some reason, the last bit made the others exchange sly glances. What the heck is going on here, Rachel wondered.

Chapter 4

AGNES

From the outside, St. Raphael College impressed with a fieldstone façade. May just sliding into June, young ivy leaves crept up to the eaves. Inside, a paint job might help to brighten the dingy hallways, Agnes figured. The dimly lit office wing depressed her.

When she knocked, her mom let her in and shut the door right behind her. Used to an 'open door policy' at her own college, Agnes raised a questioning eyebrow.

"You must be Agnes. What a pleasure to meet you, finally," the woman behind the desk greeted her. In her sixties, she made no attempt to hide her age. The bobbed hair, streaked with gray, suited her attractive features. A strong chin and dark-blue hooded eyes commanded attention.

Now she rose, one hand stretched out in greeting. "I'm Gwen. Pull up a chair. Sorry to keep your mom from your date. I know how much she's looked forward to your visit. Something unexpected cropped up."

A sideways hug from Sera. "Glad to see you in Halifax—at long last. How did your paper go?"

"Don't ask. Not counting session chair and commentator, an audience of two, is all I can say. One of them, your typical class monopolizer." Belatedly, she realized Gwen—who was not only her mom's best friend out East but also the department chair—might know Rex. "Sorry—shouldn't complain."

"No worries, dear. There will be other times." Her mother's gaunt face crinkled into a smile. Slim and trim in straight black pants and forest-green turtleneck, she hadn't aged at all. Mandatory retirement scrapped years back, Mom's likely to go on teaching forever, Agnes mused.

Sensing the tension in the room, she asked, "Should I wait for you somewhere else then? Don't want to butt in if—"

"We were just discussing an issue that has upset our keynote speaker," said Gwen. She pointed to a chair for Agnes to sit. "The grad student who volunteered to pick him up last night didn't show up. It really isn't like her to let anyone down."

"Still," said Sera, "I'm convinced there must be a perfectly reasonable explanation. A mistake about dates?"

"Perhaps… How likely, though? After all, they've been emailing for weeks. I wasn't happy when she volunteered."

The look Gwen and her mother exchanged made Agnes wonder. Before she could stop herself, she asked, "Oh, why's that?" Embarrassed, she apologized, "None of my business…"

For a moment, they hesitated. Then Gwen said, "Tania is exceptionally beautiful," as if that explained things. The grimace Agnes inadvertently pulled made her go on. "Yes, it smacks of sexism. I absolutely agree. A person's beauty has nothing to do with her intellectual or practical ability. The concern for her safety in chaperoning a well-known professor from out-of-town might be ridiculous. In the end, I did not discourage her. She's a capable and sensible adult."

"You did say she hopes to do her doctorate under him," said Sera.

"From what she told me, he encouraged her to apply and raised her hopes." To Agnes, Gwen explained, "Tania is our star MA student. She's ready to defend her thesis later this month. With the graduate scholarship she has lined up, she is receiving admission offers from every Canadian doctoral program she applied to. After their email exchange, she now wants to apply to this place in Texas."

"Well, from the way he reacted last night, she blew it," put in Sera.

"What a shame." Sounds pretty disastrous, thought Agnes. "What happened?"

"As I mentioned, Tania did not show up. Her job was to meet Dr. Potter at the airport and drive him to the hotel. Apparently, they also had arranged to go for dinner. He called me late last night—around eleven. Completely outraged. From what I can gather, he waited for almost an hour. When she did not show, he took a limousine into town."

"La-di-da—quite in style," commented Agnes.

"Oh, he's a flamboyant character. Insisted on a suite at the Harborfront Hotel. We foot the bill."

"Must be nice to be so sought after," grinned Agnes. The fact of him being stood up gave her sardonic satisfaction. "Didn't you ask her—"

The door burst open to interrupt. A middle-aged woman, wrapped in a voluminous red cardigan over a rose-patterned dress, bustled in. Ash-blond hair escaped an untidy bun at the nape of her neck. Pushing her purple-rimmed glasses up her nose, she nodded at Agnes. Without further greeting, she blurted out, "I hear our stellar student screwed up royally. Whining her excuses, no doubt?"

"Theresa, may I introduce Sera's daughter Agnes? She's here for the Congress. Meet my colleague, Dr. Martin, Agnes."

The murmured 'pleased to meet you' received no response from the woman who eyed Gwen challengingly.

"Thus far, Tania has not responded. So unlike her. In fact, Sera and I were discussing matters."

"Probably went on a binge with her followers, I bet." The nasty tone conveyed contempt. "There's been nothing but unrest and bickering since she joined our program."

16

"As far as I can tell, Tania is a serious and sober student—both in character and habits," Sera said in measured tones. "And before you ask, Theresa, I saw much of her when she took my seminar in Art Appreciation and Aesthetics. At our little get-togethers, she only drank water."

The noisy harrumph left no doubt about Dr. Martin's view on fraternizing with grads.

"Any tension we experience arises from the latent racism of some people," Gwen said pointedly.

"Fiddlesticks. The girl leads on any male, whether student or faculty. You're just blind to it. Our female students have her sussed out and don't fall for that 'I'm just a sweet innocent' act. Just look at—"

"Enough, Theresa. You're entitled to—"

A loud crash stopped Gwen mid-sentence. This time a young man barged in.

Like a subway station at rush hour, Agnes grinned to herself. With interest, she viewed the newcomer who bent down to pick up several mega-sized hardcover art books. Hence, the bang, she deduced. The slight figure in jeans and marine pullover—pale-blue shirttails and cuffs sticking out—glanced up as Gwen spoke.

"Hi, Bao. Good thing you're here."

Before Gwen could say more, he blurted out, "I looked for Tania. All over. Is she here?"

"We were hoping you could tell us where she is, Bao. All morning I've tried to reach her. I realize her mobile's often turned off—when she's at the library or working. But still…"

"I called many times. SMS too. No answer. No one in her room."

"Did you see her last night?"

"No… Yesterday afternoon. Please help me find Tania."

A snort from Theresa drew Agnes's attention momentarily away from the pleading deep-brown eyes of the young man. His straight, black hair cut at a sharp angle fell into his face. The worried expression made her assume he must be a close friend of the elusive Tania.

"We're quite as eager to talk to her," Gwen assured him. "If you see her first, ask her to contact me right away. Why not check with people she hangs out with? Here, write down your number. I'll text if I hear from her."

"Thank you, Professor. I will." He scribbled on her writing pad. With a nod, he hugged his books to his skinny chest and left.

"Well, I ask you," commented Dr. Martin. "The cheek to interrupt a private conversation. No manners at all. But what do I expect?"

"Bao is anxious, Theresa." The censure in her mom's voice told Agnes her opinion of this colleague.

"He's Tania's boyfriend, Agnes," said Gwen. "I'd hoped he'd put us in touch."

"If this young fellow thinks he's her exclusive beau, his eyes will be opened soon enough. She has better fish to fry."

Sometimes I'm quite glad not to have a permanent job in a department, was Agnes' silent comment. There might be some gruesome murder if I worked here.

"Gwen, Agnes and I will go for a quick coffee before my committee meeting." Anxious to leave, they both got up while Sera spoke. "We'll see you tonight at the keynote address."

Chapter 5

AGNES

"Isn't he just fabulous?" Rachel's milky skin glowed as she chattered on, "Didn't you just love his talk? To me, he's the greatest art historian alive."

Yeah, if you like naked satyrs and nymphs gamboling on a huge screen, Agnes mutely commented. After a long day of attending philosophy talks, her energy was too low to feign enthusiasm for a keynote address in art history. Or it's envy of the flamboyant professor's charisma, her inner voice gibed.

Not to spoil Rachel's pleasure, she mumbled, "Very interesting speaker."

"Let's hurry, so we can meet him," said Rachel, urging her along to the faculty lounge for the keynote post-mortem.

Most of the large audience meandered over to crowd the room. Free drinks and finger food drew undergraduate and graduate students like sparrows to breadcrumbs. Profs and part-time instructors showed up mostly of necessity rather than from inclination. The noise level quickly rose. Snatches of conversation met them as they weaved their way through the refreshments.

Armed with orange juice for Agnes as designated driver and Rachel's white wine, they surveyed the crowd. Not expecting to see any familiar faces other than her mom and Gwen, the sight of Jamie and Rex surprised Agnes. Before she could decide whether to say 'hi,' her friend pulled her sleeve.

"Don't look. He's over there. We'll stroll by and wait for our opportunity."

No need to ask who. This evening's star occupied center stage in the middle of the gathering. A young female fan club tittered dutifully at his conversational gambits, Agnes noticed. Loath to become part of the group, she was torn. The keynote address had thoroughly embarrassed her. Sexually explicit material aired in public made her cringe. Art or no art. To compliment him on his talk filled her with dread. Abandoning Rachel would wound her friend. So, she gritted her teeth and followed like a lamb.

Still at the fringe of the groupie throng, Agnes caught her mother's eye off to the side and, with a little jut of her head at Rachel's back, rolled her own. Parental telepathy divined her SOS. Not missing a beat, Sera left her current conversation partner with a few words that made the undergrad beam.

A moment later, she materialized at Prof. Potter's side and drew his attention to Rachel's and Agnes's approach.

"Fred, may I introduce my daughter, Dr. Taylor. She teaches philosophy."

Quite obviously, Sera must have chatted with Potter prior to his talk to address him by first name, Agnes figured. The use of her last name and title, however, indicated an arm's length approach, if not disapproval. The man's smarmy tone and effusive greeting explained why.

"A philosopher! How delightful. Always a pleasure to see a young female storm our male strongholds." The pressure of his fingers enclosing hers, accompanied by appraising scrutiny, caused Agnes to pull back.

Her mom covered her gaffe adroitly. "Meet my goddaughter Rachel Jones, an art historian like you."

"Oh, I'm still an amateur, doing an MA," a blushing Rachel hastened to correct.

Her sweet voice and lovely features conquered the great man. To Agnes's relief, Potter turned his full charm on Ray. Within seconds the two were deeply immersed in art talk.

As Potter slowly steered Rachel out of the circle, murmuring an excuse to Sera about lending an ear to this promising grad student, his disappointed admirers dispersed. From across the room, Gwen signaled for Sera to join her.

"Sorry, dear. You don't mind if I leave you to your own devices," said her mom and heeded the mute call.

Abandoned yet again, Agnes scanned the lounge for company. To work the room was not her kind of thing. Countless department parties taught her to focus on shy people who appreciated someone taking the first step. Like Jamie—now on his own—stuffing himself at the refreshment table.

An empty paper plate in hand, she sidled up to him and reached for some strawberries. The brownies tempted her—too sticky for an icebreaker, she decided.

"Aren't those delicious? I adore strawberries," she lied, waving one at Jamie. "How did you like the talk?"

"*Umm*—not my kind of thing..." The bespectacled eyes darted at her only to drop again to his plate, laden with brownies and chocolate chip cookies. Left hand grabbing a napkin, he draped it over as if to hide the loot.

"Yeah, I know what you mean." Not your most inspired small talk gambit, she admitted. Think of something more personal. "Oh, by the way, we're neighbors—sort of."

An uncomprehending glance met hers. So she continued, "Caught sight of you across the road. Rex too. My friend and I are in the blue clapboard Victorian—an Airbnb."

For some reason, that made things worse. The lights caught on his glasses when his head shot up. "When?"

"Yesterday morning."

A twitch of his mouth said, 'snoop.'

"Hey—don't get me wrong. My friend kept me waiting. Didn't want to miss my appointment and happened to be at the window checking for her." Why the heck am I justifying myself? Nonetheless, she couldn't stop. "Saw Rex's girlfriend leaving, all frazzled, and then you and—"

"She's not his girlfriend!" The vehement voice—rising over the general babble—toned down right away when some heads turned. "He's her English tutor." Pride sneaking in, he reddened as he boasted, "I coach her in aesthetics."

Not giving Agnes a chance to reply, he mumbled, "Excuse me," and made for the exit. Both hands clutched his load of sweet treats to his narrow chest.

Ends up with gooey chocolate icing all over his preppy blazer, Agnes thought and looked for her next victim.

Chapter 6

RACHEL

"Let me top up your glass and find a quiet spot for a tête-à-tête," said Potter while tipping the wine bottle for a refill.

Without waiting for Rachel's agreement, he led the way to a mustard green two-seater sofa wedged in a corner, partially concealed by a couple of dusty, artificial palm plants.

"Have a seat," he urged her and made himself comfortable facing her from the other end. Rachel cradled her glass with both hands and drew in her legs to avoid touching his knees.

"Away from these noisy people, the chatter is bearable, don't you think? Now I can lend an ear without constant interruptions." His eyes sought hers before he asked, "Are you a student here?"

"No, I just came for the Congress. I'm—"

"Ah, yes. You didn't strike me as someone who would enjoy these backwaters. Where are you from?"

"Toronto—Ontario," Rachel added, just in case it didn't mean anything to him. "Torontonian born and raised, and also where I'm doing my MA."

"Interesting. My own family hails from Boston. We came over with the Mayflower, of course."

The proud lift of the chin, as if he himself had been on the famous ship's maiden voyage, brought an involuntary smile to Rachel's lips. To hide it, she said, "Oh, I envy you. For a historian, that must be a wonderful heritage."

Gratified, he agreed, "Yes, my family's history is endlessly fascinating. We still own large estates in various parts of the country." He raised his glass and swirled its content contemplatively. Assessing her over its rim, he said, "So, I take it, you do not know the students at this…place?"

Her hesitation—she was thinking of Terry—seemed to satisfy him. For, he continued, "It has been a great disappointment to me. One of their graduate students appealed to me via email to take on her PhD supervision. I've devoted a considerable amount of my valuable time in correspondence with her. And what are the thanks I get?"

His expectant look made Rachel squirm as though she herself had failed in gratitude. Uncertain, she gave a little shake of her head.

"Stood me up at the airport! A no-show."

While he voiced his outrage, Rachel was putting two and two together. This must be the person the girls discussed at Timmies. Instead of letting on that she'd heard about it, she judged that her full attention and commiseration might be preferable to him.

"I'm so sorry. What happened?"

"Well, of course, no fault of yours." He smiled but then grew serious. "This young woman was to meet my flight last night and convey me to my hotel. To make up for any inconvenience and to show myself grateful for the service, I had extended an invitation to dinner. I'm not accustomed to being stood up, as I told the organizer last night in no uncertain terms."

Glad to have learned a lot about smoothing the waves on her travels to far-flung places with her dad—a classics professor with a penchant for archeological digs—Rachel made appropriate soothing sounds. "That must have been terribly inconvenient for you. Such a shame after all the trouble you took."

Mollified, his mood changed. With a charming smile, he assured her, "I'm sure you would never be so inconsiderate. Now tell me about your own plans. You must be eager to join a first-rate PhD program. Maybe I can lend a helping hand there."

Her own misgiving about her potential, and even desire, for the highest academic credentials momentarily forgotten, Rachel felt pleased to have gained his interest. Demurely, she clasped her hands in her lap and murmured, "That would be wonderful. Your work is so fascinating and intriguing."

"Well, well," he cautioned. "We have to see. Certainly, I'm willing to act as a mentor to such a promising young lady. To decide if I can take on your supervision, we have to get to know each other much better." His glance took in her person head to toe.

She thought she heard him say, "I think you'll do," but couldn't be quite sure. Flattered, she sat up straight and composed her face into a studious expression. The one she reserved for interviews or other important occasions. To impress an eminent scholar like Potter would open any number of path-ways for her future.

"I wonder…" Eying her speculatively, he hesitated. "Maybe… Perhaps better not," he ended more decisively.

At a loss to guess what she might be missing out on and disappointed that he'd changed his mind, she asked timidly, "You were about to say? Sorry, I don't want to intrude on your thoughts, but…" Unsure how to continue, she stopped.

He took his arm from the back of the sofa where it had rested for the past minutes and bent toward her confidentially. His glance searched her face as if to determine if he could trust her.

Very softly, he said, "You are a serious student eager to learn and to discover new things, aren't you?"

The proximity and his earnestness made her slightly uneasy. His eyes mesmerized her. Thrilled by his allure, yet anxious about measuring up, she stammered, "I…I think…so. At least… I hope I am."

Satisfied, he leaned back. "Yes, I believe you'll do. The reason why I hesitate—and this is strictly between you and me," he interjected sternly, "I've made groundbreaking discoveries. It will be sensational when I publish it. Thus far, I've only shared my discoveries with a small intimate circle." Again, he ceased speaking to assess the effect on her.

Spellbound and hardly breathing, as if entranced by a snake charmer, her eyes grew wide. It elicited a smile that she could not interpret.

Not breaking eye contact, he got up, saying, "Okay, let's go. I flatter myself to recognize true academic material at a glance. And you are it. A sample of the exhibits waits at my hotel."

He held out his hand to help her up. "Mind you, don't expect me to give you more than a glimpse for now. It'll be a real treat for someone as eager as you are."

Chapter 7

AGNES

No chance of prying Rachel away from her catch for the next little while, Agnes supposed as she aimlessly wandered along the fringes. Then, her eyes lit up. Behold, she quipped, there stands Rex, my foe—glass in hand, otherwise unoccupied. Now's the time to inquire about the motive of his questioning.

On her way over, she tossed her plate into the only available trash bin, with a pinprick of guilt for not being able to recycle.

"Hello again," she greeted him. The blank look indicated he'd forgotten all about her. Chagrined, she introduced herself. "Thanks again for your interesting questions on my paper this morning. Much appreciated you taking the lead." Yeah, right, obnoxious quibbler.

Raised eyebrow—making the forehead grow in height—told her he wasn't buying it. The lip curled in disdain. No response.

"Do you have any special interest in the topic, Rex? Of course, I was delighted to have someone so keen on discussing —" Too late. His glance went over her head to the door behind her. Clearly, he wasn't listening to any word she cared to utter.

"Where is Tania?" a familiar voice broke in from the back.

Startled, Agnes swung around. Upset and slightly disheveled —shirt now completely crumbled hanging loose under the sweater, hair sticking out as though pulled once too often by nervous hands—Bao's stare challenged Rex.

Instinctively, Agnes stepped out of the way.

"What are you asking me for?" drawled Rex.

"You always hang around her. Tania's my girlfriend!"

"Pipe down, buddy. I teach her proper English. That's my job—you hear?" To drive his point home, he jabbed the forefinger of his muscular hand at Bao's chest.

"You teach her today?"

"No, I did not. Maybe you should book some grammar lessons for yourself." With this parting shot, the tutor strode to the door.

"Don't mind him," Agnes tried to soothe away the insult. The flash of hatred on Bao's lean face disturbed her. When his eyes readjusted to her, it was replaced by anguish. To help him focus on more practical matters, she asked, "Any luck with Tania's friends?"

"Lisa don't like me. I ask. She never—"

"Who's she?"

"Roommate. Tania and Lisa are best friends."

"What about others? Or her family? Did you call Tania's people? Maybe she went home. Family emergency, or something."

"Has no one. Can't go home. She—like me. International student. No money to—how you say?—hop on flight."

"Classmates? Did you ask any of them?" As an MA student about to defend her thesis, she might not take any classes at this point. Most university students took the summer term off anyway, Agnes reminded herself.

The boyfriend shook his head despondently—the long, angled fringe falling down to the tip of his well-shaped nose. For a second, Agnes contemplated him, admiring the noble, chiseled features. Then chided herself for being frivolously distracted.

As if tuning in on her aesthetic mindset, he said apropos of nothing, "Tania is so beautiful." To prove his point, he fiddled with the mobile he'd been clutching in his hand like a lifeline.

The photo he proffered stunned her. Not merely the outstanding loveliness of the face smiling at her from the screen —but recognition. No doubt possible. The sharp image glimpsed through the binoculars had been the same—minus the smile. Distress had not diminished the beauty.

Lost for words, Agnes stalled for time.

Perhaps misjudging her silence, Bao insisted fiercely, "She is beautiful!" Then more gently, "She says, she is not. But me, I'm an artist. I take a photo and tell Tania, 'You look at it every day. Then you see your beauty.'"

Her mind in a whirl, Agnes tried to decide. To tell the boyfriend where she saw this face would be cruelty. Besides, he knew she went to Rex for tutoring. The brief acquaintance with Rex told her anyone might be upset after a session with him. After all, Jamie left with her. Or right behind her. Perhaps he knew where she went…

Shaking off the stray thoughts, she murmured, "A lovely face."

Chapter 8

RACHEL

"You won't mind if I take a quick shower, will you?" Not waiting for her response, Potter strode to a door leading toward the bedroom of the hotel suite. "After a few hours on a strange campus, I feel grubby and in need of freshening up. Turn on the TV to keep you company."

"No worries," Rachel hastened to assure him. "I'll be fine. This is a beautiful place to relax in after a long day."

With a little wave, he closed the bedroom door.

The hotel suite he occupied was, indeed, rather luxurious. Used to all kinds of ill-appointed quarters while traveling with her dad to far-flung places away from cities and any sort of tourist amenities, Rachel appreciated luxury as a special treat.

Earlier, her exclamation, "How awesome!" as they entered his living room had prompted a tour of the entire suite. A peek into the en suite bathroom revealed marble tiles and a raised whirlpool tub for two. Its elegance put the other small bathroom off the entrance hallway to shame. The spacious bedroom had a king-size bed and tasteful, modern décor.

Now she made herself comfortable on the broad couch and flipped through programs on the flat-screen TV. On an intimate dining table stood the tray that room service had delivered soon after their arrival. He must have called them while she used the washroom near the main door. A bottle, clothed in a pure-white napkin, waited in a silver cooler. Champagne flutes next to it betrayed what it held. The rest of the tray also was shrouded by white linen.

For a moment, Rachel was tempted to jump up and lift the cloth but resisted. Somehow, she suspected that he'd be seriously disappointed later if her ahs and ohs did not convey genuine surprise at whatever treat he had in store for her.

Eventually, she settled on an episode of *Beauty and the Beast* and became absorbed in Cat's and Vincent's romance…

Chapter 9

AGNES

Just when Agnes felt at a loss how to extricate herself from a sticky situation without offending the young man, Sera's voice came to the rescue.

"We'd better get going, dear—I'm sorry, Bao. Didn't mean to butt in. Are you okay?"

Instead of a reply, he gave a quick shake of the head and stormed out.

"Far from it," answered Agnes in his place. "Still no sign of Tania. Rather upsetting for him. Maybe she's staying away on purpose. Lover's tiff."

"Doesn't sound like her. From what I've seen of her, she's too caring a person to cause him gratuitous anxiety. Speaking of vanishing acts, though, have you seen Rachel? Dinner reservation's in half an hour, and we need to head downtown."

"Still talking to that charmer, I guess?"

"Can't say I spot either of them," said Sera as she scanned the room. Then, she waggled her raised arm to some purpose. A grad student, who evidently belonged to the event organizers, joined them. Asked, he told them that the great man had left fifteen minutes earlier in the company of a female. The description sounded like Rachel.

"I'll grab my bag from the office while you text her to meet us outside," instructed her mother.

"She can meet us at my car. Or are you taking yours?"

"No, I walked this morning. Front entrance in five," Sera called back over her shoulder and was gone.

Thumbs happily texting while strolling down the hallway, Agnes almost collided with the banister at the top of the stairs. Good thing. For Rachel's reply might have made her miss the steps and break her neck.

R >At Fred's hotel. Wanna see newest research.<
A >Are you nuts??? Leave! now!!!<

No response.

A >Answer me!!<

"What's wrong, Agnes? Why are you stamping your foot like a toddler?"

A gentle hand touched her forearm, alerting Agnes to Sera's return. Frustrated, she vented to her mom, "She's not answering. I'm so ticked off."

"Aren't you overreacting, dear? Maybe Rachel is in a part of the building with poor reception. These old—"

"No—read this," said Agnes, pushing her phone into Sera's hand. Before her mother could comment, she let off steam, "Marches off with a total stranger to his hotel. Newest research, my foot. Might as well say, stamp collection."

They made for the parking lot and got into the car. As they weaved their way through side streets at Sera's direction, Agnes fumed on.

"Let's not get overexcited, Agnes. After all, Potter is an eminent figure in his field. Rachel mentioned she hoped to network and build a relationship. You know how important that is for her professional future."

"Putting herself into compromising situations is not going to help. The man gave her the once-over the moment you introduced her."

"Oh, I agree. Not very prudent. Well, once we're at the restaurant, you can text her to come on over. A five-minute walk from the Harborfront, and she'll be with us before the food arrives."

The Moroccan restaurant owner bustled up to greet them at the door. Evidently a frequent customer, Sera received VIP treatment. The table for four—tastefully laid with white dinnerware, sparkling glasses, and flickering candles—complemented the natural stone and wood decor.

Her mom's, "Omar, meet my daughter Agnes," led the distinguished-looking owner to treat her with instant warmth. Asked by Sera, "What do you recommend today?" he unleashed a plethora of choices.

With few exceptions, like couscous and samosa, the names meant nothing to Agnes. On her precarious income, eating out usually meant grabbing something from an inexpensive take-out or some tiny place around Toronto's Kensington Market.

Overwhelmed by the embarrassment of riches, she delegated ordering to her parent. Left to her own devices, she would have taken far too long in questioning Omar on the composition of each and every option.

In no time, an appetizer selection arrived, tempting her to gorge. Between bites of spicy deep-fried cauliflower, she read out aloud Rachel's response to her latest text.

R >Start without me. I'll join you later.<

"Well, she probably can't just up and leave, now that she went along," remarked Sera as her own phone vibrated.

A glance at its screen, and she added, "Seems we're on our own. Gwen says she's being held up."

Despair mounting, Agnes stared at the two vacant place settings. How very awkward. She'd been counting on Ray—and her mother's friend—to ease them through the evening. The rare times she'd met up with her mom over the last decades proved exercises in tightrope walking. Both anxious to avoid any topics with the potential of rupturing their fragile truce left little to talk about. Or so it always seemed to Agnes. Sera's customary poise showed no cracks.

A sip of her wine—watered down with Perrier since she was driving—gave her courage. "Any plans for the summer? You're off until September, aren't you?'

"June, I'll stick around—gardening and sketching. For July, Gwen and I are booked on a trip to Ireland, followed by a week in London to raid the museums."

"Sounds like fun—"

"Excuse me," Sera interrupted with an apologetic smile as her mobile's vibration was magnified by the wooden tabletop.

Her expression sobered while reading. "Sorry, dear. Speaking of the devil," she aimed for a light tone. "Gwen again. Some news about Tania."

While her mom texted a response, Agnes wrote a furious message to Rachel.

A >Hurry up!! If you desert me, I'll never forgive you.<

This time the reply arrived in seconds.

R >Can't leave now. He's taking a shower.<
A >What???<
R >Cool it. Poor guy was grubby after his talk and needed to freshen up.<

"They found Tania's body," said her mom, stunned.

Chapter 10

AGNES

Distracted, Agnes placed her own phone screen-down next to her plate. "What do you mean? An accident?"

Fingers spread out, her mother hesitated. "More serious, I fear. Bao's held for questioning. Gwen's on her way to the station to arrange legal aid and lend her support. She looks out for our international students and took him under her wings when he joined us last fall."

"Not him—surely? The way he talks about his girlfriend—and he was so upset…"

"After all, you've barely met him at Gwen's office."

"Remember, I talked to him at the get-together earlier. He was desperately searching for her. Why would he—" The answer popped into her mind while speaking. Of course, he would pretend to search if he'd harmed her.

"Oh, I agree. My impression is he genuinely cares for her. Admittedly, his temper at times flares up. A true artist with a promising career but sensitive to criticism. In class, he lashes out when he feels snubbed by a peer or mocked for his English. He's fluent in French—did his BA in Montreal. Needless to say, we step in instantly if students act out."

"Still, I can't believe…" Should she tell Sera what she saw the other morning?

Their waiter interrupted to announce their Harira, a delicious smelling tomato-lentil soup. A whiff of cumin and cinnamon filled the air.

Her mom exchanged a few words with Hakim. Only after he'd left, she asked, "What's on your mind, Agnes?"

Reluctantly, Agnes told her what she'd observed the day before.

"What's the connection to Tania? You've never met her."

"Bao showed me her photo on his phone. Such a stunning face—hard to forget and easy to recognize no matter the expression."

"I see." Lost in thought—spoon held aloft—her mother scrutinized a spot above Agnes's head.

"Don't you think one of them is a more likely candidate if something happened to the girl? If no one has seen her after yesterday morning, I mean. Mom, if you'd seen her face— totally distraught it looked close-up." To admit to her mother that she'd used binoculars had been the hardest part. Like a peeping Tom—she blushed at the memory.

"We can't be sure who saw her when. No one checked. Everyone assumed it was merely a question of failing to pick up Fred Potter."

"Yeah. Still, she must have been somewhere between the morning and the no-show. Jamie followed her. Or at least hastened in the same direction." Better not go out on a limb, Agnes cautioned herself. "Personally, my money would be on Rex, though. The girl was distraught after seeing him. Smug and openly insulting to Bao —" Entangled in her own faulty logic, Agnes stopped short.

"Let's not get ahead of ourselves," said Sera. "Although—"

"What? C'mon, Mom, don't hold out on me," prompted Agnes when the other broke off.

"Only gossip and rumors—I'd be loath to share. Lots of girls have a crush on him, but... Suffice it to say, Rex's reputation around campus—"

Whatever she might have added remained unsaid as another text drew her attention.

Spoon after slow spoon lifted to her lips, Agnes observed her parent. Somehow the deliciously flavored broth was devoid of taste.

"I apologize for dragging you into this, Agnes. And for ruining our meal." Her mom half rose as she spoke. "Need to call Gwen. Be right back." Napkin discarded on her chair, Sera made for the exit.

With a clatter, Agnes dropped the utensil. Talk about a screwed-up evening.

The noise attracted Hakim.

"Finished with the soup?" The glance he gave her conveyed disapproval for leaving the last third untouched.

"Delicious. Please tell the Chef, Hakim. Just one of those nights. A bit of a problem with a friend."

Commiserating, he tut-tutted. "Should I hold off the next course until your mom's back?"

"Yes, please do. We're so sorry. The food and the place are marvelous."

With a satisfied nod and graceful smile, he whisked away their bowls.

Of its own accord, Agnes's hand toyed with her phone, her thumb choosing to unlock the display. The last SMS stared back at her. What on earth was Rachel playing at. Better tell her...

A >Serious developments re Tania - put your ass into gear<

The speed of the response gratified.

R >??<
A >Tell you when you get here<

No point in giving it all away. Curiosity might spur willful Ray into action.

R >Can't just walk out. We got on so well.<
A >Leave him a note. Say an emergency<
R >Ok. Need some paper<
A >Hotel pad check drawer<

Chapter 11

RACHEL

Reluctant to abandon Cat in a dicey spot of trouble, Rachel hit the 'off' button on the remote. The reality of the hotel room almost came as a surprise.

A glance at her mobile's clock. Potter really took his sweet time. Kind of audacious to keep a guest waiting. Despite his charm, maybe he belonged to the breed of profs who liked to remind grad students of their place in the academic pecking order.

With a sigh, Rachel uncurled herself from the couch and scanned the room. She felt torn. If she took off, her host would be offended. Being kind of stood up twice in twenty-four hours most likely would make him hit the roof. She'd be doomed to the same fate as the elusive no-show. Rank number one on Potter's blacklist.

The alternative would be to let down Agnes. At the thought, a hot wave of anger rose. Why did Agnes have to be so difficult? Most of the time, she was great fun. Lately, her job hunt made her grumpy. Then again—Rachel smiled ruefully— from their childhood onward, Angel suffered from occasional bouts of the mothering bug. Two years Ray's senior, she acted at times as if it were a twenty-year gap.

Rachel's eyes alighted on the desk near the curtained window. Might as well get it over with, she sighed. One hand on each twin desk drawer, she pulled them open and skimmed their content. The one to the right held a Halifax phonebook and a folder. Opening the latter revealed emergency numbers, restaurant menus, and all kinds of information shielded by plastic sleeves.

Her glance veered to the left and brought her up short. Side by side, inside the other drawer sat a mobile phone, face down, and a pinkish-purple lace bra. The sight made Rachel jump back as if she'd spotted the man's own undies. Without thinking, she pushed the drawer shut and listened for a sound from the bedroom. Still nothing.

Well, it's his own fault if he makes me wait for ages, she told herself. Grateful that the hotel had invested in quality material, she noiselessly eased the drawer open again. For a moment, she stared at the cell, encased in a feminine, pink protective cover.

A little further back, she glimpsed the obligatory hotel stationery, complete with a pen. About to grab it, she stopped. Of its own accord, her left hand moved to her back pocket and pulled out her phone. She unlocked it and snapped a pic of the revealing items in situ. A smile on her face, she included it in a text to Agnes.

R >Look what I found<

Her grin broadened while she waited for a reaction. Meanwhile, she slipped the writing pad and pen onto the desk surface and combed her mind for diplomatic phrases to justify her sudden departure.

Again, her glance strayed to the drawer content. The mobile's pink casing sported a delicate flower pattern. Not a likely choice for a he-man like Fred. Must be his girlfriend's. Rachel pulled a face.

The vibration of her own cell diverted her attention.

A >Rachel! You're snooping<

Figures. Angel would accuse her regardless of being the one to instigate the search for stationary. She bit her lips to cut off the oath they were about to shout. Her thumbs flew over the keys.

R >Not my fault if he keeps his girlfriend's undies in the desk!<
R >You told me to<

She stopped for breath. What made her think Potter had a girlfriend with him? There was no sign of another occupant. Maybe he had not opened the drawer at all—who uses stationary, anyway? Or the cleaning staff was sloppy. While puzzling this out, she fired off another SMS.

R >Perhaps from a previous guest<

Chapter 12

AGNES

Agnes stared at her phone. The message included a photo of the inside of a drawer. Bewildered, Agnes tapped it and used two fingers to enlarge the details. As expected, a hotel stationery pad. So what? In front of it, a mobile's back. A puzzling object confronted her as she moved the image. Part of a lacy bra in mauve. What the heck?

A >Rachel! You're snooping<
R >Not my fault if he keeps his girlfriend's undies in the desk!<
R > You told me to<
R > Perhaps from a previous guest<

"Bad news, I'm afraid, Agnes," interrupted Sera and sank back onto her chair.

"Mom, Rachel is— Sorry, what did you say?"

"Things don't look good for Bao. Please remember, this is absolutely confidential." When Agnes's hands flew up—palms down—in reflex reaction, Sera appeased her. "Yes, of course, you realize—"

Their waiter's reappearance in her line of vision stopped her.

"Everything alright, Sera?" he asked in low tones to avoid alerting other patrons.

"No worries, Hakim. A little matter at campus that requires my attention. Just give us a moment to decide whether to switch to take-out. My apologies."

With assurances to let them sort things in peace, he withdrew.

Not wanting to rush her mother, Agnes did her best to suppress her fingers' urge to drum the tabletop. On autopilot, her mind grappled with potential complications of driving her mom back to campus and Rachel being on her way over to the restaurant. The way the evening played out, further screwups wouldn't surprise her.

Of their own accord, her hands grabbed some strands of hair that escaped the braid as if to pluck them out. Instead, she looped them back behind her ears.

Only when Hakim disappeared through the swinging door into the kitchen did Sera bend forward to continue.

"None of this is to go further, for now, Agnes." A deep sigh, "By tomorrow, some of it will be public knowledge, I fear.—The info comes via Gwen's former partner who's with the police. They've remained close friends, and quite naturally, she immediately contacted him. So, you understand, he went out on a limb in sharing details."

Resigned to a longer lecture, Agnes nodded. As academics, they both valued the need for confidentiality. Yet, no one had illusions about insider knowledge remaining within the inner circle for long.

Again, making sure no one was close enough to overhear, her mom leaned in. "Barring contrary post-mortem evidence, it appears Tania was strangled and dumped into the outer harbor at Point Pleasant."

Shocked, Agnes sat back, trying to digest this. "Horrible, that poor girl," she whispered.

Her agile mind outpaced her emotions. Eyes scrunched, she frowned. "But what's the connection to Bao?" When her mom sighed wearily, she insisted, "Sounds like a random assault to me. Isn't that a park area? Ray mentioned something about jogging trails out by your place."

"Yes, of course. And you're right, Point Pleasant is popular with runners and walkers. It's a wooded, narrow land tongue crisscrossed by trails and has gorgeous views onto the bay."

"Anyone might attack a woman alone in a park. Why suspect the boyfriend? Someone beautiful like her might be in far more danger from creeps. After all, during low season and with the crappy weather yesterday, not too many people go to parks. Beats me why she would."

"Tania is—was—keen on jogging. Not sure if out at the Point," her mom said.

"Then why is Bao in trouble?"

"Because of what Lisa told police. She's—"

"Yeah—he mentioned her—the roommate, isn't she? Apparently doesn't like him."

"In any event, Tania and Bao had an argument yesterday afternoon. Or, more precisely, she claimed they were 'fighting.' Seems he had one of his fits of temper and yelled at Tania and smashed some dishes. They were Lisa's and—knowing Lisa—I assume she got into the shouting match too."

"Any couple might argue once in a while. Doesn't mean they end up killing each other. Maybe it was just about who left the kitchen in a mess." Her own vehemence in defending a guy she hardly knew brought a flush to Agnes's cheeks.

"Well, no. Jealousy was at issue. From what Gwen says—and she got it straight from Lisa who heard the quarrel firsthand—Bao resented Tania volunteering to pick up Potter."

"Big deal. Surely no one murders for that."

"It went deeper, Agnes. For weeks Bao grew increasingly angry at Tania's email exchange with Fred. Before all this arose, they spoke of applying for permanent resident status in Canada. Tons of international students plan to do so once they finish their degrees. I imagine Bao realized that her move to Texas might jeopardize their relationship. As students on a tight budget, they couldn't afford to jet-set forth and back to visit each other. We all thought she was idolizing Potter. A boyfriend might feel wounded and threatened by such hero worship of a charismatic man twice his age."

"Wait—at least the roommate's testimony tells us Tania was still alive later in the day," said Agnes. Come to think of it, so did Bao's—she mused. His claim wouldn't count, though. Aloud she asked, "What time? Did this Lisa say?"

"Close to five. She couldn't pinpoint the exact time. In any case, Tania got ready to leave for the airport."

"Then why would she end up dead in a park? Makes zero sense to me."

"The information is scanty, I admit."

"What about a car? Did he go with her?"

"Bao, you mean?" When Agnes nodded, her mom went on, "No, he stormed out shouting 'blue murder,' as Lisa dramatically put it. One hopes she didn't use that expression when questioned by the police. No sign of Tania's car yet. Presumably, they checked at the airport and around where she lives."

"The poor guy. Really has it in for him, doesn't she?"

"Who, Lisa? Oh, she's high strung. At times, she can't help being a bit of…"

"What? A drama queen?"

"You said it." At least, it elicited a little crooked smile from Sera.

A movement at the kitchen entrance caught their attention. Their waiter stood hesitantly, glancing in their direction, undecided whether to butt in. With a hand sign and a mouthed, 'another moment,' Sera stalled his approach.

"Well, we'd better make up our mind about take-out or

finishing here," she said. Picking up her mobile, she suggested, "How about taking it home to my place? If Gwen still needs me to pop over, it won't take me a couple of minutes. You and Rachel can stay even if I have to leave suddenly. Is that alright with you, dear?"

"Shoot! Forgot all about Rachel. Why isn't she here yet?" Frazzled, Agnes turned over her phone and unlocked to 'Messages' again. And froze.

Chapter 13

RACHEL

No further response from Angel. Nothing for it but to think of some way to formulate her excuses to Professor Potter. Her eyes strayed again to the bedroom door. No sound came from inside. Goodness, but that man took a long time. Must have decided to take a dip in the whirlpool instead of a shower. Just hope he didn't fall asleep in the tub. And drown…

Shocked by her own thoughts, her head snapped up. Get a grip, she admonished herself. Obediently her fingers cramped around the pen, unused to handwriting instead of keyboarding.

How to begin?

'Dear Prof. Potter.'

The pen ceased to move. Too formal? Well, he was a formal kind of person, wasn't he? Another line flowed with more ease.

'I'm so sorry, but I can't wait any longer.'

Then she reconsidered. That sounded accusatory. Drawing attention to having been kept waiting unduly. True enough, but not diplomatic. Resigned to starting all over, she ripped the sheet off the pad and tossed it into the waste bin. Then, realizing he might find it, she fished it out again and stuffed it into her back pocket.

By now frustrated, she aimlessly pulled open the left drawer again and contemplated the flowery mobile as though it might inspire her. Curiosity got the better of her. Gingerly, using the tip of the pen, she flipped it over. Of course, the screen was dark.

Idly, she stared down at it. Did it belong to the owner of the bra? Or did items accumulate in hotel drawers over time? Highly unlikely. Not in a place of this class. Must be one and the same person who left it behind.

Twirling the pen between two fingers, her mind felt oddly dissatisfied. Why would any woman put her bra in a desk drawer? Who stuffs their cell phone in drawers?

Probably his girlfriend's, after all. Perhaps, he swiped her things into the next best hiding place in order not to embarrass his guest. Might have done so while she, Rachel, used the bath-room upon their arrival.

As if aiming for a bullseye, her pen pushed the home button.

Nothing happened.

Turned off or dead battery. Curiosity killed the cat, she thought, as her thumb held the 'on' button. Flimsy pay-as-you-go cell...

The screen lit up, and an eerily beautiful face smiled at her from below.

Involuntarily, she smiled back. One finger touching the screen to prevent it from going dark, she used her other hand to take a close-up photo of the abandoned mobile. With a grin, she sent it off to Agnes.

The same moment she heard a sound from the bedroom. In a flash, she stuffed pad and pen back into the drawer. A few steps took her away from the desk, her thumbs all the while furiously typing.

R >Can't leave now. He's coming out. No worries. His dame's a beaut. I'm safe<

Chapter 14

AGNES

"What's wrong, Agnes? Are you feeling ill? The food—"

Her mother's anxious voice penetrated her mental stupor. Wordlessly, she passed over her mobile.

"That's Tania. I don't understand," her mom said. "Did Bao send you this? Why?"

"No—Rachel did…"

"Where on earth did she—"

"Let me—" Fingers stretched across the table; Agnes grabbed the phone from Sera's hand, her nails connecting with soft flesh.

"Ouch—you could just ask, dear."

The mild rebuke scarcely registered as Agnes scrolled up. She'd missed the next message, both sent more than ten minutes ago.

R >Can't leave now. He's coming out. No worries. His dame's a beaut. I'm safe<

Nausea rose in Agnes's throat. Eyes filming over—unseeingly, they remained fixed on the screen. Her tongue moistened her lips. Still, her words rose barely above a whisper.

"Oh—my—God—"

"Agnes, please. What's going on? You've gone all white."

In slow motion, Agnes's left hand went up to cover her mouth, fingers digging into her right cheek. Mental haze paralyzed her.

With one fluid movement Sera jumped up and was by her side. Ready to give CPR if needed, Agnes's mind registered irrelevantly.

The action shattered her stupefied inertia. "We've got to get her out of there! Now, Mom," she cried out louder than intended.

Half rising from her chair, she knocked over her wine glass. Sera caught it before it clattered to the stone floor.

Omar's head poked out of the kitchen, and some other diners turned their way at the disturbance. With a little wave and a murmured apology, Sera assured them all was well.

"Hold on, Agnes," the quiet parental tone brooked no opposition. Gently, her mother's hands guided her back into her seat. "Calm down. Take a deep breath." After stroking Agnes' shoulders for a moment, she herself sat down again.

"Now, tell me what this is about."

"Mom, don't you understand? We must hurry. It's him!"

Chapter 15

RACHEL

"My dear young lady, I do apologize for the long wait. Unforgivable, I'm afraid."

Relaxed, Potter leaned in the doorway and grinned charmingly, a wave of expensive aftershave preceding him.

Murmuring that she didn't mind one bit, Rachel eyed him shyly. In a white toweling robe and satiny lounge pants in a rich wine color, his dark hair carefully styled, clean-shaven, and scented appealingly, his masculinity struck her.

What disconcerted her was his intense direct gaze that seemed to suck you right in. Nervously, she fiddled with her phone. His eyes let her go and focused on her fingers.

"You young ones are all the same. Can't be parted for a second from your lifeline devices. Now, be a good girl. Turn it off and put it away." He waited until she complied hastily and then walked across to the table and grabbed hold of the tray.

As he bent forward to deposit it on the low coffee table in front of her, his bathrobe gaped open to reveal a muscular, tanned chest. His face came up to catch her staring. Amused, he looked deeply into her eyes.

"Ah, do you find me too casually dressed? Again, my apologies," he said mockingly. "It seemed too late in the day to dress formally again. I was sure you don't mind a relaxed look."

A perfunctory tug at the belt of his rope, which did nothing to hide the manly chest from view, he sank into the cushions next to her. With a deep sigh of content, he undressed the champagne bottle. The cork cooperated and dislodged, issuing a satisfying *pop*. Hardly a drop spilled when he filled the flutes.

His warm smile embraced her as he offered the first to her. Glass raised to clink hers, he proposed a toast.

"To a beautiful friendship."

Rachel took a sip—high-end bubbly, she acknowledged to herself—and sat up straighter to avoid his disconcerting gaze.

"Now, let's enjoy our little refreshment before I show you my treasures."

As she'd expected, he delighted in revealing the content of the tray with a theatrical flourish.

Chapter 16

AGNES

Eyebrows raised in demonstration of her disbelief, Sera remarked in a reasonable tone, "Leaving aside the grammar, who is 'it'—or more precisely, who is what?"

"He killed her!"

"Agnes, I'm losing my patience. Who are you talking about?"

"Potter, of course. He killed Tania."

"Don't be absurd, dear. The man didn't even meet her. In-person, that is. She didn't show up at the airport, remember?"

"She must have! How else would her phone end up in his desk drawer?"

"You've lost me. Whatever makes you think that? That's a wild association." Brows knitted together now, Sera scrutinized her, evidently fearing for her daughter's sanity.

"No, it's not. A sound deduction based on facts. Let's not quibble and get Rachel out of there before it's too late." Frustrated, Agnes started to rise, clutching her phone as though it could keep her friend alive.

"Okay, Agnes," her mom humored her. "Since you really believe this, spell it out for a less astute mind."

Ignoring the sarcasm, Agnes fought for control. On the edge

of her seat now, she let go of her phone to list off the points on her fingers.

"First off, Ray found a phone with a pink flowery case in Potter's hotel desk drawer. It was next to a lacy bra. She assumed it belonged to his girlfriend or a previous occupant of the room. When she sent me the pic, I got mad, thinking she was sticking her nose into his private affairs."

By now, she had Sera's undivided attention. Encouraged, she mustered more ammunition for her punch line.

"Then this photo of Tania. Now, look closely." A quick thumbprint unlocked the device, and the image lit up in the message thread. "You notice, it captures the home screen of a cell phone where you can still make out the rim of a pink casing. The wallpaper is Tania's picture. Same shot as on Bao's own mobile."

Her speech grew faster until she ran out of breath. Sucking in air greedily, she watched understanding dawning on her mom's gaunt features.

"Only her murderer would have gotten hold of her cell. There's no normal way for it to end up in Potter's desk."

Expression all serious now, Sera nodded and pushed herself up. "Correct or not, let's call the police. They're the ones to deal with this effectively."

"No, Mom! It'll be too late! It takes far too long to explain and convince the police. They've no idea who we are. If we call 911, the dispatcher at best sends a patrol car who have no clue what this is about. By the time you reach the person in charge, Rachel might be—"

"Okay, Agnes, I do see your point. Gwen will be able to connect directly to the investigation team through her friend. They'll take immediate action, I'm sure. I'll call her as soon as we're outside. The cops," she added, falling into colloquialism, "will have our garters for butting in." With a stern look at Agnes, she instructed, "No dramatics, and don't panic."

Relieved and exhausted, Agnes let out her breath.

"I'll have a quick word with Omar. No time to wait for doggy bags," she added with a strained smile and moved toward the kitchen entrance.

Her weight shifting from one foot to the other as she waited at the exit, Agnes's thoughts raced ahead. Surely, the man wasn't a maniac out to kill two women within 24 hours—or was he?

Chapter 17

RACHEL

"A little more caviar?" Prof. Potter tempted her.

Not overly fond of the stuff, Rachel declined politely and devoured the last tiny bit of the thinly sliced baguette with liver pâté. Her fingertips already touching her lips; she just stopped herself in time from licking them. A covert glance at him met with a smile that disconcerted her.

Quickly wiping her fingers on a napkin, she said, "Thanks so much. That was delicious," hoping he would speed things up. Agnes must be ready to kill her for being left in the lurch.

"Now for my little treat," he said and got up and went to the bedroom.

For a moment, Rachel felt panic rising. But then she told herself not to be stupid. Obviously, he kept his research material in there. Probably didn't want the maids to mess with it when doing the rooms. Her dad was fussy about that kind of thing too. When traveling, he locked his stuff in his luggage.

Sure enough, Fred reappeared moments later, a fat folder tucked under his arm. Without thinking, she stacked the debris of their snack on the tray and restored it to the side table. A quick swipe with the linen napkin that had clothed the bottle removed any remaining crumbs.

He nodded approvingly and sat down.

"Come sit with me and have a look," his right hand patted the soft sofa cushion next to him while his left opened the folder to fan out glossy eight-by-ten pictures.

Curious, Rachel moved in close to see. From his bathrobe pocket, he produced a magnifying glass and handed it to her. "Here, you need this to appreciate the finer details."

He let her study the photos for a few moments before asking, "You know what this is?" Not giving her a chance to reply, he answered himself, "We call it a krater. Fifth Century BC and—"

For once, she interrupted him, eager to shine with her own knowledge. "Yes, I know. Kraters are large pottery vessels. The ancient Greeks used them at their symposia to mix wine with water. The Master of Ceremony at the drinking party determined the proportion of the mix. My—"

Not a good idea to mention her dad. Most profs like to instruct the uninitiated. Potter might be put off if robbed of the pleasure, she figured. Better to focus on the now and the glossies in front of her.

Her father specialized in the classical Greek period and had taught her tons about it. Symposia she'd read up on by herself, though, and learned that the males aimed to get systematically drunk while entertained by flute girls and dancers—and boys. At times, these parties turned into orgies.

The photos showed different angles, sides, and aspects of a red-figure vessel. The ancient potters coated what was to be the background with black liquid clay so that the ornamentation pattern and figures stood out in the natural red clay color of the vessel or other pottery. Black-figure technique used the opposite method by painting on the figures and patterns in liquid clay that turned black during the firing process, leaving the background red.

Holding the magnifying glass aloft, Rachel realized that she kept her mind on method to avoid thinking about the lewd imagery of the actual painted details. They were far more sexually explicit than what Potter had shown during his keynote address. And kinky to boot.

Very aware of the man beside her, Rachel found herself babbling, "Fascinating. Unbelievably well-preserved example of the period. Where was it discovered?"

"Now, that would be telling," he laughed. "We don't know each other well enough yet for me to share specifics. This is only one of the amazing finds we've made."

He leaned forward to pull a closeup from among the images fanned out on the table. Rachel felt his knee's pressure against her thigh as he asked, "What do you make of this little scene? The ancients sure knew how to amuse themselves."

Not a prude by any means, Rachel felt herself blushing to the roots of her hair.

Chapter 18

AGNES

"Leave this to me," ordered Sera when they hastened down the carpeted corridor, which smelled faintly of deodorizer and recycled air.

At the reception desk, her mother had pulled the 'formidable professor' act to obtain Potter's room number. The simultaneous arrival of a large group that clamored for service gave hope that the young receptionist might forget to notify him.

Sera's firm knock on his door reverberated unnaturally loud in the hallway. Yet, it took three repetitions before the door opened a crack.

Shielded by her mom's back, Agnes's knees trembled. Her mouth went dry.

"What?" came his clipped and rude question. Through the opening gap of only a couple of inches, he could not possibly see his visitors and must assume it to be room service. For he growled, "Can't you read? 'Do not disturb'—I got all I need."

"Dr. Potter—Fred," said Sera firmly. "May we come in for a moment? An emergency, I'm afraid."

A moment's hesitation before he replied, "Give me a minute," and made to shut them out.

To Agnes's amazement, her mom put her foot in the gap

while stemming her left hand against the door. The action caught him off guard. The door flew open and revealed a gaping Potter who retreated into the suite as Sera advanced. All that cycling, skiing, and gym stuff her mom indulged in paid off, Agnes thought with an appreciative little grin.

The sight of Potter in a luxurious fluffy white bathrobe over burgundy, silky lounge pants, however, made her stomach lurch. A nightmarish image of Rachel sprawled on the man's bed intruded. On wobbly legs, she followed in Sera's wake.

Their unwilling host blustered yet backed ahead of them into the living room.

To Agnes's immense relief, a fully clad Rachel jumped up from the sofa facing them. Champagne glass still in hand, she sputtered, "Aunt Sera! What in hell are you doing here?" The voice broke and grew petulant, "How could you do this to me?"

For a second, Agnes feared Rachel might either throw her glass at them or break down in tears. Instead, she sank back onto the couch, defiantly.

The large coffee table was littered with photos that, to judge by the man's research interest, Agnes suspected to be of the ancient pornographic variety. Anger at Rachel's foolishness overrode any compassion for her mortified friend.

"Yes, may I ask the nature of your unexpected visit, Ms. … Ms.," inquired a haughty Potter, taking disdain as the best line of defense.

"Taylor. We met earlier today, you might recall," replied Sera with dignity. "Needless to say, we apologize for the intrusion. An emergency situation requires my goddaughter's immediate presence."

"What happened? Are Mom and Dad okay?" cried Rachel and jumped up again.

Perhaps weighing the need to ensure Rachel's immediate cooperation over causing her unnecessary anxiety, Sera stalled—and opted for the latter.

"I'm sure they are, dear. Let's talk about it later. Please come along now."

Wrong move, Agnes mentally warned, too much like coaxing a stubborn kid.

Predictably, Rachel bristled. Crossing her arms, she sat down and leaned back into the cushions.

"In that case, I think, you'd better leave. Other emergencies are unlikely to affect me personally. You've interrupted an important conversation," she added with uncharacteristic arrogance.

Unnerved, Agnes wanted to shout at her, 'Don't be a bloody fool!'

"I do believe, Dr. Potter will agree with me that whatever conversation you might have can be continued at a more suitable time in more suitable surroundings," her mom said and mustered the man with a severe glance.

Chest stuck out, about to bluster again; he changed his mind. Nonchalantly, he picked up his champagne flute and refilled it from a large bottle in a cooler, dripping ice water onto the photo display. Over the rim of his glass, he contemplated Sera—his smirk reminding Agnes of a satyr.

A slow sip before he drawled, "By all means, take her away."

"That's so unfair!"

Upon Rachel's outcry, he slowly turned to give her a once-over only to find her wanting. Nose lifted high to glance down its ridge to muster her contemptuously; he said, "Please don't bother applying to my department. You just don't measure up to our standards."

A howl of outrage from Ray would not have surprised Agnes. To prevent an outburst, she stepped forward to pull her away from behind the low table and hissed, "Cool it. I'll explain outside."

As she sensed Rachel's resistance and fearing she might revert to the type of tantrum she'd outgrown a couple of decades ago, Agnes murmured their secret childhood formula employed solely in the face of danger. "Trust me. Blood-sister's honor."

A light flickered in Rachel's eyes. Then her shoulders sagged.

She remembers, thought Agnes. Relief flooded her whole body as her friend meekly tolerated being guided to the hallway. Ray only stopped to grab her satchel from the floor.

Behind them, Agnes heard her mother apologize to the arrogant monster for their intrusion. Angry, she wheeled around. From a few steps away, Sera's face appeared an immobile mask.

Realization hit Agnes. Of course, it was essential to delude the man into a false sense of security. The slightest suspicion and he would destroy the evidence. Only the photos on their mobiles would be left to trace the atrocity back to him. Circumstantial evidence at best, she feared.

Her mom forming the rear guard, Agnes propelled Rachel along to the elevators, not giving her time to pause for questions.

Just then, the doors of one lift parted to disgorge a small group of people. One didn't need the uniforms and black bulletproof vests of the three following behind a man and a woman in work-a-day suits to recognize who was coming to call.

Chapter 19

RACHEL

"Will they make it stick?" asked Rachel, still smarting from last night's humiliation. Despite the midday sun shining on her back through the open window, she shivered. Her mind struggled to take in what Potter had done.

"With your evidence, there's a good chance," said Gwen, returning to the kitchen table. "Who knows what DNA and other forensic testing might turn up, now that they've found her car. Immersed in saltwater or not, the interior might retain traces."

"How the heck did he manage to dunk it?" Rachel reached for a handful of strawberries from the bowl Gwen placed in the middle of the table. Her appetite had slowly returned when Aunt Sera's friend served homemade strawberry shortcake for dessert.

During lunch, they'd studiously avoided the topic on everyone's mind. Even now, all of them were focusing on the perpetrator and the chances of proving his guilt, she realized. None wanted to face the horror of what had happened to the girl.

"Submersing the car would be easy," replied Sera. "Most likely, he drove it onto the abandoned pier, put it in neutral, and pushed from the back. Tania gave me a lift into town once in her small hatchback—standard transmission like mine. When the gears are disengaged, it rolls without much of a push."

"Must have opened all the windows to avoid it sticking upright, nose buried in slick," Agnes remarked. "But why did Tania go to a park with him at night? I don't get it."

"Point Pleasant is a must-see for visitors. Whole busloads come out. We're inundated with tourists out here, aren't we, Gwen?"

Aunt Sera's friend sighed and nodded. "If he asked her where they could go for a stroll after sitting on the plane for hours," said Gwen, "she'd naturally think of the park. After all, she jogged there quite often."

"Totally," agreed Rachel. This was easy for her to relate to. "First thing I would suggest too. Places you go running become so familiar you never imagine anything bad could happen to you… To take her phone with him really floors me—so stupid. And her bra. If it was hers."

"Fetishism, I believe, is a common phenomenon. The trophy of the predator," said Gwen.

"Makes you wonder where they spent the time after she picked him up at the airport." Trust Angel to spot the logical loopholes.

"Presumably, they must have gone for dinner after all—forensics will determine that," said Gwen. "The police had no time to appeal to the public yet. Now it will be far easier to find witnesses who saw them somewhere together. From what my friend tells me, they always are inundated with reports of sightings in such cases. Most of them unreliable—"

No longer able to avoid facing the worst, Rachel blurted out, "Did he—" but couldn't bring herself to spell it out.

The older women glanced at each—they understood.

"No. Based on what I heard, only her—" Gwen's voice faltered. Then she rushed on, "From what Lisa told me, Tania was wearing a baggy sweater and skin-tight jeans. The top would come off easily if he tried to—you know—"

"You think he planned it?" Skin crawling, Rachel thought of her own naivety in going to his hotel room. Her arm muscles contracted in a shudder that hunched her shoulders and pressed her elbows against her ribs.

"Somehow, I doubt it." Gwen held up the teapot questioningly. They all declined, and she poured the dregs into her own cup—then pulled a face when tasting.

"Pure speculation on my part," said Aunt Sera, "but I think he took her compliance for granted. My brief impression of him is that he's so conceited and presumptuous that he cannot even imagine any woman wanting to resist him. Meeting vehement resistance would spurn him on to impose his will. And in a lonely place at night, there was nothing to stop him."

"I agree," said Agnes. "The guy struck me as the type who takes conquest and submission for granted. The kind that gets their kicks out of a woman struggling against them. Flatters their macho ego, I imagine. If he came to his senses at all, he might have feared she would report him for harassment. Illustrious career on the line, he'd do anything to shut her up."

In a flashback, Rachel again felt herself freeze when Potter's knee had pressed against her thigh. Had she been worried about making a scene by withdrawing in an obvious manner? Was it his status as an eminent academic that had daunted her? If it had been any other guy, she would have had no qualms about drawing a clear line and telling him off. Thank God for Aunt Sera and Agnes barging in...

"I assume he'll plead accidental death—if he admits to anything at all," remarked Gwen.

Rachel could feel Agnes tensing next to her on the window seat. "His sense of self-preservation will prompt him to try any means to weasel out of this," Agnes said. "If only the cops find enough evidence to close any possible loopholes to prevent him escaping justice. He's bound to bring in a star lawyer to get him off somehow..."

The four women sat in silence. Each, Rachel supposed, contemplating this horrific possibility.

Gwen's voice cut into her mental musings. "Police are likely to dig into Potter's past. Though I haven't heard anything concrete—well, Sera, I told you already last night—the man has quite a reputation. Keep in mind, even a few years ago, virtually no one reported an eminent professor for having affairs with his students. Through the grapevine, I'd heard rumors that I found disturbing—"

"Why on earth did you invite him as keynote speaker?"

"I didn't, Agnes. Our committee did despite my veto. Unfortunately, I could not share my reasons. Mere hearsay. From reliable colleagues in the States, mind you. Disclosure on my part would have been actionable as no official complaints existed. The reservations I voiced targeted the unsuitability of his talks. Needless to say, I was overruled."

"Do you think I'll have to testify in court?" With dismay, Rachel thought of herself being questioned in public about going—eagerly—to the man's room. Her folly made her grind her teeth.

"Sure, you do, silly," said Agnes.

Rachel could feel her mouth pucker in response, which made Angel hug her and say gently, "Much will hinge on your testimony. You ought to be proud of being instrumental in bringing Tania's killer to justice."

"Did I mention? Bao asked to come for a quick visit," said Gwen." I think I hear him now." She rose to go to the front door.

Chapter 20

AGNES

Giving Ray's back a final rub, Agnes thought they really needed a sisterly talk on their long drive back to Ontario. Eighteen hundred kilometers—and their planned day in Quebec City on the way home—left a lot of time for a heart-to-heart, she smiled. The fear for Rachel's safety had left its mark. Last night she woke up in a sweat several times. Only Ray's steady breathing in the other bed had reassured her that she'd escaped unscathed.

From their earliest childhood, Agnes had felt responsible for Ray. Two years her senior, it must have felt like decades of greater wisdom or something to her infant mind. How self-determined Rebel-Ray later revolted against being mothered—she grinned at the recollection. And then always showed herself truly grateful when Agnes rescued her from the scrapes she got into. 'You're my guardian angel,' she used to say. 'Angel' stuck to this day. Agnes cringed at the thought of how nearly the angel failed last night.

The thought prompted her to ask her mom, "Was Gwen the one to break it to her people?"

"There's no one," Sera responded. "Tania was brought up

by her grandmother. She decided to come to Canada when her granny passed away. No other family left."

"Unbearably sad…" Agnes felt her throat constrict.

To shake off the despondent mood that threatened to descend, Agnes focused on the voices now wafting in from the front hallway.

Her mind sought to recapture the pleasant first impression of Gwen's place at their arrival for the lunch date. It was to be their last stop before leaving for Ontario right after.

She'd been all gooey-eyed over the downright adorable gingerbread-trimmed Cape Cod. Straight out of a Century Home magazine, she'd remarked. Only in wow-factor, for it was much lived in. Books all over the place and a chubby calico cat curled up in the wing chair by the fireplace. Rather stand-offish or anti-social, the smug feline repelled any advances from the visitors.

Since their early lunch, they'd been sitting in the kitchen around the scrubbed pine table. Sera and Gwen picked the mismatched chairs facing the window. She and Rachel opted for the cushioned window bench; their backs warmed by the sun shining through the half-raised sash panes. A glorious summery late-spring day.

A sudden movement next to her recalled her to the present. Her buddy sat bold upright, eyeing the entrance. The keen interest and something undefinable in her glance made her face radiate. As quickly as it had appeared, it vanished to be replaced by a somber expression of empathy.

From her contemplation of Rachel's reaction, Agnes followed her friend's glance to see a diffident Bao hover at the kitchen door.

A bright midday sunray lit up his striking features. The deep-black hair slanted forward in a point. Yesterday's crumbled clothes that he still wore did nothing to detract from the nobility of his features. The face, tired and drained of any emotion, no longer expressed anxiety but looked deadened by shock and grief.

Her mom rose with outstretched hands and solicitous murmurs to welcome him. While she quietly introduced her daughter and godchild, their host offered tea and a bite to eat, which Bao politely declined.

"I come to thank you again," he said to Gwen. "You help me always and are true and good."

"What happened to Tania devastated all of us. We're most sincerely sorry for your loss, Bao. It was the least I could do to stand by you. The police won't worry you again now."

"Me, I do not matter. Punish Tania's killer. Revenge. That is all I want." The fierceness of his tone and expression made Agnes shudder. Potter could count himself lucky to be in custody.

By now, they all were standing in the middle of the room. Bao turned to Rachel.

"I thank you forever." His voice vibrated with solemn pathos. "You found the murderer."

"Hey, I didn't do anything heroic," a blushing Rachel warded off his gratitude. "Totally clueless about what I'd found, I'm afraid. In fact…"

"Yes, Bao, the only astute one among us is Agnes. My daughter's quick wit deduced the meaning of what Rachel discovered. Without her fast reaction and insistence on immediate action—and I admit, I stalled by doubting her insights— who knows how it might have ended." A stern look at her godchild caused Rachel to shiver visibly.

When her mother's arm hugged her close for a moment, and Bao earnestly thanked her, Agnes blushed crimson and started to stutter.

"I— I— Took me way too long. Only dotted the i's and crossed the t's when anyone could see what it meant." Realizing the implication, she got even more flustered, mumbling, "Sorry, Mom, didn't mean—"

"No worries, dear, I was as dense as an oak log. I need my resident philosopher to lead me out of the cave," Sera assured her ruefully.

"It was actually Tania herself who brought to light the murderer," Agnes said in a sudden insight, "with your help, Bao. Without the photo you took and told her to look at every day, we might not have discovered the truth."

For a moment, no one spoke—almost as though Tania had reached out to them. The spell broke when Gwen urged Bao to stay, her face grave with concern, "Won't you sit down for a moment?"

He shook his head without responding.

Agnes had to suppress an urge to take him into her arms to comfort him. He looked utterly lost. How he must suffer—not only by losing Tania. To have parted from his beloved in anger, and no chance ever to tell her he was sorry, would haunt him for a long time. He might not even have friends to turn to, she thought in dismay.

"Bao, Sera and I will come by tonight. The three of us can go to the vigil together." While Gwen turned to Agnes and Rachel to explain, he nodded stoically but dazed as if he did not really take in the words. "A number of students, with the help of faculty and staff, have organized a vigil for this evening. Small comfort, I know, but…" She didn't finish whatever she was thinking.

"I'm so sorry we can't stay. Our thoughts will be with you and Tania," murmured Agnes and felt how inadequate it sounded. She reached out to Bao, who slowly backed to the door, clearly needing to be alone with his grief.

"Will you be okay?" she asked. "Is there anyone—"

"I'm not important," he repeated. "I'm strong. Do not worry about me." The dark eyes, dull with pain, belied his words.

Tentatively, Agnes touched his sleeve. "Please, take care. My mom and Gwen will be here when you need someone."

Unexpectedly, he hugged her very briefly and rushed out, Gwen closely following behind.

Helplessly, Agnes shook her head.

"Try not to worry too much, Agnes," her mother told her. "We do have very good student support services. And you were right to say that Gwen and I will be here to help him."

Ray had been uncharacteristically subdued, her ready empathy only evident in her pained look. Meeting Bao must have driven home the reality of what had happened to Tania. Both of them had only been names for Rachel, Agnes reflected. Even to her, Tania was a fleetingly glimpsed figure. No more real perhaps than people one passes in the street or reads about in the paper. Now, the agony Bao was going through had materialized for all of them in the room and still lingered.

While she helped a pensive Rachel clear the table, Agnes regarded her with compassion. In retrospect, she shivered at her own denseness. To suspect Jamie and assume he, or far more likely Rex, must have been responsible when all the while her dearest friend was in danger from a predator and killer... The image of a lovely mocha-toned face, distorted by distress, resurfaced and overlayed the live image in front of her.

Horrified realization dawned. Was the assault that led to her death not the first one? A tutor who receives his female student clad in an undershirt instead of being properly dressed deserves to be regarded with grave suspicion. Why, if not from a feeling of guilt, this intense interest Rex showed in Hobbes's view on self-accusation?

Her mind inevitably went back to Hobbes and her talk the other morning on self-accusation. Of course, Hobbes was right that self-preservation was the major driving force in humans as in all other animals. Self-defense against an attacker is only natural. But she strongly disagreed with Hobbes that a natural right to self-preservation entitled an aggressor to use any means reason might suggest in preserving his liberty.

Even in a state of nature, with no legal system and no political or societal structure—she firmly believed—no one has a right to harm others. In this, she was entirely on John Locke's side who took a 'no harm principle' to be the first law of nature, much more fundamental even than any civil law could be.

True enough, any self-accusation under duress was null and void because, if in fear, people might admit to things they never did. Yet—Agnes thought—surely, we are morally obligated to admit voluntarily to grave wrongs we have committed. If we humans have a natural tendency to try to evade punishment as we try to avoid any pain, she thought, that does not mean we *ought* to evade justice. The realization that she should have clarified and explained her own position to Rex made her uneasy. Not that mere words could change a man... But before leaving, she'd take her mom aside to share her concerns. Someone needed to keep a closer eye on the tutor.

Even her philosophical musings were mere attempts to keep the dismal horror of Tania's final day at bay. The thought filled Agnes with deep sorrow and regret of never having met this absent beauty.

As if sensing her emotional state, her mom came up to her and said softly, "Despite it all, I'm so glad I had this rare chance to see you, even if we had no quality time to reconnect. Maybe on another occasion?"

Pulling both Agnes and Rachel close, she added, "For now, let's get you two on your way."

Up next: *Silent Sands – Agnes Taylor Mystery – Book 1*

AGNES TAYLOR MYSTERY
-BOOK1-

Silent
Sands

EVA BERNHARD

Silent Sands

AGNES TAYLOR MYSTERY - BOOK 1

By Eva Bernhard

Prologue

"She's coming around."

Words dimly penetrating. Searing pain wells up from her abdomen—obliterates time—fading away into damp darkness…

Time expands and contracts—separates like plasma. Heat scorches inside and out.

Drops pass lips cracked like dry mud. Dribble down her chin —slowly break a path down her throat, puddling in the hollow of her collarbones. Evaporates on sticky, sweltering skin. Not enough to still the craving for cooling relief.

Half-open eyes meet deep blue concern that melts into a smile.

"Took your sweet time," greets her efforts to hone in to the now.

Calm features superimpose and exude serenity and kindness.

Nothingness settles in…

Mellow early morning light.

"You've made it, kid," another smiling face intrudes, casts her into shadow.

"Don't try to talk," meets her move to part lips sticking fast, parched, and disused.

"She needs fluids. We need to get her to a hospital."

"How the heck—"

The effort to shake her head makes it spin.

"Hey, take it easy. Relax." Hands cradle her shoulders—tender and reassuring. She dissolves again into lethargy.

"See, she doesn't want to. Told you she's not legit."

"Yeah, I guess... Well, we got no motor anyway. The locals ain't gonna help none."

"Hang in there, kid. Got you through the tough part. Takes time. Now you'll be up an' runnin' in a tick."

"Here, try to drink."

Tepid water deliciously runs over her tongue. She swallows —painfully. Can feel it trickle down. Easing her constricted chest. Her throat begins to expand and absorb the flow.

Time stands still. Drift in and out—out and in...

A bony small brown hand comes into focus cupping an earth-brown vessel. Droplets sweat down its side. One disengages, languorous as resin. She anticipates its impact on her face. Anxious, yet yearning.

"Look! She's drinking!"

"Told you so." Smug, as though he'd done it himself.

No sense how long there's been nothing. Tenacious twilight...

"She's waking up." Warm breath on her cheek. "Boy, do you ever sleep a lot."

"Whoa—chill. Don't try to sit up." A gentle arm under her back props her up.

Light blazes—burns red behind gooey eyelids.

"Here, drink. Some tea or stuff to make you strong."

She obeys. Then memory returns—clutches her stomach. "Where is—"

The voice sounds utterly strange; yet she feels its vibration in her chest. Painfully opening her lids, she seeks an answer. Blinding light floods in. A hand quickly shades her vision.

"Sorry, kid, couldn't save—" Words tinged with infinite regret, never finished.

"We'll get you out of here. Take you home with us. Promise —" The other voice was drowned out by the scream that tore her chest.

Chapter 1
AGNES TAYLOR

I must have been in the grip of temporary insanity to agree to this trip. Pure masochism, Agnes thought.

Seizing the handle of her suitcase yet again, she inched forward in the queue aiming to board the ferry. Waves of anxiety and desperation welled up. Three weeks! Trapped on an obscure German North Sea island with a mother she'd rarely set eyes on in ages.

Suspicious her mother might be able to tap into her mental chatter, Agnes surreptitiously glanced over her shoulder. But Sera, oblivious to any turmoil, focused on the task at hand—her lean, lightly tanned face serene despite the hustle and noise around them.

The train had disgorged them, together with hordes of other holidaymakers, right next to the ferry terminal. Carried along by the steady stream making its way to the narrow gangplank, Agnes saw little of the surroundings.

What she could make out appeared disappointingly utilitarian. No picturesque harbor here. Huge parking lots—much of the island was car-free—and holding lanes for the access bridge, now lowered to admit vehicles. Seagulls screeching mixed with clanking and crunching of metal and a general cacophony. Air, salty and rank from rotting fish maybe, assaulted her nose.

Earlier, when they disembarked from the train, a delicious scent of deep-fried fish in batter had pervaded the air.

"Let's grab lunch now," she'd said to Sera as they passed the vendor's truck.

"You'll be seasick," was her mom's only reaction. As though she were still a little kid who couldn't hold down her dinner on a boat. Besides, Sera didn't have a clue what was good for her or not. They hadn't vacationed—or been together for more than a few hours at a stretch—in a couple of decades. Not since Sera had left her behind to take up a professorship in the fine arts department at the university in Halifax. The thought still rankled.

Lost in her own mental maze, Agnes failed to notice the end of the gangplank. She stumbled stepping onto the ship deck. "*Vorsicht Stufe*," a belated caution by a uniformed crew member to watch her step drew everyone's attention to her literal misstep. Furiously blushing, she hurried on.

If anything, the boat itself was far more crowded. People ascended not only from the foot passenger catwalk but now also from the cars below.

Afraid to lose her mom in the throng, Agnes turned around to find her right behind—a slender figure clad in slim-line black pants. A pearl-gray top accentuated the silver in her close-cropped hairstyle. In her seventies, Sera looked trim and fit, her hair still retaining some of its original black.

Next to her mother, Agnes felt pudgy and inadequate. Not that she was really overweight. The coloring she had inherited, as her own dark tresses—now caught in a scrunchie at the nape of her neck—showed.

With a sigh, Agnes dragged herself into the present as Sera pushed up stylish sunglasses to scan the deck.

"Do you want to stay up here or go inside? Probably rather windy once we—" Agnes broke off.

Sera looked at her strangely.

"What? Did I say something funny?"

"At times you truly amaze me, Agnes. Don't you think twenty years of living by the ocean taught me all about wind?" Without waiting for a reply, Sera hoisted her large backpack, instead of wheeling it on its casters, and made for a spot on one of the deck benches that a young man had just vacated.

Several deep breaths of salty air, gulped in an effort to de-stress, Agnes resigned herself to three weeks' confinement on the island.

Chapter 2

AGNES

"*Ju—huh!! Willkommen auf Bosum!*"

Tall, sun-bleached blond, and well padded, a woman bore down on them. Welcoming them to the isle of Bosum, she waved a magic marker placard 'Sera & Agnes' one-handed over her head. Agnes caught Sera wince and step back as though afraid of being enfolded in sunburned arms. The flaxen lady instead grabbed Sera's wheeled backpack and—not heeding any signs of feeble resistance—hauled it onto her own back. Her left hand seized Agnes's luggage, while she commanded, "Follow, here along!"

Parting the sea of a disembarking crowd with Agnes' suitcase, the woman steered them through to a tiny hatchback parked on the pier. Baggage wedged into the back, she urged them on, "Let us leave quickly before the cars come. My little house is ready for you."

They all piled into the small vehicle and their chauffeuse took off with squealing tires. To Agnes's relief, she instantly slowed down and at a crawling pace weaved through the holiday crowd clogging the wharf.

Nevertheless, they'd beat the worst crush. Once on the upper harbor road, they avoided the town and made their way sedately along marshes and salt meadows towards sandy hills glimpsed in the distance.

Abruptly their hostess twisted in her seat to eye Sera.

"*Geschafft*—done it. Now we can talk. How was your trip over? I'm Mathilda." The broad smile over her shoulder was directed at her rear passenger.

"Yes, thanks. Great," Agnes hastened to assure her—adding mentally, 'watch the road or we'll end up in this swamp.' The narrow road wound along wetlands to the right and deep dune sand land inward.

Later Mathilda pointed at a campground. "There. A general shop."

"We picked up a few things on the mainland, thanks." Agnes patted her backpack only to regret it immediately when Mathilda's head craned back.

"I have put some goodies for you into the refrigerator. In just ten minutes you are here from the house on the bicycles we keep for our guests."

When they murmured their appreciation, Mathilda—intent on practicing both her English and her generosity—said, "Do not worry. Once a week I can drive you to the store in town. For little money. The bus stops at the cul-de-sac. One must walk back to the house. Too heavy with shopping bags."

Presently, they entered a small pathway hidden between dunes. No house or sign of life showed. In fact, the campground and a Café two or three kilometers back appeared to be the only habitations.

As though reading her mind, Sera wondered, "No one lives close by?"

"*Nein, nein.* No—you have this all to yourself. It is now a *Naturschutzgebiet*. How do you say? A nature preserve. Building verboten. You cannot now put houses here."

A sudden stop, arm stretched out, she pointed to a quaint cottage with thatched roof and picturesque wild roses climbing trellises that framed the front and exclaimed, "My little house. Very old. The only one left."

To be alone with this fairy-tale cottage, Agnes yearned and diagnosed 'love at first sight.' Dreamily she contemplated the whimsical place nestled in greenery and blossoms suffused by the midday sunlight. Once inside, she longed to explore. Accompanied by the owner reciting the essential workings of the little place—all mod coms except for phone or TV—they inspected a cozy kitchen with a patio out back.

"Quite isolated, isn't it?" Sera glanced at the dunes visible through the back door.

"*Ach ja*—but the Café and camping place have telephones." Somewhat severely, Mathilda raised a finger at Agnes. "I explained in my email. No Internet or *Handys* here. Your mother has angst?"

What's handy? wondered Agnes. Oh, she means 'cell phones.' Aloud she said, "No worries. We'll survive. Without international plans, our Canadian mobiles are useless in any case. Wireless at a library or coffee shop in town will do."

The appeasement worked and, leaving Mathilda to show Sera the downstairs amenities, Agnes snuck up the stairs and viewed the two bedrooms and white tiled, modern bathroom. The whole place was beautiful—original plank flooring, white-washed walls, and natural wood furnishings with summer-fresh scented duvets. Vintage lace drapes gently stirred by a breeze from the open windows.

Half an hour later—house inspection accomplished—Mathilda folded herself into her little contraption and with a last, "You have my number," she was gone.

A deep inhale and exhale of rose-scented air before Agnes faced Sera who fussed over the tea kettle. Perhaps to convince herself rather than her mother, she said brightly, "So, here we are. Let's have a wonderful holiday. Are you game to explore the dunes this afternoon?"

Chapter 3
POLLY HOLT

Polly Holt zipped around, startled by a bony hand grabbing her right shoulder.

"Hell, Nancy! Do you have to scare me like that! Enough to give a person a heart attack."

"Bad conscience, Polly? Glad you heeded our call for action and decided to join us after all."

Involuntarily Polly stepped back to peek at the gaunt, serious face, skin stretched taut over prominent cheekbones. Dark brown eyes locked on to hers.

"Nah, you know me, Nancy, I don't do joining." To break away from uncomfortable scrutiny, Polly half-turned. A flock of backpackers—single file like ducks—lumbered across the marketplace toward a stage erected on the opposite side. "Got tons of groupies—no need for me," she said.

"They are not my *groupies* but committed activists. Some-times in life, Polly, we do need to commit."

"Oh, yeah? A bit rich coming from you, Nance."

No reaction. Instead, Nancy's glance swept the crowd milling around them. "To adopt a cause larger than oneself makes life worth living."

Polly scuffed the pavement with her sandaled foot. "Yah, well," she mumbled.

"I must go." Briskly, Nancy moved on.

"Hey, wait! Wanna do coffee sometime?"

"Text or email Shady to arrange it."

"You gotta be bloody kiddin'. Make a friggin' appointment for an interview with you?"

"Suit yourself, Polly. I came here to achieve our goals, not for a trip down memory lane." Without another word, she left.

A vicious kick at the cobblestones stubbed her toe so badly Polly yelped in agony.

"*Ouch!* Wow, that hurt," said a high feminine voice from behind.

Embarrassed for her near tantrum, Polly sheepishly turned, head bent low. The girl grinned so conspiratorially it disarmed any resentment. The next words, however, made her gape.

"Moms are a pain, aren't they?"

"Uh...she's not my mother. She's..."

Fully engrossed by texting on a mobile, the other paid no further attention.

With a shrug, Polly scanned the assembly for Nancy's slim, somber-clad figure. No sign of her.

Slogan chanting set in loudly from various directions of Bosum's central square, now packed with people. Tourists mingled with gawkers, activists, and demonstrators alike. Tough on the locals to be forced to endure all this commotion, Polly thought. Bad enough to have your isle conquered by a mob every summer, let alone mass rallies.

"Didn't you say wind energy is good?" whined a different female close to her. "I don't understand," drawing the last word up and down.

Before Polly was able to make out the face, two huge breasts —barely contained in a padded bra, spanned by a shiny tank top—leaned forward. The golden skin glistened satiny and well cared for. Luxurious, blond curls flowed over bare shoulders, caressing the cleavage.

"I think they are demanding a stop to the wind park project slated for the island." Helpfully, Polly jerked a finger in the general direction of placards, banners, and posters waved by protesters.

WINDKRAFT NEIN DANKE—WIND POWER NO THANKS

WINDRÄDER MACHEN KRANK—WIND TURBINES MAKE SICK

FUNPARKS NO WINDPARKS

"Yeah, I get that." 'Stupid!' her expression said. "But what's wrong with it?" An impatient shake of her mane.

Giant jean-clad legs came into Polly's line of vision. As her glance wandered up, she met calculating eyes above a spotless white, loose shirt giving her the once over, only to contemptuously dismiss her diminutive, skinny, androgynous frame.

"You always say wind and solar are the thing. Didn't we see like zillions of wind things on the mainland on the way up?—Guess what—they like hate them around here!"

Big guy hugged bosomy woman to his hip. "There're two sides to everything, silly. These dudes are the con side."

"So weird," the gal commented. "I thought enviros are all for this stuff."

"A lot of people think wind farms are dangerous to wildlife and a human health hazard," Polly ventured, unasked.

That earned her a sweet, sisterly smile. "You don't say? Are you like protesting, too? Do you live here?"

"Nope. Just watching."

"So, what's so bad about them? Like for the environment and stuff? Isn't it totally the green thing?"

Distracted momentarily by the sight of someone in a hoodie at the rear of the group in front of them, Polly responded mechanically, "All depends on what perspective you take. Some say wind turbines make people sick."

"You mean you get sick of them, like?"

"Haha, you could say both. Fed up watching them turn round and round. I meant it literally. People claim the noise causes medical problems. Though objectively, placed at a proper distance they're no louder than your fridge."

All the while, the girl nodded and fidgeted—her eyes shifted to her companion who ignored both of them.

"Plus, some people mind the aesthetics." A frown threatened to pucker the flawless skin, and Polly hastened to explain, "Beauty of nature kind of thing. Gigantic turbines are a blot on the landscape, they say."

"No way! They're so pretty with cows and sheep in all that green grass. We saw zillions driving up here. I put them on Instagram." As though eager to show the evidence, she scrolled on her phone.

Macho was having none of that. Without a word, he grabbed his girlfriend by the arms and marched her off into town.

Perfect timing, Polly thought when crackling from the loud-speakers drew everyone's attention. Let the show begin.

Chapter 4

AGNES

"What a din! *Kurgebiet*—If this is what 'health spa areas' are like nowadays; I'm surprised anyone recuperates."

"Wasn't my idea going into town," Agnes shot back. "I'd rather be out on the beach."

"Quite the maddening crowd." Though the sign at the entrance of the car-free zone read 'cyclists must dismount,' Sera only now conceded, "Better get off our bikes here." And—to Agnes's dismay—almost collided with a bearded vacationer pushing a toddler in a stroller.

The little girl ogled Sera wide-eyed, her ice-cream cone perilously tilting over the side of the buggy. A fatherly hand—used to multitasking—straightened it in the nick of time. "*Achtung! Passt auf!*"

The caution to 'pay attention' made people stop to enjoy the spectacle. With an apologetic grimace in all directions, Agnes pushed her own bike out of harm's way.

"You sure did pick the busiest time to come into town," she hissed at Sera. "Let's leave them here and walk."

They found a lamppost next to an overcrowded row of public bicycle racks and locked theirs together with the chain lock discovered in Mathilda's shed. What an organized woman;

enough to make one sink into hopeless depression of inadequacy, Agnes thought wearily.

The cacophony—a mix of chanting, shouting, and clanging—grew louder the farther they moved from the leafy spa area into a pedestrian zone lined by cafés with market umbrellas and wicker chairs, elegant boutiques, and stores that beckoned with beach toys. While Agnes dawdled, Sera sped ahead.

"Hey, do you know where we're going? Have you been here before?"

Half-turning her head, Sera countered, "It's not exactly Paris, is it?"

"Slow down! What's the rush? Aren't we on holiday?"

"Suit yourself. I need exercise after my tedious flight and the train rides."

"Precisely why I wanted to hike in the dunes."

"Don't sound like a broken record, Agnes. You were free to do as you please."

"And let you go into town on your own on our first day here?"

"Let me? Are you intending to play your mother's keeper? I've lived and traveled on my own for over twenty years. I don't need you to watch over me, thank you very much. If anything, it would be more natural the other way around."

"Well, you haven't done much of that in my lifetime." The retort slipped out. Her mom's stricken look deflated her anger. Too late.

"Perhaps we'd better take some time out, right here and now." Sera's voice was expressionless. "Why don't we meet later where we left the bikes? Let's say in a couple of hours?"

The contrite, "If that's what you want…" petered out as Sera was swallowed up by the mingling multitude.

Shoot! Put my foot in again, Agnes berated herself. Why is it always my fault? Only tried to be considerate. Mothers are so darn touchy.—Well, Rachel's mom never was. All the years I lived with them, Faye stayed calm no matter how impatient

Professor Jones might get. He can't abide the little inconveniences of daily life. Too focused on esoteric textual problems to bother with mundane tasks. An academic herself now with a PhD, his intellect still overawed her.

Morosely walking on, Agnes fretted, this vacation is jinxed. Need time out after being together for twenty-four hours—and you can't count nighttime, can you?—imagine three weeks of this! We'll end up killing each other by day three.

Almost tripping over a sidewalk planter spilling gorgeous blooming plants, snapped her back into the moment. She had let herself drift along with the pedestrian flow. The sudden brightness of sunlight and deafening cacophony stemmed from the town square she'd entered.

People everywhere—shouting and chanting, waving banners and posters. Agnes couldn't quite make out what they said—too many gawkers blocking her view. Impossible to stand still without being pressed against the onlookers packing the sidewalk and street surrounding the cobblestone square. Not sure yet whether to retreat or to stay, Agnes stopped to ask in halting German what was going on.

"*Och, 'ne WKA Demo,*" the woman next to her said. A demonstration about the new *Windkraftanlage*, she explained when Agnes frowned.

Aha, Agnes thought, a 'wind power installation.' Why make such infernal noise about it? Wasn't Germany at the global forefront of generating wind energy? Their much-publicized *Atomausstieg*—the 'exit from nuclear power' after the Fukushima disaster in Japan—depended on it, she'd read.

Puzzled, she tried to get closer to see what was happening. People were drifting all in one direction. A raised stage with electronic equipment and mega-size speakers at each end attracted their attention.

Just then a man mounted the platform—ratty, grayish ponytail, black jeans, and black shirt with casually rolled-up sleeves proclaimed, 'young at heart.' The general uproar of shrill whistling, cheering, and booing did nothing to affect his swaggering stride.

A tall guy in baggy khakis and loose-fitting, natural linen-type shirt, joined him. Bearded and wearing his long, reddish hair combed back in ample waves, he towered over the now, by contrast, much older seeming fellow in black.

From the other end, a woman—slim in bluish-black trousers and top, her short dark hair mottled with gray—strode onto the stage to shouts of "Nancy!" "Nancy, go for it."

These vocal fans jostled with their bulky backpacks for space in the front row. They wore t-shirts with bold peace signs on one side and crossed-out turbine symbols on the other. Some younger passengers on the ferry, Agnes remembered, sported such logos.

Now the towering man raised his hand in a manner befitting an ancient orator. A hush descended over the multitudes—only to be broken again by laughter rippling through the waiting audience. A small, rotund man in suit and tie waddled across to climb the dais, crying in German, "Wait for me! Please!" The other guy chuckled, passed him the microphone, and stepped back.

"*Freunde, die ihr hier versammelt seid,*" the newcomer greeted his 'assembled friends.' As their mayor, he said, he knew everyone wanted the best for their beloved island. No decisions on the turbine installation would be made by the council until all sides were heard. Hecklers shouted that he'd long made up his mind to sell out to *WKA* developers. They momentarily ceased when the bearded man interfered by raising an imperious hand.

Frazzled, the little mayor attempted to announce the platform party. The Ponytail, he presented—to loud booing and whistling—as Ronny Rosso of *Niederwinder & Co* who proposed the *WKA*. Desperately waving both hands at his red-haired rescuer, the mayor sought to divert the protesters' attention.

In complete command of the situation, the bearded redhead stepped up laughing. Cheers and shouts erupted. "Danny,"

"*Unser Danny Boy!*" and "DD we love you." No doubt Daniel Dregger, representative of *Die Umwelt Partei*, the local chapter of 'The Environment Party,' was a high-acclaimed favorite before he introduced himself.

The much-loved Danny smiled benignly. "Allow me to recommend to you Nancy McLennon, a well-known pacifist environmental activist, whom I admire greatly." Both his and her followers broke into a riot of cheers. DD's translation was drowned out.

Always a sucker for speeches, Agnes stayed to enjoy herself. Rosso's was quite brief. In strongly accented German, his spin set out a win-win situation. Renewable energy was vital in times of global climate change. The windy north marched into a green future. Bosum could cash in and could expect huge profits. A sure-fire "grow rich quick gig," he promised.

Protestors started to interrupt Rosso. On cue, Daniel sidled up to Ponytail to come to his aid. With an irritated sideways glance, Ronny continued his upbeat sales pitch. Not only would the island overall prosper, but Niederwinder was willing to share their success. Everyone might secure a piece of the pie.

Despite cries of derision, this quickened the interest of bystanders. In imitation of Dregger, Ronny held up his hand and let the surprising moment of silence settle in before he explained. Niederwinder proposed an ingenious plan to involve local stakeholders—Agnes had to admit—to offer them shares that promised large long-term returns. A 25% return on one's money might be an exaggeration. Still, a lucrative deal when interest rates hit rock bottom.

A practically-minded woman asked when and where she might buy-in. The windy agent said all would be arranged soon and handed the mic to the head of town who announced McLennon's speech to much cheering.

Just like Ronny, Nancy spoke with an accent. Puzzled by Ronny's, Agnes recognized Nancy's as American. When expressions eluded her, Nancy resorted to English. Appeals to emotions figured prominently as she vividly described the environmental damage wind farms cause. Turbines, she argued, kill large colonies of birds, bats, and waterfowl in collision with blades the size of jetliner wings.

As though on cue, a small infant near the front launched a loud wailing which eerily was picked up by the loudspeakers. It stopped Nancy mid-sentence, her hands going up to her ears. What a sound, Agnes sympathized. A pro, the woman recovered her poise quickly and explained the island's role as a vital nesting ground and resting place for many rare species and migrating birds.

The talk drifted to melting icebergs, starving polar bears drifting on ice floats, floods, tsunamis, and general global mayhem. Spread out arms to include the gathered people, Nancy urged them to let nature be. "Humans," she said, repeating her final words in English to the cheers of her fans, "are only one of the planet's species and have no right to play God. We can no longer rape nature with impunity. We're not masters of the earth but plain citizens."

Though Agnes appreciated some points—after all, who is not concerned about climate change these days?—she objected to the wholesale condemnation of wind power. What was the alternative? Was Nancy advocating going nuclear? Hardly credible.

Daniel's calm voice chased away the gloom that had settled not only on Agnes. Fittingly, the cloud that had obscured the sun for the last ten minutes or so, gave way to brilliant sunshine. Thoughts of the beach floated up and were dispelled as DD riveted her attention.

It wasn't really what he said but how he said it that made it spellbinding. Awesome orator, Agnes acknowledged with a grin. A smart move to praise the previous speakers' forthrightness and to express sympathy for their views. Of course, everyone cherished Bosum's and the environment's well-being, he asserted. The tremendous boom of renewable resources held great potential for economically challenged regions. Why not harness what Mother Nature—in her infinite wisdom and generosity—provided at no cost?

Here some brave fans of Nancy interrupted with albeit polite calls, "What about the birds?" "Mother Nature's own free children have equal rights!" A benign nod into the general direction of the callers, Daniel responded with apparent pleasure.

"You're absolutely right. Other living beings are important. As candidate for *Die Umwelt Partei*, the local Environment Party, I for one, assure you we won't forget their well-being." In his own language, he emphasized the need to protect sentient life—as far as possible.

Hah, thought Agnes, the caveat at the end is nicely ambiguous.

Shamelessly he played the nimbyism card. Until islanders took charge of their own power generation, they lacked control over how it was sourced. For all they knew, it could be wind, or nuclear, or even coal. Wasn't it rather disingenuous to shout 'not in my backyard,' while accepting wind energy from the mainland?

Here a few people, Agnes noted, regarded their neighbors somewhat sheepishly.

Clever to seize the moment, he delivered his punchline—bilingual to reach all listeners, "With our own wind installation, we become autarkic—*plus* make a solid profit by feeding the power-hungry cities."

An elderly local asked in dialect what Danny Boy would tell the council to do. Accomplished orator that he was, DD pondered for a moment—head bent, fingers cradling his chin. Before the expectant silence turned into restlessness, he responded, "I'll vote for sustainability and self-sufficiency"—as though they had all deliberated together.

"Let's use the biggest turbines available to maximize the highest capacity with the lowest footprint. The area of the campground and nudist, or *FKK*, beach is just the place for it.

They've already scared away the birds," he said with an exaggerated wink.

The crowd broke into loud laughter. It raised chuckles even from the most serious of his listeners.

Leave on a high note—Agnes gave mute kudos. A quick check of the clock on the church tower dismayed her—she needed to run to meet Sera. Best to avoid the shopping mile. From a brochure provided by Mathilda, she recalled a less busy route via the dike which spanned the periphery of this end of the island and turned into a promenade.

Sure enough, the first side street she took led straight to it. Beach to her right—bustling with sunbathers, clamoring kids, and yapping dogs—and a bird's eye view of leafy streets on the left. Red and dark-brown clay-tiled roofs contrasted attractively with the abundant greenery and blooms of every shape and color. The prettiness of it all rooted Agnes to the spot.

While she looked down into a street closer to the embankment, she thought she spotted Sera in front of a house with a wide sun porch. A second later the woman ducked under a rose arbor, presumably leading to the front door.

Must have been mistaken, she concluded. What chance, Sera going to a private residence here. Her mom wasn't nosy. Nor was she the 'Photo! Photo!' tourist type. Admittedly, she always carried a sketchbook. After all, Sera wasn't merely a fine arts professor but an artist. Why go inside, though? Who on earth might Sera want to visit? Or did she have a doppelgänger?

Chapter 5

POLLY

Polly Holt shivered in a thin t-shirt and skinny roll-up jeans. Figures! Come the weekend the weather had to change. After the awesome sunny day yesterday, the bleak overcast sky made for a dreary late Saturday morning. A temperature drop of ten degrees or more.

The goose bumps brought a smile to her face, nonetheless. It hadn't been a come-on. More like letting her in on a joke. Upon seeing her exposed by an errant ray of early sunlight, the guy on the ladder sung out, "*Ei, ei was hab' ich da entdeckt? Zwei Erbsen auf ein Brett gesteckt!*" Loud enough to share his discovery with his mate on the roof, yet intended for her ears.

Idly, her mind played with his little rhyme. 'What do I spy? Two peas on a board, oh my.' Well, she'd prefer to think of them as Hershey Kisses. Either way, her boobs were nothing much to ogle at. Braless outlined under her skimpy t-shirt— they'd served well as an icebreaker.

Ready for a break from their work, they enjoyed airing their grievances against Windy Ronny. They feared the end of their business once the island was solidly covered with cheap wind energy.

Any hope the islanders might harbor of low prices was

naïve. Still, she felt sorry for Kai and Udo. Decent blokes scraping a living from a small solar company. No environmentalist but, hey, if the results were the same, who cares?

Polly rummaged in her backpack and knotted a fleece sweater over her shoulders to cover her back. Out of the wind, inside the Dune Café, it was not as nippy as outside. Old and drafty with large windows, it retained the night chill.

Quite a lunch crowd. *FKK* beach must be empty. Too frigid today. Keeps the nudists at bay—she chuckled to herself.

Not that she had anything against bare tits or bums. Unbidden an image of her first accidental encounter with a nudist beach filled her mind—an old geezer, true to nature, leering at her. Made her cringe from distaste. All he'd worn was a sleeping infant in a carrier strapped to his back.

"For Christ's sake," she'd cried indignantly. "Get the child out of the sun!" He'd smirked—knowingly.

The mere memory contracted her muscles to shudder under her skin.

"*Was darf's denn sein?*" The waitress' sudden appearance, asking what she might like, shuttered the mental striptease. Without thinking, Polly ordered a *Matjes* herring sandwich and coffee.

To distract herself, she moved over to the window seat and scanned the path into the dunes. A woman came into view pushing a bike awkwardly through the deep, loose sand and onto the boardwalk. The unrelenting wind whipped long dark curls across the woman's face, obscuring it. Ouch, how painful, thought Polly.

"*So. Ein Kännchen Kaffee für die Dame,*" the waitress announced while unloading 'the mini coffee pot for the Lady' and a cup and saucer plus a diminutive cream jug. Tickled at the thought of being labeled a lady, Polly assured her she didn't mind a little delay about the food.

The brew was still inky after she upended the tiny creamer. Crunching her bonus cookie, she saw the cyclist stand uncertainly in the middle of the Café. A helmet dangled from her left arm, her right hand gripped a small backpack. No idea where to park herself, Polly deduced.

Now she came closer and for a moment stood next to Polly's table. Shoulders slumped, she faced the exit, resigned to give up hope of lunch.

"Grab a seat, why don't ya?" The woman whipped around and regarded the speaker. "Hey, it's okay," Polly beamed at her. "People around here don't mind sharing a table—honestly."

"If you're sure… Don't want to intrude."

"Relax. No worries. In fact, I'll enjoy your company."

"How did you guess I speak English? By the way, I'm Agnes." The newcomer sank onto the proffered chair.

"Elementary, dear Watson." Voice dropped sonorously, Polly winked. "Not the hound but the helmet gave you away."

Puzzled Agnes glanced at the red helmet lying innocently on the floor.

"The back. Dig it? Says Bell and a tiny Canadian flag, eh?" Delighted, Polly watched as her companion's Madonna-like features lit up. As in Raphaelite Madonna, she thought, not the current aberration.

"Could have bought it there on vacation, couldn't I?"

"Was worth the risk. Ontario, I presume."

"How do you make that out, Holmes?"

"You talk like a Torontonian, Watson."

"Didn't know we sounded like anything special." Unconvinced Agnes puckered her brow.

A triumphant grin—Polly slapped the table. "Gotcha! Knew you'd admit to it when I entangled you."

"Oh, your friend is here too," interrupted the waitress in German and set down the food.

While her chance companion placed an order by pointing to a choice on the menu, Polly's mind and eyes wandered in tandem. Beautiful hands she has…

"Don't wait for me. Enjoy your sandwich."

"No sweat. Was never taught the finer points of manners." Her mouth full of delicious herring—mayonnaise dripping down her chin—Polly mumbled indistinctly.

A big gulp and a swipe at her lips—she inquired, "So what brings you here? Chilly for nudist sunbathing.—Not quite the type either."

"What's the type like, then?" All innocently arched eyebrows.

"Touché."

"No, you're right, though. Only came for a peek. Oh no—not at the nudists!" Face growing pink, Agnes explained, "Yesterday I was at a kind of town hall meeting. Someone said this area was the perfect site for a wind farm."

"Yeah, DD did. Heard him, too. Lots of folks beg to differ and resent it."

"You were there? Didn't see you."

"How could you with that many people milling about? Off to the sidelines I keep." Too new an acquaintance to share more, Polly decided.

"I still can't make up my mind about it." A puzzled expression crossed Agnes's features. "When the demonstrators gathered, I was shocked how many were against wind energy."

"Never heard the fuss about such projects in your province? The lonely turbine down at Lakeshore in Toronto can't have fooled you into thinking Ontario has gone green."

"Are you a Torontonian?" The Madonna face lit up eagerly.

"Been there, bought the t-shirt, yadayadayada." Polly hurried on, "Common knowledge—local residents are up in arms as soon as you mention a wind farm site search. Unless they are short on cash and own land to lease out. Wealthy landowners usually join the resistance."

"Come to think of it, I did read about a case some years ago in a small town north of Toronto where Hydro bought a place because someone sued them for health damage or something."

After a moment, Agnes added, "They likely imagine being sick because they hate the sight of turbines."

"Was just talking about it yesterday. No, the effects can be palpable for the homeowner. Psycho-somatic."

"What did you think of Daniel's point about making the island sustainably self-sufficient? An important consideration for locals, I believe. Especially if they personally profit through a buy-in."

With a shake of her head, Polly laughed. "Not all of them, I can tell you. A couple of dudes I nattered with are installing solar panels for the Café. None too pleased at Niederwinder's scheme, they are. Their outfit offers minor solar installations for the islanders. The two of them hoped to cater to summer residents too. Not that the two are environmentalists—they've jumped on the green bandwagon when their dad's store went broke. Small electric supply shop, and Dad rather a grump, I gathered."

"Wow. A whole life history they spilled to an incomer like you? You're not from around here, are you?"

"Nah. They liked my boobs." Polly pushed her chest out and chuckled deeply.

The shock and incredulity when Agnes stealthily eyed her neighbor was comical.

"Yah, yah, don't say it. Not much to write home about. Exactly why they joked about them."

"You chatted with such males?" Disbelief bordered on disgust in Agnes's voice.

"Let's say it served my purpose." Evasive now, Polly feared to lose her audience. "Kai and Udo mainly blame Windy Ronny —the geezer with the ponytail yesterday—for all evils about to descend on them."

"Why not DD too?"

"Without Rosso tempting the islanders with profit share, Daniel would stick to a mix of renewable energies supplemented by power imports, if need be."

"Makes no sense to gripe about the agent instead of the company who pushed the deal."

"Must fix on a person as scapegoat. People pick a clear enemy in any battle, and companies are amorphous." Pleased with her sagacious comment, Polly sat back.

Soup and salad almost finished, Agnes might leave in a moment. Somehow, Polly felt loath to let her companion go—or pedal, for that matter—out of her life again.

"How about you come into town tonight? Join me to find out more. At one of the pubs-cum-restaurants—*Zur Krone*. Can't miss it. The crown in its name is big on the sign outside." A paper napkin served to jot down directions for Agnes. "Our Ronny plans to reveal a money-making scheme too good to miss —or to be true, haha. Lots of fun—the opposition's bound to attend in full armor."

Now you're gushing, Polly thought as Agnes pocketed the note, forehead creased into a frown.

"Not sure if I can make it."

Disappointment welled up to Polly's chagrin, before Agnes continued unaware, "My mom and I are on hols together. So, to go out tonight…the whole thing's kind of difficult…"

"No sweat—" Slow down, Polly told herself, count to ten— or to three. "Why don't you bring your mom along?" To heap on a little persuasion can't hurt. "Such an opportunity for her to enjoy the local flair. Tourists usually miss the real atmosphere. Kicks off at eight-thirty. Place serves a decent dinner—your mother might like it. Say, an hour earlier?"

Uncertain or nervous, Agnes bit her lip. "Can't promise, but I'll ask her. By now she might be back—better leave, or she'll wonder—"

"Did she go shopping? Takes a while on a Saturday morning." Let her go! Polly ordered herself. "Are you staying at a hotel?" Immediately, she regretted appearing too insistent and curious.

Preoccupied, Agnes responded, "No—at a cottage out in the

dunes. Farther out from here." Frowning deeply, she muttered, "No idea where she was going. Went in the direction to the tip of the island. To the dead end." A headshake as though needing to dislodge an unwanted thought. "Well, maybe she's gone sketching."

"Didn't you ask her?"

Resolutely, Agnes rose and fastened her helmet. "Nope," she said, swinging her backpack over her shoulder, wallet ready in hand to pay on her way out, "When I noticed her from the window upstairs, she was too far…"

Lost in her own world, as though the image still held sway, Agnes visibly forced attention on Polly. "Anyway—so nice meeting you. If not tonight, we'll catch up another time. Or you can drop by. They call it Road's End. Ominous name for a delightful sunny cottage, don't you think?" A final wave and Agnes made for the exit.

Settled back in her chair and—skinny legs stretched out—Polly grinned at her sandals.

Chapter 6

AGNES

"Hey, Agnes! Over here!"

Her new acquaintance waved and bounced up and down at a table toward the far end of the packed dining room. *Die Krone* was a traditional German *Gasthaus* and combined hotel, restaurant, and pub. A sign in the foyer also pointed to a *Saal*—'a hall' for dances and other gatherings.

Upon their entry, an overwhelming smell of fried and baked fish and meat hit them. Waiters and waitresses juggled overloaded trays, held up precariously high above their heads. No one offered to seat them, and no 'Please wait to be seated' either.

Relieved Agnes, with Sera in tow, walked over to the table.

"Brilliant! Glad to meet your mom." The little jack-in-a-box bowed to Sera with a broad grin.

"Good thing you found an empty table," Agnes said, "I didn't think we stood a chance when we came in."

"Oh, fought off the onslaught like a knight," an impish, smiling face responded. "Told them I was expecting friends."

"You were quite confident then. Sorry, apparently Agnes didn't catch your name. Yes, I'm Agnes's mom. You can call me Sera, if you like."

When she told her mother of the invitation, Agnes realized she'd no clue who her lunch companion was. To her amazement, Sera appeared intrigued and accepted without hesitation.

"Polly. Polly Holt at your service." The little imp beamed and bowed again with a flourish like a Renaissance gent taking off his feathered cap. "So happy you decided to join me. Have a seat."

Minutes later, after they'd placed their order, Sera and Polly were absorbed in an animated chat. Taken aback by the immediate rapport, Agnes observed with envy. They're getting on like the proverbial house on fire, her mind commented. Odd metaphor, considering what happens in a blaze... For Christ's sake, they are discussing Sera's art! Never volunteers any comments about it to me, does she?

During one of her mother's funny anecdotes about students, Agnes became aware of Polly's eyes seeking her own. The warmth of her gaze sought to include Agnes while, nevertheless, remaining attentive to Sera, laughing at all the right spots.

"Did Agnes mention the commotion in the marketplace yesterday?" asked Polly, changing topics. At least she remembers my existence, Agnes thought.

"Yes—the first speech I heard for myself. So interesting to find out from my daughter what followed afterward."

Why didn't she say a thing when I told her about it today! Agnes bristled again—made her feel stupid to tell people things they knew. It gave her the sense of being tripped up into a false rendition of facts.

The waiter's clatter, piling up their plates with some of the plentiful food left over, prevented her from sinking into deeper resentment.

"Let's mosey on over to Windy Ronny's meeting." An eager Polly cut off renewed mental meanderings.

Inside the hall, Sera suggested remaining at the back.

"Suits me just fine. Sideliner is my middle name. You okay too, Agnes?"

While her mother asked about the evening's program, Agnes took the chance to scrutinize Polly. Can't be more than five feet at the most, she judged. At first glance, one might take the imp for a teen rather than an adult woman. Not over twenty-three or -five, at a guess. Hard to say, though. The light, wispy short hair and boyish figure remind one of an elf. The eyes—at times without warning—express wisdom well beyond the apparent age. A fun person, Agnes smiled remembering their banter at the café.

Meanwhile, the place filled up. Similar types like the attendees at the town gathering—off and on Agnes believed to recognize a face or two seen the day before. To judge by the peace sign t-shirts, Nancy's fans showed in full force. Some others emitted a hostile, fierce vibe. Don't be fanciful, Agnes scolded herself. You never know what might happen when people clash in a confined space, her more anxious self worried. Being close to the exit definitely was a plus.

At the front, a stage—equipped with a lectern and microphone, flanked by a table with several chairs—buzzed with activity. Three or four guys mucked about, readying the audio equipment, under the direction of a rather red-faced, beer-bellied man in shirt sleeves—perhaps the hotelier—who was in everyone's way.

Nervously, Agnes wondered about crowd control. No cops in sight. Hope it doesn't turn nasty, she fretted.

"What's worrying you, Agnes?" Perceptive Polly leaned over Sera to be heard despite the din.

"Usually, you expect officers to monitor this type of event—in case of trouble."

"You mean in riot gear?" her mother asked, eyes shooting up in astonishment.

"No, merely regular police presence, I meant."

"*Moin! Moin!*" The dialect greeting—used by locals any time of day—distorted now by sudden feedback and loud tapping, reverberated over the general babel. A gray-bearded man, attired like the very picture of a sea captain, stood at the mic. Only needs a pipe dangling from the side of his mouth, Agnes smirked, and the image would be complete.

Beside the speaker, Ronny the Ponytail now lounged at the table, preening at the impressive size of his audience. A woman and a man, both in dark business suits, sat next to him, the guy shuffling papers and checking his mobile by turns. Hands hovering over a laptop, the woman's eyes remained glued to the screen.

"Hello, people," the announcer began, "most of you know me, but for the rest: I'm Hinrich Dieken, proprietor of the Dunes Campground." The reason for his prominence eluded Agnes. Yet the reaction of locals and apparent summer residents bore him out.

"It's a great honor to present Mr. Rosso, who has asked us to schedule this meeting," he boomed. Ronny Rosso, he added, was accompanied by two representatives of *Niederwinder & Co.* In all the laudations Agnes missed their names.

As agent, Dieken assured them, Ronny was authorized to make a fantastic proposal. His assistants were happy to answer any questions about the *WKA* and how to become involved.

A rumbling of unrest and dissent emanated from the ranks of Nancy's followers. Their leader herself was nowhere in sight, Agnes noted.

"*Immer mit der Ruhe,*" Dieken held up his hand in a placating 'calm down' motion that mirrored his words. His arm swept toward Ronny, inviting him to take over the mic.

Again in youthful black, Ponytail jumped up with elasticity —energetic entrepreneur personified. Without preamble, he launched into a sales pitch for shares in the wind farm. Examples of similar projects—peppered with figures and stats—were to prove the gains for private investors "*wie du und ich.*"

'Like you and me'—yeah right, Agnes rolled her eyes at his folk rhetoric.

A PowerPoint presentation ran in the background, operated

by the woman at the laptop. Images of wind turbines rotating against a blue North Sea sky, dotted with puffy white clouds, sometimes soaring gulls and cuddly white sheep and lambs in the foreground. All very picturesque. Peaceful coexistence of turbine, bird, and beast—a neat touch, Agnes reflected.

A Nancy fan interrupted him in English, "There's yet no permission to build. You're taking your victory for granted!"

The sales agent did not miss a beat but continued his spiel. Once the council announced their decision in favor of the *WKA* in the best interest of everybody on the island, he would hold another meeting Monday night. Anyone ready to commit could sign-up for a buy-in. "Early bird gets the worm," he concluded.

"*Vögel die am Morgen singen, frisst am Abend die Katz,*" shouted someone in the back, and was drowned in a general rumpus.

"What did he say?" Sera asked. "I didn't catch it with all this noise."

"He said, 'birds that sing in the morning get eaten by the cat at night,'" translated Polly.

"Sounds like a threat." Her heartbeat increased in tandem with her unease, making Agnes hypersensitive to nuances.

The tension rose when a belligerent voice shouted in German, how many windmills Ronny intended to plant in front of their noses. The massive man, a purplish color rising up his broad neck, gesticulated wildly and shook his fist at Ponytail.

In answer, Ronny laughed and promised enough turbines for all of them to buy shares. This infuriated the yeller into a stream of obscenities. Another person screeched DD would stop such rape of nature.

After a chopping motion across his throat to prompt the tech guy to cut off the extra microphone, Rosso countered in flippant tones the decision was up to the council and the regional planning commission. In Bosum's best interest, they were bound to vote to max capacity and profit. The necessary cables were in place to export to the mainland. Property owners plus the municipality, he claimed, expressed strong interest in hosting turbines.

Cries of "Shame, shame…" and "Turbines kill" and similar slogans—the dissenters were strategically positioned all over the room.

A man—perhaps a prosperous vacationer to judge by the impeccable white slacks, navy blue sweater crowned by a white shirt collar—grabbed a mic. Approved by the sound techie, his educated voice now came over the speakers, drowning out chanting and shouting. Into the momentary silence, he voiced his disgust at the destruction of this paradisiacal island for base mammon.

A sure recipe for adding fuel to the flames of outrage. Some locals yelled, "Speak for yourself!" The campground owner-cum-moderator tried to take center stage but proved inapt at crowd control.

Disturbed by the hostile atmosphere, Agnes turned to Sera and Polly. "Stay, or leave now?"

Her mounting anxiety made both eager to assent.

"Let's go for a stroll on the promenade. Ice cream or tea after? My treat," said Polly and ushered them through the double doors leading to the adjacent pub.

At the bar, a group of young males—skinheads and short-shorn types—jostled each other, snickering, and pointing at the women.

What a mean and nasty bunch, Agnes thought and chided herself for her snap judgment. Nonetheless, she linked arms with her mom to hurry her to the exit.

A skinhead made to block their path and jeered, "*Olle Lesben!*"

In reaction to his intended insult, 'old lesbians,' little Polly stepped in front of Sera to shield her.

Suddenly two older, brawny males muscled their way in between the women and the skinheads. The taller hissed something at the aggressor that made him flinch and turn tail. To save face, he shouted for another round for his buddies. Their cheering and shoulder slapping evidently restored his macho image.

The familiar way Polly thanked their rescuers led Agnes to assume they must have met before. An odd couple for the imp to be chummy with, she wondered as she regarded them more closely. Spotless, conventional short-sleeved dress shirts over equally clean jeans, both of them were in their late forties, she guessed. The tall one gave Polly a quick sideways hug and the other patted her head affectionately. As the guys walked them to the door, Sera and Agnes added their thanks.

Once outside, Sera—although visibly shaken—made an effort to sound off-hand when she said to Polly, "You are quite adroit at making friends."

"Oh, that's just Kai and Udo. Met them this morning. All in a day's work."

Ah, the fellows who insulted her, Agnes deduced. The way they'd treated Polly tonight was sort of big-brotherly and by no means impertinent.

"Let's fill our lungs with some bracing sea air to blow away that bar stench. Well, perhaps you…"

"Too true, Polly. A brisk little walk is just what we need," Sera said kindly.

When they reached the west side of the promenade, the sea wall was packed with people, all gazing at the sun sinking into the water horizon. Within minutes, Polly found them a spot on the slope of the dike where a group of sun worshippers greeted them with the obligatory '*moin*'—readily adopted even by tourists—and courteously made room for them.

Whether it was the peaceful atmosphere emanating from the crowd focused westward in contemplation, or any other cause, Agnes rarely had felt so at peace next to Sera. The presence of Polly—the natural exuberance serenely muted—had something to do with it.

Focused on the waves rolling ceaselessly onto the beach and draining back into the sea, the tension drained from body and mind. For a moment she felt her mother's hand rest on hers, warm and soft. As she turned, Sera was facing the setting sun. With a sigh of content, Agnes let go.

Chapter 7

POLLY

"*Hab' ich dir doch gleich gesagt!*"

The 'I told you so!' earned a shushing sound and a hissed "*Mami!*" The end vowel drawn into a long 'eee.'

In vain. The deep and penetrating elderly voice continued unabashed in German to malign cake and Tea House alike. The daughter's desperate, 'Not so loud. People are listening,' was met with, 'I don't care! They'll never see us again.'

Across the bench from Polly, Agnes and Sera buried their faces behind the menu. Earlier, when the three of them came in, Polly had noticed the women in the next booth because of the elderly woman's outfit—youthful turquois-white striped blazer revealing tons of chunky bead jewelry, white hair held back by a folded pink, gauzy tulle scarf. The middle-aged daughter was downright dowdy.

Curious, Polly unobtrusively glanced back. The rebel mother, who enjoyed her offspring's discomfiture, now summoned the waitress, clinking away with a spoon against the porcelain teacup. A timid, '*Mami*, one doesn't do that anymore —so rude,' made her cackle. Told the cake was 'disgustingly stale,' the server hastened to add up the bill.

Hell, I sure know how to pick places tonight—Polly clenched

her teeth. Unnerved by her own companions' evident embarrassment, Polly blabbered about the history of the venue—embossed on the placemats—and translated how to brew a perfect cuppa the East Frisian way.

When their neighbors passed their table on the way out, the mother in the lead, Polly fleetingly caught an expression like 'there but for the grace of God' on Sera's and Agnes's face.

To distract them, she asked upbeat, "What did you think, then, of that meeting tonight? You understand the language, don't you?"

"Sera brought me up bilingual, and I went to German school every Saturday morning for years on end."

"As a teenager, she refused to speak it. Never quite knew why," said Sera.

"I took it again at Uni—for academic purposes. Professor Jones suggested it as vital for my dissertation research—and he was right." The tone was smug and Agnes's expression defiant.

"Professor Jones? I can't think why you still don't call him Michael." To Polly, Sera explained, "She lived with them for years when I got a position at a university in the Maritimes. A self-determined teenager of sixteen, Agnes chose to stay in Toronto with our friends to finish high school."

Two familiar faces entered and passed on to the vacated booth behind theirs. With a twitch of her shoulder, Polly motioned to draw attention to the newcomers. Why Sera would ask a moment later to switch seats, puzzled Polly. Still, it suited her well to be able to observe Ronny and DD who were settled at the table occupied before by the outspoken octogenarian.

Not wanting to make her interest in the guys too obvious, Polly focused on her companions and returned to the interrupted conversation. Neither Sera nor Agnes wanted to share more. A sensitive topic, Polly assumed as Sera instead said it was getting late and they still needed to cycle back.

"Why don't you come visit tomorrow?" Sera gave Polly's

hand a gentle squeeze. "Say, eleven or so? Road's End, they call it—can't miss it past the campground."

"Sweet of you to invite me—thanks so much—I will."

Pleased with the outcome, Polly watched them walk to the front to pay. From the door, they gave her a last smiling wave and were gone. Too late she remembered her intention to treat them to a nightcap. Oh well—next time.

In a fluid motion, she sidled over to the other bench again, her back towards the men at the adjacent table. The joint was almost empty now. Rummaging in her scuffed messenger bag, Polly brought out her iPhone and attached earbuds loosely to her ear. Another deep delve and a tattered paperback surfaced. Thus equipped, she settled back comfortably to focus on her neighbors' conversation.

Not a moment too soon. Right into an argument they were. At least, Ronny was. In English too, presumably hoping other patrons were linguistically challenged. Unless it just came more naturally to Rosso.

"Don't try and throw a spanner into the works now," he hissed. "You promised to back me. No one dictates how many turbines we'll put up. Your party is *for* wind energy. The more the merrier, I'd say!"

"Yes, my party supports its expansion. My mandate, however, is to reconcile human needs with environmental," a pompous, yet calm, Daniel responded.

"Spare me your political propaganda, DD! Save it for your fan club. We're talking business here—not bloody ideology! You let me down at the council tomorrow, you'll pay for it big time!"

"Are you threatening me?" A chill, like January's north wind, infused Daniel's tone.

Insufficient to cool off Ronny's wrath. "You'd better believe it, buddy. The Guttenberg scandal was nothing compared to what's going to blow your way if you cross me. I've staked my life on this deal—Niederwinder depends on me."

"I've no idea what you are talking about," stonewalled DD.

A kingdom to watch their faces, groaned Polly. Too obvious to take a selfie now to achieve that. The bench backs were far too high to get the occupants into her line of vision. Made for decent cover for eavesdroppers though.

"Don't give me that crap, Danny Boy! No need to spell it out. Got some councilors in my pocket. They know which way the wind is blowing." Rosso laughed menacingly. "Without me, no deal. With me, everyone wins. Don't you forget it, man."

"I won't listen to more of your threats. It's clear what action to take." Apparently, Daniel had already gotten up and now passed her table in large strides to the exit.

Though tempted to catch a glimpse, she kept her eyes glued to the book and tapped her iPhone in tune to an imaginary beat.

A few minutes passed in which Polly maintained her pose. Then a shadow blocked out the overhead light.

"*Hallooochen, Mädel. So ganz allein heute Abend?*" All syrupy seductive for a 'gal, so all alone this evening,' Ronny cooed.

Only when a hand was casually placed next to her own, did Polly react with a simulated start. An elaborate fumble to squeeze her mobile's side to stop the non-existent music, she pulled one earbud to let it dangle. Glazed eyes lifted to the old geezer, emerging from another world. Perfect show.

"*Wie bitte?* Her polite, 'Pardon me?' secured another pause to punctuate her pretend confusion. While he ogled, fake recognition hit her. "*Moin, Herr Rosso. Was bringt Sie denn her?*" Inane question—'What brings you here?'—yet, worked like a charm.

"*Na, darf man sich dazu setzen, kleines Fräulein.*"

Yuk! her mind commented in reflex to his question whether he might join the little Miss. Face muscles under full control, she beamed a welcome and made sure to giggle her permission. So thrilled, she gushed in German, delighted to talk to him. Totally fascinated by his speeches at the rally yesterday and at tonight's meeting… Love to hear more!

Make it snappy, she mentally added, the place is about to close.

As soon as he'd made himself comfy—expansively spreading one arm along the top of the bench across from her—she coyly began to question him. Quite a challenge to balance sounding naïve with getting some worthwhile info. Harder with a guy who's on autopilot, mixing sales pitch with sexual innuendo. Made her queasy, yet amused at his antics and her skill to fend them off, all the while fluttering eyelids to rivet his attention.

"Gosh, Polly, did you see Nancy?" an anxious voice interrupted without warning.

Shoot! The last thing needed just now. A frazzled guy in dreadlocks came up to her.

"Was supposed to meet her here. Did she come by?"

Before she could answer, the intruder turned and saw Rosso.

"What the hell are you doing with that scumbag!" Outraged, and stunned.

So was Ronny.

Now, I've done it—Polly prepared herself for waves of wrath to crash upon her poor head. Nothing for it—aim for efficiency.

"Sorry, Mark." Calmly, she switched to English. "No hide or hair of her tonight. Took the opportunity to inquire into Mr. Rosso's intentions though."

"You little bitch!" Rosso jumped up sputtering. "You a ruddy reporter or what?" Without waiting for her reply, he pushed Mark out of the way and stormed to the door.

His objective received a setback. A man from a large table in an alcove up front cut off Ronny's retreat by diving in his path. Ah, the incomer-cum-sailor who bemoaned the destruction of paradise for mere money, Polly presumed, as he accosted Rosso loudly enough for everyone to hear.

"*Nur damit Sie's wissen. Wir nehmen uns einen Anwalt.*" A vague gesture to people out of view at his table implied their involvement in the announced threat that they were getting a lawyer.

The windy agent didn't want to know but thrust out both

hands to push the man out of his way. Before he could make contact, however, a strong hand reached out from the alcove and pulled the fancy mariner back by the tails of his navy blazer.

"Hermann, ich bitte dich! Keine Szene!" A blond head of a woman came into view.

Her begging him not to make a scene exasperated Hermann all the more. Swinging around, he thundered at her that people still had the right to voice their opinion. 'Stay out of this, Mattie,' he growled—in German, of course—and denied her this very freedom of speech.

In the meantime, Rosso dodged to the exit. On the way, he stuffed a bill into the spell-bound waitress's open money pouch strapped to her ample waist. No bill-dodging for him.

Mark, who'd been brooding over the scene, stormed out after him.

No time like the present to bow out, Polly decided. First, need a loo. She hurried toward the washrooms at the rear.

Crap! Did I leave my iPhone in the booth? Annoyed, she turned back—her hand fumbled through her bag and latched on to the phone. The sight of a person sorting heaps of paper in a booth separated by a flimsy room divider from the one Rosso and DD had occupied, stopped her short. The woman seemed utterly engrossed in her work. Polly stepped closer. "Fancy seeing you here."

A head with short dark hair sprinkled with gray lifted to face her. Earbud cables emerged from both ears connected to a tablet. How ironic, Polly admitted mutely—nah, nowhere near as convincing as me.

"Hi, Polly. A trifle late for tea. They are ready to close." Elaborate shuffling of papers.

"Oh, c'mon, Nancy. Gimme a break." With a sigh, Polly plunked down on the opposite bench. "No way you missed over-hearing Ronny."

The older woman merely raised her eyebrows.

"Why didn't you say anything when Mark came for you just now?"

The other stuffed sheets into a backpack.

"Yeah, well—stupid question." Tired of waiting, Polly answered herself and got up. "I'd love to stay and chat but my bladder's bursting. See ya around."

"Take care, Polly," Nancy said softly. "I mean it."

By the time Polly left the loo, the booth was empty. In fact, the whole place was deserted.

Chapter 8
AGNES

"*Ju—huh*...anyone home?"

The cheery voice reverberated through the kitchen and reached them on the stone patio out back. A careful peek around the small back window to the inside revealed to Agnes a heated red face framed by blond hair.

Superwoman Mathilda hollered from out front. Poked her head right into the window.

"Should we pretend no one's home?" Agnes asked softly as she turned to Sera next to her at the little bistro table. So much for a peaceful Sunday morning. They both sighed.

"No use. She'll track us down," said Sera with a smile.

For almost an hour, they'd enjoyed the warm sunshine—lingering over breakfast, off and on gazing at the dunes where a tiny gap allowed a glimpse of the sea.

Bumblebees buzzed in the wild roses climbing the back of the cottage at one end. The sweet scent of their blooms and warming sand spiced the air. A fresh breeze caressed them in the shelter of the sandy knolls.

The prediction proved correct. For an indomitable Mathilda stormed in from the side path with a cry, "*Ach, da sind Sie!*"

Well, there they were, indeed. Both of them echoed Mathilda's *moin*, and Agnes mustered her German to remark on the beautiful day. So far Sera had been strangely reluctant to address their host in her own language. Maybe she lacked the opportunity in Nova Scotia and lost the knack of it over time.

"Have you everything you need?" Determined to practice her English, Mathilda relieved them of the need to make an effort. "I brought you a basket of fresh vegetables and berries from my garden. It is on the little table under the window."

Their thanks heightened the beaming red complexion. "*Och,* one does what one can, *ne?* Happy guests come back—that is my motto!"

With an audible thump and an "*aah*" of content, she sank unbidden onto the little bench at the side of the flagstone deck. Well, she owns it, Agnes told herself.

"And how do you like our little island? Is beautiful, *ne?*"

Very much, they assured her. Politely, Sera offered coffee. Mathilda declined but regaled them instead with local news. Without fail, the conversation turned to the hottest topic: the *WKA*, the wind power installation.

Her English somewhat deserted her at times. Yet, outrage at any plans to place turbines in the vicinity of Road's End, or close to her other properties came across loud and clear.

From what Agnes could gather, their rental was the smallest of Mathilda's many vacation units. Must be quite a lucrative gig, Agnes supposed. Hubby appeared to be a physician. No wonder they could afford a spacious villa in Bavaria, the scenic alpine south of Germany, as their main residence.

The mention of her home near Munich made Mathilda fretful. Down south the same problem plagued them as here up north. "*Windmühlen überall,*" she exclaimed exasperated. Frau Merkel was nuts to allow 'windmills everywhere,' their hostess insisted. What's more, Merkel as the Chancellor, must shoulder the blame for causing all this by "stepping out of the atom contract from one day to the next, just like that!" She snapped her fingers at them.

All this insider lore bewildered Agnes whose head started to swim. The gist; Mathilda's *Männi* was fed up and would put a stop to it.

Was *Männi* her spouse's nickname, or did she use it for 'hubby?' Equally likely. Either way, Agnes wondered, how's hubby going to put an end to it?

A rapping on the open window out front interrupted. As she rose to check, Agnes was thrilled to recognize Polly's grinning face. A little hand waved a salute.

"C'mon over," she called out. "Little gate to your right."

A moment later Polly came into full view.

"How nice to see you," Sera greeted her. She'd been very quiet, leaving Agnes to hold up their end of the conversation with their landlady. Not much was needed—the woman could well prop up any discourse single-handedly.

"*Ach*, a visit," said Mathilda and pushed herself up, ready to leave. "Then I do not want to…*stören*… What is the word?"

"'To intrude' you mean," Agnes murmured but hastened to assure her that she was welcome to stay.

Lunch for *Männi* demanded Mathilda's attention, however, and she rushed off.

"Hope it's not me who's butting in?"

Such diffidence was the last thing Agnes expected in Polly.

In answer, Sera smilingly patted the chair next to her own. Agnes went inside for a mug and kitchen stool. While she poured coffee for Polly, her mom moved raisin bread and jam closer.

"I shouldn't let you, but I love a warm welcome." The trademark impish grin spoke for itself. "So, what's up today? Ready for adventure?"

Like a happy, carefree child, Agnes thought.

"Glad to put a smile on your face, Agnes. How about a hike to the tip of the island? We can go out along the beach and back through the *Naturschutzpark*. Awesome bird sanctuary."

"Sounds scenic. What do you think, Mom?"

"My kind of thing. A picnic lunch? Mathilda's veggie basket comes in handy."

"Packed a boring peanut butter sandwich. Any addition to the menu is most welcome." In anticipation, Polly bounced in her seat.

"Why not go the other way around—return by the shore to cool off?" Agnes asked.

"High tide," replied both in unison.

"You two are quite the sailors."

"You better know your tide tables around here," said Polly. "Don't want to be cut off in an awkward spot."

By ten-thirty they trooped down the dune path to the sea.

The water hardly ripples and is far out, Agnes mused. Unless I'd stay rooted here for a day, I'd never be able to tell if it's coming or going.

"How did you ever luck out finding this place?" Sandals swinging in one hand, Polly sidled up to her. "Wicked location."

"Ask Sera. She sent me the email address to book it. No kudos for me, I'm afraid."

In her brisk gait, her mother strode far ahead. They scampered through the deep warm sand to catch up. Down at the shoreline, the hard-packed surface was easier to walk on.

The wind blew snatches of her mom's conversation with Polly in Agnes's direction as she loitered behind.

For several miles, the beach stretched all the way to the tip of the island. Off and on they passed other walkers. Some threw sticks or floating balls into the waves for their dogs to retrieve. Barking and voices, buffered and muffled by the incessant sucking and rolling of the surf. Shrieks of gulls pierced the air.

The three of them moved inward with the tide, barefoot splashing through the lowest waves that chased each other only to dissolve. Soggy sand oozing between her toes, Agnes stopped at times to wriggle them in the suction of a retreating wave. Salty foam bobbed against her calves and made them tingle.

"Good for your feet. Massage and pedicure rolled in one."

"Where do you pick up all this sea lore?" Surprised Agnes gaped at her mom.

"I do live by the ocean," said Sera mildly sarcastic. "For decades now, if you remember?"

"Silly of me. Of course. Guess I've lost touch…" Heat rising, Agnes floundered under Polly's astonished gaze.

Perhaps as a distraction, Polly launched into an anecdote from Bosum's checkered past. About to ask how Polly knew all this, Agnes groaned mutely—googled it, as any sensible person would do. Never occurred to me to browse for the island's history, she chided herself. Too preoccupied by anxiety about three weeks with an estranged mother.

By midday, they reached the tip of the island—if that wasn't a misnomer. The beach simply curved landward into the shallows and marshy terrain. The sun burned intensely despite the steady wind. Only tiny cumulus clouds dotted the endless blue.

"Let's find a spot for our picnic. Not too far into the dunes, though, Agnes." Her mom called her back. "They belong to the restricted area." Made Agnes feel like a moron who needed signs to avoid treading on Mother Nature's toes.

After a leisurely lunch, laid out on Sera's lightweight beach blanket, Agnes succumbed to drowsiness. As though from far away, her mother's voice—asking about ferries to neighboring islands—faded in and out. "…want to go… Tomorrow? …dear? Means getting up…"

"Agnes, wake up sleepyhead." A gentle touch on her shoulder. "Gotta get going before the tide cuts us off."

That woke her up alright. Being stranded—literally—was not her kind of sport. She reached up to rub her eyes. Mistake —*ouch*—grit. Polly's, "Hold still," followed by some water trickling over her eyes and gentle dabbing with something cottony soft.

"Sorry, didn't mean to startle you." Contrite, Polly helped her to sit up. "We do need to start back."

"Did I really doze off?"

"Out like a light for three-quarters of an hour or so," chuckled the imp.

All packed up and ready to leave, Sera smiled down at her. Agnes scrambled awkwardly to her feet.

"Here, have a drink of water." Practical as usual, her mother offered her the cup lid of a thermos.

The coolness of the water brought her back somewhat. Still woozy after soaking up too much midday sun, Agnes walked quietly along.

The low-lying path through the nature reserve proved narrow and stifling. Tons of insects of all types swarmed over the marshy ground. Boggy smells of decaying vegetation permeated the afternoon heat. Buzzing critters everywhere around them.

A large sign—*Nationalpark Wattenmeer, UNESCO Weltnaturerbe*, World Heritage Site —announced the reserve's boundary as they moved inland. Part of its writing was no longer legible, defaced by black spray paint. What bleeding jackass does that? Such senseless, willful destruction…

Perhaps in response to her deep sigh, Polly reeled off information about wildlife, habitats, and all kinds of fun facts about the park and bird sanctuary.

"How come you know so much about it?"

"My hobby horse, so to speak," said Polly with a dismissive wave of her skinny arm. "Compulsive reader, too." Before Agnes could ask more, she turned to Sera behind them to point out some birds in a nearby pond.

Watching them, Agnes's mind freewheeled. What luck we found her. Well, she found you. Whatever. That moment we stopped on the ride home last night…got all emotional when Sera put her arm around me…pointing to the Big Dipper in the night sky. Never were so close for ages. Not since I was twelve or thirteen… Polly actually picked you up. You know she's lesbian. So what? I'm not. Can't even manage hetero relationships. Not after the last fiasco…

As though tapping into her mind, Polly turned around and caught Agnes contemplating her. Sort of startled, the grin froze on the elfin face—for a moment it grew…sad. Yet she rallied immediately, while Agnes marshaled her own features into a smile.

It was going on five when they finally reached the cottage, all sweaty, gritty with sand. A shower—yearned Agnes—followed by a nap in the serene bedroom, how heavenly.

Though she accepted some icy cold mineral water, Polly declined Sera's invitation to dinner. On her way out, she offered, "If you like, I can make reservations for your trip tomorrow when I'm in town. You'd better leave early to make sure—"

"What trip?" Puzzled, Agnes frowned. "Aren't we trying to sit in on the council meeting? Didn't you say the public can attend?"

Both of them gave her a funny look.

"If you'd rather stay here, that's fine. Of course, I can go on my own." The resignation was unmistakable in her mother's tone.

"Go where?"

More forthright, Polly put her straight. "Don't you remember, sleepyhead? You agreed to go on an island excursion. You'll enjoy it. No worries, I'll report on council proceedings—aye aye, Madame Capitaine!"

Unsure, Agnes hesitated—but seeing her mom's face—

"Tell you what," the imp hastened on. "Why don't I pick you two up at the ferry terminal—do dinner? There's a seafood place on the old fishery wharf. Awesome and quaint." To Agnes's amusement, she grotesquely winked at them, her index finger across her lips. "Psst—mum's the word. A Bosum insider tip."

"*Oold Fischhus.*" Dreamily, as though far away, Sera spoke the words.

"Do you know it? Been there already?" Deflated, Polly slumped.

"What?" With a start, Sera re-entered their universe. "Sorry, Polly, what did you say?"

"The *Oold Fischhus*. Have you tried it? We can go somewhere else."

"Oh, no. The ratings and reviews on the internet… Yes, let's." A determined pat on Polly's arm punctuated Sera's reply.

"Can't wait. Bye, Polly. Thanks!" In a serious hurry now, Agnes was halfway up the stairs, shouting "Me first!" before the door had closed on her new friend.

Chapter 9
POLLY

Grubby and sweaty, dried up salt and sand still caking her feet and legs, Polly wriggled on the hard chair. The Sunday night meeting—called by the local chapter of the *Naturschutzverein*, an organization for the protection of nature—dragged on painfully. Intended as a last-minute information session and discussion forum for a concerned public, the aim to strengthen the anti-turbine side became soon obvious. Bosum's Town Council hearing on Monday afternoon loomed largely. Environmental groups and activists outnumbered the islanders the organizers hoped to target.

Without AC, the stagnant air stifled. A shower would be heavenly. Earlier at the Doll's House—as she'd dubbed her tiny backyard rental cabin—Polly automatically started to undress when she returned from Road's End. Last minute, she'd figured grubbiness helped to fit in with the guys she'd planned to hang out with. Most of the enviros either pitched their tents at the campground or crashed at the crowded youth hostel. The old pub-cum-dance hall the event now took place was around the corner from it.

An angry voice brought her back into the present. A woman

demanded for Niederwinder's application letter to the council to
be read out. The moderator complied.

"What's he reading?" Mark leaned over. "Can't you translate? You understand German, don't you?"

"Are you kiddin'? I'm not a friggin' synchronous inter-
preter," she protested.

To forestall more whining, she said, "OK, bud. The gist is
they're filing an initial application for a wind park with six
turbines 150 to 190 meters high.—Hey, that's a maximum
height of over 600 feet.—Their capacity will make the island
autarkic and allow for energy export to the mainland. Proposed
sites span Zone 3 and border Zone 2 on one side.—By the map
posted on the website it goes from here to the campground—"

"Whoa, slow down," interrupted the ungrateful dude.
"What this zones stuff are you talking about? What does it
mean?" The vowels of the last word drawled like some petulant
toddler demanding candies.

Eyes widening, she mimicked him, "Man, you must know
that? Call yourself an enviro activist and no clue what gives?"

"Don't jabber at me, Polly. Just tell me."

"Zone 3 is for general human use. Zone 2 is restricted use
area. Take the marked paths through the dunes, for example.
You can go there but can't simply walk into the sand-scape as
you please. Zone 1—designated as *Ruhezone* or 'resting zone'—is
for the birds, not us. Off-limits to all except researchers with
special—"

To stop the barrage of info, Mark threw up his hands.
"Polly, give a guy a break! Stick to the topic."

"I *am*! Never mind… To make their case, Niederwinder uses
the federal government's support of wind energy. Germany
plans to phase out nuclear power. So, alternatives are in
demand."

"Bound to tickle the council's fancy," her neighbor muttered
darkly. "The Green faction will lap it all up."

Someone in the audience echoed Mark's prediction.

Sarcasm only too obvious, the man asked if anyone in their right mind preferred radiation from nuclear waste and accidents to wind power.

"What's he saying?" fretted Mark.

Yet again, Polly translated—exasperated. First, when she ran into him outside the hall, he'd accosted her as a traitor for talking to Ronny. Her explanation of doing research to broaden her information base swung him to the other extreme. Praised her for bravely infiltrating enemy lines; his words. Afterward, he stuck to her like old gum to the pavement.

Now with his constant interruptions, her focus slipped. The debate moved to accusations and counter-accusations. Some blamed all evil on Rosso. Others hailed him as a blessing for the island. The more level-headed declared him to be irrelevant to the real issue.

"This is effing madness," a livid male shouted down everyone. "We've got to stop this NOW! The entire landscape is gonna be plastered with wind turbines!"

A man of indeterminate age—died flame-red hair wildly flowing over his shoulders and hanging into his face—jumped up at the front and swung around to glare at the assembly. A dark beard obscured the lower part of his face. Only of middle height, his voice, appearance, and gesticulating made him larger than life.

On the roll, he raged on, "Whatever isn't cluttered with turbines, they plant with bio-fuel crops. Soon, no nature is left in this bloody country for you to protect!"

Well, well—our Torch, ready to throw a trademark tantrum. Despite the new disguise, Polly felt certain to recognize the self-proclaimed EcoLib spokesman. The Eco Liberty Lovers, an international organization fighting at times ruthlessly for environmental causes, attracted all sorts. Always operating undercover, Torch changed his appearance like a chameleon. Otherwise, the FBI might have cuffed him long ago.

The nickname said it all. Wanted for any number of arson

attacks, EcoLibers disowned him for his right-wing eco-fascist love of violence. In fact, she knew their website now disavowed torching things or any violent aggression as means of protest. Those who play with fire will die in the flames. Not likely the Feds or the general public believed EcoLib had become pacifist. The FBI labeled them a domestic terrorist threat, a bunch of eco-terrorists.

From her own impression of Tor, he qualified as a firebug looking for an excuse. Any cause would do.

His shouting, however, got everyone's attention now. Hadn't come alone either—others chimed in, or encouraged him, "Way t'go Torsten."

Ah, his current incognito. Stupidly close to home, Polly reckoned.

As more and more English speakers took over, some locals and what looked like well-to-do summer residents started to leave in obvious frustration.

Stuck in his groove, Tor barraged willing and unwilling listeners alike with virulent calls for action. A reasonable person's caution of moderation incensed him further.

"If you're not on our side, what are you doing here?" thundered Tor.

One of the *Naturschutz* organizers—too timid or polite to interrupt—used the tiny pause before Torch could bellow with renewed force, to interject, "We appreciate your support." With mechanic nods in the madman's direction, "We really do. Please understand, our people want to live in peace and protect our nature. The problem is not wind energy. Only—our small island cannot sustain it. Most is designated environmentally sensitive—"

"So, you are saying you're just a bunch of NIMBYs, is that it?" Typical bully, Tor closed in on the organizer who gave ground, intimidated.

Shaken, he nevertheless responded, "Sorry, I do not—What are Nimbies?"

"Not In My Back Yard! Get it? Do it anywhere else but not here!"

More and more of the non-activists got up during this exchange and headed for the doors. The session deteriorated by the minute. Defeats the purpose, Polly wondered, or do Tor and Co aim for chaos?

The moderator desperately tried to regain control—to no avail.

"Think you can pick and choose who gets to be downwind of this?" Determined to close in for the kill, Tor swiped at all and sundry. "It's all a corporate money grab! Land and sea will be littered with onshore and offshore wind parks. Oil rigs clutter the North Sea! Plastic trash's choking the oceans!"

Now he's lost it, Polly diagnosed. No stopping him when he raves.

"Torsten, please… That's not the point here. It doesn't help to antagonize—"

Polly recognized Nancy's voice.

"Me? Antagonize? I just tell him how it is!" The maniac lashed out at her instead.

As people left in droves, Polly spotted an elegant man in a blue designer shirt. Accompanied by a blond woman, the pair talked loudly on their way to the rear exit.

Her curiosity aroused, Polly's mind went into full gear. If that isn't the woman at Sera's and Agnes's this morning… Yup, it's her. Just spruced up now. Wonder who she is? … The man looked perfectly groomed from close-up as they walked by. Hah! The couple from the Tea House! Pissed off at something, they are.

By now disorder reigned. Half-hearted closing remarks of a brave *Naturschützer* petered out in the hubbub of scraping chairs and venting tongues of a general exodus. Only some protesters and activists remained for a post-mortem.

Suddenly ravenous, Polly got up to leave. Almost at the double doors at the far end, she succumbed to her inquisitive streak. Stairs led to a corridor with a sign WC. A steep climb further up, and she reached a narrow columned gallery. Concealed by a pillar, she gained a bird's eye view of the hall below. The stragglers congregated in distinct groupings. Why Torsten chatted among a flock of skinheads, didn't puzzle only her. The unease of his supporters showed in their furtive glances and unrest.

Her focus shifted when Mark disengaged himself from his buddies to make a beeline for Nancy. No luck. The side door swung shut before he had reached his target. Steps behind the pacifist leader followed a woman in her mid-twenties, sporting granny glasses—her body swaddled in home-knit woolly stuff. A pink, flat, fluffy hat set off her ash-blond braids.

Yah well, that figures. Where Nancy is, Shady's never far off, Polly thought.

Still in hot pursuit of the older woman, Mark got inter-cepted by faithful Shady. Maybe his running footsteps betrayed him. For she whirled around and launched into monologue mode, from the looks of it. Watchdog guarding pacifist from unwanted encounters, Polly surmised as she moved further along the narrow gallery for a ringside seat.

A glimpse of another onlooker huddled behind the next column stopped her dead.

At Friday's rally, she thought she'd recognized him. Quite a reputation he garnered for unilateral direct action in the name of ALL. The Animal Liberty League most likely had no idea of his existence. Everyone called him Flipper. An asocial recluse; no one knew much else about him. Other than him being psycho—big time. Appeared out of nowhere when some spec-tacular action was in the wings. And disappeared like a spook after it blew up. Sometimes literally.

Unnerved, Polly tried to creep back unnoticed but alerted him by a creaking board. For a second, vacant, light-colored eyes met hers. Then his head dropped, dark hair obscuring his face. His eyes, she guessed, stared down now again into the hall.

A pale, sinewy hand groped over his shoulder to yank up the hood of his black hoodie.

Gives one the creeps, Polly shuddered. Half-ashamed of doing a rabbit, she scurried down the stairs and straight out the double doors.

Out in the cool evening air, her stomach grumbled and gurgled. A sudden vision of French fries laden with mayonnaise distracted her. A Kebab joint at the town center made incredible fries. The thought of their Greek salad with goat feta and tzatziki let her mouth water.

The church clock struck ten as she reached *Eddies Döner* in a little street off the market square. By now her tummy growled viciously. No doubt, she'd be drooling by the time the slow-moving lineup thinned out. The guys behind the counter—still unfazed and efficient at the close of a long day—bantered and joked in Turkish and German while serving customers.

As she waited for her order to be prepared, Polly strolled over to the tight passage that led to tables in the back to secure a vacant seat. What she saw instead prompted her to hide beside a fridge with soft drinks and beer.

At a small table at the rear wall sat Nancy with Ronny of all people! What on earth brought them here together? Nancy doing fast food with the *WKA* sales rep?

To scope the action, Polly crept forward. Bet the old lecher is up to his tricks again, she figured. His paw on the table casually inched awfully close to Nancy's. Instead of slapping him, she actually smiled! That's not her kind of thing. What's wrong with the woman? At least she did move her hand to the safety of her beer bottle.

"*Hier, deine Fritten,*" the guy at the cash called her over, wrapping up her fries. Salad packed, she grabbed both and put down a twenty Euro bill. When he held out her change, she waved her package and made her exit before Rosso could spot her. Becomes a habit, she smirked. Polly the Fugitive. Makes for a tacky title.

Now, where to park herself and dig in while keeping an eye on events? A scan of the street revealed steps to an unlit alley diagonally across from the *Döner*. At the risk of being tripped over, she hunkered down and unwrapped her dinner. The smell! Famished, she fell over her fries, hot and crisp from the fryer.

Ten minutes later, she gobbled salad like a hare when Nancy appeared. Left the blighter behind and now hurried off in the direction of the marketplace. Better make myself scarce before our Ronny espies me, Polly muttered to herself.

Sure enough, Ponytail emerged. Illuminated by the bright overhead lamp, he preened himself—expansively stretched—lit a cigarette and exhaled in evident enjoyment. For a few moments, he stood there, while Polly sought to melt into the steps she sat on.

Windy Ronny, however, didn't have a care in the world. The dude started to whistle a tune and—no better word, Polly thought—sauntered toward the square. Pleased with himself. The proverbial cat that got the canary. What the frig was he doing with Nancy that tickled him so?

Chapter 10
AGNES

"*Seraaaaah!*"

Agnes surfaced with a shout reverberating in the recesses of her brain. Sweat soaked, the thin t-shirt stuck to her body.

She threw off the duvet and sat up—too fast. Dizzy, she swallowed hard. Only a dream… Her heart thudded.

Yet, a real scream, she felt certain. A creature in agony that penetrated her subconscious mind. A gull?

Hand trembling, she reached for the travel alarm. Bird twitter filtered into her awareness. Heavy blackout curtains swelled in between the old windowpanes that opened inward. 6:07 AM.

Dazed, Agnes padded to the window. One arm holding back a curtain panel—damp to the touch—she leaned out. Light drizzle condensed on her bare forearm resting against the frame. Not a good morning for a boat trip. Kind of foggy too.

The hammering in her chest ceased. Diffuse anxiety still tightened it. Dream images gnawed at the back of her mind, eluded her grasp. Let it go, she told herself.

In semiconscious habit, her right hand went up to her head. Spread fingers pushed back strands of dark hair, stringy with sweat, loping them behind her ears, one at a time.

Might as well stay up. Grab a coffee and catch breakfast later on the ferry.

The bedroom was clammy, not cold. She grabbed a clean white t-shirt and pants before she tiptoed barefoot across the hallway. Needn't worry about noise—her mom's door stood open, the room unoccupied. Must be up too. Silent downstairs though. For some reason, Agnes hurried going to the bathroom.

Zipping up her jeans, she descended the stairs to the kitchen. A water glass on the table—maybe from last night. No smell of coffee. No dirty cup. As far as visible through the back window, the patio lay deserted.

Unease mounted. Restless, Agnes crossed the foyer and stepped out front. The rose arbor dripped from dew and mist. The road stretched empty both ways. Puzzled, she followed the walkway along the sidewall and entered the backyard by the little gate. Of course, her mom wasn't there.

No use grabbing sandals now, she decided, and made straight for the dune path they had taken with Polly the day before.

During the night, the wind must have whipped up sand to cover much of the boardwalk. Vague outlines of fresh footsteps appeared once she left the boards behind.

The tide far out, neither human nor beast out where the three of them had walked yesterday. Mist blurred everything—its saltiness made her tear up. Toward the other side—south-west, she guessed—a promontory jutted within a hundred yards or so to her left. Seagulls screeched overhead. A whole flock of them winged clamoring in that direction.

Still scanning the ground, she traced the footsteps to the shoreline. They aimed right into the water. For a second her heart contracted and skipped. A forced laugh at her own fanciful premonition. Why the heck would Sera want to drown herself? Ridiculous. Quite serene she'd been last night after her nap. They'd read companionably until both drooped with drowsiness by ten-thirty.

Obviously, Sera went water-treading. A dim memory from her childhood resurfaced. *Kneippkur?* Named after the nine-teenth-century pastor, Sebastian Kneipp, the therapy involved early morning excursions into icy cold river water or over dewy grass. Summer memories—when all was well with her and Mom.

Cut it out and go meet her. Time to head back and pack for the day trip. Unlikely Sera would aim for the tip of the isle today. Better to roll up her jeans and trudge around the promontory.

It took forever to reach the farthest point of the jut to obtain any view of that side. The hard-packed sand at the water's edge allowed for a faster pace, but still. The dunes rose steeply from the upper beach. No way for Sera to be walking up there—too aware of the restrictions.

Need to go back, Agnes thought. What if she's taken the trail into the nature reserve? Can't give up now. Pointless to come this far and not check out the other side. For all she knew, there might be promontory after promontory. Lost count of time without her mobile. A sense of urgency permeated her. She wanted to jog—never been her kind of thing.

With keen anticipation, she rounded the land's end. Only to be disappointed—shrouded in gray haze in the distance, the immediate vicinity appeared as devoid of life.

How could she be so dense? The *FKK* stretch from Saturday morning, near the Dune Café where she'd met Polly. Stupid not to realize before. The land did jut out again in the direction of the town. Too far for her mother to have gone. Not on a morning of an all-day outing. Or could she?

Apprehension slid into irritation.

From what she recalled; benches framed a platform where the track went inland to the Café. Nobody would be about this early in this weather, she thought. Conceivably her mom sought a dry spot for a break before heading back. Might as well check it out. No footprints led up from the water—the suction of the waves likely erased them.

Over the rhythmical splashing of the incoming tide, harsh discordant screeches penetrated. A formation of gulls crowded higher up on the beach. Others spiraled above, swooping down to scatter their kin. Something disturbed her in their behavior.

Instead of aiming for the resting place a couple hundred yards off, she crossed diagonally to the squabbling birds. Propelled on by an urge to run, like in a nightmare the deeper clammy sand trapped her feet with every step.

Frustrated as much as anguished, she shouted, "Sera!" "Mom!"

Distant crying—or her imagination supplied it on cue? The mist swallowed sound here. Made her hair stick to her face in stringy strands, beaded with salty moisture mingled with sweat.

Now she saw her. Twenty, thirty yards away.

Huddled in the sand—surrounded by flapping wings and stabbing beaks—Sera alternately hugged herself and lashed out with flaying hands. Soft moans dissolved into keening.

"Sera!" The shout left her lips almost soundless.

She fell to her knees and made to shelter her mom in an embrace. Stopped—arms raised wide.

Something lay in the greenish-gray sand—mostly covered. A foot, sole up in trainers, exposed.

No one could lie face down in sand—and still breathe. Weird thought, but then it hit her. The birds. Came closer again, pattering in circles, mincing almost, pecking others to keep them at bay. Vigilant eyes stared at her, daring her to shoo them away.

The weight of Sera now clinging to her, sobbing, broke the spell. Agnes hugged with such force, her mom's breath escaped violently. A murmured, "sorry," she eased her grip—stroked the short, damp hair, mumbled inanities.

A whisper, "The gulls." The crying subsided.

All Agnes could think, need to get away. Go for help. Too late for what is lying there. Make sure…

With an effort, she raised herself and coaxed her mother into sitting up.

"Stay here. Have to check. Try CPR or something."

"Did…," whimpered Sera. "He's dead… Cold—"

Revulsion choked Agnes when she lowered herself next to the immersed figure. She gingerly brushed grit off the neck and felt for a pulse. What her fingers touched was horribly chilled and clammy. Bile rose from her empty stomach.

Close-up, she realized only one side of the face lay buried, the other bare. She scooted over and met one staring eye, covered by a fine layer of sand-corns. The skin on the temple and cheekbone tinged bluish—mouth and nose stuck in sand. A huge luminescent green bottle fly—she shuddered and turned away. Focused instead on longish wet hair spread out in wispy strands tangled with grit.

There was no way he could be resuscitated. Frantically, she wiped her hands on her jeans. As though that would wipe off the image.

"We need to go for help, Mom."

People at the Café. Someone will take over. Call police. Before these vultures peck—

"Can't leave him—gulls—" A violent shudder shook the thin body—weak flapping of the arms caused agitated wings to whoosh.

"You're not staying! Mom! We both go. Somebody's going to be sent right back here." What's lying there is beyond caring. The thought floated into her consciousness unbidden—dehumanizing.

Too exhausted to put up any resistance, Sera staggered along when led—almost dragged, Agnes feared.

The going was excruciating—deep, dank sand sucked in her bare feet. Something hard and sharp pierced Agnes' sole, and she cried out in pain. Sera's nails dug into her forearm.

"Nothing, Mom. Only a shell. I'm okay." As if to prove it, she tugged her mother along with renewed energy.

They reached the path next to the deserted platform and were able to go faster once they got to the boardwalk. The Café was still another fifteen-minute walk among dunes, she remembered from Saturday. Twice they stopped for Sera to recover from the exertion. *This is too much for her at her age. For anyone. People don't stumble over bodies in the morning and not be upset. They freak. I would if I were alone,* Agnes told herself.

From the back, the Café showed dismal and forlorn. No one about. *Must be going on seven or so.* Metallic clatter from out front drew her attention.

"Leave me here. Call help," her mom urged. Legs buckling, she slid down onto the steps to the deck. *Chairs all stacked and chained to the back wall,* Agnes noticed irrelevantly. About to argue, her mother waved her off with a feeble, "I'm okay. Go."

When she rounded the corner to the front entrance, Agnes saw a white van and a couple of guys busy unloading a ladder from its roof. *What does one say? As though that mattered.*

"*Bitte helfen. Ein Unfall,*" was all she managed; her academic German deserting her in an emergency.

The 'please help—an accident,' startled them in mid-action —ladder aloft. Lowering it against the vehicle, they approached. Familiar somehow. Close up, she realized—Polly's acquaintances. The names escaped her.

Recognition lit up their faces to be replaced by solicitude.

"*Was ist passiert?*" asked one. The other asked if she was hurt.

Ignoring the question, 'What happened?' she shook her head. "*Polizei. Ruf Polizei.*"—she urged them to call the police.

They escorted her inside. On a foggy morning, the Café proved dim and—chairs stacked on tables—unwelcoming. It took a moment for her eyes to adjust. A young, unusually tall woman—a neon-blue scarf wrapped around her hair—was mopping the floor. Blue plastic clogs supported muscular calves in beige capris.

"*Wir haben noch nicht auf!*" Irritation paramount in declaring they weren't open yet; she gave Agnes a tired, exasperated glance.

"*Karl! Karl, kumm man her,*" the taller guy called, ignoring the cleaner.

In answer to this summons, a man, drying his hands on a dishtowel, entered from a door next to the bar counter. Impatiently he asked what they wanted—they'd already got their coffee, he grumbled.

Intimidated by his tone, Agnes stumbled over her words as she repeated her request for help.

To her relief, his manner changed as she spoke and— pegging her stammer and accent correctly—he responded, "What happened? You do speak English, don't you? No use letting everyone in on it when something happens." A meaningful nod in direction of the cleaner included the two men by her side. "Bad for staff morale and business," he added under his breath.

In a few words, Agnes explained about finding a body. Her main anxiety focused on her mother, she was ready to turn responsibility for the dead over to others.

"Some drunk passed out last night maybe. Better call an ambulance."

"If you wish… Police too. The person was face down in the sand. No pulse…" She shuddered at the memory.

"Let's keep our cool." A worried glance at the workers watching them. "I ring them both."

"May I bring my mother in, please? She's out back. Was her who found him. Terrible shock for—"

"Yes, of course.—Hey, Erica," he called over the cleaner and told her to unlock the door and bring coffee for the ladies. The young woman, torn between sullen annoyance at being disturbed and obvious curiosity, let Agnes out to the deck where Sera sat bent over on the stoop.

Moments later a table close to the counter waited for them. The woman banged cups and a thermos pot, plus a pitcher of cream in front of Agnes to help herself.

Beside her, Sera shook as from a bad chill and lost control of her hands. Agnes had to hold the cup to her mom's lips.

Armed with a blanket, Karl reappeared to swaddle Sera in it and, soft enough for only Agnes to hear, "They'll be here soon."

With a few words, he shooed the guys back to their job. As they departed, Agnes smiled at them and mouthed her thanks.

Karl went over to the young woman and spoke to her quietly. She disappeared through a side door.

A chair—one-handed plucked from a neighboring table—he straddled across from Agnes. As he leaned forward, it tilted precariously on two legs.

"Won't be too long. Don't worry; Mom will be alright."

"How come you speak English so well?" asked Agnes, just to say something ordinary.

"That's a long story, as they say. Wanna hear it?"

A nod and a smile prompted him to go on.

"Will take your mind off things." He jutted his chin in Sera's direction, who sat hunched forward oblivious to them. Her chair drawn closer to Sera's, one arm around the bony shoulders, Agnes nodded at him.

"Well, for starters, I'm from the Midwest of Germany. Ugly mining town and the mines were shutting down. Lots of unemployment and no future for us young ones. Anyhow, getting stoned in a dead coal hole of a place didn't do it for me in the long run. Planned to beat it real quick. First to Düsseldorf. Studied fine arts at the Academy. Didn't last long. London next. That was totally rocking back then," he grinned at the recollection. "Improved my English no end. A stint in California helped. Went anywhere the drugs flowed back in the day. Music and art too. My passions."

While he spoke, Agnes mustered him, covertly, as she believed. The man seemed fit and muscles spoke of workout. Slim around the hips. Well into his fifties? A much lived-in, bronzed face. Longish hair—brushed back by his fingers as he talked—so bleached from the sun, it might be blond or going white. Silvery two-day stubble showed not unattractively in the gaunt, weathered visage. Quite a nice face. Greenish-brown, kind eyes that regarded her with amusement now.

Embarrassed she realized her impolite intense scrutiny. To her chagrin, he winked at her.

His wide mouth pulled up at the corners as he refilled their cups. "Did you have breakfast?"

Still crimson, hair curtaining her burning cheeks, Agnes shook her head. Her mother, who leaned against her shoulder now, did not stir.

"Make you something later, then. To make a long story short. I landed on Majorca." Not sure if that meant anything to her, he said, "Heard of it? Spanish Mediterranean island? Party mile?"

Perhaps taking her nod for recognition, he went on, "Loved the sunshine, after California. Friend asked me to join her running a beach café. Awesome time all around—for a few years, at any rate. Non-stop revel. Booze, drugs, pills, you name it, I've popped it. Takes its toll. Washed out, burned out, sliding downhill with a vengeance. Couldn't stand myself in the mirror whenever I was sober enough in the morning to greet my mug. Whatever. Then my uncle died. No kids. Left me this place. No idea why. Likely couldn't think of anyone else. He and my mother had been close as nippers. Last of the family I am. Mom passed away a year before him—cancer…"

Awkwardly, Agnes murmured, "So sorry to hear."

"Well, so was I. Shook me right up. Hurried back home when Dad told me she was going down fast. But, too late. My uncle came to the funeral. All in a haze for me. It hurt. You see, I didn't visit the old girl in her last illness. She'd been a good sort. Terribly fond of her I used to be. Too doped to realize time was wasting."

A painful half-smile creased his features. "Water under the bridge. Not the kind of thing to mention today."

With an effort, he picked up the thread. "Drove up here to put the house on the market and go back to Spain. Came—and stayed. Fell in love with the ramshackle joint. My gut told me it was my wake-up call."

A sudden glance around as though waking up. "Rather run down it was; just like me," he laughed softly. "Not much business despite the summer crowd. Spruced it up and concentrated on getting it going again. Years in the Balearic hotspot taught me the ropes. A going concern this dive is now." His chest swelled with pride.

"Live music events weekends during the season. The *FKK* bunch proves a loyal clientele." Eyes rolling. "No more dope for me, thank you. Took me almost two years to go clean and get fit again. Been here three years. Lots of people come out this way, well into autumn."

A movement made him swivel toward the door. "Speak of the devil. There's the fuzz now, I think."

Both hands grabbing the table, he got up. "Don't worry. Mom's alright. She's one tough cookie, I can tell."

Chapter 11
AGNES

Pushing past Karl, a cop in a blue uniform barked some introductions. Neither his name and rank nor that of his female colleague registered with Agnes. The proffered metal tags showed only number IDs. Too worried about Sera, she didn't care. If the cop was the bullying type, things could become rough.

Offended on their behalf, Karl told the man to cool it. In a calmer tone, he offered to translate since the "ladies" spoke English. The woman officer started to say something. Her colleague snapped at her to take down their personal information. Eibo—as Karl called the male—launched into rapid-fire questions. Unfazed, Karl translated at his leisure.

Asked about the morning's events, Agnes explained briefly. Whenever possible, she also answered for her mother who said very little.

The paramedics arrived, and Karl wanted them to attend to Sera first. She declined, insisting she only needed rest. The Eibo person told his second in command to carry on and barged out ahead of the ambulance crew.

The young constable, or whatever her rank was, chewed on

her pen before she took courage to reveal her English as adequate to continue the interview.

"Good for you, Maike," said, Karl. "I'll make myself useful and rustle up breakfast."

As he disappeared through a door beside the old-fashioned counter, Agnes felt abandoned. The clatter of pots and dishes reassured her somewhat.

―――

"Right. That is all for now. Thank you for your cooperation." The officer eventually ran out of questions and, closing her notepad, crossed the room to the front window.

Despite Maike's evident effort to ease the tension, Agnes worried about the strain on her mom. "How are you holding up? They won't keep us here much longer, I hope."

A tired nod was all Sera managed.

"There we are. A light little breakfast. Made enough for you too, Maike," said Karl as he loaded the table with fresh orange juice, fragrant buns in a wicker basket, cold cuts, cheeses, and more. The used coffee cups he whisked away and replaced them with thin porcelain ones instead. Back to the kitchen he went, only to reappear with yet more.

"Made some stiff *Ostfriesen* tea. A tad of my famous scrambled eggs?"

He looked so comically disappointed when Sera shook her head that it elicited a whisper of a smile from her. "Ah, knew I could twist your arm. Here, take some baby tomatoes. Planted them myself."

With aplomb, he served and chattered away. Like a bubbling rivulet, the prattle soothed and relaxed. Off and on even Sera picked at her food. Ravenous, Agnes wolfed down delicious seed buns with homemade jam and didn't say no to eggs and fresh fruit with quark. The hot tea warmed body and soul.

Quite indecent to gobble like a starved puppy, she told

herself. Guilt made her glance up at their host, only to meet his amused grin.

To entertain them, he chatted about the container garden he planted last year with amazing success. "All organic, of course. Hey, I might go vegetarian now. Not for the restaurant though. The *FKK* folks love their meat." Realizing the ambiguity, he winced and amended, "On their plates, I mean."

A cup of tea next to her, Maike leaned against the windowsill. Every few minutes, she glanced out. When she straightened with a jerk and walked to the front entrance, Agnes's throat constricted. If only she hadn't gorged like a glutton.

Another uniform entered. A clipped, "*Moin,*" and a quick sideways twitch of his head to the door, he prompted Maike to leave wordlessly.

The off-hand tone of Karl's greeting smacked of dislike and was reciprocated. At the offered tea, the newcomer curled his lip. Legs apart—hands with fingers slightly spread at his sides, a vigilant glance hovering inches over their heads—he blocked the exit. For reasons she could not pinpoint, he made Agnes more nervous than the bully. Fan of American cop shows, was he? Just needs mirrored sunglasses to perfect the image, she thought.

"Karl! Karl!" A deep male shout and the side door opened with such force that it banged against the wall. Instead of a man, a huge black and tan German shepherd barged into the room, leash dragging behind. One look at the copper, and the beast lunged across, growling menacingly.

"Castro, stop!" A sharp command from Karl brought the dog to an immediate halt in the middle of the room. "Sit." With a final snarl, Castro sank down on his haunches. Karl redirected his canine's attention to their side of the room and coaxed, "Be nice and say hi to our guests."

Now the happiest, sweetly smiling dog came up to Sera, tail wagging so vigorously that his whole rear-end swayed from side to side. Crouched down, Sera let him sniff her hands and allowed him to lick her face with ardor.

Amazed, Agnes watched the change and could have sworn both were smiling. A true dog person, her mom was. Once, for a year after a favorite passed away, she used to stop and ask people to pet their mutts. A great embarrassment to Agnes's teenage self. She herself liked pooches as an inevitable part of their little household, often needing far too much attention.

"*Mensch, Karl, was machen denn all die Bullen hier?*

The disembodied voice, asking what the fuzz was doing out there, belonged to a fellow who hastened in after the shepherd. At least six foot five, by Agnes's guess, his dark wet hair fell into his tanned face. Navy blue sweatshirt over black track pants with UCLA logo hung loosely on his huge, lank frame. He stopped, his mouth still open, and gaped at the cop who had his hand on his holster, as Agnes noticed only now. Stunned, he asked, "*Was is' denn hier los?*"

"Yes, you may well ask what's going on here." Pointedly ignoring the officer, Karl stretched up one arm to his friend's shoulders, but only his hand reached far enough to touch one. "Let me introduce my buddy Guido, or Guy—the French way —for short. Guy, meet Sera and Agnes Taylor from beautiful Canada. And we wish the occasion was a happier one. Nevertheless, I'm delighted to have made their acquaintance this morning. What occasioned it, indeed, was quite sad."

A pause for effect, before his voice changed—quite solemn; no more joking around. "These poor ladies found a body on the beach, Guy. Hence, the fuzz swarming and stopping you. Hope you didn't allow Castro go for a uniform."

Guy had listened spellbound. "Holy sh—" he said softly. "Beg your pardon, ma'am," he bowed to Sera. To Karl, "No, I kept a tight hold on your brute's leash when I saw their cars from afar. Ran all the way. A drunk from last night, you reckon?"

"My thought, exactly. Who knows? Quite a few of the guys

were plastered by the time we closed." Head shaking in frustration at the senselessness, perhaps, Karl continued, "Maybe passed out and drowned when the tide came in. Poor bastard."

The four of them remained mute for a few moments. To her horror, Agnes realized she hadn't fathomed how the man might have met his end.

"So sorry that you seem trapped here for a while longer," said Karl." Regret it on your behalf—me, I very much like your company. Is there anything I can get you? Maybe something to read? Magazines?—That's it. Wait—I fetch some to browse. Make yourselves comfy."

A slap on his thigh brought his canine fan to attention. "Hey, buster—come along. Din din." They disappeared in direction of the kitchen, Castro bouncing with boundless energy and anticipation.

The other three sat down again—watched by the officer who had withdrawn to guard the exit and glared now at them from a safe distance.

"Are you from the US?" In polite inquiry, Sera turned to Guy. "The UCLA wear, I mean."

"Did my stint there. That's where I met our Karl. Nah, I hail from D'dorf." In answer to Agnes's puzzled frown, he clarified, "Düsseldorf—you know—Rhineland? Wine?" He winked at her. "Where in Canada are you ladies from?"

"My daughter lives in Toronto and I live in Halifax," Sera responded.

"Never been to those parts. One year Karl and I made it up to the Sunshine Coast. Man, was it ever gorgeous. Liked it almost better than down in California. Vancouver's tame though. The island, however—wow! We stayed for a while in Tofino. Later we drove up—"

"If you are ready, I can now drive you to your cottage," a voice interrupted him. Maike had returned unnoticed.

"Here the mags. Locked the beast in the kit—" Arms cradling a stack of magazines, Karl stood still. "Want to take some for a quiet read at home?" Deflated, he turned to Agnes, apparently at a loss what to do with his load. Guy came to his aid; relieving him of the glossies, he placed them on the bar counter.

"I can't thank you enough, Karl, for all your kindness." Sincere appreciation showed in Sera's face as she reached out her hands to clasp his. "We're sure to be back. Have to pay for our breakfast then," she smiled apologetically. "I'm afraid I came away without my wallet this morning."

"Oh, don't mention it. On the house, of course. Allow me to come by later today to make sure you're okay. Worries me to think of you out there all by yourself. If you want, I can find you something in town instead."

To her own surprise, Agnes wanted to say, "yes, please." Missed her chance, because her mom said, "Very kind of you. We'll think about it. Don't go out of your way. You've done so much for us. I'm sure, we'll be alright now."

"Entirely my pleasure, believe me." An idea lit up his face. "I'll bring Castro," he appealed to Sera like a little boy offering to share his favorite toy. "How can a dog lover like you say no to that? Sold you on it, didn't I?" In a quick squeeze, he hugged her shoulders with one arm and received a genuine smile.

Dog lovers always stick together, Agnes thought.

No one spoke during the drive in the blue-and-silver police station wagon. Upon their arrival, Maike insisted on checking the premises before letting them re-enter their cottage. Within a few minutes, she reported back, "All clear. Please do not be alarmed if you see any officers close by. It's for your own safety. The colleagues from our *Kripo*—or the 'criminal investigation service'—will be by later to speak to you."

Their thanks gracefully accepted—a smart salute from the cruiser before the driver pulled a U-turn in the narrow road—and Maike departed.

With a deep sigh, Sera went inside. After a final glance to

both sides, Agnes followed and locked the door. No more intruders, police or otherwise, she determined.

"Agnes, dear, I know you might want to talk now that we are by ourselves… I'm afraid, I need to take some Tylenol and lie down. My head is splitting, and I feel quite shaky."

"Oh, Mom—I'm so sorry! I wish I could have brought you back here much sooner." As if she had deliberately neglected her mother, Agnes was suffused by remorse.

"You're not responsible, Agnes. Nothing that happened is your fault. Let me just rest for a while, and we'll talk later."

Several steps up the stairs, Sera paused, "Would you just pass me a bottle of mineral water from the fridge, please?"

"Go ahead. I'll bring it right up." Eager to be of any use, Agnes rushed to do her bidding.

A few minutes later, she entered her mom's bedroom to find it empty. She placed the bottle and a glass on the nightstand next to the bed and went to draw the curtains, assuming Sera would prefer semi-darkness to recuperate.

"Have a good rest," she called out at the closed bathroom door.

Back in the kitchen, she paced, wavering. The clock showed 11:23 AM. Her body quivered, wound up from too much caffeine and adrenalin coursing her veins. Unsure whether she wanted to cry, or was on the verge of hysterics—she asked herself wryly, what does one do on a day that starts with finding a body?

Chapter 12

AGNES

Loud knocking. Someone at the front door. Must be the cops. A towel wrapped tightly around her body, hair in wild tangles from toweling, Agnes opened the bathroom window. A woman and a man below were scanning their environs; she closer to the door, he standing back. No uniforms—he in a windcheater, and she in an oilskin, Barbour-type jacket. Both wore dark slacks.

"Hey," Agnes called softly in case Sera was asleep. Two heads swiveled in her direction.

"*Kriminal Polizei*." Dog tags proffered, as though she could read them from this distance. The female cop continued, "Could we please speak to you?"

"Give me a minute. I'll be right down."

Barefoot, Agnes padded to her bedroom, the towel twisted together in front of her chest. She tossed around stuff in the old armoire until she unearthed a faded indigo sweatshirt and clean jeans.

When she got to the door, her hands were still trying to squish her tresses into a messy wet ponytail, drops running annoyingly onto her forehead and down her neck. To keep the intruders at bay, she offered a curt "hi"—one hand on the opposite door frame, thus barring entry.

"If you wanted to talk to my mother, you can't. All this is way too much for her. By the time we got back here, she was in agony from one of her migraines."

"Sorry to hear it. We can start with your statement. May we come in, please?" the female asked. Again, they held up their metal ID tags.

"Those things don't tell me anything. Don't you have proper IDs?" At least, this cop spoke English, so she needn't muster her pathetic German.

In response, they dug out photo IDs printed on some water-proof type of green linen. Agnes took one at a time and scrutinized them with deliberate slowness. The first—picture on the left, signature below—showed a serious, well-groomed woman in a white shirt collar with shoulder epaulets. Andrea Collins, it read on the right side of the fold. Beneath the name, *Polizeikommissarin*—Inspector. His ID declared him to be a *Polizeioberkommissar*—Chief Inspector, she guessed, so one rank higher—called Mobias Dickering.

Unable to stall any longer, Agnes pointed the way to the kitchen.

Does one offer cops coffee? Or tea? She stood irresolutely. "Have a seat," she said instead.

Dickering crossed to the small window overlooking the back-yard. Her attention attracted, Agnes believed to see movement at the mouth of the dune path. She flinched. Then was annoyed at herself—stupid really, she should have expected forensics to search here.

To her dismay, she realized the Inspector observed her. Professional and sharp inside and out Collins appeared. Stylish, short chestnut glossy hair, and a face weekly pampered by an aesthetician, no doubt. With a defeated slump, Agnes—shoeless, unkempt, in washed-out favorite sweat top—felt awkward and inadequate. At a disadvantage against this model of career woman efficiency from the moment go, she thought.

In an attempt to take charge, Agnes offered her a chair. Yet the way Collins slid into her seat, shedding her coat in a fluid movement with catlike elegance, overawed Agnes. A sardonic glint lit up the woman's eyes, fully aware of the powerful impression she made. The charcoal cashmere top flattered in its classic chic. Surely not on a copper's salary. Must come from well-to-do background to ooze this sort of self-confident sophistication and poise.

Mesmerized like a cornered mouse, Agnes fought to break the spell. She turned to Dickering only to find herself under scrutiny there too. His glance at once lost its sharpness and became the personification of caring concern. All smiles, he joined them at the kitchen table, waiting until she chose a chair before opting for the bench opposite from her. Relaxed, one arm stretched out over the backrest, he regarded her expectantly.

A well-tuned pair. Without exchanging as much as a glance, Collins opened proceedings and asked permission to record the interview.

When she requested personal information, Agnes lost patience. "How often do you ask?"

The other officer—Maike…don't know her last name—took down everything. We told her all we know."

"Yes, indeed, your preliminary statements are on record. You appreciate, I'm sure, procedures must be followed. Moreover, the person who acted as translator is not officially qualified."

"How come you speak English?"

"I happen to be of British descent and have spent part of my life in English-speaking countries. My formal accreditation qualifies me to conduct interviews," said the Inspector and fiddled with the recording device. "Are we ready to begin?"

"Yeah, sure. Go ahead."

An official formula, date, location, persons present, was followed by personal info. Asked about marital status, Agnes bristled, which was duly noted by Collins who went on to explain the interviewing method. They were to start with general questions to allow the interviewee to understand the questioning style.

How dare they? Impotent, Agnes fumed. What did they take her for? Some nitwit, or what?

A supercilious smile from Collins added fuel to her wrath.

"With regard to your occupation, you stated that you are a sessional instructor. Could you explain this and describe your work?"

Gladly, Agnes thought sarcastically; at least, it'll show you I'm not a complete idiot. "A sessional is hired on term-by-term contracts to teach university or college courses. Common practice for the first years after completing your PhD, until you land a tenure track position."

"Thank you. May I ask you to clarify those terms, please? What are you referring to?"

Eyes rolling at the tedium of this, Agnes snapped, "In North America, it's the career path from Assistant Prof, to Associate, to Full Professor. You get tenure after a few years and sufficient publications and advance to the second level."

"Very good."—Sounds like she's praising a doggy for sitting on command, Agnes's temper rose another notch.—"So do I understand correctly? No one achieves this type of position immediately after graduation?"

Wow, the cat shows her claws. Don't let her rattle you. A deep breath still didn't help.

"No, of course not! I mean, they are difficult to come by. Some people land them at once. Well, I didn't."

"I see. Explain please, wherein lies the difference between those who do and those who don't succeed in this?"

Zeroed in right on the sore spot, Agnes cringed, about to lose control of her rising anger. Before she could say something she would live to regret, the Chief Inspector bent forward to intervene.

"Let's change topics," he said amiably. "Would you describe to us please how you traveled to this island?"

So, he too spoke English. Quite an accomplished pair. Rather gruffly, Agnes set out their itinerary from meeting her mother at Frankfurt's airport to taking trains to the coast. Instead of giving her the verbal equivalent of a condescending pat on the head, he asked her what made them choose Bosum for their holiday. After all, "Canada," he smiled, "is so famous for its fantastic coastal areas."

With no intention of baring her heart to him, Agnes said, "Northern Europe sounded fun and Bosum popped up on Google."

A clipped nod and he instructed her to go over the morning events, ending, "Please don't leave out anything, no matter how unimportant it may strike you."

In the hope to finish things soon, Agnes sped through a recital of all she had done from the moment she'd noticed Sera's absence, to Karl's call to emergency forces. They let her talk uninterrupted. Despite the recording, Collins took notes.

When she stopped, Chief Dickering sat up straighter and proposed, "Now let us go back to clarify a few points."

Not able to suppress a groan, Agnes eyed him.

The question came from the Inspector, instead. "Why didn't you wait for your mother in the cottage? Wasn't an excursion planned for today?"

Some sort of criticism of her action—or doubt of the veracity of her account—appeared implied and made Agnes snap back, "Because I was worried, don't you see?"

"Yes, I do. What I'm asking is, why? Is it disturbing if your mother goes out to catch a breath of fresh air in the morning?"

Heat rising up her throat, Agnes glanced at Dickering. Embarrassed she muttered, "I woke up with a start from a bad dream. Alright? Dreamed badly of my mother, I guess, and thought I'd heard a scream."

"You did not mention this before." Trust Collins to spot any omission.

"Well, you didn't ask, did you?" To shut out the annoying

woman, Agnes twisted her upper body to address the Chief Inspector. "Didn't think of it before—I awoke, calling my mother's name before I became fully conscious."

"You said 'a scream.' Can you describe it?" The calm in his voice soothed.

"Oh, I realized after—a screech from a seagull."

"When you bent over the body, you say, you knew 'he was dead,' and that there was no point trying CPR. What made you sure?"

This question of Collins threw Agnes and caused her to stammer, "I... I... I just... The eye... It was the eye, mostly. Covered in sand and wide-open. No one could be alive like that! Surely...?"

"Did you try to turn him over?"

"No, I did not!" The smug expression on the cop's face acted like a burning sting and she upped her volume. "Are you telling me I did wrong? I'm not a doctor! My CPR training is outdated. Took it as a teenager."

Thou profess too much, came unbidden. Couldn't stop though.

"Look, I did what came natural. Protect my mother. Get help.—My mother freaked over the gulls. Almost did myself. First dead body I've ever... Horrible—" She shuddered at a sudden flashback of the eye.

Both scrutinized her now like an interesting specimen between glass slides. Never imagined how vulnerable such people make you, she thought.

Unfazed, Collins resumed, "Did you recognize the deceased?"

"No, of course not! We don't know anyone here. I couldn't see much of the face, anyway."

"Have a look at this photograph," Dickering held out a print at which she recoiled in horror. "Don't worry." A fatherly smile. "An older likeness—not of the body."

Hesitant, not quite trusting his reassurance, Agnes took one corner of the picture between two fingertips. The man—slicked-back hair and a loud suit—struck her faintly familiar. Unable to place him, she slowly shook her head, "I don't think so."

From an envelope, the Chief removed an eight by ten shot and asked, "How about this one?"

"That's the *WKA* guy! Ronny something," Agnes cried out in astonishment. In half-profile with ponytail and in black jeans and shirt, behind him a wind turbine, no doubt was possible. Promotional material, like the stuff shown at the meeting. "Is he the dead man?"

"*Sprechen Sie deutsch?*"

Dickering's unexpected question of whether she spoke German made Agnes frown as she replied, "A little bit... Why do you ask?"

"You pronounced *WKA* correctly the German way. Where did you meet Ronny Rosso?"

"I didn't meet him. Only listened to his talk at the rally in the market square on Friday. Well, and again in *Die Krone* Saturday night." Better skip the brief glimpse at the Tea House.

"So, you were very interested in Rosso," the Collins cat cut in.

"No, I wasn't! I happened to be in town and the commotion was hard to miss. Danny's speech appealed more to my fancy. The ridiculous fuss about wind farms intrigued me."

"Intrigued enough to spend a holiday evening listening to Rosso once more?"

"Gosh! A friend asked us to join her for dinner, and we stayed on. Big deal."

"I thought you said you did not know anyone on the island? Who is this 'friend?'"

God—can't say anything without that bitch hitting on it like a sharpshooter. Afraid she by now must appear as utterly harassed and frazzled to them as her mind felt from inside, panic welled up. Sweat trickled down her armpits. Might drip from her cuffs any moment... No longer capable of enduring the tension, she crossed her arms and got up. "Need water," sounded constricted to her own ears.

"Here, let me get you some." Collins all helpful now.

"No!—I can manage." In haste, Agnes grabbed a bottle of mineral water from the fridge. It slopped onto the counter as she poured. Without turning around—their eyes drilling holes in her back—she raised the glass with both hands to her lips and drank, her teeth chattering against its rim. Calm down, calm down—she talked herself into relaxing her jaw muscles— take a minute or two. They were at you long enough. For God's sake, you're just a witness. What do they do with the guilty?

Another deep breath—her hands calmed somewhat; she drank. Not until she had finished did she turn around to face her tormentors. Amazingly, they hadn't said a word. Now they regarded her with detachment.

"Look, all this is a bit much for me," Agnes rationalized. "The shock's only catching up with me now, I guess." She slopped more water into her glass. Belatedly, she held up the bottle, "Want some?" In unison, they shook their heads and murmured thanks. "Or maybe tea?"

"Why don't I make it, while you explain about your friend?" A courteous sweep of the arm to encourage her to take a seat accompanied the Chief's words. He got up, grabbed the water kettle, and asked where to find things.

Resigned to her lot, Agnes faced the Collins person who sat pen poised.

"Her name's Polly. Just met her Saturday morning at the Dune Café. I'd stopped there for lunch. We got talking. Polly mentioned the do planned for the evening. My mother was interested. So, we went and did dinner with Polly."

"How did you get into town?" the insatiable Collins asked.

"We cycled."

"You intended to go back by the same means in the dark? Is your mother not already in her seventies?"

"I might be in my seventies, but I'm neither senile nor too frail to use a bicycle!" Strident, Sera's words cut in.

"Oh, Mom!—Are you feeling better?" Agnes jumped up and stood with her hands half-raised, uncertain whether to hug Sera or plead to be hugged and comforted by her.

Her ambivalence prompted her mother to cross the room and put an arm around Agnes' shoulders. A quick squeeze to say, "I'm here now, don't worry."

For once Collins lost her composure as she scrambled to her feet inelegantly—Agnes noted with satisfaction. Her superior turned without haste, open teapot in hand. Now he set it down beside the stove and walked up to Sera. Hand stretched out, he introduced himself and apologized for intruding without her permission and explained their presence.

"I won't have you harass my daughter." Her mom's face was an implacable mask. 'The formidable professor facade,' Agnes used to call it. Serious, unbending, unyielding, and strict, in short, 'no more nonsense from you, please.'

"We have no intention of harassing your daughter, or you, for that matter," the Inspector tried to reassure them.

A glance from Sera quelled her. "My daughter's agitated voice woke me. It conveyed that she *felt* harassed, which is the defining factor. Intention of the harasser plays little or no role. The German police, I take it, are no more permitted to harass witnesses than the Canadian."

Awed, Agnes regarded her mom's stance—tall and straight, shoulders back, commanding attention and compliance. Impressive! The mother ardently admired as a kid. Back then, Sera insisted not to give way to bullies—stand up for yourself with confidence. "If you sense a real threat, it is quite honorable to retreat from the situation—with dignity, not fleeing helter-skelter. Never—never ever—turn your back on a bully," she had urged.

"Our apologies. After a cup of tea, we all feel better," Dickering aimed to pacify. A rueful smile at Sera, while he went to attend to the hissing kettle. Already filling the waiting teapot, he said, "With your permission, I carry on here. We are sorry if anything has upset you, Ms. Taylor," he nodded at Agnes. A bow to Sera, "Mrs. Taylor, provided you agree, we take your statement once we are all refreshed."

"Ms. I am not married. And my daughter is Dr. Taylor," with uncharacteristic fastidiousness Sera corrected him.

"As you wish, Ms. Taylor."

Eager to appease, the Chief is—or wants to soften her up for the interview, Agnes surmised, not trusting either cop by now.

Quite at home, he brought the teapot to the table and went back to fetch cups, saucers, milk, and sugar.

Though Sera allowed him to serve her, she placed her chair to distance herself physically from the proceedings. Not wanting to sit on the bench with Dickering, Agnes went into the little parlor across the hallway and brought a leather sling chair. Gentleman that he was, Dickering jumped to come to her aid. She declined politely.

The conversation over tea was stilted as though unloved neighbors with whom one has a nodding acquaintance had invited themselves over. Hard at work to put them at their ease, the Chief did most of the talking. Yet, Agnes did not trust any remark or question to be innocuous. Mind made up to be formal and unapproachable, her mom stayed mute unless directly addressed.

To end the annoying chit-chat, Agnes asked Dickering, "Once you're done interviewing my mother, are we free to get on with our lives?"

"If you mean, can you carry on with your holiday; yes, please do so. The dune path behind the cottage, the beach, and the *Naturschutzgebiet* trails will remain off-limits for a day or two. There is no objection to going into town, of course."

"Are you treating this as homicide, then?" inquired Sera.

"We treat any sudden death of this nature as suspicious until we can determine otherwise," Collins replied in his stead. "It is not common to find dead bodies on our beaches."

"Well, it's uncommon for us to stumble on them," snapped Agnes.

A sideways glance from her mom, who took charge before things deteriorated further. "If everyone is quite finished, perhaps we can move on to the interview." She rose and carried her cup to the sink, a clear sign that teatime was officially over.

"I want to be present when you question my mother." Agnes moved close to Sera.

"We prefer to speak to witnesses separately," countered the Inspector. "Unless they are minors, or pressing reasons exist—"

"Don't worry, Agnes, I'll be fine." A gentle squeeze of Agnes's hand and her mother faced the interrogators.

Chapter 13
AGNES

Like the rumbling of distant thunder, hollering penetrated her subconscious and issued in bizarre images of a canon dodging her every step.

An electrified zap coursed her body and jerked her awake.

"*Halli*—*hallooo?* Anybody home?"

The voice drifted in through the tilted window. Heavy with sleep, Agnes dragged herself into an upright position. The alarm clock displayed 2:33 PM. Unconscious to the world for hours—

"*Juh*—*huh*—where—are—you?" Singsong, up and down—well-familiar in its intonation.

Resigned, Agnes lifted her legs over the side of the bed and padded over to the window to open one wing fully. "Hello, Mathilda. Give me a minute."

The indomitable woman beamed up at her. "I can wait."

First, make sure Sera's alright, she told herself on the landing. The door to her mom's room swung in a crack without any creak. On her back—a damp white towel covering the upper half of her face, arms stretched out loosely at her sides—her mother lay motionless. Still dressed in the black slacks and dark polo-style top, she must have dozed off uncovered.

Somehow the slender bare feet seemed terribly vulnerable to Agnes. About to retreat on tiptoe, Sera's soft voice recalled her.

"Is that Mathilda?"

"Yes, Mom. Sorry—did she wake you? Is your migraine back again?"

"It never quite left. Could you check what she came for? I can't—"

"No worries, Mom. You just try to rest."

She eased the door shut and went downstairs to let in their landlady.

"The police tried to stop me going to my own house! Can you imagine?" An outraged Mathilda burst in, the affront evident in the crimson patches on her cheeks.

"*Na*, I told them! Road's End is my house. No one can forbid me to go there! No dead body was found in my backyard, I said. He lay on the beach, a kilometer, *nee*, two or more away. I must go to my summer guests." Her chest thrust out—chin stretched forward, arms akimbo—she recounted her tale. Silently Agnes sympathized with the cops at the roadblock.

Pleased with herself, Mathilda ended, "That did it. *Basta!* Here I am, presto!"

As she spoke, she walked ahead to the kitchen.

After all, it's her house, rented out or not, Agnes mutely admitted.

"And how is *Mutti*?"

What mutt? frowned Agnes. Then it clicked; a diminutive of *Mutter*, mother. She herself had called Sera *Mama* as a child and only switched to 'mom' as a teen. Later, as they went their separate ways, she'd addressed her by first name. Maybe to mark the distance...or her own maturity.

"She's resting—her migraine's acting up." To divert attention from her mother in case the good Samaritan intended to sneak a peek, Agnes changed topics. "So, you heard about the body?"

"*Ach*, everybody knows that." Dismissively. "Two English

ladies found him. Well, I said, that are my summer guests! Right away I wanted to come, but the *Wattwächter* meeting… We guard the *Watt*—"

"The mudflats," murmured Agnes.

"Oh? Would one call us mud guards?" Puzzled, she regarded her tenant, before rushing on, "We needed to discuss what council decides this afternoon. Now it is not on anymore! There you have it! *Der Mensch schaltet, Gott waltet.* The human manages, God rules."

Quite at a loss, Agnes asked, "What's not on?"

"The *WKA* application, of course!" The slow headshake pronounced Agnes to be regrettably dense. "They say the dead you found is Ronny Rosso."

A sharp eye challenged her to contradict the wisdom of the 'they.' Pause for thought was needed.

Did the pair from the *Kripo* caution non-disclosure? No recollection. Most likely her abrupt departure at the end, when she stormed upstairs, had prevented any instructions.

Better to prevaricate for the moment. "Sorry, I'm a bit out of it." In wild association, her mind jumped to Polly, who would be waiting for them at the pier tonight.

"No food left either." Only Mathilda's jerking back, eyebrows raised, told her she'd spoken out loud.

"I'm so sorry. It's all rather overwhelming. We had planned a trip, and a friend was to meet us after to go out for dinner. Now I must cancel and get stuff to eat—" Another thought hit her, how could she abandon Sera, lying up there in pain? Nor was her mom able to cycle into town.

"Need to wait and see if my mom is well enough later. I can't leave her here on her own."

"*Och*, that is no problem. I remain with *Mutti*. You go shopping with my little car. The roses need cutting back. *Mutti* can have her lie-down."

Tempted, yet unsure, Agnes decided to check with Sera.

Her hesitation prompted their landlady to throw in further

temptation. "I brought you a cake for *Kaffeeklatsch*. Afternoon coffee, you know? Then you can tell me what happened this morning."

When Agnes opened the bedroom door moments later, Sera lay prone as before.

"Mom, I remembered our dinner date for tonight. Our guardian angel is lending me her car to grab groceries, and I'll try to find Polly."

"I'm glad, Agnes. It worried me to think of her wondering if we missed the ferry back. Go to the *Rathaus*—the Town Hall—she'll be there for the council meeting. Would you ask her to come stay with us overnight?"

Surprised at Sera's request, a stab of jealousy pained Agnes. Simultaneously, she realized she herself craved Polly's company. The thought of the little elf removed some of the weight that had been pressing her down since the morning. "I'll find her, I promise. If you need anything, Mathilda's here pruning her roses. Before I go, let me rinse the towel for you. How about a cold drink, or something?"

"Thank you, Agnes. A cool compress is all I need right now." Lifting the damp cloth off her face carefully, she attempted to smile and winced in pain from the facial movement.

Shortly after, Agnes was driving toward the town. On the passenger seat lay a map of the island on which Mathilda had marked the location of the best grocery store accessible by car. Bins and crates with empty mineral water bottles took up the trunk space of the little hatchback.

When Agnes passed the Dune Café, she yearned for Karl's

cheerful face but resisted. He had promised to come by later. At present, her top priority was to track down Polly.

A stern officer waved her to a stop at the roadblock, then became courteous when she showed her Canadian driver's license and mentioned renting Road's End cottage.

To reach the *Rathaus* where Bosum's council was to meet, she needed to park in one of the lots on the periphery and hasten through the pedestrian zone to the market square. Tons of people hung out in an air of expectation. Environmentalists predominated.

The Town Hall at the opposite end from the church attracted her attention by the number of folks crowding in front of its double-sided staircase. Vacationers or summer residents, conspicuous by their dark tan and leisure clothing, mingled in groups. Most locals might be at work on a Monday afternoon. More likely, they'd tapped in the same grapevine as Mathilda, Agnes assumed.

On tiptoes, she scanned the assembly for Polly—and worried. Given the imp's petite size, she could be standing a few feet away and be completely hidden by taller onlookers. As she started to walk around, Agnes noticed a shift in general focus. Heads turned to the balustrade-enclosed landing, flanked by the staircases on both sides.

The *Rathaus's* wooden portal opened, and a man in a dark suit stepped up to the balustrade. Another man and a woman huddled closer to the huge doors in the rear. Like others, Agnes stood still—expectantly. In preparation for an announcement, the man lifted his arm and shushed the spectators. Hushed silence rippled outward.

The town official announced in German that the item they waited for needed to be removed from today's council agenda. With dexterity, he switched forth and back in languages to reach the majority of constituents.

While he spoke, Agnes moved on in her search. No sign of her quarry. When he repeated in English, Agnes came to a halt.

"As I said earlier," the official began, "many of you are here because of the *WKA* application, the third item on today's list. Niederwinder & Co requested a postponement. Their main agent, Mr. Rosso, has met with an unfortunate accident last night."

A low murmur grew into a loud buzz. Comments of "told you so," and "*der is' doch tot*," "sure he's dead," issued from all sides.

"As news travel's fast on Bosum, rumors may have spread. The sad fact is Mr. Rosso passed away." His hand lifted to stop the renewed hum, he resumed, "I am not at liberty to release any details. The police, however, urge anyone with information about Mr. Rosso's activities yesterday, or other pertinent knowledge, to contact them immediately." Voice raised over the restless audience, he gave a phone number and web address for the local police.

Without heeding questions fired at them, all three officials turned on their heel and disappeared into the *Rathaus*. The heavy, iron-studded, wooden doors closed behind them to shut out the clamor of an unruly public.

Unsure what to do, Agnes remained immobile. No clue where Polly lived, or where else to search, the only other option was to cycle to the wharf at night. Would mean leaving her mom on her own… Her heart sank at the prospect of admitting her failure to find their friend. Shoulders slumped, her head drooped in anticipated defeat.

A light touch on her left arm startled her. Too small to be threatening, a hand rested on her forearm.

"Looking for someone," a deep, yet familiar voice inquired.

Agnes pivoted to see Polly standing right behind her, smiling up. Joy welled up, and she grabbed the imp with both hands and hugged her tight.

"Oh, Polly! Am I ever glad I found you!"

"Oho, *you* found *me*? My dear Watson, the honor is wholly

mine!" Two skinny arms hugged her back. "Now don't crush me, though."

"I'm so sorry!" Embarrassed, Agnes stepped back. "Didn't mean to—was—was just so relieved…"

"What a disappointment. I so hoped you meant it." The trademark grin split the little face. "Okay, Agnes, no more teasing. You've had a grotty day. Was about to come out to the cottage. Figured the cops might let a wee thing like me pass."

"You have heard already?"

"Yeah, of course. Like the man said; news travels fast around here. No other 'two English ladies' rent a place out in no man's land. Had to be you. All kidding aside. Been worried about you and your mom. How is Sera?"

"She's come down with a terrible migraine. It's all too much for her. Still, she coped well where it mattered most. Formidable with the police."

"I can well imagine. Let's go somewhere quiet, and you fill me in," Taking Agnes by the hand, she started to weave her way through the dispersing crowd. On the way, Polly waved at a few of the activist types. Some called out to her.

"Didn't realize you are friends with people here." Perplexed, Agnes mustered a guy in dreadlocks who greeted her companion.

"Oh, one gets around. Small island and all that," said Polly and marched on.

When they entered a quiet, narrow side street, Agnes stopped dead.

"Polly, you will come back with me, won't you? My mom asked for you and would be so disappointed if I came without you. And me too—" Conscious of the pathetic pleading in her own voice, she broke off.

Vocal pitch descended by at least one octave, "My dear Watson, of course, I see it as my duty to investigate." An impish grin. "It warms my heart to be expected so keenly."

"We'll need groceries first. Mathilda—you know; our landlady you met yesterday?—lent me her car. She's with Sera now, so I could search for you and grab stuff for dinner. Say you'll stay over. Please?"

"A sleep-over? What fun! Do we roast marshmallows and indulge in pillow fights?"

Despite all her worries, Agnes laughed with abandon. Life was good with Polly around.

Chapter 14

POLLY

"Just let's not talk about it with Mathilda there," said Agnes as she switched off the ignition.

"Okay by me," replied Polly and followed to the back of the car. "Tell me the rest later. I'm rather curious now about your Mathilda anyway."

Hatch opened to unload the groceries, Agnes stopped, arm still raised.

"Why's that?"

"Speak of the devil," whispered Polly. Her elbow nudged Agnes before she busied herself with one of the shopping bins.

"*Ach*, there you are!" Garden shears stretched out, as though in attack, Mathilda came bustling down the walkway to the rose arbor. "*Mutti* is still having a lie-down."

At her approach, Polly and Agnes stepped aside. No one would stand in Mathilda's path. Shears tucked under her left arm, she grabbed a case of mineral water from the trunk.

Inside, the kitchen table was laid for three and a rectangular cake sat in the middle. Kettle on the boil, a thermos pot, crowned by a plastic filter, waited on the counter.

"Why don't you run up, Polly? If Sera's awake, ask whether she's ready for coffee. Her room's on your right at the top."

"Wouldn't you better go yourself, Agnes? I can't go and barge into Sera's bedroom."

"Oh, no worries. She's expecting you alright. In fact, she'll be delighted."

An odd sideways glance from a disapproving Mathilda decided Polly. Grinning at Agnes, she saluted, "Aye, captain," and took the stairs at a double. On the landing, she nonetheless hesitated. The old banister was painted white, as much of the interior of the whitewashed cottage. All original plank flooring, she guessed. The only decoration consisted of black and white stormy seascape photos in narrow frames. Very minimalist and effective. Pretty good taste our Mattie's got. Stop dawdling, she ordered herself.

With the tips of three fingers, she tapped a tattoo on the door and called out softly, "Sera, it's me Polly. Are you awake?"

"Polly, dear. Come in, please"—the words muffled by the solid wood.

Still fearing to intrude, Polly eased down the handle and peeked in.

"I'm delighted you're here, my dear. Don't be shy; close the door for a moment, and we talk." Behind her reading glasses, Sera's eyes crinkled in welcome. Several pillows propped against the wooden headboard of the bed, she sat, knees drawn up. A sketchbook lay face down next to her.

"Hi, Sera. So glad to see you."

"Pull up a chair from over there, Polly. Now tell me, how are you, dear? Did Agnes find you at the meeting?"

"But, Sera, the question is, how *you* are. Me, I'm fine, of course, thanks." Gently, she took the older woman's left hand in both of hers. It felt bony, cool, and fragile.

Sera patted Polly's hands with her right and replied, "Don't worry about me. I'm alright, child. The migraine has retreated into the background after adding some Advil to the Tylenol I took this morning. So, I'm quite doped." She raised a quizzical eyebrow. "Did I shock you now?"

"No, no. I'm glad you're all better. Can I tempt you to join us downstairs? Homemade cake, courtesy of your landlady. Fresh fruit—plums, I think—on a fluffy layer of dough."

"Ah, *Pflaumen Blechkuchen*," replied Sera with perfect German pronunciation. "One of my favorites. I'd intended to come down to thank Mathilda for all her kindness. Let me freshen up a little. Won't take long."

"Brilliant. I'll tell Aggie!" In her haste, Polly knocked her leg against a chest at the foot of the bed.

"See you shortly," she called back from the stairs when at eye level with Sera's door that she'd left dangling.

Not able to stop herself from beaming, Polly burst into the kitchen. "She'll be down in a tick."

Over at the counter, Agnes poured water into the filter. A delicious aroma of freshly brewed coffee permeated the room.

"Almost ready. Let the *kaffeeklatsch* begin. Could you take the round plastic container with the blue lid from the fridge, please? Mathilda brought whipped cream."

"Where is she?" asked Polly. "We'll need another place setting."

"Oh, it was getting too late for her. Apparently, hubby's back from the golf course by six. Potatoes needed to be put on, she said. Why are you so interested in her?"

"Ran into her a couple of times. With hubby or, at least, I think, it's him—"

"Mom! Are you feeling okay?" Attention diverted, Agnes rushed forward. "Come, have a seat. Like some coffee? Or can I make you a tea? Perhaps something cold, first?"

Her hand on Agnes's forearm, Sera said, "I'm alright, Agnes. No need to fuss over me...dear," she added. "So, Mathilda is gone? Too bad, I've missed her." She walked over to the back window and glanced out towards the sea.

"Take the bench, Polly, so that I can play hostess," directed Agnes when Sera pulled up a chair. "Mathilda invited us for a 'grilling' at her place tomorrow night. I take it, she means a barbecue. Unless she really wants to interrogate us." A momentary grin turned into a blush. "Sorry, stupid joke." With more care than needed, she busied herself sliding slices of cake onto each of their plates. She handed the bowl of cream to Sera. "Wasn't sure you'd want to accept."

"Let's see how things are tomorrow." Sera passed the container to Polly without taking any.

"What a color—that's the real thing. Yummy!" Manners forgotten, Polly smothered her cake in it.

"Mom, Polly's going to stay over." Like a puppy who'd retrieved a bone, Agnes beamed.

"I thought you might persuade her." To Polly, she said, "There's a folding bed tucked away in Agnes's bedroom. Or, of course, we could check out the crow's nest."

"A crow's nest? You mean with big black birds in it?" Visions of giant wings at night made Polly wary. "I don't do indoor birds."

"No, no, Polly. You watch too much Hitchcock." A tinkle like a Christmas silver bell, Sera's laugh teased her. "Or did you read du Maurier's original? Not to worry. The trapdoor under the eaves has a ladder to go up to a small attic, a kids' room, Mathilda told me. We didn't inspect it."

"Wow! Let's check it out!" Halfway out of her seat, Polly stopped herself, grabbing the table with both hands. "That sounds like fantastic! I love it!"

"Slow down, Polly. I'm not sure whether the cots can accommodate an adult." Her hand lightly patted Polly's. "We'll go up after coffee, I promise." 'Kids!' said Sera's expression as she winked at Agnes.

Aware her scrunched-up face must resemble a spoiled brat's who's been told to wait for ice cream until after dinner, Polly sought to regain her adult status. "Did read the book years ago. Never caught the movie, yet. Any good?"

"Oh, that one! Mom and I watched it when I was thirteen or so," Agnes chipped in. "Frightened the hell out of me."

"Ah, I recall now. When it got tense, you huddled behind my back in the old wing chair we used to have. Remember?" She reached over and stroked Agnes's arm. "I read to you every night—you and me cuddled in that chair together—when you were a child."

Mother and daughter smiled at each other with such deep intimacy for a moment that Polly's chest constricted with an unbearable yearning.

"One of my best childhood memories, Mom," the voice was tinged by nostalgia.

Head lowered, eyes fixed on the remaining runny cream on her plate, Polly stared at her fork drawing lines through the puddle that disappeared as quickly as they were drawn.

"Well, Polly, if you are ready, why don't you and Agnes investigate the crow's nest."

"Hey! Look who's out there."

At Agnes's exclamation, Polly raised her eyes to find herself alone at the table. A man waved outside the kitchen window. His muffled greetings could be more seen than heard. The large head of a shepherd dog—fangs exposed, paws on the sill—came into view, only to be ordered down immediately.

The room was filled with noise as they returned—a joyful yapping dog danced around Sera, who crouched to pat and scratch its ears. Her calm endearments were answered by sonorous groans from the brute.

"Meet Karl and Castro. This is our friend Polly." Extended right arm in a bow of presentation, Agnes's face glowed her pleasure.

Stiff from sitting or from embarrassment, Polly couldn't tell which, she scrambled to her feet and moved around the table to inspect the Karl person. The dog immediately shifted attention and regarded its master. Californian beach bum was Polly's first impression. Aging surfer, tanned and sun-bleached. He oozed a laid-back 'don't give a damn' vibe.

"Castro, say 'hi' to Polly." A nudge prompted the pooch to approach. "How are you with man's best friend, Polly?"

"If they don't eat me, I love them." In a cautious movement, she offered her palms for Castro to sniff. Seems to pass muster—sits and observes me expectantly. Better be sure though, she concluded. "May I pat—is it a him or her?"

"He'd like that," Karl assured her. "Next thing you know; he wants a tummy rub."

"Would you like some coffee and plum cake?" asked Agnes, opening the cabinet for a cup and plate.

"No thanks. Over-indulged today. Made me wonder if you gals are up to a little walk. Cooped up all day, I wager. You'll need some brazing air."

"Aren't the trails still off-limits?" A worried glance at her mother betrayed Agnes's concern.

"With the barrier in place, the road's all empty. Can't open the shop today either. The fuzz says they don't mind us walking as long as we stick to the road."

Both he and Agnes waited for Sera's reaction, who was busy stacking dishes. "Are you game?" he asked and began to carry plates for her. "Castro would love you to take him for his constitutional." At the sound of his name, the shepherd left Polly to join his master, bushy tail wagging agreement.

"Gotta work up an appetite. Brought your dinner. Homemade veggie lasagna. Made it all myself." In imitation of a chimpanzee, he drummed his chest with two fists. "The way you feasted on cake and cream, I increase your daily quota by a couple of miles."

"Could Agnes and I first peek in the crow's nest?" Though it reduced her to a whining toddler in her own opinion, Polly couldn't help herself.

"A crows' nest?" echoed Karl. "Are you into—"

"Nah, it's where I'll sleep," she interrupted and enjoyed his baffled expression.

"Mom, if you're up to a stroll, why don't I show Polly the attic and you and Karl go ahead. We'll catch up with you later."

As he shifted his inquiring glance to Sera, she appeared amused. "Give me a moment to grab shoes and jacket, Karl."

While the three of them cleared the table, Castro crouched on his haunches—head cocked to one side—eyes following forth and back like a spectator at a ping-pong match.

"What an awesome mutt!" Pot in her hand, Polly stopped to adore him. "Gorgeous. Those tan markings; they're all symmetrical. Even the little patches over his eyebrows. You trained him a fair bit, didn't you?"

A complacent nod from the handler. "Yeah, he's doing okay. Just has a thing about uniforms. Can't stand them."

"I know the feeling," quipped Polly in her best baritone parody. "Did he have a run-in with the fuzz that left him traumatized?"

"Not sure. I assume someone tried to train him to sell him as a police dog, but something went wrong. Perhaps aggressive training method or whatever. Got him as an older pup from a shelter after he'd been abandoned, or he absconded. Given his loyal nature, only serious abuse would make him leave, I'd say."

"Ready if you are." As Sera moved to the front door, Castro ran after her, tail beating in anticipant staccato.

"Right. So much for the loyal nature," Karl said deadpan as he followed.

Pulling Agnes' sleeve, Polly asked, "Can we go now? Please, Mom? I've been good."

"Okay, kid. You deserve your treat."

They found the trapdoor and a pole. A newer metal ladder folded down to give easy access to the center of the roof. From below, the brightness promised the attic window to be sufficient to let in lots of late afternoon sun.

Unable to suppress her explorer excitement, Polly skipped from one foot to the other, raring to ascend.

"Why don't you go check it out? The ceiling is too low for my taste," said Agnes.

Halfway up before the sentence was finished, a moment later Polly poked her head through the opening and grinned at the adorable kiddie nest.

Chapter 15

AGNES

"Anyone, more lasagna?" Karl held the serving spoon aloft, hovering over the tray. Under the table, Castro's tail beat an affirmative tattoo on the floor. "No, not you, brute. Fed you earlier."

"Stuffed to the gills, thanks." Polly rubbed her tiny stomach. "Awesome though." She licked her fork.

"Delicious," agreed Sera as she crossed her cutlery on her plate.

Pleased that her mom had finished the portion Karl had dished out, Agnes was amazed how much she herself enjoyed this evening with new friends. She raised her plate, "Just another sliver for me, please. The best pasta I've had in ages. Are the veggies from your garden?"

"They sure are. Handpicked, minutes before I chopped them up." A blob of sauce dripped from the spoon onto the table as his hands demonstrated a chopping action.

"He told us this morning about his organic veggie plot," explained Agnes.

Cocked eyebrow, Polly regarded him. "Quite the green thumb. Jumped on the eco bandwagon, did you? What with the solar panels and all?"

Noticeable different tone when she speaks to Karl, Agnes thought. Hardly talks to him at all—not during the walk nor after.

"How come you know about my solar? They're still in the box."

"Oh, I have my sources and ways and means."

"She talked to your workmen Saturday morning," said Agnes.

"Udo and Kai, you mean? They speak English?"

"No idea if they do. No need to—Polly is fluent in German." Proud of her new friend's accomplishments, Agnes wanted to pique his interest in the imp and succeeded.

"Oh. How long have you lived in Germany? The way I learned English—thrown in at the deep end; speak or drown," he laughed. "So, what's your home country?"

"Questions, questions. Let's say, kicked around lots of places. The eternal nomad, that's me."

As Polly's face shuttered, Agnes began to realize how little the elf revealed of herself. The clatter of porcelain diverted her attention to Sera clearing the table. Castro, keen on action, scrambled out from under the table and, as nothing happened, plonked down in the middle of the kitchen. To prevent anyone from tripping over the dog while they did the dishes, Karl told him to lie by the entrance. From there, soulful canine eyes followed their every move.

By the time everything was tidied away, Sera said her good-nights. She hugged Karl and Polly in thanks for their support and cuddled an ecstatic Castro.

"I'll run up with you, Mom. Need a sweater from my room."

On the landing upstairs, Agnes hesitated whether to hug Sera. "Do you have everything... Been quite a day, hasn't it?" she babbled.

"Please don't worry. Quiet time and a good night's rest, and I'll be back to normal." Her hand on Agnes's arm, she urged, "Go back now. Those two remind me of dogs unsure what to make of each other yet," she said, her mouth and eyes crinkling. "They'll be okay in the end. Glad Castro is so sensible." She leaned in and her lips brushed Agnes's cheek lightly. "Sleep well, dear."

About to close the door, she turned back. "I forgot; the police said to expect them for more questions.—Routine, apparently."

"Aka harassment of innocent witnesses. Guess, there's no choice. Hmm…dial a local lawyer," mused Agnes, only half in jest.

"Try not to worry so much." The tired smile showed how exhausted Sera was.

"Sorry, Mom. Sleep tight."

Back in the kitchen, Agnes found Polly cross-legged on the floor, stroking Castro, his head in her lap.

"Tea's ready," announced Karl as he carried a pot over to the table. "What are you shaking your head at, Agnes? Too late for a cuppa?" He sounded concerned as though fearing to have done the wrong thing.

"Not at all. No, my mom told me about the cops coming back to pester us again tomorrow. I'd love some tea," she lied— don't want to hurt his feelings, she rationalized, am afloat and wired from caffeine all day.

"You never did say what the police did to make you so mad this afternoon." With a yawn, Polly dropped onto the bench seat and stretched out her legs. "Castro, stop licking my feet. It tickles."

"Yeah, how did it go?" asked Karl as he filled his own cup.

"Hm…not sure if sharing a police interview is permitted. They didn't prohibit it. Actually… Never gave them a chance." With glee at the recollection, she said, "Walked out on them in the end."

"You did? Atta girl!" He underlined his praise by setting down the teapot with a bang.

The approval on Polly's face encouraged Agnes to recount

her ordeal in detail, painting Collins's interrogation style in lucid tones. "To be honest, the Chief wasn't much better," she concluded. "They make quite the pair, the two of them, with their 'good cop—bad cop' act."

"So, are they treating it as a homicide, you think?" Trust Polly to recognize what matters.

"Not sure—they didn't tell me. Dead bodies don't litter the beaches around here, the Collins woman implied. Ergo, a suspicious death."

"If I may venture in boldly," interrupted Karl in mock pomposity, while he heaped sugar into his cup, "I might shed some light on this. Homicide most likely—they believe."

In astonishment, Agnes sat back and nodded when Polly asked for both of them, "How did you find out?"

A devilish grin as Karl aped her, "Got my sources and ways and means." After a pause to enjoy their expectant faces, "Oh, alright—you'd squeeze it out of me sooner or later. Eibo let on." Upon their uncomprehending expressions, he said to Agnes, "Remember the first cop? Maike's partner?" When she nodded, he explained, "Constable Eibo Hennigen. Quite the lad."

"Friend of yours?" inquired Polly sardonically.

"Nah, not Eibo. One of the regulars at the Café. God's gift to women, he fancies himself. Spends his leisure time at the *FKK* beach all summer schmoozing with female tourists. Comes out for all our live-music dos. Rumors are some girls complain about him. We'd kick him out if he harassed the gals at my place. Castro keeps an eye on troublemakers. Don't you, my boy?"

The shepherd's head emerged from below when his name was uttered, and his master fondled the raised ear. The image of the dog's reaction to uniforms was still fresh in Agnes's mind. Such canine protection would serve well to discourage patrons acting up.

"No, Eibo thinks he owes me some. Very forthcoming he's been when I asked him this afternoon. Mind you, he's at the bottom of the pecking order. Limits his usefulness. There are grounds for suspicion, he said. Must await forensic results to be sure."

When neither one of them reacted, he hastened on, "Makes a huge difference. A drunk who passes out on the beach and drowns by accident is one thing. A murder inquiry is quite another. Both are bad for business. Homicides in your front yard scare people away or garners the wrong publicity. Gawkers, ghouls, and paparazzi, and all that jazz."

"Oh, no!" groaned Agnes in dismay.

"Sorry to sound selfish and mercenary. Have worked my ass off—pardon my language—to make a go of this over the past three years. One lousy season throws me back far more than I can afford.—Means *finito* kaput for me."

"I'm the egoist here." Anxious to set the record straight, Agnes justified herself, "My worry is what it will do to me and my mom. What if they suspect us? I don't stand up well to being given the Third Degree. They twist the words in your mouth until you've no idea what you're saying." She shuddered at the memory. "You read so much about wrongly convicted people. We're foreigners. Totally scary—" Heart racing, her palm covered her mouth as if to hold back her anguish.

"Mark my words, Watson," boomed Polly's imitation baritone. "We need to investigate to help them out. Them flatfoots can't be relied on to discover the truth."

Before Agnes could scold her irritably for her insensitive levity, Polly resumed in her normal voice, "Quite seriously, Agnes, we'd better find out for ourselves. Knowledge is power."

"And absolute power corrupts absolutely," chipped in Karl. "Yeah, sorry. Doesn't fit, does it? She's right though, Agnes. For Mom's and your safety, we must prove someone else did the dirty deed."

"You told us no one can say it *is* homicide." As much as she disliked raised voices, her own went up a notch. Polly's chirpy,

"A stitch in time saves nine, and all that," made her want to shout.

"If we wait until they get the lab results, it could be too late to redirect their attention," explained Polly in appeasement.

"Right you are," agreed Karl, only to query, "Pray tell, Sherlock, how do you intend to go about this?"

All serious now, Polly regarded him and Agnes in turn. "First, Aggie, you walk us over what precisely happened this morning. Every teeny detail of it. Same goes for Sera, if possible. Next, we create a list of people with reason to off Ronny Rosso. To figure out what they did last night, we need to divvy them—"

"Are you crazy! For one thing, don't dare badger my mother. The shock makes her fragile enough without reliving the horror of it. Plus, how the heck do you propose to learn who had a grudge against that man? I'm a total stranger here. Talk of opening cans of worms! You end up chatting to the murderer and get killed too."

"Get real, Agnes. Of course, sooner or later we'll be speaking with the killer. That's the idea. Must be careful how we do it. Don't worry—you'd be the only one discussing any of this with your mom. If you decide not to, so be it."

"Your point is valid though, Agnes," said Karl, his fist cradling his chin. "Are us three suspects as well as inquirers? I mean, can we exclude ourselves only because we investigate together? It's not as though we're old friends. You, Polly, are quite an enigma, for example."

"Don't pick on Polly." About to reach to touch his arm, Agnes pulled her hand back. "Honestly, Polly, what help could I possibly be? A few glimpses of this man—you saw as much yourself. What's more, Karl, you probably have no clue who he is. Or was…" she corrected herself.

"As a matter of fact, I ran into him last night."

"Where?" The revelation caused Polly to bounce up on her bench.

"Dude came with Hinrich Dieken—the owner of the camp-ground down the road; can't miss it on the way to town." They both nodded, Polly rather impatiently. "Owns quite a bit of land around here—as far as there still is private property. Anyway, they walked in around eleven-thirty. Didn't pay much attention to them. Me and my faithful brute were on a mission to sort some rowdy skinheads outside. Barred them before—they never learn. Passed by Hinrich who led this ponytail guy to the alcove at the back. I told the police about it today when they showed me a picture of their man. Recognized the face. The hairdo caught my attention." Unconsciously his fingers weaved through his own long strands.

"Our first clue!" Excited, Polly wriggled on her seat. "We should start writing all this down. How did they act?"

"What do you mean?" The puzzled tone of his handler must have penetrated the sleeping dog's consciousness. With a yip, he awoke and poked his head out from under the table and received an absent-minded pat.

"Were they friendly-like, or arguing, or what?"

Puckered forehead, the tanned skin wrinkling under sun-bleached hair, Karl focused on the recollection. With a sigh, Castro subsided. "Dieken did most of the talking," Karl said slowly. "Led the way. Ponytail trailed after him—smoldering. Not a happy man. Maybe he didn't like the music.—Come to think of it, the band was on a break. The skinheads were giving us agro about the lull."

"How did your Hinrich sound? Angry, or chummy, or what?"

"The grand inquisitor, are you, Polly?" Exasperated, he tried to clarify. "No, neither. I'd say… Dunno, got the impres-sion he was in control. Then again, he usually is. Being sort of neighbors and in a lonely spot, we're on quite familiar terms. Was more—Well, like laying down the law for the Rosso person."

"You didn't overhear any details?"

"No. As I said, too busy. Hinrich just waved in passing—ordered beer and schnapps."

"Could you question your staff? Or any customers who heard them talk?"

"Polly! You can't ask Karl to spy on people!" Though intrigued against her will, even forgetting her exhaustion, Agnes now was uncomfortable with where this was leading.

"As the man said earlier, Agnes. The faster it's cleared up; the less damage it can do to his business. Besides, if he solves a murder, he'd be the local hero." The imp regarded Karl speculatively.

"Haha. Yeah, you've got a point there," conceded Karl with a self-conscious grimace. "Will do my best to dig up the juicy bits. What's your contribution? Eh, Sherlock?"

"Well, Aggie?" An attention-grabbing pause. "Should we tell him?" When Agnes showed no sign of comprehension, she straightened up to her full diminutive height. "Duh? Tell the man what we've discovered." Satisfied with Agnes's 'ah,' she tucked her legs under like the Buddha.

Both took turns describing the meetings they'd attended on Friday and Saturday. Unimpressed, Karl remarked that his customers kept him up to date. Everyone, of course, griped about the *WKA*. Not him, he said. The greener, the better for the island, in his view. That Rosso and Daniel Dregger chummed at the Tea House made him chuckle.

Kind of deflated and tired, Agnes was glad they were finished. Her mind on snuggling under her cozy duvet, she started to collect cups.

"Wait, not done yet. After you and Sera were gone, the action started. Those jerks started to argue."

With a jolt, Agnes admitted to herself that Rosso and DD slipped from her radar the moment they sat down. Her most vivid memory was of an exchange between a querulous elderly mother and her flustered daughter at the next table. So deeply embarrassing a pair, she couldn't get out of the place fast enough.

"Earth to sleepyhead on cloud nine." The elfish sing-song recalled her to the present. "Care what happened after?"

"Sorry, Polly. Yes, do tell us. Right after, we'll have to call it quits. I'm dead beat. Oh, God! Gosh, poor choice of words—"

"No worries, I'll be quick. They were in a tizzy, what with Ronny accusing Dregger of going back on his word over the number of turbines to be erected. In short, Rosso threatened Daniel with some sort of revelation. Said the Guttenberg scandal would seem nothing by comparison." She turned to Agnes, "Are you familiar with—"

"You mean the German minister of foreign affairs who resigned a number of years ago after the news broke of his plagiarized dissertation back in the day? Rather old hat."

"Got it in one. A landmark case. Spurred on a pack of plagiarism hunters. Beats me what Rosso meant. Baffled Green Danny too. Maybe he played dumb. Said he knew what to do and up and left. Pissed off, he was. Speaking of which—you asked me about Mathilda. Later on, a guy—in a lather about the *WKA*—blocked Ronny's exit.—Remember Fancy Pants at the meeting accusing Rosso of destroying paradise for mere mammon?"

A dim memory surfaced to make Agnes nod. It sufficed for Polly to continue, "The very man. Gave Rosso a piece of his mind. Told him *they* would get a lawyer—I take it, him and the people at his table."

"Where does our landlady come in?"

"A hand materialized from the alcove and grabbed his coat tail. Begged him not to make a scene. He called her Mattie. Guess who?" An eyebrow raised quizzically. "Yes, my dear, Watson. T'was our waltzin' Mathilda. There you go." Smug, Polly concluded an octave lower, "The plot thickens, me dears!"

"My head's swimming—is all." Hands dug deep into her hair, Agnes groaned.

Concerned, Karl regarded her. A scrabbling sound from under the table brought to light an excited canine, sensing a homerun. "Yes, my friend. Some of us have to trudge back. Let's sleep on this, gals. My place for brunch tomorrow? Decide wide awake if we want to take it further.—Gotta say though, I do feel sort of hooked."

Chapter 16

AGNES

Rain drumming on the roof and window. Shoot! Left it tilted! Whoa—slow down.

Agnes sank back onto the bed to let the dizziness subside. Bad idea to jump up still half-asleep. 9:23 AM! Dead to the world for almost ten hours. Oh shoot, must all metaphors be so deadly?

She grabbed her jeans and padded barefoot to the bathroom. A faint whiff of coffee and toast hit her nostrils. The aroma became irrefutable when she was halfway down the stairs.

"Here's Sleeping Beauty," greeted Polly while she poured steaming water into a filter cone. "Toast's ready in a tick. Want some?"

"My dreams come true," said Agnes. "Perfect way to wake up."

"Always aiming to please," joked the elf and brought over the coffee pot.

"We seem to spend our life at this table lately." Legs stretched out, Agnes took a first sip. "Ahhh—delicious."

"If you care to contemplate the great outdoors—we'll be

marooned here all morning. Unless of course you, like me, love to splash through puddles."

"I'm more the 'curl up with a good book' type," laughed Agnes. "Is Sera still sleeping?"

"Just went up for a sweater—" Head swiveling to the stairway, Polly announced, "Here she is."

"Good morning, Agnes." In passing her mother touched Agnes' shoulder. "Did you sleep alright?"

"Hi, Mom. Except for weird dreams—at least I slept long. How are you feeling?"

"Don't worry about me, dear. I'm fine." With a smile, she thanked Polly who handed her a steaming cup.

"Your mom and I are early birds. Enjoyed her tea when I got back from my walk."

"You were out in this weather? Weren't you soaked?"

"Nah—started to pour in earnest as I came up the path."

"You went to the *beach*?" Such an act struck Agnes as almost sacrilegious, if not downright ghoulish. With unease, she glanced over at Sera who busied herself filling the toaster on the counter.

"After all, it's merely a beach. And thankfully, no one's around at dawn. The cops are gone. Sooner or later people will want to reclaim that stretch of sand. Life goes on." Her tone calm and matter of fact. She leaned close to whisper, "Wanted to check it out after what we said last night."

Involuntarily, Agnes glanced at her mother. With forced brightness, she asked, "Sera, what would you like to do today? Or should I ask, what can we do on a rainy day?"

The toast popped, and Sera offered Agnes the fragrant slices before she replied, "Go into town once it lets up, I thought. The central reading room and perhaps a *Kurkonzert*, if classical music is on the program. Maybe do some sketching. Polly, what are your plans? You'll want to return to your own place, I assume."

"Oh, I'm easy," said Polly, her eyes on Agnes.

"What about Mathilda's invitation, Mom? Not sure, if it's

still on with the weather. I'd better call her in any case." As helpful as Mathilda proved to be, Agnes didn't take to the woman.

"If they want to go ahead with it, we ought to accept. She's been kind to us. Let's pick up a decent bottle of wine to take along." As an afterthought, "We'll be in town anyway." As though that clinched it, Sera reached over to pat Polly's forearm. "How was the crow's nest?"

"Loved it! Up with the birds, so to speak. They literally did wake me at sunup. Or, what passed for sunrise this morn," she grinned.

"Weren't you too cramped in a kid's cot?" asked Agnes, stuffing the last of her second, thickly cut whole-grain toast into her mouth. Jam dripped down her chin. She quickly leaned nose-close over her plate.

A dismissive hand wave from Polly, "Nay, not a wee tot like me. You don't mind if I go up while you finish breakfast?"

The moment Polly sprinted up, knocks at the front door alerted them.

"Who the heck calls this early?" mumbled Agnes, still chewing.

"The police most likely. Please see to them. I'll be upstairs." Without waiting for a response, Sera made for the stairs.

In no mood for the encounter, Agnes took another gulp of coffee to unglue her teeth before she went to check.

A couple of steps back stood Maike, glancing indecisively at the side gate. At the sound of the door, she swung around. The rain had almost petered out. Only the dripping foliage and puddles on the walkway reminded one of the downpour.

"*Moin.* I am glad to find you at home. My superiors need to ask more questions. Could you come to the station with us now?"

"Why me?" Instantly, Agnes regretted her petulant query. Better her than Sera. "Oh well, whatever—give me time to dress."

"Of course, we gladly take your mother along." Must be a mind reader—got to be careful, Agnes thought. However, Maike's next words showed concern rather than telepathy. "It might not be prudent to leave her on her own in this isolated cottage."

"Right. I'll ask her." Agnes turned and closed the door in the cop's face.

When she reached the top landing, Sera motioned to her from her room. Perched on the foot end of the bed, Polly sat, legs tucked under.

"They require me at the station and will give you a ride into town." No way, Agnes intended to repeat Maike's rationale, or her mother would bristle at such paternalistic interference or implied ageism.

Her mom raised eyebrows in question at Polly.

"You'd better go along. I'll catch you later. Don't want to get on their radar. Just pretend I'm not here." Polly winked conspiratorially, despite Sera's serious expression.

"Fine with me. There's a kid's bike in the shed you could borrow," suggested Agnes and grinned. "Should do you nicely."

"Gee, thanks, pal. Let's all meet around one at the kebab joint in that little street behind the church. Can't miss it. *Eddies Döner*. They make a mean *Bauernsalat*—Greek salad, to you."

"Okay by me," agreed Agnes. Her mother nodded assent. "Right, give me ten minutes for a quick shower. Oh, and Polly, can you stop by the café to tell Karl, please?"

"Will do. No worries."

"If you need rain gear—"

The word petered out as Polly snuck into the hallway and up the ladder as though she expected spies to be lurking around every corner.

Headshaking, Agnes made for the bathroom. Careful not to be visible from below, she peeked out the window. A silver-and-blue police vehicle parked outside the hedge bordering the road. On the passenger side, one hand braced against the car roof, stood Maike surveying the path to the cottage. Swiftly, Agnes pulled down the blinds, thinking, we'd better hustle…

———————

Forty minutes later she was kept waiting herself with plenty of time to scrutinize her surroundings. By the standard of American cop shows, the place didn't have the vibe of an interview room. More likely it did double duty as someone's office.

An elderly PC with a monitor occupied a desk shoved against the wall that ached for a coat of paint. Scuffed, olive-green plastic chairs and a couple of padded office chairs, one of better quality with armrests, cluttered the smallish space. Metal shelving stored boxes and a jumble of stacked loose paper and journals. A rookie in uniform, seated close to the door, appeared fascinated by a spot on the ceiling whenever Agnes glanced in her direction.

"Sorry for the delay." File folder in hand, Collins breathed into the room. With one foot—elegantly shoed in low-heeled, sleek pumps—she hooked and pulled over the captain-style chair. Today she wore well-tailored, slim-line pewter pants with a matching charcoal top of a deceptively simple cut. Under the bright LED, her hair shimmered even glossier. Without another word, she sat and busied herself with the files.

Could swear the darn woman can recite the content in her sleep, Agnes fumed and suppressed her fingers' urge to drum on something. Impatience would underscore the Inspector's power.

How she missed her mobile to punctuate her nonchalance by texting.

Instead, Agnes visualized how Polly might conduct herself; slouch back—expansively—admire the view. Quite a large window for a cop shop. Impressive vista, they've got. Hey, you can catch sight of the sea from up here. Weather's bound to pick up…

The ruse worked since Collins sprang to life. "Ms. Taylor…

Pardon me—Dr. Taylor," she met Agnes's lazy glance sardonically. "We need you to clear up a few points that arose from your previous statement. The transcript of our initial interview requires your signature. Would you please read it over and sign at the bottom?" The manicured hand held out some sheets.

Two can play this game, Agnes decided. Take your sweet time to peruse the drivel. Imagine the woman is a tiresome, aggressive student trying to prove herself by attacking the Prof. —Piece of cake—dealt with the type before.

Her mental commentary ran on while she read. Actually, an advantage to see it transcribed. All familiar and nothing unexpected. Off and on she'd sounded petulant. No wonder—revisiting Collins's questions now threatened to raise her hackles. Did the beast intend to rile her? The cop would hardly give her the benefit of a mnemonic aid, otherwise. Forcing her facial muscles to remain immobile, she grabbed the proffered pen.

"Thank you." A mere glance at the signature. The papers were dismissed to oblivion. "If you don't mind, we will also record the present session."

"Be my guest."

Same spiel again—identification and date. "May we begin?"

Like a dull puppet, Agnes nodded.

"You will have to speak. Body language is not recorded."

"Yes, you most certainly may start your questions."

"Dr. Taylor, you mentioned in your statement that a friend you had met on Saturday morning, told you about the public meeting the deceased was holding in *Die Krone* the same evening. You and your mother agreed to join—"

"For the record, I did not say 'we agreed.' I'd no idea if my mother would want to."

"Right. Who is this so-called friend? We need the full name and address."

"Are you kidding? Do you ask everyone you meet for their particulars?" Attack is the best defense. You love debates in class. So, enjoy yourself. "In Canada, we're on first-name basis.

Tons of people I'm familiar with for years without a clue of their last names—never mind addresses. Thousands of students walk in and out of my life and leave no trace."

"Am I to take from all this that you are neither apprised of this person's last name nor her address?"

"The *person* is called Polly. If she ever mentioned her surname, it didn't compute. So, yes, the answer is, 'No, I've no idea.'" The verbal sparring elated Agnes. In absence of Chief Dickering, she could focus on one foe. Two against one was unfair anyway. The mute and immobile rookie didn't count.

"Have you seen this—Polly—since our last talk?"

Don't hesitate now, Agnes, she urged herself. "Yes, sure."

"When was that?"

Did the cops keep tabs on them? Were they being followed? Well, at least they can't bug our phone, haha, Agnes thought. "Last night. Kept us company." Info glut serves to distract. "Plus, Karl and Castro joined us for dinner. Brought lasagna. Oh, Mathilda dropped off a cake. In between—"

"May I interrupt? Which Karl and Castro? Surely not Marx and Fidel?"

Ah, Collins aimed for humor. Lost the scent, though.

"Well, their last names elude me. My most recent new friend is Karl, proprietor of the Dune Café. Met him yesterday morning. Come to think of it, if his first name is Fidel, then I do know his last—"

"Who is Castro?" cut in Inspector Collins, her voice strident.

"His German Shepherd, of course. My mother is very fond of him." Delighted with her red herrings, Agnes grinned.

"Where were you between eleven o'clock on Sunday night and six on Monday morning?"

Wow, talk about non sequiturs. "Quite apropos of nothing, isn't it? I told you yesterday; after our long hike, we were utterly zonked by eleven. So, in short, we both slept. I woke six-thirtyish."

"Are you and your mother close?"

"What business of yours is that?"

"In an inquiry like this, we have to ask all kinds of questions that may appear irrelevant. Believe me; we know what we are doing."

"That I can well believe!"

"Do you see each other often throughout the year?"

"How's your geographic knowledge of Canada? Toronto is about eighteen hundred km from Halifax. Doesn't make for a comfy commute."

"Could you simply answer my questions?"

"The response is, 'no, of course, not.' As professionals, we are too involved to afford time or money to jet set."

"When did you last see your mother before this joined vacation?"

"Oh, a number of years ago when I attended a major congress in Halifax."

Eyes narrowed, Collins regarded her—like an insect about to be squashed.

"Am I to understand that the relationship is not very close?"

"Your inference is a non sequitur. People might not meet physically, yet be very close nonetheless. What with texting, tweeting, Facebook, etcetera—some relationships function far better at a distance than face-to-face."

"So, you and your mother are in frequent digital contact?"

"My leisure hours are too limited for virtual or other socializing. Countless student emails require attention when I'm online. In short, no, we do not text or tweet. Period. Infer from this what you wish. To my mind, none of this reflects on us or has anything to do with the death of a person unknown to us." Time to assert myself here. "If there are no pertinent questions, I would like to join my mother. Our vacation is precious *because* of its rarity." There! How's that for turning tables?

"Do bear with me for a little longer." For a minute the Inspector shuffled papers—an obvious power grab.

To resist, Agnes focused on the rookie by the door. Until she realized the tormentor scrutinized her intently.

"You said one of the deceased's eyes was visible and open when you bent over him and was partially covered with sand. Did you notice flies or other insects near or on—"

"Yuck! What kind of question is that! Are you deliberately trying to gross me out?" The b—beast! Knew how to get back every time!

"The presence of flies, maggots, and other insects, and so on, is useful as a forensic indicator," responded Collins with exaggerated calm. "You saw the body considerably earlier than we or our specialists did. Hence, the question is highly pertinent and of importance."

"Yeah well, your job is certainly not to my liking. I prefer the theoretical realm." Nausea still rising, Agnes dug her nails into her jeans-clad thighs.

"Please, do try to remember," the woman coaxed her.

For a moment, Agnes allowed her mind to unveil the image she was trying her best to bury. Staring at the blank wall, she shuddered. "Yes, I think there were flies… One black, yellowish-green, shiny, fat thing buzzing…"

Stomach gone acidic, revulsion fought with fascination. Had she been conscious of the flies at the time, or was this false memory syndrome?

"No, I don't recall more," she said, her gaze returning to Collins. Did the woman actually hide a smile? "Sorry, but this is all I can help you with. I assume I'm free to go? You don't detain me for anything—surely?"

"Yes, of course, you may leave any time you wish. Police cannot force anyone to speak to them. Only a prosecutor or judge can."

While Agnes rose, the Inspector spoke the concluding formulae for the interview. At a glance from her superior, the uniform jumped to attention.

"The officer will make arrangements with you to come in to

sign the transcript. Please inform us if you plan to go off-island. In regard to your friend Polly, ask her to call us. And do let us know her full name and contact info as soon as possible."

"That I will not! I've no intention of doing your job for you, or to pressure my friends, or to spy on them."

In the hallway, accompanied by the patient rookie, Agnes declined a ride back and barged for the exit. Outside, she took a deep breath of salty, moist air. The rain had stopped.

At a clipping pace, she strode through the town to outrun her anger. It still took her about a fifteen-minute, brisk walk on the promenade, eyes fixed on the beach and the sea, to ban the image of the elegant beast.

Time to call Mathilda.

Zigzagging her way through a warrant of streets, trying not to get totally lost, it was midday by the time she reached a familiar pedestrian zone. From here she might retrace her steps into the *Kurgebiet*. The ambiance of high-end clinics, sanatoriums, and exclusive spa hotels sporting manicured lawns, calmed. Her step slowed to a leisurely pace. The air smelled earthy from the damp soil of the park-like grounds of upscale health resorts. A profusion of greenery, wherever one turned. Maybe the health effect spilled over into the botany.

Relaxed she crossed the wide pedestrian zone—its old-world charm recreated by ornamental benches, lamp posts, flower urns, and shading trees—and strolled in direction of the tourist office. Glancing into an adjacent street, she noticed a longish building with a low rhododendron hedge bordering a front yard. The blooms of a rose arbor marked the entrance.

Idly she perceived a woman who moved purposefully towards the steps to the front door flanked by an access ramp. The person resembled her mom. Odd.

Caught in an eerie sense of déjà vu, Agnes stood still. Fully expecting Sera to come back into the street—in fact, about to hail her—she saw the woman disappear through the entrance. Why would Sera go into a building here? Must be the public library or something. Much bigger than the residence she spotted a Sera look-alike enter on Friday afternoon. The difference could be explained by the bird's eye angle from the top of the dike that day.

Perplexed she approached to read the sign next to the wrought-iron gate. *Senioren Residenz Lüüt Mööv*. What on earth would her mother want in a residence for seniors? For a few minutes Agnes hung around, but the woman did not reappear.

Just a fluke, she decided. Someone on the island shared a similar appearance and taste in dress. After all, dark slacks and tops were popular. Many women in late middle age and beyond wore their gray hair fashionably short and were trim and fit. Still, rather strange. Must tell Sera later of her doppelgänger.

Chapter 17

POLLY

Here's Agnes. Polly jumped up, waved, and ran to the door. Pure luck to secure a table at a back window with a view of the entrance to spy anyone coming into the *Döner*.

No reaction to Polly's, "Hey, how's it going, Partner?" Instead, Agnes asked, "Is Sera here yet?"

"No—only got here five minutes ago myself." She'd made sure to be early, in case the servers recognized her from Sunday night. The cashier sure did.

"Want a drink from the cooler? Told them we're still waiting for someone before ordering grub."

With an absent-minded nod, Agnes grabbed a beer and paid in cash. Surprised, Polly noticed her taking a swig of the brew as they went to sit in the back. Anxiety issued from her friend's deep-brown eyes and threatened to become contagious.

"Seriously—how are you? Was the fuzz grueling?"

"Most annoying. The Collins woman tried to nail me with irrelevant, impertinent questions about my relationship to my mom. At one point I started to enjoy fencing—Until she totally grossed me out! Asked about flies on the man's face." A shudder and another long swig from the bottle.

"Ah, hence you now needed some fortification." Time to lighten up, thought Polly.

"Partially," said Agnes, her eyes staring at the wall. "What freaked me out came later." Her gaze returned to Polly's face without connecting. After a quick glance at the entrance, her voice dropped to a whisper, "I think I spotted Sera earlier." Handwaving as though to ward off any smart-ass rejoinder. "Be serious for a moment. This woman, who resembled my mother, entered some sort of retirement residence."

Exhausted, Agnes leaned back. "If you ask me, it's uncanny. First, I see her look-alike go into a house in town, and now this. Might be the same place—not sure. Does she have a doppel-gänger? The more I think about it—totally creepy! Or what's she up to?"

"Ahem," Polly vied for Agnes's attention. "You can ask her yourself now." Half-rising to be visible, she yoo-hooed.

"Did I keep you waiting?" Rucksack stowed under a chair, Sera sat down next to Agnes. "Are you alright, dear? You look distressed."

Concerned how things might pan out, Polly slid back into her seat across from them.

The way Agnes stared unfocused at Sera's hand that stroked hers was disquieting. The tone of her, "I'm okay—really," belied her words.

Relax, Polly wanted to say. Instead, she opted for, "Let's order some grub. I'm starved."

All three of them decided on salads, and Sera insisted on paying. To give them a chance to work things out in private, Polly waited for their stuff up front. No luck—when she returned with the laden tray, an unnatural, strained silence hung over the table.

"How was your morning, Sera?" Make conversation, chatter for three, and so on, Polly urged herself.

"Thanks, dear," said Sera, as Polly dished out their fare. "A sheltered spot at the harbor proved ideal for sketching."

"Oh, can I see?" begged Polly.

"Not yet. This afternoon I plan to compare different light conditions. Did you manage with the kiddie bike?"

"Yup. Not too bad," replied Polly, her eyes on Agnes who pushed lettuce leaves around her plate. "Spoke to Karl—he'll be in town and wants to meet at three."

A piece of cucumber on her fork held Agnes's attention as she nodded assent.

"What did Mathilda say, Agnes? Are we on for tonight?" Salad finished, Sera made to scoot off again.

"Sorry, Mom, I almost forgot. Actually, took me forever to find a payphone. That's how I came by the senior residence, see?" Faced with Sera's blank expression, Agnes stumbled on, "So, yes, Mathilda wants us over for six. They live between the wharf and *Kurgebiet*. I can meet you at a quarter to at the main bus terminal."

What caused this sudden verbosity? wondered Polly.

"Perfect. I'll pick up the wine." One hand grabbing the rucksack, Sera got up. "Polly, dear," she bent down, lips brushing her cheek. "Stay in touch."

"You bet." With a grin, Polly regarded Sera who squeezed Agnes' shoulder and left.

"Okay, Watson, let's mosey on. No use brooding. Tell me all about what's bugging you."

Out in the street, Agnes held her back. "Hold on. Where are we going? Aren't we meeting Karl?"

"First need to walk off your steam," chuckled Polly, and linked her arm with Agnes's. "Ever been to the tiny lake out by the youth hostel?" In answer to a shake of the dark curls, "Thought not. Local beauty spot. A trail circles it. Plus, Karl's got some errands in the area."

Both were quiet as they made their way through the residential streets. Eventually, Polly zoomed in on an overgrown, narrow entrance to the footpath to the lake. She sensed Agnes relax once the silence of the path engulfed them. Sudden sunlight filtered through the canopies of the towering chestnut trees. Like a stage effect, the vista now opened onto the water. Audibly, Agnes caught her breath and stopped dead.

"Wow—so beautiful," she exclaimed. "You were right. It'll do the trick."

"Let's stroll on a little. Not much time before we meet Karl at three." Polly skipped ahead.

"The swans glide along so majestically… Nothing seems to worry them."

"I bet not. Ever witnessed a swan attack a pooch who bothers it?"

For a few minutes, they walked in companionable silence.

"How quiet it is. Where are all the people?"

"Oh, they'll come out all too soon. In the morning and evening, joggers, dog walkers, love birds, and whatnot take over." Gently Polly squeezed Agnes's arm and let it go. "Now tell me what's on your mind. Your mom did not react too well to your doppelgänger theory, Watson?"

A deep breath sucked in noisily through her nose, Agnes burst out, "To put it mildly. Evaded my question altogether, she did. Typical."

"Whoa, Agnes. Keep your knickers on. Thought you had calmed—"

"Easy for you to say. She's not your mom—"

"More's the pity."

"Every time I ever asked about important personal things, she's done the same thing. Would you believe it? She's never told me who my dad is!" One hand pushing her mane back impatiently, she glared at Polly. "Whenever I asked her as a teenager, I got weird answers. She'd say, I seemed to assume she herself knew who the father was. There was no guarantee of that. For Christ's sake, all my friends had dads. Even Tina whose parents were divorced. When I was fourteen, my mom said, 'We believed in free love and sex. So different from Canadian conservative attitudes.' Said to a teenage kid!"

"A woman after my own heart." The guffaw brought on another glare from Agnes. "Seriously, Agnes, I understand a Canadian fourteen-year-old might be shocked. Still, aren't you now a grown woman with experience in life? What if she simply is uncertain who fathered you? Who needs a father anyway?"

"Well, I always wanted one like my friend Rachel's."

"No use yearning for it. Tell me, what *did* Sera say today?"

"First, I described the woman entering the senior residence and joked it was she, or her doppelgänger. When I asked what on earth she would do in such a place, she prevaricated. Said, if it were her, she might be exploring places to retire. She's old enough."

"She's not—"

"Her words, not mine. So, I wondered aloud why in the world she'd want to spend her retirement here. Annoyed me by repeating her formula. If it had been her, could it be Bosum suited her? I got so ticked off! At least, I deserve a straightforward honest reply, I argued. Absurd, to think she'd leave a place as beautiful as Nova Scotia. A coast she's loved for decades—to move to a conservative, touristy German island? So hurtful to say I'd seen little of her over the past twenty-odd years and had no clue what she loved or not. Left me speechless. Good thing you came back just then."

"Guess she wants to keep her private life private, Agnes. You gotta respect—"

"Polly, I do respect people's privacy. We're talking about my mother! Over the last couple of days, I'd begun to believe she loves me. And I love her and realized I even like her a lot."

"Of course, she does and you do! Doesn't mean you share all your thoughts."

"Sure, I can agree in principle. I don't snoop. This is different—perplexing and counterproductive. The Inspector is already suspicious. Why else would she quiz me about my relationship to my mother?—Speaking of which, she also inquired about you, and I protected your privacy. Told her to shove it—

more or less—said I wasn't privy to your particulars and would not find them out for her."

"Atta girl! Thanks, pal. Appreciate it."

"What if Sera hides something?"

"Don't be ludicrous, Agnes. Your mom's one hell of a special person. I believe in her completely—and so should you."

"After a mere three-day acquaintance? Besides, being special doesn't preclude having secrets."

"Tell you what. If it bothers you so much, I'll go and find out for you. Shouldn't be hard to chat up the staff. What's the place called again?"

"Something like *Lüüt Mööv*," responded Agnes automatically —only to burst out, "Polly! You can't go and spy on her! She'd never forgive you. Or me. It violates her right to privacy. Didn't you just lecture me—"

"Yah, well, extraordinary circumstances require exceptional measures. Every rule has its exception," waffled Polly. "Let's go meet Karl. Can't keep a busy man waiting." The reminder of Karl did the trick. Hand on her elbow, Polly steered Agnes off onto another path leading to the northwest side of the island.

Chapter 18

POLLY

Fifteen minutes later they arrived at a pub that sported an old wooden sign with a willow—*Zur Weide*. A smaller one—*Bier Garten*—suspended above an arbor pointed to the back.

From a bench encircling a huge willow tree, Karl waved to them. While zigzagging around tables and chairs—red and green paint peeling with age on the wooden slats—Polly scanned the beer garden but found it nearly empty.

Drawing back his sprawled-out legs—clad in dark brown calf-length cargo pants—Karl got up to greet them. A quick hug for Agnes, he nudged Polly with a friendly elbow and a 'hey, pal.' His forearms—exposed by the rolled-up sleeves of a blue denim shirt—Polly noticed, were quite as muscular as his tanned calves.

"No Castro?" Amazed, Polly registered her own disappointment.

"Got to make do with me. Castro's anti-consumerist—hates shopping." He scrutinized Agnes's face and asked softly, "How did it go?"

A chair pulled up across from Karl, Agnes now stroked back her heavy, dark hair. Voice vibrating with suppressed emotion, she said, "Could've been worse. Chief Dickering wasn't there. Collins is a b—beastly nuisance. Reminded me of obnoxious students. They don't worry me, so why should she?"

"Way to go, my girl!" Karl beamed encouragement straight into Agnes's eyes.

"Agnes worries they're too interested in her mom." Assertive, Polly broke the spell. "Let's figure out who's done the dirty deed. Only thing to set her mind at rest."

"Got something interesting to tell you." Reluctantly Karl took his eyes off Agnes. "First, I'll go grab our drinks. What's your poison?"

Supplied with coffee a little later, Polly emptied the creamer over hers and slowly added a pinch of sugar—keenly aware of Karl watching Agnes stir lots of cream into her cup.

"So, are you ready?" They both nodded at him. To heighten their anticipation, he took a deep swig of water.

Still gazing at Agnes, he asked, "Remember Erika, the gal yesterday morning?"

"The cleaner?"

"A kind of factotum is Erika. Cleans and helps in the kitchen, does my apartment upstairs too, stocks up, and what-not. What with all the stuff going on yesterday, it didn't hit me that she was unusually jumpy and frazzled."

He stared into his cup as if lost in memory. "You've got to know Erika. One hell of a time she's had as a kid. Now she's —och, what? Twenty or twenty-two? Tough and big and does not take any nonsense from the lads. Anyhow, last evening after I got back, she was all glum, yet nervy. Put it down to the fuzz swarming the place. Always spells trouble to her. Too often came to sort her old man and kid brother back home."

Once more Karl paused and sipped coffee. With his listen-ers' undivided attention—Agnes engrossed, head tilted, and

Polly herself on the edge of her chair fidgeting—he resumed in a conspiratorial tone.

"This morning I found her crying quietly over her cleaning pail, leaning on her mop." When both of them regarded him incredulously, he insisted, "No, I'm serious. Erika has a *Putz-fimmel*. I mean, she's an obsessive cleaner. Loves to scour and make things shipshape. To be left alone at seven AM to wave her wand until the world is in order again is her idea of a good time. A marvel she is. Am truly blessed with her." The guileless green eyes—no, brown speckles too—all sincere, Polly acknowledged. So, Erika's a protégé rather than his woman.

Was the man a mind-reader? For he clarified, with a glance at Agnes, "I'm not involved with her, in case you were wondering. A great kid, she is. Served as her ersatz father from way back when she started shortly after I took over. Not frontline staff—prefers to work her ass off in the background."

"Karl! Come to the point, will you?" With a thud, Polly brought her chair down from rocking backward.

"Well, anyway. So, I simply prepared her favorite breakfast —quiet-like, not disturbing her—and dished it out with a flourish." An arm sweep demonstrated the action. "Belgian Waffles, piping hot, loaded with fresh berries and whipped cream."

"Brilliant!" Envisioning the taste, Polly licked her lips. "Way to start the day."

"Make you some next time," promised Karl. "First, the sight caused a minor emotional meltdown. Soon the waffles did their magic. Perked up after gobbling half of it. Still took a pot of strong tea before her worries spilled out in bits and pieces."

His eyes sought Agnes's. "Here goes. Our Erika intended Sunday night to tie down the patio umbrellas, a bit after midnight. Most people had left by then. An old fart leaned against the railing, smoking. No reason for Erika to pay him any attention. Lots of customers smoke out back. Then, when she bends over to fasten a stack of umbrellas—a chain is bolted to the wall for the purpose—the guy creeps up behind her and feels her up. Literally! Tells her what he'd like to do with the chain. Well, he hadn't reckoned with our Erika. She's fierce. Turned around and slapped him soundly and tried to kick him in the privates."

"Good for her!" cheered Polly, clapping her hands in glee. Even Agnes's concerned face crinkled into a smile.

"The kick didn't connect—more's the pity. The geezer took off toward the beach path, swearing at her and shaking his fist. Held a liquor bottle in his other hand. Counts herself lucky he didn't throw it at her."

"Awful," commented Agnes, yet appeared baffled. "Don't get me wrong—I empathize with her terrible experience. Why would she be so anxious and worried about it the next day? Surely she reacted confidently and effectively—well capable of defending herself."

"What's the connection—" Realization dawned and Polly stopped herself,

"Guess what?"—Forefinger raised to halt their answers.— "Old fart sported a ponytail. The police questioned my staff and showed them photos. Totally shocked, Erika recognized the dead man and denied ever coming across him. Mere instinct with her. Later, she freaked—what if the fuzz finds out and think she followed and topped him?"

"Well, are you certain she didn't?"

Karl sat back—stunned.

"I'm afraid you're right there, Polly. Said she rushed straight inside. Didn't go out to fasten the umbrellas until an hour later." Another pause before he resumed, "Came back out just when someone skulked to the dune path."

"Oh, how convenient!" The outburst might be unfair, Polly admitted to herself. Maybe Erika was an honest person.

"You gotta know Erika." All patient but partisan, Karl said, "I tend to take her word at face value. Lacks imagination."

"Did she tell you more?" Leave it to Agnes to be reasonable. As long as it did not involve her mom, of course.

"Yeah. Unsure if man or woman—shortish hair, she thought. A mere glimpse she caught. Slim figure in dark pants and loose hoodie or anorak. Pulled up the hood right that moment. Average height, meaning anywhere between 160 or 175. She's around 180 herself. That's what—six feet? The person was somewhat shorter, she says. Could mean a few inches."

"So, how did you react?" asked Polly.

"Said, she must tell the fuzz. Could help to track down crucial evidence."

"Is she going to?"

A shrug. "No idea, Agnes. Can't force her and won't rat on her either."

"Hey!" Indignant, Polly spoke for both, "We won't snitch."

Despite her nod, Agnes radiated anxiety. Her right hand twirled a strand of dark hair around and around while her eyes sought consolation up in the willow tree.

Thinks it sounds like her mom—the sudden insight flashed in Polly's mind. Oh no. Ridiculous. How to clear Sera of any suspicion? Aloud, she said, "We'll have to check this out. Did other people mention anything? Your staff? Any point quizzing Erika again?"

"Yeah, got a feeling she's holding back.—Must tread lightly, or she'll retreat into her shell and won't speak at all." He eyed Polly. "Haven't heard from anyone. Patrons were long gone, anyhow."

"Do try to find out," begged Polly, now anxious about her friend. "Please, Karl?"

"Sure. Won't hurt to give it a shot."

To divert Agnes from Sera, Polly took charge. "Let's change tack. Why would someone want to off Ronny Rosso?"

Both Karl and Agnes considered her skeptically. So, she raised a finger to count off the first item. "He certainly had loose paws. Helps to list possible motives."

"Ah. Sherlock strikes again." He elicited an involuntary smile from Agnes.

"Yup. Have me Watson already." Polly leaned in to nudge Agnes.

"At least, I'm as befuddled as Holmes' sidekick. Or I could play Hastings to your Poirot, Polly."

"Haha, my size is about right for that role. But let's get cracking. Who starts? Your favorite reason for killing somebody."

"Me first!" Karl's hand shot up. "Sex, love, and drugs."

"Money," said Agnes.

"Add, gain of any kind," offered Polly.

Warmed up now, Agnes rattled off, "Revenge, fear, jealousy, hate—" Only to be trumped by Karl's, "Power, reputation—"

"Competition, diffidence, and glory—or reputation. Says Hobbes."

"Come again, Agnes? You mean, Calvin and—"

"Sorry—no. Thomas Hobbes' state of nature theory. Ruled by fear, every man is at war with every other, he claims. Self-preservation—as a pre-emptive strike—is a natural right. Humans compete for the same things. Scarcity and envy make them covet what others have. So, diffidence makes us enemies. Diffidence means distrust. Old English... Sorry, to ramble..."

Flushed crimson, Agnes' speech flow trickled out.

"Quite smart for an old fart, Hobbes was."

"He's got a point—Hobbes, I mean, not you, Karl. Well, you're right too," laughed Polly. "More philosophical insights, Agnes?"

"Well, John Locke says people might kill in defense of their inalienable right to life, liberty, and possession, or to defend someone else's rights."

"Wow, Agnes, impressive!"

"Basic stuff I teach. Enough of me," yet, clearly pleased at Karl's praise, no matter how off-hand Agnes spoke.

"For starters, we did brilliantly!" Briskly Polly clapped her hands. "Question is, which motive fits Ronny's killing? We can prove he was a lewd old geezer. Sex angle?"

"Secondly, he was involved with the *WKA* company, which leads to gain for some, and loss for others," said Agnes.

"Who stood to gain?"

"Dieken," Karl answered Polly without hesitation. "Owns a lot of land with the right type of zoning. You can't touch the restricted zone—*Naturschutz*—nature protection—off-limits."

"Righto. Who else?"

"Maybe the town," suggested Karl, only to throw doubt on his words, "Aren't we looking at this topsy-turvy, Polly? Hinrich and others who gain from the *WKA* need Ronny alive, not dead."

"Yeah sure—unless Ronny interfered with the deal *they* hoped to make with Niederwinder."

"Whoa, too complex for me." Perplexed, Karl threw up his hands. "Can't we keep it simple, Polly? Who profits directly from the man's demise?"

"Sure, whatever."

"The environmentalists out to stop the *WKA* do," remarked Agnes.

"Plus, locals who don't like the wind-dings," added Polly.

"What about those guys you hired for your solar panels? They'll lose if the island is serviced by wind power."

"You're assuming wind energy is going to be dirt cheap, Agnes. I'd be doubting that."

"I think you're right, Karl. Residential solar installation might still be attractive. Not sure, though," said Polly. "Would activists gain all that much? The death of a rep won't stop Niederwinder."

"The enviros scored time to sway public opinion." Not convinced by his own point, Karl continued, "You've gotta be one hell of an extremist to kill for a breather."

"Don't some eco-terrorists use arson, or set free caged

animals in labs, and so on. Like the Animal Liberty League. Or do dangerous stunts?" pointed out Agnes.

"A crackpot infiltrating them might from sheer hate," he admitted.

"Exactly. Also, what about the locals? Would tempers run high enough to murder over a disagreement about a wind farm?"

"Well, I've only been here for three years, Agnes. Yeah, there are some bullheaded people—here like anywhere. People do have long memories. Especially islanders."

"Got to include the incomers too," said Polly. "People like your Mathilda and her Hermann, Agnes. They're passionately against the *WKA*."

"Interesting point," agreed Agnes. "Their real estate investments might be affected."

"Paradise lost, and all that, as the man said."

"Gals, this is great fun and I'd love to stay and chat, but a man gotta do what a man gotta do." Karl double-tapped the table with his palms.

"Can we quickly divvy up tasks?" As Karl and Agnes waited expectantly, Polly proceeded, "Do tackle your regulars and staff to find out more, Karl. Chat up Dieken. Such a local bigshot must be heavily involved and bound to hoard insider info. At your barbeque, Agnes, attend to Mathilda and Hermann tonight, okay?"

"Shouldn't Karl also check out those solar suppliers? They did feel their business threatened and blamed Ronny; you said so on Saturday, Polly."

Glad Agnes's on the ball now, Polly thought. Would prefer to talk to Kai and Udo myself, though. "Yes, definitely, on your list they go, Karl."

"What about you, Sherlock? You gonna sit back, stoke your pipe and take a pinch of morph again?" A broad grin split his face as he got up.

"Gotta suss out them enviros, bud. No rest for the wicked."

Chapter 19

AGNES

"And this is the terrace," Mathilda flung out her right arm with a flourish, hand spread open.

The evening proved windy and cool. Obediently, Sera and Agnes stepped through the glass double doors out to the flagstone patio overlooking a rock garden ravine. Eager to show off his barbecue, Hermann hurried after them as his spouse advertised the stunning vista. Their house faced southwest and rested on an elevation high enough to afford a view over the dike onto the *Wattenmeer*. The water lapped close to the embankment—leaden and churned up, mirroring the leaden shades of the racing clouds. A ferry just departed along the fairway a little east of them.

"I do hope you like fish," called out Hermann, busy putting packages wrapped in foil on the charcoal burner. No gas barbecue here. As though to prove its authenticity, it issued tiny puffs of smoke.

"Of course, the weather does not put the view into the best light." Their hostess ignored the interruption. "You must come again on a sunny day." She turned to hubby, "We now go inside, *Schatz*. Come in for an aperitif with us when you are finished." Not waiting for her 'darling's' response, she led the way back into the living room. "Make yourself comfortable," a hand sweep indicating a dark brown leather couch and steel and leather-sling armchairs on one side of the room, opposite to a huge panorama window spanning floor to ceiling.

Glad to rest, Agnes took an armchair, while her mom aimed for the sofa. The chair was surprisingly comfy despite its minimalist appearance. Espresso laminate flooring and abstract art prints in deep colors lent the room warmth. The dining table on the other side gleamed—tastefully set with contemporary white porcelain on lime green placemats.

"What can I offer you?" asked Mathilda. "Martini? Sherry? Cointreau? Or do you like something else?"

"A small dry sherry would be delightful," nodded Sera with a smile. "Thank you."

Never fond of aperitifs to begin with, yet not inclined to more mineral water, Agnes hesitated. Their host's return—hand rubbing, beaming jocularly—saved her.

"Nothing like a hot tea with a dash of rum in this weather. Anyone join me?" His encouraging glance rested on Agnes.

Her, "Yes, please," met Mathilda's hissed, "*Aber Männi, doch nicht vor dem Essen.*"

"Before dinner, after dinner; what's the difference, Mattie? We are on holidays. Grog's coming up for the young lady." With a wink at Agnes, he headed for the kitchen.

Spectacular, high-tech, sleek and pricey, the culinary center comprised part of the guided house tour earlier. If this is their vacation domicile, Agnes had wondered, what might their main residence be like? Where do people find this kind of money? Sure, if he's a physician, he might make a bundle. Most likely old money, she mused. In his tailored white linen pants, dark blue silk shirt, and Italian loafers, he appeared accustomed to riches.

By contrast, Mathilda was down-to-earth and prosaic. Dressed similarly, she didn't possess the knack of wearing it with ease. Her skin lacked the well-cared-for gloss that her husband's face exuded, Agnes noticed, as his Mattie leaned over the sofa table to arrange some bowls of chips and nuts ready to hand.

"*Ahh*," a satisfied sigh from their hostess. "Now we can munch and have a cozy chat."

What the heck were they to talk about all evening? Anxiety mounted as Agnes sought for common topics to air. Besides, I'm socially challenged at the best of times, she fretted.

Two steaming glass mugs in hand, Hermann came back, whistling a tune. The amber liquid sloshed when he placed one mug in front of her.

"*Männi, der gute Tisch!*" With a paper napkin, Mathilda hastened to wipe up the small spill marring the 'good table' and dried the bottom of Agnes's mug. "Rings on the wood it leaves." Exasperated, she shook her head and grabbed coasters to prevent further disaster. Hubby, who had ignored her, returned with a glass teapot and stainless steel warmer, tea light lit.

Muster your best behavior, Agnes told herself. No dripping of sauce, or something, on the shiny dining table later.

"How are you enjoying our little cottage." A benign smile, favoring each of them, their host joined the circle.

Well, other than the beach being littered with dead bodies, quite paradisiacal, Agnes inanely smirked at her own wit. An irritated frown from her mother, who responded politely, "Just adorable. Needless to say, we wish the circumstances were not so dire."

"Yes, yes." Vigorous nodding from Mathilda. "Such a shame to spoil your nice vacation."

Most inconsiderate of people to get themselves bumped off and lie around for innocent tourists to stumble over. Puts a damper on the old holiday spirit, doesn't it? Haha. Blame the rum for this audible snicker. Agnes! What's wrong with you? Her super-ego lashed out. Lay off the booze! Catching a censorious glance from Sera, Agnes bent forward—ostensibly to grab a handful of nuts from the bowl—and let her hair curtain her wayward face. Straightening up, she met Hermann's gaze, saturated with geniality.

"Awesome grog, this." Glass raised in grinning salute to him.

"Warms the old bones," he agreed. "Not that yours are old," he hastened to add. The man's no more than ten or fifteen years older than me, Agnes figured.

"So, you are a fellow academic," was his next gambit. "Always a pleasure to meet an intelligent woman." An involuntary glance strayed to his wife.

Wow, if ever there was an ambiguous remark, Agnes commented silently. Aloud she replied, "I work as a sessional instructor at some universities and colleges around Toronto. As a physician, do you teach as well?"

"A physician?" he laughed. "What gave you that idea? I'm a nuclear physicist, attached to a research institute. Am also a corporate consultant. Yes, it does involve some teaching."

"Oh, I'm sorry, I thought Mathilda said physician."

"Most likely she did." Still chuckling, he leaned towards his spouse, interrupting her description of an island attraction. "Mattie, you've changed my profession and made me a doctor?" The voice rippled with suppressed amusement.

"A doctor, Männi? Why would I say that?"

"I'm not a physician, my silly girl, but a *physicist*." The last word emphasized with heavy irony at which Mathilda blushed purple. Instead of a reply, she waved her hand in impatience. With a shake of her head, she mouthed to Sera a silent, *Men!* Poor Mattie; Agnes felt a stab of feminist empathy for the woman.

Taking her cue, however, Agnes embarked on the task Polly had assigned for the evening. "As a nuclear physicist, you can't be too fond of the planned wind park project; I take it?"

"Hah! There you're hitting a raw nerve." Took the bait and evaded the hook. "Excuse me for a moment. Our fish needs me before it gets scorched." Off he went.

H'm, interesting—a contemplative sip from her grog. To

reduce its potency, she added plain black tea from the glass pot —careful to avoid any drips.

A few minutes later, the cook sank back into his chair— crossed elegant legs and, swinging one loafer playfully from the toes of a slender, tanned foot, he addressed her.

"Apologies for the interruption. As I was saying, you quite touched a nerve there. To put it bluntly, I'm firmly set against this wind farm. So are numerous other property owners and naturalists. A crying shame how these unscrupulous, mercenary opportunists intend to destroy this island! Let's face it; this is one of the last bits of natural paradise. As a scientist, I have no objection to diversifying our energy sources. By all means. Not here, though."

While he paused to replenish his drink, Agnes ventured, "Not in your backyard; anywhere else is okay?"

"Ah, young woman, I see what you're driving at. Said I like an intelligent woman and I do. You call it Nimbyism, pure and simple. Yet NIMBYs, as is often forgotten, are also rightful stakeholders. In this case, it is the voice of reason based on scientific facts."

Bent forward to rest his mug, he regarded her speculatively before inquiring, "How much of Bosum did you explore thus far? Despite this deplorable incident."

"We hiked to the north end and through the nature reserve, and we've cycled into town."

"Then you'll understand what I'm talking about." An approving nod. "This isle is a crucial part of the world's natural heritage. Unique as nesting ground and resting place for a myriad of avian species. The mudflats provide habitats for countless aquatic species. The Frisian island chain is precious, not only for Germany but the living planet. Do you realize, my young friend, that the *Wattenmeer* is one of the last *natural* biospheres worldwide?"

Downright condescending. Time to assert my academic credentials, Agnes decided.

The man regarded her expectantly.

"Yes, so I've been told. Such view is quite in line with deep ecology. Doesn't the nuclear lobby favor a quest for human supremacy?"

"Ha! I so love a woman with brains!" A delighted chuckle. "Nonetheless, you are mistaken." An admonishing forefinger raised high. "Did you read your Lovelock?" Any attempt to answer ignored, he lectured, "His Gaia theory gives the impression of ecocentrism, yet James Lovelock advocates nuclear and condemns wind power as a waste of energy." A sputtered hahaha at his pun. "A waste of time and money. He's one of the few environmental spokesmen for our belea-guered guild. Of course, he's a fellow scientist and not a tree-hugger."

"His theory of Earth and its atmosphere as a self-regulating system is fascinating and persuasive, I grant you. His laudation of nuclear reactors, however, is irresponsible. Saying, radiation from accidents benefits the environment as it keeps people away for decades, I consider utterly offensive. Sorry, I know you must think me rude."

"No reason to apologize. What would we do without acad-emic freedom to argue?" Rhetorical eyebrow arched. "We scien-tists are used to this unfortunate attitude that you share. It results from a deep-seated fear of the invisible. Lovelock recognizes this too. Fewer people die in nuclear incidents than from mishaps related to other energy sources. Consider coal mining or oil rigs at high sea. Not to mention the environmental impact of major spills."

"There might be less accidents. Yet Fukushima proved again how horrendously terrifying they are," countered Agnes, her hackles rising. "Countless reactors are built globally without anyone in the world having a clue how to deal effectively with such disasters. With climate change phenomena like earth-quakes, tsunamis, hurricanes, and floods on the increase, the likelihood of nuclear catastrophe rises. For Christ's sake, no solution for basic nuclear waste disposal is on the horizon either!"

Exhausted, she stopped, aware of Hermann watching her encouragingly as though she were a promising but retiring student who, after much coaxing, finally erupted into a discussion to defend her stance. Across from her, her mom regarded her with a frown. Better not rock the hospitable boat.

After a deep breath, Agnes toned down a notch. "Shouldn't permanent disposal have been the top priority before building the first plant?"

"A valid point. Yes! Germany is actively trying to solve the long-term storage problem, as we speak." A slap punished his right knee in emphasis.

The sound inadvertently alerted his wife. "Männi, is the fish not ready?" She waggled a finger at Agnes and said indulgently, "You academics. Always arguing." Heaving herself up, she pointed to the table. "You make yourself comfortable. I fetch the food."

"Can I help with anything?" offered Agnes.

"Nö, nö," the hostess declined. "I have a server wagon."

Moments later, she wheeled in a two-tiered trolley laden with bowls that filled the air with their delicious aromas. The outdoor chef brought in steaming fish on a platter, foil already removed. When he deposited it in the middle of the dining table, Agnes's eyes bulged. The fishes were looking back openmouthed. Her stomach heaved. Sprigs of parsley dangled dashingly from fishy lips like fags of diehard smokers. Lemon slices added their mock grin.

Her face evidently betrayed her, for Hermann whipped up the platter and placed it at the far end of the table.

"Agnes," he asked quietly, "would you like me to prepare a fillet for you?"

"Oh, yes, please." Grateful, she passed her plate.

"Not everyone's cup of tea, to come eye to eye with their dinner, if I may mix my metaphors here." Although Hermann might lack sensitivity where his spouse is concerned, he's quite easy to take socially, Agnes conceded.

For the next ten minutes, their remarks circled around polite table talk. The fare was indeed praiseworthy. Apparently, their hosts were passionate cooks. They expanded on the advantages of organic produce, although neither Agnes nor her mother needed to be persuaded. Some ingredients were fresh from their container garden, they stressed. Both professed to be ardent gardeners as well as culinary enthusiasts. Quite an accomplished couple.

Curious about Mathilda, Sera asked whether she worked full-time. To Agnes's amazement, their landlady ran a property management and consulting firm. Apart from owning several rental properties, she scouted for wealthy clients to match them with the properties of their dreams. For some clients, she found lucrative investments, and advised on, or organized, the management. As she put it, her time was her own and enabled her to seize opportunities.

An accomplished businesswoman with a nice portfolio of income properties. So, the money was not a one-sided affair at all. Was rather sexist of you to assume so in the first place, Agnes chided herself.

Her mom's voice recalled her to the now.

"Hermann, you mentioned to my daughter earlier that you favor diversification of energy. What puzzles me, why not utilize wind power where wind is plentiful?"

"Let me ask you: Can we, at present, determine the effects of widespread massive wind parks? No data is available. Don't misunderstand me; I'm not saying, 'don't use wind energy.' It would be irresponsible, indeed, to put all our energy eggs into the nuclear basket." He chuckled fondly at his metaphor.

"Why not, then, a moderate number of turbines on Bosum?" asked her mother to Agnes's astonishment.

"Do you know how high these windmills are?" broke in their hostess, cheeks aflame with hectic dark red blotches. "These monsters are dangerous! Did you not hear of this terrible thing on Norderney?" Her eyes darted from Sera to Agnes and back, expecting them to ask the inevitable. When neither of them spoke, she continued, "Down they came. Crashed into the living room. *Kaput!*"

"Now, now, then, Mattie," cautioned her spouse. "Calm down. Remember your blood pressure."

"*Is' doch wahr*," grumbled she—more blood rising.

"Yes, of course, it is true. Our friends, I fear, might not quite follow."

An understatement, thought Agnes, though she could guess what happened on one of the neighboring islands. The explanation confirmed this.

"What my wife is referring to occurred way back in May 2000. On the islands we have long memories," he added, as though he and his wife were insiders. "The rotor head and blade of a turbine disengaged and penetrated the wall of a house over a hundred meters away. Many of the locals over here, and we have to count Mattie among them, perceive this as a clear indication that wind power is hazardous to humans."

Ah, she's a Bosum native. Pleased at the discovery, Agnes filed the info for future reference.

An indulgent glance at his spouse, he pushed his chair away from the table and crossed his elegant legs again, one arm resting expansively along the top of its back.

Everyone else seemed to feel quite knackered by the topic. The expert soldiered on, determined to cover the full terrain and leave no aspect bunkered.

"Mind you, I strongly object to the pressure the wind lobby exerts on the residents of any northern German community. A common phenomenon everywhere, I suspect. We see it even down south in Bavaria."

Before he could elaborate, a resolute spouse took the reins. "*Männi, lass gut sein*," she told him to give it a rest. "Let us have coffee and dessert." Without further ado, she got up and Sera helped to stack the plates.

Bushed and in need for a quiet moment, Agnes asked to use the powder room next to the front entrance. The mirror, framed in walnut, matched the wooden washstand with its beautifully shaped elevated basin. A tired face frowned back as she stared. Time to tuck you in. All this vacationing turns out to be quite draining.

Chapter 20

POLLY

"A fugitive couldn't be more of a pain to hunt down!"

Polly had the devious satisfaction of seeing her quarry literally jump out of his boot. She dropped down heavily—as far as a lightweight like her could manage that—onto the wooden step next to Mark.

"What the hell are you scaring me like that for!" With one hand Mark tried unsuccessfully to retrieve the heavy hiking boot he'd been trying to put on when she'd pounced on him. Jumping up had propelled it out of reach—now he fished for it with his foot stretched out to the limit of his lanky leg.

"Guilty conscience, Mark?" inquired Polly with exquisite guilelessness.

For a moment he resembled a cornered weasel; his eyes darted in all directions, sending sidelong glances up the staircase they were sitting on, and along the long triste corridors branching off its base. The boot straightened; he devoted his full attention to getting his foot in.

Addressing himself to the floor, or maybe the recalcitrant boot, he managed to respond in a gruff growl, "What're you talking about?"

Enough, Polly. Or he'll never talk to you... She touched his arm with two fingers. "Sorry, Mark. Bad joke." When he swiveled to regard her, still suspicious, she mustered her most innocent smile. After all, she didn't hang around the youth hostel for an hour, searching high and low, to antagonize him now. No matter how much fun he was to tease.

"Been looking for you all over the place. Come, let's grab a bite to eat. On me." To break his silence, she nudged him gently. "Or did you eat already?"

Finally, he pulled himself up and glared down at her still sitting on the second step.

"Nah, thought I open a can of tuna. Yeah, if you pay, I do dinner with you."

"Dinner? Who says dinner, man? Was going to buy you fries and a bratwurst," she teased. The deeply disappointed face made her relent. "Oh, alright. Your pick. What would you like?"

"Pizza." Mark licked his lips. "Caesar salad and German beer," he grinned. "Little Italian place down the road."

Perked up now, he was all eager. So, she extended a hand for him to pull her up.

"Do they serve Caesar salad over here? Never mind, we'll find out."

They left the youth hostel with its smell of steamed cabbage, damp sand, and ill-washed humanity and made their way towards the town center. Didn't have far to go—Polly had noticed the place in passing. The outside was painted in green, red, and white. An awning above the storefront read *Pizzeria Mio Piccolo*. Its wide window was curtained halfway up with white net curtains clipped to a brass rod.

Upon entry, a powerful blast of food odor hit them. Wooden tables flanked both sides of the center aisle dividing the narrow and long dining room. Checkered red-white tablecloths and Chianti bottles with runny candles provided a tacky Mediter-ranean flair.

So be it, Polly thought. The joint proved noisy, hot, and busy, as they squeezed through to a table for two, way in the back. A harassed-looking waiter in his late twenties, sporting a black shirt and a long white apron held together by a money belt, banged a menu on the table without stopping to greet them.

Caesar salad was indeed on offer, and they decided to split a large Pizza Margherita. To appease her culinary conscience, Polly opted for a side salad. She flagged down another waiter who rushed by. Reluctantly, he took their order. Instead of beer, Polly took a spritzer.

While they waited for their drinks, she entertained her companion with witty comments about the décor. Set his mind at ease. The beer will do the rest, she figured.

"*Jeez*," muttered Mark as beer foam sloshed over the table-cloth, spilled by the waiter unloading their glasses from a precariously balanced tray. No tip here. The extra-large tankard would put Mark into a talkative mood in no time.

Her glance still wandering over the kitschy wall decorations, Polly asked indifferently whether Mark caught up with Nancy the other night. No response forthcoming, her eyes slowly returned to sweep over the boyish figure huddled forward, dreadlocks shadowing eyes engrossed in the half-empty beer mug. Hard to tell what color his hair might actually be, maybe ash blond, Polly speculated irrelevantly. With a jerk his head came up—tresses flung back violently, the flickering candlelight burnishing the gray of his eyes, making them almost fierce.

"Gives me the slip! Man, I've so tried. Shady's doing a watchdog. Bloody nerd."

Sapped of his strength by the outburst, Mark's eyes latched on her face as if sucking ersatz energy from it.

"What do you want with her anyhow?" No way she'd rat on Nancy in the *Döner* with Rosso late on Sunday.

"My mom and dad were besties with Nancy, like back in the day, you know. Early '90s, Clayoquot Sound. Vancouver Island, eh?" His glance roamed dreamily.

Sounds like a kid bragging about his new tablet.

"Ah, that's how you got involved with the activists. Your parents are part of the scene."

"No, totally not! Don't even talk to them. Traitors!" fumed Mark. "Guess what they do now?" Without waiting for her prompt, he blurted out, "Dad's a CEO of a lumber outfit! Can you believe it? Reforming the industry inside out, he calls it." The voice mimicked a sonorous pompous ass. A deep gulp from the dripping mug to wash away the memory.

"Mom teaches high school. Tries to do her bit," he conceded grudgingly. "You can't fathom their place. Ever heard of McNeill Bay? Coast off Victoria?" As Polly shook her head, he continued, "Filthy rich. Not one of the smallest mansions they built, I tell you. Friggin' waste. Of course, drive SUVs." In disgust, he brandished his locks like arrows. Then he leaned closer across the little table. With covert glances left and right as if expecting wiretappers, he confided, "Nancy used to spike trees."

Energy expended, he leaned back. And not a moment too soon, for the waiter unceremoniously slapped pizza and salads onto the table. Hot sauce spattered. In reflex, Polly jumped up only to find herself eye-level with a bronzed, hairless chest framed by a black shirt. A heavy gold chain hung loosely. Must get it waxed, *ouch!* Hypnotized, she stared.

Without an apology, the server turned and instead offered a view of a firm butt in skin-tight black jeans. Ignoring the quality of service, Mark slashed away at the pizza to tear off a huge slice, his lips coated with Caesar dressing. Man, when did they last feed the dude? No use trying to chat him up until he's filled his face, she guessed.

"Hey—uberdelish!" Her exuberant praise after her first mouthful wrung a grin and a nodded 'told you so' from Mark. A thin red rivulet forked in the soft crevice of his chin. Mesmerized Polly watched, waiting for the drops to dislodge. Alerted by her gaze, he swiped at his mouth with a paper napkin just missing the end of the trail. Instinctively her fingers swiped at her own chin, a move mirrored by him. The realization irritated him and brought on a glare.

Afraid to be paying for his grub to no purpose, Polly resuscitated the Nancy motif apropos of nothing.

"Nancy's not into heavy action, is she? Split from the ELFs, didn't she?"

"Nah, doesn't do aggro. PPS is pacifist not only by name."

"Yeah, I know. Stick with them. More up your alley to save the planet peacefully." An offended stare was all she earned. "Most of the guys decamped by now, I assume? After what happened to Ronny Rosso, I mean."

"Freaking piece of s—"

So much for speaking ill or not...a chance too opportune to be missed. No exertion required—Mark beat her to it.

"Did you get anything from him on Saturday? Thought I don't believe my eyes when you two were all cozied up there."

"Me? How? Blew my cover." Mimed indignation. "Barely got to work when your untimely entry spooked him." A speculative glance at him before she pounced. "You went after him, didn't you?"

"Told you; I was looking for Nancy." Gruffly he fenced her accusation. "Besides...he was gone. Puff," he blew out his cheeks, lips bulging, "into thin air."

"So did you find her, or what happened?" Clear he couldn't have, she figured, but never hurts to check for an alibi.

"Nah, had to give up. Mom's friends expected me to spend the night. Got a fancy place here," he sneered. "Suited me fine for one night. Hostel shower sucks."

Satisfied, Polly harked back. "Must be so convenient someone offed Rosso."

"Yah, kinda. Buys us a bit of time," agreed Mark complacently.

"You figure the guys did for him?"

"Are you nuts!" Alarmed, he blustered, "We don't do offing dudes."

No, only torching stuff. Kind of ironic… Aloud she said, "Yeah, I figured it kinda didn't make sense. Wasn't part of some direct action. Not with him lying on that beach out there in nowhere land."

"I don't friggin' care, who's done for him. Deserves a medal for ridding the planet of another cancer cell. The less the merrier, I'd say."

"Oh, c'mon, man. Don't get on to your pet peeve again. Overpopulation is hardly the cause of all ills, environmental and otherwise." Ridiculous sentiment in someone who's such a softy at heart as he is.

"It is so," came the petulant reply. "If two-thirds of us were gone, the earth would be far better off. A malignant cancer, us humans."

Deep ecologists, Polly sighed inwardly, got a lot to answer for to have spawned this attitude. In all fairness, they were innocent. None of the truly deep thinkers suggested genocide or the extermination of humanity. The cavalier misanthropes were opportunists.

At the risk of shutting him up, she set the record straight. "Us in the West use up most resources. Could keep thirty people in less affluent countries for each one of us. So, it's not about numbers but rate of consumption and the sort of stuff we consume. We could easily develop benign consumptive habits and cut out much of the crap killing the environment."

"Yeah, read your articles." He scowled at her. "Don't lecture me."

"Sorry—got carried away." To make amends, she asked, "Wanna coffee? Dessert? Another beer?"

She leaned sideways to stop the waiter who came into her field of vision. Not shy in exploiting the freebee occasion, Mark ordered tiramisu and cappuccino. In hope of drawing things out at will, Polly ordered a latte and spumoni ice cream.

Yet when their order arrived, he devoted his full attention to his dessert, completely ignoring her. Only after he'd downed his coffee was she able to steer him back on track.

"What's next on the agenda, you reckon? Can't see Nieder-winder withdrawing their plans for the wind farm only because Rosso is no longer in the picture. You said yourself, it's only going to buy time."

"Don't you know?" His eyes raised from his empty plate, he regarded her oddly.

"Nah, haven't seen anyone since Sunday," explained Polly. "Stayed with friends and kept busy."

"Something's up Thursday." At his most cryptic again.

"Well, are you going to spill?"

"Go see for yourself. Town Hall at three." With that, he got up. "Thanks for dinner." He signaled a high five. "See ya. Peace."

Puzzled, she watched him go. He flapped the hood of his army-green cotton jacket over his head before he reached the door. Jeans sagged baggily, his awkward gait made him look far older. If he'd been around at all yet, must have been an infant in arms when his parents joined the war of the woods at Clay-oquot. Would anyone take a babe along to such protest action?

It cost her another ten minutes to draw the waiter's attention once more to pay. His disdain for customers struck her as suffi-ciently entertaining to warrant a large tip after all. Far larger than customary in Germany, but well worth seeing his face. Didn't move a muscle. Nor did he thank her. Real class, Polly grinned to herself.

Chapter 21

AGNES

"Sehr zu empfehlen. Ein exzellentes Buch."

Book in hand, Agnes swung around expecting to see a salesperson. To her surprise, it was DD of all people who beamed his recommendation of the book as excellent. The sudden encounter made her completely tongue-tied. Painfully aware of cheeks afire, a stammered "thanks," quickly amended to *"danke,"* escaped. Don't be an idiot and blush like a friggin' teenager—she chastised herself. And Daniel Dregger is amused. Smirks, the jerk!

"Do you speak English," he asked and picked up a copy of the book she clutched to her chest now.

She managed a nod. Perhaps to give her time to regroup, he flipped through. Absorbed in its pages, he commented, "Lovelock got it quite right."

After a minute, while she studied intensely the back cover of *Gaias Rache,* he went on, *"The Revenge of Gaia* led to his 'final warning'—*The Vanishing Face of Gaia.* Not his last word either; he'll still be publishing as a centenarian." An amazed chuckle underlined his point.

Calmed by his chatter, she replied, "I've read a few of his scholarly articles. The popularized account held little interest for me." A raised eyebrow prompted her to explain, "The title caught my eye because his name came up in conversation last night."

"Oh, I don't know. Pop versions tend to be far more influential than scientific writings. Most people are incapable of understanding an academic text."

"I guess you're right. Scholarly publications rarely reach a general audience."

"Speaking from experience?"

"Haven't published enough to lay claim to much experience, one way or another."

With unwarranted care, Daniel restored Lovelock's book to the pile. "If you're not in a rush, we could go for a coffee." Perhaps afraid this sounded too much like a come-on, he stumbled on, "The espresso bar upstairs... I was on my way up there. Just thought..."

Nice that he's gauche now. Reassured, Agnes put down her copy firmly. "I'd love to."

"You aren't buying it?—Silly of me. Of course, you'd prefer the English original."

"Oh, I do read German." Eager as ever to underline any petty accomplishments—she scolded herself.

"You do? Impressive! Let's go up here," pointing to the wide staircase, "and you tell me what you do professionally. I'm honestly curious." A warm smile engulfed her.

Wait until I tell Polly about this marvelous opportunity to quiz DD, she reveled in her luck. Should she pretend not to know anything about him? Or flatter his oratorical ego by praising his speech on Friday. Could involve disclosures. Like finding Ronny. Or more precisely, finding a mother who stumbles over dead bodies. Quite awkward.

"What will you have?"

No idea how long Daniel had been watching; Agnes resurfaced to find herself in front of the glass display of a coffee bar. The pastries looked delicious. She tore her eyes from the seductive goodies to study the chalkboard list of beverages.

To the young woman behind the counter, she said, "*Eine Latte bitte.*" On second thought, better no jitters inducing caffeine. "*Coffeinfrei,*" she amended.

"No sweets?"

"Oh well, before you twist my arm… I'll take one of those." In absence of a label to name it by, she pointed to a fancy flaked pastry with sumptuous fruit on some sort of pudding cream.

By the time she'd dug out her wallet from her backpack, the barista assured her all was paid for. "My pleasure," her companion waved off any thanks and suggested a table at a window facing the street. Latte glass and plate safely on the table, Agnes took in the vista. "Wow. Amazing view. You can actually see the sea in the distance."

"Isn't it?" agreed Daniel complacently as though he'd personally been responsible.

Large frame balanced precariously on the dainty chair, he bit into his sensible smoked salmon wholegrain bun. Not until he had swallowed and sipped some black coffee did he speak. All the while, Agnes wrestled with her pastry.

"I'd better introduce myself. Don't want you to think that I'm going around town of a morning picking up women… No matter how attractive." A rueful grin and then, "As it happens, I'm the local representative of the Environment Party. Daniel Dregger—or DD for short, if you wish."

Since Agnes was struggling with a particularly big mouthful of viscous fruity cream, she was spared the need for a response. Undeterred, he carried on the monologue.

"Hence my interest in Lovelock and things environmental. Are you aware of our current local controversy? Opinions clash over a proposed wind turbine project on this island. My party, needless to say, is all in favor of expanding alternative energies in general, and wind power in particular."

An encouraging nod sufficed—DD, the natural orator, didn't

need any prompting. His voice, seductively caressing and attractive, was a treat to listen to.

"The company filing the application is aiming too high. In my opinion, there is no need to go beyond the required capacity for local independence. My public stance, by the way. Between you and me," conspiratorially he lowered his volume, "some people are in it purely for the money. Never mind the environment."

Wow, how perceptive of you—Agnes camouflaged her uncharitable thought through enthusiastic nods.

"Things should by rights be long decided. Council met on Monday afternoon. However, no motion was ever put forward." Skillful pause; eyeing her intently. "Their man was killed Sunday night." He lifted his cup, regarded her over the rim, and waited for a reaction.

This is getting seriously awkward, Agnes fretted. Better do something. Like drop your latte glass? Too messy. She burrowed in her backpack for a swathe of tissues and deliberately wiped her mouth.

"Ehem…I…," wide-eyed. Means anything from incredulity to speechlessness and communicative labor pangs. Did the trick for now.

"Yes, hard to credit, isn't it?"—Nod, nod—"It's made the national papers by now. I'm afraid the island will soon be swarming with reporters."

Oh, no—appalled Agnes's mind went into overdrive—the local rag rooters left us fairly in peace so far. Except for the car sitting out front this morning. She suppressed a grin, remembering how she and Sera had evaded attention by cutting through the dunes to the bus stop at the end of the road. … Better check out the newsstand on the way out—

"Not sure what impact it will have," combing his fingers through his long hair, Daniel spun out his lonely musings. Trust a politician to hold up a conversation single-handedly and then some.

"All depends on who is going to replace Rosso," he muttered to himself. "*Ach*—I'm sorry, this is of little interest to you. Tell me about yourself—"

"No, no. Absolutely fascinating," Agnes hastened to assure him. "Did you take a degree in environmental studies to qualify as candidate for your party? I've always wondered what it takes over here to make it in politics. Dr. Merkel, whom I greatly admire, certainly is far better educated than your average politician anywhere."

"Nice of you to put me into the same class with Frau Merkel. No, I'm afraid, I can't compete educationally with the Merkels of this world."—An unconvincing hahaha.—"Nor with Obama—those were the days…" A sigh and wistful shake of his mane.

"I'm your practical, hands-on kind of guy. Not for me the hallowed halls of academia." He bent close to confide, "Tell you the truth, I dropped out of university as a freshman. Traveled the world and worked in the US and Canada—tree planting."

When Agnes uttered a surprised "oh," he appeared gratified.

"My old man was none too pleased, I can tell you. He's Professor Emeritus now, but a well-known scientist in his day. I was to follow in his illustrious footsteps." The chuckle struck her as malicious. "No way I would spend my life in a biology lab. Give me the real world any time." No love lost between son and father.

"Surely you must do some writing in your line of work," Agnes persisted.

"Not unless you count speech scribbling. Quite frankly, I merely jot down a few notes and speak extemporarily. My old man, to the last, clung to his yellowed batch of ancient scribbles to give his lectures. Must have bored his students to tears."

A deep sympathy for the old man cured Agnes from her initial reaction to DD's charms. Alas, how to extricate herself now? Glancing around for inspiration, she noticed a wall clock.

"Oh, my goodness. Eleven thirty already! Got to dash." She jumped up and slung her backpack over her shoulder. The suddenness left Daniel momentarily speechless.

"Thanks so much for the delightful snack and talk!" Okay to gush now. "A great pleasure to meet a real politician—and from my favorite party. Best of luck with your project."

Before he could unfold himself from the chair, she'd reached the stairs.

"But—I don't even know your name. Can I see—"

"Sorry—must run. Someone's waiting for me."

His expression spoke eloquently of disillusionment. Pleased, she realized that he might believe the 'someone' to be a husband or lover.

Only when she hastened up the street, did she remember the papers. Too late.

Chapter 22
POLLY

"Kannst'e nich' aufpassen!"

Frig— Righto. Better do watch out. Now her feet were soaked and her legs spattered up to her thighs. Good thing the water in the puddle that had accumulated in a pothole was fairly clear. Might dry up without leaving her jeans in too much of a mess.

While rooting for her phone, Polly offered a token apology for her evident inattention. The woman pushing the stroller appeared none too pleased. Understandably, as the toddler now hollered to get out and splash in the puddle. Always setting a perfect example, that's me—Polly grinned encouragement at the infant rebel and hastened on. If she didn't want to miss her chance to catch Sera in the act, she'd need to run a lot faster.

The iPhone displayed 10:10 AM when she checked it on the fly. Just over fifteen minutes since Agnes's call to report their arrival at the bus depot. Sera's insistence on spending the day by herself might mean she intended to visit the seniors' residence. Perhaps a long shot. Worth a try. Once she spotted Sera enter or depart, she could make inquiries. Googled directions to *Lütt Mööv* last night. Also found out it meant "Little Gull."

When she turned the corner, a street sweeper meandered

along picking up errant wrappers that spoiled the high-end ambiance. As she strolled closer to the residence, a young man appeared, pushing a wheelchair through a side gate onto the sidewalk. An elderly person with short frizzy white hair leaned over the armrest in a terribly uncomfortable position, by the looks of it. A plaid blanket of muted colors drawn up to the chin left anyone guessing at the gender of the occupant.

Instinctively, Polly drew back behind a lamppost—insufficient cover even for her skinny little frame. A gap farther down in the old-fashioned cast-iron fence on her side of the road caught her eye. She slipped through and cautiously proceeded through the park-like grounds until level with the walkway to *Lüüt Mööv*.

A huge tree provided shelter, and an ivy-covered fence made her less noticeable to anyone leaving the place. If need be, she might pretend to be examining the impressive chestnut. To disguise her features, she pulled on her black rain jacket, its deep hood hiding the upper part of her face. From afar someone might take her for a child. Hoods keep ticks away—assuming any dared to invade these manicured grounds, she smirked to herself.

Eyes glued to her mobile—its camera trained on the entrance arbor—she hunkered down against the tree. To any passerby, it would be yet another kid busy texting.

Meanwhile, her mind wandered and marveled at digital tech's ability to obscure all kinds of behavior considered whacko back in the day. If you walked around all by your lonesome, whispering softly—never mind talking loudly—people gave you a wide berth. Or worse, you'd end up in a loony bin, as they used to call it. Now sport an earbud or headset and you can yak non-stop, and no one gives a damn.

Incredible—she mused—what you can overhear strolling the aisles of supermarkets. Makes you wonder why phone booths ever needed doors to pull shut tightly. Either humans have drastically changed, or they never did value their privacy. Maybe they always yearned to shout out their quarrels and intimate secrets to all and sundry. In this brave new world, they can and they do. Might be we are hardwired with an incessant need to share our—

A sudden movement across the road shook Polly out of her mental meanderings. Watching attentively over the rim of the iPhone, now held in front of her face, she observed someone coming down the walkway to the gate. Shoot, why hadn't she asked Agnes what Sera was wearing today? Well, impossible without drawing Agnes's attention to what she was up to.

No doubt. She was in luck. Perfect photo op—Sera stood still in the arbor and looked to each side. One hand fumbling in her knapsack, she put on sunshades before moving slowly in direction of the promenade rather than into town. Definitely preoccupied—head bent as if staring at the pavement.

Frozen to the spot, Polly's eyes followed until her quarry disappeared into the drizzle of the miserable day. A no-brainer what she needed to do next. And pronto if she were to get to the wharf on time to meet Agnes and Karl at eleven-thirty. Only question, is it my great-aunt or uncle that Sera's been visiting. Gotta play it by ear, she wagered.

Chapter 23

AGNES

"Hey, Agnes! Over here!"

The motion of a waving arm drew Agnes's attention when she swerved full tilt upon hearing her name. Bum resting on the hood of his van—its tail-end doors wide open—Karl loafed, one hand bracing himself. His hair windblown and tousled, dark shirt hanging haphazardly over faded shorts—boyishness dominated the impression, at least from twenty yards off. The smile enveloped her like a cocoon the closer she got. A dangerous man.

A thud from the rear broke the spell. Their eyes refocused on the man who emerged from the back.

"Hello, Agnes." Guy's face lit up. "An unexpected pleasure. Our Karl had it all worked out, sending me home with this stuff," he pointed vaguely in direction of the van's interior, "so he could keep you all to himself."

"No such luck, man. Got to share with Polly."

"Hi, there. Nice to meet again." With the full force of her smile on Guy, Agnes tried to ignore Karl's comment.

"Better get going, buddy. Or we'll have a soggy mess." He slapped his friend on the back.

A mock salute, Guy banged the rear door shut and swung

himself into the driver's seat. With a wave and a honk, he was off.

In reaction to Agnes's evident surprise at such promptitude, Karl explained. Perishables were packed on ice during transport from the mainland. Any delays might cause havoc. "Can't stay long," he concluded. "Our Polly should be here soon. Said she wanted to do something first before meeting us at the tavern." His outstretched arm indicated a traditional harbor pub across from the wharf.

"How are you going to get back?"

Instead of a response, Karl grabbed an old bike that leaned against the guard rail of the quay wall. Close up, the pub appeared to be the real thing, not a touristy imitation. '*Oold Schipper*' read the faded lettering above its mullioned, narrow front windows.

The interior proved dusky and dank. An odd mixture of odors hit them. Spilled stale beer and more than a hundred years of pungent tobacco smoke mingled with fry-ups and strong bitter coffee. The more recent smoking ban could do little to combat the legacy of ages. A slight whiff of bad drains crept in from the hallway leading to both kitchen and washrooms.

After her eyes adjusted to the gloom, Agnes noticed several tables were occupied; all local males and most of them sexagenarians and beyond.

"Let's sit over here. No one to listen in." With two gentle fingers on her elbow, Karl steered her to a corner table. "Coffee's fine. Kinda strong. Stay away from the grub."

Their order arrived a few minutes later, together with a breathless Polly. Given his earlier remark, Karl greeted the little elf fondly, Agnes thought relieved. Why did she care so much for these two to like each other? Won't meet them again after the holidays. The reflection cramped her stomach to make her wince in pain.

"Something wrong? You are all pale and greenish," exclaimed Polly. "Hell, you didn't eat the food here?"

"Not a chance. Don't look so appalled."

Breathing a noisy sigh of relief, Polly slumped into a chair across from her, next to Karl.

"So, what's up, dude?"

"You tell us," Karl shot back.

"No fighting, kids. I go first." Flattered by her audience's instant attention, Agnes reported on yesterday's barbecue. Riding the rhetorical wave exhilarated and energized—until she realized how mesmerized they were. *What are you getting into? You'll end up in a mess here.* Annoyed, she drowned her inner voice in a gulp of god-awful acidic coffee that made her cough.

"Hey, Agnes, take it easy." Concerned, Polly leaned over to tap her back but barely reached her shoulder. "You do spin a good yarn once you're on a roll, pal. What a pair," she chuckled.

"Sure hate the wind-dings, don't they? Unlikely they'd off Rosso for that," said Karl and refilled Agnes's cup with tar-colored brew from the tiny pot.

"True.—Equally doubtful the activists would. My contacts said," here Polly winked at them with comical emphasis, "extremists torch or sabotage things but avoid killing intentionally."

"Can we assume it to be an intentional killing?"

"You've got a point, Agnes," conceded Polly. "Still— someone followed Ronny. Sudden fights involve intention, I'd say."

"Hey, guys—or ladies, to be more precise. Sorry to butt in. Gotta run soon. Want more on Erika before I split?"

"Let the man talk, Agnes. He's burning with news."

"Quit mocking, Sherlock. Remember I thought she didn't tell all?" He bent forward and lowered his voice. "Well, last night me and Hinrich sat over a beer—I'd invited him over to pump him. Erika, busing tables, stops to gape at us all in a tizzy. Quizzed her after, and finally, she spills the beans—Sunday night's episode with Rosso wasn't—"

"Yah, yah, someone went down the dune path. Old news."

"Wait! Stay tuned for our next installment."

"Get real. Another mysterious stranger pops up later?"

"Jeez—hold your horses." Impatiently, Karl waved both hands. "In fact, this happened earlier. Hinrich's voice last night triggered it. Odd… He's a regular…she's heard him often," he shook off his stray thoughts.

"Sunday night she was in the storage room sorting when people started to argue outside. Par for the course. Dudes out for a smoke, or drunk—takes only a spark or two. But our Erika turns antsy when things heat up. Could hear everything through the little window higher up—all the climbing vines and stuff makes it invisible. What with Dieken booming on last night, it suddenly clicked for her—matched the loud voice arguing Sunday night. Triggered another connection in her brain—the second voice was Rosso's!"

"Yeah, neat story. So, what did they say?"

"Now it gets interesting, Polly my pal."

"C'mon—speed it up. Thought you need to leave."

A glance at his ancient flip phone and Karl swore. "Yikes— better hurry. Here's my take on what Erika told me. Dieken claimed Rosso had promised him exclusive rights and now was back-paddling. When Ronny told him where to put their deal, Hinrich threatened to let the cat out of the bag—to tell everyone about Rosso. The little weasel begged Dieken to keep his mouth shut. Then the voices faded away," said Karl with a straight face.

"Haha, how anticlimactic."

"Hang on, Polly! Not finished. All curious, she used the stepladder and peeked out the window. Spied two guys aiming for the parking lot—too dark to recognize details. One walked off. A car started and drove away. End of story."

"Interesting. Would make sense if Ronny had killed the campground owner to prevent a disclosure—of whatever. Yet Dieken does not profit now."

"Right on, Watson," agreed Polly. "Odd for your Erika to recall only now."

"She's not *my* Erika! Told you why she didn't think of this before. The voices didn't click until last night. Likely mad at herself about dawdling in the storeroom and forgot it all."

"Why would Dieken kill Rosso?"

"Never said he did. Pay attention, Sherlock."

"Please, Karl, just tell us, what are you inferring from this?" Sparks flying induced stomach cramps—discord phobia, Agnes diagnosed and empathized with Erika.

"Think about it. If Rosso was afraid of Dieken exposing him, and if Hinrich believed it would ruin Ronny, then can't we assume someone else knew the secret too?"

"Pretty torturous—"

"What secret, Karl?" Agnes interrupted.

"How should I know? Maybe shady stuff about his *WKA* connections."

"Unlikely—Dieken would be shooting himself in the foot. He'd lose his deal."

"Brilliant, Watson! Hey—your point may still hold, Karl. Say, the disclosure affected only Rosso's credibility, and Hinrich figured with a different Niederwinder rep he'll wangle a better bargain."

"Sherlock, you're answering your earlier question. He could have killed Rosso for that." Stretching his arms, Karl got up. "Alas—not likely since he drove off.—These skeptical looks tell me you're wondering how I can be sure the car was Dieken's. Elementary. Shortly after, Rosso hit on Erika on the patio."

Pleased at scoring, he slapped the table. "Time to say good-bye, my friends.—Oh, I tried Udo and Kai this morning—no luck. Beer with Hinrich didn't loosen his tongue either."

"Leave those guys to me. With an idea now what to quiz him about, your chum Hinrich should be easier to tackle."

"Be careful, Karl." Surprised at a stab of fear, Agnes cautioned, "With high stakes, it might turn nasty."

"Glad you care about the old man's safety. I'm more worried about you gals." With a "Call me about next steps," he was gone.

Well into lunchtime, the fry-up smell in the musty tavern was overpowering. The two of them hastened outside. The fresh sea breeze invigorated Agnes. Her stomach audibly gurgled, which made the imp giggle.

"You too? Wanna grab a shrimp sandwich at the *Imbiss* over there?" She pointed to a seafood takeout truck that was parked at the roadside, apparently permanently, across from the ferry dock.

"H'm, not sure. Let's check first." Usually, Agnes avoided all catering vehicles and vendor carts as potential germ traps. Squeaky clean display and appetizing food here, she admitted.

As if reading her mind, the large man stooping behind the counter—almost entirely covered by an apron over a short-sleeved shirt, both white and spotless—praised his wares as fresh from the sea. Any fresher, it would bite you, he joked lamely. They ordered sandwiches loaded with tiny dark-pink North Sea shrimps and soft drinks.

Westward from the wharf, the quay wall gave way to a rocky shore. The boulders, flat enough to sit on, offered a panoramic view out to the mainland. The mist had lifted, but storm clouds were brewing.

"Mathilda's place cannot be all that far from here." Sandwich in hand, Agnes waved further west.

"Watch it! Your shrimps slide."

"Oh God, this is so delicious." Creamy juice dribbled from Agnes's fingers to her wrist. "So glad you suggested it."

In companionable silence, they munched until the last delectable bite.

"You were right about your mom, you know."

"What do you mean?" Instantly alarmed, Agnes sat up straight, all mellowness evaporated.

"Like—she's visiting someone." A sideways glance and Polly gazed out over the water again. "Like at that residence, eh?"

When Polly starts to blabber, Agnes realized, alarm bells clamor. A shriek escaped.

"How do *you* know? What have you done, Polly!"

"Calm down, Agnes. Don't panic. Nothing bad. It's just—well, I happened to spot Sera go into the place this morning. Kind of asked around later. Visits a woman called Ellie Schneider. Ring a bell or something?"

"Not off-hand... How did you find out anyway?"

"Oh, I simply went in and asked."

"Polly!—You can't spy on my mother!"

"Agnes, come off it. You're worried sick about her, and I want to prove you've no reason to. I'm convinced she'd never do anything seriously bad like."

"You know my mother for all but a few days."

"So what? Call it *Menschenkenntnis.* Gut intuition about human nature, or something. Your mom's a good person. Doesn't go around offing people."

"I never said she did! Trust me to have some faith in my own mother." Words spoke with pomposity—a lying assurance. Faith in her mother she'd deleted from her vocabulary over two decades ago.

While she fretted, curiosity won out. "Did you find out anything about this woman?"

"I saw her," said Polly, all airy—then grew serious. "Merely peeked into the room. She's ancient. Well into her nineties, I'm sure. Not quite there upstairs and in pretty bad shape physically. Babbling and drooling. A frightening relic."

"How the heck did you manage—"

"Easy. Told reception I'd just missed my aunt going in to visit. Kind of tricky. No clue if it's a man or woman Sera came for. Babbled vaguely, convoluted like, and Nurse promptly cued me. 'Ah, Frau Schneider' and the old darling would be thrilled with two visits today. Buzzed me right in—no ID or nothing."

Their carelessness still appeared to amaze her. Never mind her own audacity. "No chance anyone'd be stealing one of the old dears, eh?"

In a flash, realization hit to make Agnes jittery. "Did you say 'Schneider?'"

"Yeah, thought so myself," replied Polly, deliberately off-hand. "Your granny, you reckon?"

"She changed the name!" Why this deeply offended her, Agnes had no idea.

"Nothing wrong with anglicizing your name when you emigrate," said Polly. "Many people did back in the day and do now. Taylor is easier to pronounce.—Tell you what. Why not ask Sera?"

"Ask her—How? Am I to tell her now, 'Mom, Polly did a spot of sleuthing—just amateur for fun, and stuff—dug up an old granny. Is it mine by any chance?'"

"Yeah, I guess—awkward that…" Arms hugging her skinny legs, Polly stared at the waves, avoiding Agnes's eyes. "We need to figure it out on our own then."

"Bloody hell—" On her feet in one leap, she hissed, "You—are—not—going—to—dig—deeper!"

"Be reasonable, Agnes. You don't want to stop here. If you can't talk to your mom, how else will you find out?" Upturned face pleading with her. How can a little imp like that be so persuasive—and yet wrong?

"Please, Aggie. You wanna go home and forever wonder about your granny and your mom's family? All this secrecy bothers the hell out of you. So let me dig just a wee bit. Please? For your sake?"

Drained of energy and wrath, Agnes sank back onto the boulder. Her foot dug among the pebbles on its own accord.

"Don't say anything. Leave it to me. Feel free to give me hell again after." The full force of her impish little grin sought to win over Agnes. Apropos of nothing, Polly asked, "Hey, how was your morning? What were you up to?"

To her own amazement, Agnes had completely forgotten to report on her encounter with Daniel Dregger. Her friend listened, clearly pleased the distraction worked. Within moments Agnes was too immersed in the tale to care. Such fun characterizing DD and how his shine waned on scrutiny.

"You've got to admit; though the man is a bit of an asshole, his minimalist approach to writing hardly leaves him open to a plagiarism scandal of Guttenberg magnitude," commented Polly in the end.

"I wouldn't go as far as calling him that," Agnes qualified this judgment. "The father he maligned might be a better candidate."

"What? For asshole?"

The expression of incredulity on Polly's face delighted Agnes. "No, silly. For possible plagiarism. As Professor Emeritus, I assume, the dad did a dissertation and published research findings. Research—after all, he's a scientist—itself could be plagiarized."

"An old retired geezer—who would care now? Danny wouldn't murder for that."

"I didn't say he did, or he would. Though—people murder for less. Not recommended for politicians, I grant you. Don't forget—we wanted to figure out what *Rosso* thought he had on DD."

"Caught me out, Watson.—True, Danny said nothing to Ronny's threat. Maybe he didn't worry at all. You say he dislikes his old man—conceivably planned to denounce him publicly if the poop hits the proverbial fan."

"Keep in mind, this is pure speculation. We're maligning the old gentleman without any evidence whatsoever."

"Right again. Do investigate him, though. Academia is your forte."

While Agnes mentally listed what she wanted to google later, she sensed Polly watching her intently.

"Listen, why don't you go for a trip with your mom tomorrow? Quality time."

"Remove us from harm's way, by any chance?"

"Kind of. No idea what's planned—some direct action, I hear. You've had enough hassle for one holiday. Not a bad idea to be out of reach."

"What about you? Stay away from sketchy things. Do come along. My mom would love it—" A moment's hesitation… "Me too."

"So sweet." Was Polly blushing? Recovered herself fast enough to say, "Need to keep an eye out and stay informed. No worries, a little thing like me is invisible most of the time," she laughed and hugged Agnes. "Call me from the café tonight or tomorrow morning. I'll meet you at the ferry, and we do dinner after. Don't forget to sign out with the cops."

Rain spattered with sudden force, bouncing off the boulders. Before she had time to pull her waterproof from her backpack, Agnes was soaked. The elf had vanished. Shaking her head, Agnes ran for cover.

Chapter 24

POLLY

Holy crap. Hope she's not really her granny. What an old hag!

Polly barely managed a "*Wiedersehn*" (damned, if that'll come true!) in her haste to get out of there.

Staff must be used to this kind of reaction from younger visitors. Not many feel comfy with the truly aged, infirm, or dying. A mirror of our destiny.

And the stench! Do we start to rot inside when we reach our 'best before' date? Yuck—and I thought I wasn't ageist.

Sucking deep gulps of sea air, she ran up the street towards the waterfront, welcoming the downpour that soaked her hair and made its way into the back of her jacket. Rinse out the smell. She offered up her face to the rain, letting water trickle into her nostrils.

When she reached the promenade, she scanned the sea wall for the next steps down to the beach in the direction to the west side of the island.

The broad expanse lay deserted. Only a lonely walker further ahead—head bent low against the driving rain, soggy dog cringing close by. At least, the sand was too water-logged to be whipped up by the wind.

The sense of abandonment that saturated the greenish-gray of the beach and sky resonated with her mood. Sandals strapped to a loop of her jeans, she relished the cold creeping from the sodden ground up her bare calves. Incoming tide.

With a deep breath, Polly sprinted. She only slowed to a trot when her sides ached. The stabbing pain revived her spirits.

Admittedly, no matter how nasty, the outcome paid for the effort. Almost funny. A theater of the absurd. They totally fell for the bouquet, coyly spilling from its doily. Not to mention the pink bow on the silver box of pralines. Touch of genius. Sure ticket of admission.

To give them credit, they were thrilled the old hag got any visitors at all. They'd admitted she could be a trifle difficult. The understatement of the year. The screech, when the chocolates weren't forthcoming fast enough, still rang in Polly's ears. What a greedy, nasty old—Okay, enough, Polly. Forget it. You've got what you went for, she told herself. Count yourself lucky the nurse loved to chat.

All left now was to hang around the place Friday morning and hit on the old neighbor. Came on the dot, twice a week at ten on her way to the market, they'd said. Despite ancient Ellie most often these days in no shape to appreciate the loyalty. Mind gone down the tubes.

Used to be neighbors for a lifetime, the nurse said. Something about doing the household. No idea, though, who did whose. Either way, an acquaintance of long-standing would know where Sera fit in the picture.

A change in the surface under her feet brought her up short. Without noticing she'd mounted a ramp onto the dike. The promenade ended a hundred yards or so behind her at the town limits. She shivered in the wind.

Time to make her way back to the Doll's House. Strip off this wet stuff before catching cold. Belatedly, she pulled up the hood of her jacket. At least might warm up her soggy head. Hot shower and a pot of tea. Plan how to catch Kai and Udo tonight. Maybe a bout of bar hopping. On a night like this, what else could anyone do in a touristy town?

Chapter 25

AGNES

What makes her look so self-contained? Like the proverbial island in the stream—God, you're getting trite! True, though. Something about Sera sets her apart. An impression of solidity and serenity among the surging crowd ready to board the bus at the terminal. Better hustle, Agnes chided herself, instead of waffling pseudo-poetically.

Sera spotted her. Arm raised in a wave—her backpack was bouncing against her side—Agnes trotted the last meters across the pedestrian path.

"Sorry I'm late," she gasped catching her breath. "Tried to outwait this shower—no chance."

"Glad you've made it. The shelter keeps out the elements; so, I was well protected." Hands buried in her anorak pockets, Sera jerked her chin at the queue in the front of the bus where paying passengers boarded. "No point rushing."

"Shoot! We'll never—"

"No big deal—another one leaves at six-thirty."

To prevent herself from swearing, Agnes mustered the lineup. Lots of backpackers and, by their choice of clothes, a number of the activist types from the demo last Friday. Headed for the campground? Most likely destination. Hardly worthwhile taking this bus for the youth hostel Polly had mentioned. An air of suppressed excitement seethed under the surface of banter and chitchat as the throng moved on.

Ten minutes later all her annoyance proved groundless. Though packed to the hilt, a couple of girls offered their seats. The heavenly sluice gates opened with a vengeance as the vehicle pulled out onto the road.

"Did you have a pleasant day despite the rain?" Anxious for her mom's goodwill—now that they sat in close proximity—guilt threatened to corrode Agnes's psyche. Chatter might ban it for now. God knows what Polly is up to next. If Sera finds out, she'll—

"Surprisingly relaxing." Absorbed by the study of her own hands, intertwined in her lap, her mother said, "I do like to sketch drizzly or stormy seascapes"—a mischievous smile at Agnes—"preferably through a window."

As though to demonstrate, her mother gazed out into the downpour—the glass fogging over from the inside. Doesn't ask how my day went, Agnes's mind chattered on. Yeah, sure were going to tell her, weren't you? About plotting with Karl and Polly—especially the imp. Go right ahead, confront her about this granny person.—Do other people's brains produce these non-stop dialogues as soon as they sit still?

No longer able to contain the flow, she burst out, "Guess whom I met this morning?" "Well, met is not the right word," she rushed on under the politely questioning gaze, "ran into—"

"Polly?"

"Well, yes, we had lunch. No, I went to the large bookstore in town. Remember, we walked by—" Her mom nodded. "The candidate from the Environment Party. DD." A blank expression spurred Agnes on, "Daniel Dregger. The guy who spoke at the rally in the marketplace on Friday. The last speaker?" Still no recognition on Sera's face—uncomprehending headshaking. "Never mind. You might not have stayed to hear him. Doesn't matter anyway..." her voice trailed off. Let's not get into where else we saw him.

"How is—"

Oh, no. Not on to Polly, please! "I did go to an Internet Café. Thought we could go for a trip tomorrow. The weather is supposed to be gorgeous. Sunny, warm, and dry. Would you like to?" Without giving Sera a chance to respond, Agnes jabbered on, "A day trip off-island, I thought. Better than yet another isle with limited cycling. An old town popped up in my search—a bike trail on the mainland dike goes southwest to it. Picturesque —a little harbor, tiny streets, famous windmills—"

"Greetsiel." Murmured softly.

"You know it?" Well, sure she would—if Polly's right about the family connection. Hard to fathom the idea. Take your cue. Question her now.

A non-committal—"Who doesn't? Apparently, hundreds of thousands every year flog to it."—robbed her of the opportunity.

Deflated, Agnes slumped at the implied dismissal of her idea as too touristy.

A light pat on her hand. "Doesn't mean we wouldn't enjoy a cycling tour and lunch there. In fact, I do miss my usual workout."

"Are forty or fifty kilometers too much? Over the whole day, of course."

"A little evening spin, as they say." Her mom's melodious laugh caused a guy in front of them to crane his neck backward.

"Sorry—sounds like bragging. Long rides relax me, a much-needed counterbalance to teaching and committees. Unless it snows, I use it also to commute to campus and—"

"I had no clue." Awed, Agnes gaped. "Hope I can keep up then... Silly of me, rather obvious, you're in top shape."

Their arrival at the campground distracted her. As expected, almost everyone disembarked. Only a few had gotten off at previous stops. Three other passengers remained when the doors closed but left shortly after at the Dune Café stop.

Before he continued on, the driver turned around and asked them where they were going. Though the bus route led to the road's end, on an inclement evening no sane person would aim for a nature hike, his glance said. In broken German, Agnes told him they rented the last cottage out this way.

To their pleasure, he offered to drop them off at their door, rather than making them walk back on a wet night. Irregular stop but, he joked with a wink, try to catch him in this weather.

Indeed, dense fog now rolled in from the bog.

Minutes later, as they neared the cottage, a dark-colored sedan parked by the roadside. Unmarked cop car, Agnes deduced from the sharp stab in her chest the sight caused.

"Did you stop by the station to sign your statement?" Maternal mind-reading at work.

"Yes, this afternoon. Only took a moment. Mentioned we might day trip tomorrow. What do they want now?"

A hooded head was visible on the driver's side when they passed. Not police garb. Or was it?

The bus pulled up outside the rose arbor. Twisting to glance back at the parked car about fifty yards back, their solicitous chauffeur promised to wait until they got safely inside. Both of them thanked him profusely for his kindness.

He waved, saying, "*Hoffentlich habt ihr 'nen Hund.*"

Wish your hope was justified, and we indeed had a dog, the bigger the better, Agnes silently agreed. Too bad there's no 'rent a mutt' service.

Within seconds of entering the bathroom, a knock on the front door startled Agnes.

Still on the upstairs landing, Sera whispered. "Let's not open to anyone." Instinctively, Agnes flipped off the lights and, careful to remain hidden, they peered through the glass.

From above, they glimpsed a figure in a dark, hooded rain-coat. The fog was thicker than Agnes first realized. Now the head moved to stare upward. Bathed in a yellowish glow from the exterior light, switched on earlier, a bearded face emerged.

Heart beating furiously, Agnes gasped both with fear and anger at the intrusion. The nerve to try to barge in here at night, her mind shouted. Coming out of the fog. Yah right. London pea-souper, Jack the Ripper—her better sense scoffed. Hadn't Erika mentioned a hood—

"Look. Another car... Police," she added as roof lights flashed blue. Why did Sera whisper when no one could listen in?

Two uniformed cops appeared and accosted the man below. The guy carefully and gingerly dug in his breast pocket.

"Must be asking for his ID," said Agnes aloud, while her thoughts raced on. Is he worried they think he's pulling a gun? Unreal. On my holidays. What did we get ourselves involved in?

"The press come to hound us." Her mom's words only served to remind her of DD.

Media or not, the cops now ushered the intruder off the property. Neither Sera nor Agnes moved when their visitors disappeared into the mist. Their silent vigil paid. Both uniformed police returned to the door. One of them knocked while the other stepped back to survey the facade. The outdoor lamp revealed Maike, the female cop. With an exhale as if to release tension, Sera opened the window.

"So sorry to bother you. Would you mind coming down for a moment? I would like to explain this to you," their friendly officer called up.

When Agnes went to let them in, she recognized the male as her favorite US cop impersonation. Without a word, he walked back to the arbor.

From behind, Sera invited Maike to join them in the

kitchen. Though Agnes needed the bathroom more than anything, she didn't want to abandon her mother.

"I must apologize for the disturbance," Maike reiterated. "The man is from the papers."

As Sera and Agnes nodded at each other, she explained, "We had been watching for a while for your return. Please do not speak to the press and never open your door to strangers."

Her expression displayed genuine concern. "This cottage is very isolated. I hope you don't misunderstand me. Two ladies alone are not safe out here."

Sensing Agnes bristle, she hastened on, "Women are not weak. Sometimes we need to use extra caution."

"Female police officers like you prove our strength," said Sera, her eyes crinkling. "We appreciate your caring for us."

"Our constables cannot remain here. We come by on our patrol. My colleague and I are on duty all night. Please lock up after me." A salute acknowledged their sincere thanks as she left.

Her hand shutting the door, Agnes felt she was pushing out the yellow fog. The sound of the bolt shooting home reassured.

Chapter 26

POLLY

Time to get systematic again. Too much unrecorded info cluttering up the brain. Far too keyed up to sleep anyway. Polly changed into old, green-black checkered flannels with elastic waistband and tie strap, and a black fleece top over her white t-shirt. Her feet ached from cold. She rummaged through the dresser drawer and unearthed merino wool socks, one brownish, the other in bluish tones.

The Doll's House she rented didn't offer comfortable seating. The white wicker armchair exuded the cute factor but left your bum stiff and covered in a weaving pattern. IPad and mini keyboard in hand, she bounced onto the cot. Additional pillows and the duvet pummeled into a warm nest, she burrowed deeper. Forgot a solid surface to type on—up again. The tiny kitchenette provided a mid-size wooden cutting board. Should do.

The clock on the iPad read 12:48 AM. Where to start?

She reviewed her notes on the events, starting with the previous Friday and reread brief entries on all people involved. For Sera, she now added this morning's discoveries at *Liüüt Mööv*. Brand-new and yet to be entered—her encounter with Kai and

Udo earlier this evening. A sweet treat from the mini-fridge first to jump-start the recollection.

Cuddled back into her nest, Polly bit off a chunk of 85% dark chocolate and let it dissolve in her mouth—delicate sweetness bursting on her taste buds. A glass of milk served as an extra health kick.

The replay of events unfolded in her mind, while her fingers flew over the keys to make brief notes...

An online Bosum business directory listed them by last name as Harms, proprietors of *Sandy Solar*. Images of sandy beaches, blue sky with snow-white cotton wool puffy clouds, and roofs covered in clean, crisp, shiny panels, danced in her mental vision. Not so. The story the blokes shared burst the illusion.

Not the easiest job to track them down. First assumed they might frequent the corner pub, accurately called *Eckkneipe*, at one end of the street their office was located. The phone eBook identified it also as their home address. A landline, plus two mobile numbers listed. No other Udo or Kai Harms.

Phoning them, or ringing the doorbell, Polly reckoned, would be a last resort if nothing else worked. Preferably the encounter should appear coincidental. Neighborhood pubs drew a blank. On a hunch, she tried *Die Krone*, a fifteen-minute walk from their place. At Ronny's meeting, they had blended in with the regular guys—not the nasties—propping up the bar.

Around nine o'clock—damp and chilled through and through from foggy drizzle—she entered. The food smell from the dining room hit her stomach to make it growl. Short-shorn types, who closely resembled the nasty batch encountered on Saturday night, horsed around with the bartender and a waitress. Stereotype? Perhaps. The mean and sneering vibe was real enough.

Neither Kai nor Udo in sight. Check the restaurant. Might as well warm up and grab some grub before continuing this bar crawl, she reasoned. A quick scan of the dining area revealed only a few familiar faces. Nancy at a table toward the rear—

doing dinner with Shady and two long-haired dudes. Gave no indication of noticing Polly.

Next moment she struck gold. Only steps in front and facing her sat Udo. Before she could figure a credible maneuver, he glanced up. To her amazement, his expression transformed. What about me makes him bloom into such a brilliant smile? I'm not exactly Cool Kid personified.

Dropped his napkin as he jumped up. His brother across from him spun around, his face split into a wide grin of welcome. They waved away her protests of not wanting to intrude. Minutes later, her food ordered, they enjoyed a drink together like old buddies—liter mugs of beer for the guys and a white wine spritzer for her. Plus, a bottle of mineral water to spin things out if needed.

Piece of cake to involve them in a chat. Despite the East Frisian reputation for being monosyllabic, they opened up. True enough, they both tended to be ponderous and took their time. Proved quite endearing and relaxing.

Questions about the future prospects of solar on the island led them to vent on Ronny's death. Didn't make a hell of a difference, they argued. Niederwinder was here to stay. Made no pretense of spilling a tear over Rosso's untimely demise. Didn't gloat over it either. Might echo Rhett Butler's famous last words to Scarlett.

Over dessert, the conversation turned personal. A fluke really. It started when they fussed over whether to treat her to rhubarb crumble with cream, or vanilla nougat mousse.

"You two couldn't be sweeter if I was your long-lost sister," she'd joked.

Talk about a conversation stopper! Their faces shuttered and —bent over their empty plates—they fell silent. Made her jabber like an idiot. Dismayed, she caught Nancy watching her from afar.

In memory, Polly fidgeted in her now too warm cocoon. A

scramble to discard the duvet and a sip of cold milk cooled her down.

In the end, Kai told her. Their sister indeed was long-lost. —*Jeez*—did I ever put my foot in. Just thinking of it, she cringed in mortification. Speak about mouse holes to disappear.—The pain in the older brother's eyes.—Appalling. Decades did not lessen the hurt.

Young—and likely immature—yet the girl represented their idol, their world, and lifeline. Understandable—Kai barely seven and Udo nine when she jumped ship. Literally. In the opposite direction from the usual way, though. At fifteen, she left on the sneak with her boyfriend. With a man, Kai said. A bloke almost double her age. Seduced her and lured her away, according to Udo. One day, she hopped on the ferry with him and vanished.

The brothers never found out whether the drunk of a father tried to find Sandra. Done nothing; they suspected now. Missed the cheap housekeeper. To the boys, Sandra had been mother and protector. The younger brother's memory veiled in goddess worship—no wonder, she'd been his ersatz mom after their mother died when he was four. Can't say I blame Sandy for giving up, Polly thought. Living with a virulent alcoholic—and trying to look after and shield two brothers—would do for anyone, never mind if you're just a teen.

Why Udo, however, should sound so inordinately shocked at how Sandy let herself go, Polly couldn't tell. Gobbled sweets and fry-ups as midnight snacks and became chubby, he said. As if losing a slender figure amounted to the utmost betrayal. Dyed her hair from brown—no, almost black—to brazen blond. To attract that asshole who probably grew tired of her before the color grew out, Kai figured in retrospect.

What totally devastated them, no word from her ever since. Not phoning, or writing to an abusive drunkard of a dad, made sense. To leave her kid siblings without a message, they found incomprehensible. How a girl of fifteen should have managed back then to communicate with them without alerting the father, they did not say.

True, odd omission, unless… On the whole, Polly agreed with their unspoken assumption. The rational explanation for Sandra's silence was that she had not survived on her own. Papers are full of stories of teenage girls living on the streets and how it ends for many, said Udo.

In her fifties or so—if she did survive—calculated Polly, judging Sandy's age based on the brothers'. Can't be sure about their age and didn't ask. Would she still be a chubby blond? Ergo the company's name. Nothing to do with beaches, or dunes and sunny skies.

By then, Polly felt rotten for ruining their evening and dinner. Instead, they both went out of their way to comfort her. Did them good to talk about it, they said. Alone, without relatives, they did not mention her these days, not even to each other.

When Kai admitted he almost daily thought of Sandy—the apartment over the shop reminded him with a thousand little things—Udo nodded despondently. Why not move to escape the reminders, Polly asked. Too afraid to lose her for certain. "How would she find us if she comes back?"

Unbearably sad. The reason why they didn't marry? To avoid changing address—or at least one of them? Their parents' relationship served as a deterrent too. Abusive alcoholic dads have that effect. Her involuntary shudder brought her back to the present. Time to call it quits.

Chapter 27

AGNES

"Agnes, I do think we should ride single file here—in case someone comes from the opposite direction, or people need to pass," Sera said over her shoulder while speeding up.

Beats me why we go cycling together if we can't ride side by side, Agnes grumbled to herself. The path's wide enough and anyone coming is visible a mile away. At Sera's clipping pace no one's likely to sneak up from the rear.

Slightly out of breath after no more than an hour on the bike, Agnes foresaw trouble brewing. Furious clanging from behind startled her. A guy in skintight gear tore past her. Rides a beautiful racing machine and then such an ugly bell. Far more effective in getting people out of his way, she admitted.

Suited Sera well not to be able to talk, Agnes brooded. On the ferry over, she'd hardly said a word. Fair enough, to catch the eight-ten boat, they got up at a quarter to seven. Before boarding, she had called Polly. Of course, the prospect of a three-some dinner at the *Oold Fishhus* pleased Sera no end.

Ouch, that hurt! Pay attention to where you're going instead of moaning like a disowned child, Agnes' superego scolded. The dike's surface did have some nasty deep cracks in its concrete paving, and the front tire lacked shocks to absorb the impact.

C'mon, Agnes, she pep-talked herself. Let's enjoy this. Such a glorious day. Listen to the waves crashing, gulls screeching… This is true holiday stuff. Gorgeous views. You can see for miles out onto the North Sea. That must be Holland across the water. Invigorating salty air. The breeze. The sun—especially after yesterday's rain and fog. What more do you want? Come, you do like cycling. Just need more practice. Yah right, my bum is sufficiently sore to make standing upright for the next week a comforting thought. If my legs will ever straighten again…

Her mother twisted around to call, "We turn inland here."

"Do you know the trail?"

"No need to. The path leaves the embankment on the ramp there," forefinger pointing it out, "follows the little road on the inner side."

Well, so much for the glorious sea view. Dike wall on one side, the vista stretched now over wildflower studded meadows, vivid green fields, and reed thatched low dwellings land-inward. Bathed in sunshine, attractive in a pastoral way, Agnes acknowledged. Inevitable wind turbines reached out into the sky.

A tractor pulled past them, dragging a giant mower, or whatever the thing might be. The farmer watched them, leaning sideways, one hand on the steering wheel, the other holding a pipe. When Sera waved a greeting, he raised his pipe in salute.

Closer to midday the temperature became uncomfortably hot in the wide-open flat country. Agnes yearned for a cool drink and pedaled furiously to catch up with Sera.

"Getting tired?" Her mom smiled serenely. Not a bead of sweat in sight.

"Oh, I'll survive. But can we stop for a sec? I need a sip of water."

"How about over there? The open gate to the field—we can pull off the road."

Irritated Agnes paddled on. A memory flash surfaced from childhood. Desires ought not be immediately satisfied—Sera made her wait. Even if only for a few minutes.

Meanwhile, Sera had reached her goal. It was indeed a good spot to take a break. A hedge sheltered from the intense sun. While Agnes unscrewed her stainless steel water bottle—another product of Mathilda's foresight—Sera opened her knapsack and offered a muesli bar. Chocolate covered. Who can resist?

"Better have them now before they melt," said Sera as though to justify the early indulgence.

Predictably, she showed no sign of tiring, Agnes perceived in envy. Amazing woman. The helmet accentuates her gaunt, tanned features. How beautiful mom had been—to a little girl, nothing short of a goddess. But an unpredictable one. Well, wasn't that the trademark of the Greek gods and goddesses? In her way, quite predictable. Foreseeably choosing the unconventional.

"Ready for more?" Hand extended for Agnes's wrapper, Sera shoved it into her own pocket.

Her mother had anticipated the green movement long before its inception in Canada. Waste not, don't over-consume or litter. Compost, reuse, and recycle—all a natural part of Sera's way to bring up a child.

An image suffused Agnes's mind; the two of them huddled over the scrubbed pine table with colored paper left from a school project—a few thin stalks from Sera's tomato trellises and a pot of glue—crafting a kite.

"Gone into dreamland? Did I wake you too early this morning?"

"Sorry, Mom. Spaced out—Remember the kite we built in the kitchen? When I was eight, or so?"

"Think that was the end of the summer holidays when you started grade three," Sera mused, crinkles radiating from her eyes and well-shaped lips.

Let's avoid an emotional meltdown and be placid like those cows in the pasture. Time to say it, nonetheless.

"Did I ever tell you? Thanks a lot for spending so much time with me when I was small. I cherish some awesome memories."

Not giving Sera a chance to respond, Agnes remounted and for once pulled ahead. Must've left her mom speechless anyway.

Another half-hour of riding on in companionable silence brought them to the outskirts of Greetsiel.

"Should we find the tourist office to pick up a map?"

"Let's explore. I'm adventurous today," Agnes heard herself say.

"Not sure how much scope for adventure a historical town like Greetsiel is going to offer," Sera laughed.

"Oh, you used to find something out of the ordinary every time we went somewhere when I was a kid."

"Yes, I recall you expected me to invent the extraordinary if none was to be had. With the years, we grow sedate." A mischievous little grin. "Before this vacation, I took a solemn oath not to embarrass you anymore."

"Oh, Mom…" Cheeks burning, Agnes cringed at her juvenile pompous self.

"Let's not block the way here." Resolutely Sera led on.

In fact, they ran the danger of being jostled by sightseers milling forth and back. Pushing the bikes now, they entered the town core. Unbelievably picturesque. Of course, off-limits to traffic. Only pedestrians and bicycles cluttered the pink paving-stone streets. Some houses shimmered in whitewashed plaster, while others glowed mellow from well-worn crimson brick patina. Lattice windows lent the predominantly small buildings a nostalgic charm. Ivy shaded entire house fronts—their steep gables curved inward. Roofs in shades of red, anthracite, and brown were tiled in well-weathered clay.

Little boutiques, craft stores, leather goods, and, inevitably, touristy knick-knack shops flourished side by side with cafés, tea rooms, and restaurants. The outdoor tables and chairs, sprawled into the car-free lanes, invited sojourn—to become part of the privileged observers rather than the masses being observed.

Obviously, the place lived by the tourist trade these days. To judge from the postcards, Agnes thought when turning to peak over Sera's shoulder, the area is littered with windmills. Every other card on the stand that Sera pivoted with one finger featured them. Not the modern turbine type but of the traditional Flemish variety. Other cards sported the local harbor studded with fishing boats. Her mom held out one of them.

"Want to go there now?"

"Sure. Definitely a must-see, I'd say."

"Later on we might enjoy a picnic on the wharf—or at the famous twin windmills perhaps?"

"Anything you like. I'm game." Hope I won't regret it, Agnes qualified her rash claim.

Chapter 28

POLLY

Talk about preaching to the converted. Polly surveyed the mottled gathering—it couldn't be called a crowd—forming discreet islands in front of the steps leading to the town hall.

Hermann's voice thundered over the megaphone, reverberating from the buildings enclosing the marketplace. From his elevated position on the landing outside the portal, he gesticulated to emphasize his points. Impeccable again in a marine blazer and white open-necked shirt, today worn with tan chinos, he advertised prosperity and success.

The speech was on behalf of the *Wattwächter*, an association for the protection of the Wadden Sea, or mudflats. Members were easily identifiable by their positive disposition towards the speaker, evident in nods and murmured affirmations. Reticent, dedicated, and earnest—not noisy cheerleader types.

In the meantime, clusters of activists and other enviros of the incomer variety paid little heed to Hermann. Wasted effort to deliver part of his speech in English to be more inclusive. At the fringe, Polly recognized Mark belaboring Shady—his body language intense and insistent. Still vied for an entry into Nancy's intimate circle.

Passersby only lent a momentary ear—to judge by their

glances—reluctant to stay and get drawn into this motley throng. The iron-studded doors of the venerable building remained shut; no official in sight. Remarkable to permit the event on their front steps. Ringed at the outskirts of the happening, however, Polly now perceived uniformed police. Stoically observing and, most likely, taking note.

Upon his perch, Hermann inundated those who listened with figures. Lots of valid points—yet dry like desert sand. Predictably he concluded with a plea to reconsider "selling paradise for mere lucre." Muted applause issued from his associates and polite or charitable souls in the other groups.

What's the big deal? Why did Mark think this is worth my while? wondered Polly. Nothing new here. Idly, she watched Nancy ascending the stairs. The gait nimble like a girl's. With a courteous bow, Hermann passed the bullhorn to her on his descent.

Ethereal and forlorn, the pacifist leader stood at the top, wordlessly surveying the assembled groups. The megaphone, when finally raised, hid her face from view. The black, long-sleeved t-shirt over skinny black pants accentuated fragility. Not actually small like Polly, a timidity of voice and demeanor diminished her today. Facing her own people, she started to speak.

"Though the last thing you expect me to say, but I will say it nevertheless: I regret the untimely death of Ronny Rosso."

The prediction hit the mark. For her own followers—never mind those gathered around Torch—as Polly now saw, were bewildered or outraged. Catcalls and booing burst forth. Raised left hand, fingers spread wide, Nancy silenced them.

"Let me finish. Mr. Rosso was not our friend. The death of a human being—" For an agonizing moment, her voice failed her. The bullhorn wavered. She recovered and said softly, "I regret."

The sinewy hand again shot out in a stopping motion to forestall further reaction.

"Enough. I'll be brief today and won't repeat what I've said last Friday. Only so much. We must take this unforeseen event as a marker. A sign to pause and reevaluate."

Wow, is she ever ambiguous, Polly frowned. Does she realize, or is she oblivious to the implications? Not heeding the telepathic call for caution, Nancy went on.

"There is still time to change the course of events. Nothing is firmly decided yet. Let us take stock and reconsider."

Who's the all-inclusive 'us'?

Her followers wondered too and got antsy. Perplexed faces galore. Torch pushed aside onlookers and, arms akimbo, sneered up and taunted her.

"Lost your nerve, Nancy? Bit late for a turnaround." No need for a bullhorn—his roar reached every nook and cranny of the marketplace.

From Polly's elevated position on a pile of pallets off to the side—left by the weekly marketers—she had the advantage of a gawker at a collision.

Sensible orator, Nancy ignored the heckler. "The application for the *WKA* is not formalized yet. Bosum can still determine its own future—protect the natural heritage and take serious the needs of other creatures. *Every creature* has the right to flourish—not merely humans."

Here, for some reason, her voice broke again. At least, she was back on course. Familiar territory for her listeners.

What's the point of all this? Puzzled, Polly scanned the audience. Maybe the odd representative of the press might still kick their heels around here. The majority left the island after the weekend to cover a far more sensational case of child abduction and suspected killing on the mainland.

Few listeners regretted Nancy's departure after some lame closing remarks. Combative Torch virtually tore the megaphone from her grasp when he ascended the steps.

His flaming hair, pointedly wild attire—blazing red and orange hewed open shirt over a black torn t-shirt and ripped black jeans revealing patches of whitish flesh—drew attention as much as the alacrity of his movements and grandiosity of his gestures.

Despite the bushy dark beard, no one could miss Tor's sneer as he thundered over the amplifiers.

"Cut all the crap! Yeah, Nancy, we all love you. But—this ain't the occasion for love and peace! Enough is enough. Stop the talk! Walk the walk!"

Cheers of "Torsten, Torsten!"

Wildly glaring at the mottled crowd, he raised a fist and punched it up three times, shouting, "Let's occupy!"

Shouts of "Yay!" "Way t' go, man!" from his admirers.

What the heck is he planning to occupy? Town hall, or what? Incredulous, Polly scanned the reactions. Either his disciples knew beforehand—which is likely—or they don't care what's to be occupied—equally feasible. Enlightenment was not far afield.

"We'll march to the sodden campground and won't budge until the corporate bastards give in!" Fist stabbing the air, "Who's coming with me?"

A storm broke loose in his camp. You gotta hand it to them, Polly conceded, a couple dozen of them produce a racket to shame a hundred.

The *Wattwächter* and *Naturschützer* physically started to distance themselves. Some of them appeared to translate the message for others. Head shaking, they made to leave.

The uniforms moved closer. One of them mounted the steps, mocked by Torch.

"Hey, man. Coming to arrest me? What happened to freedom of speech in this country?" His gaping audience he incited, "Follow my call for action—no matter what happens to me!"

Playing the wronged martyr, our Tor, is he? Pleased to realize the cop burst the bubble of a dramatic scene, Polly awaited developments.

Momentarily, the silent uniform was joined by a plain-clothes superior who quietly addressed Torsten. Whatever he said was evidently non-threatening. A hesitation and Torch relinquished the megaphone. Unease rippled through the diminished gathering. Isolated catcalls and one or two "pigs go home," was all.

"Allow me a few words of caution," the plain-clothes began. "Although you are entitled to protest, demonstrations must be registered. You do not have the right to occupy any property, no matter whether private or public. Should you choose to do so, law and order will be enforced. The Dunes Campground is private land. Some of you paid to stay there, as we know, and are welcome to do so unless you break their ground rules. Anyone who is not a legitimate camper and enters without permission will be prosecuted for trespassing. Thank you."

With a dignified movement, he turned to hand back the megaphone and found the makeshift stage empty. For Torch had slunk to his cronies. From a distance, Polly watched them disband into different directions to impede pursuit. The cops observed. No need to follow—the whole place must be under CCTV surveillance.

Suddenly a familiar shape scurried off from the fringes. Flipper. Figures he'd be here, Polly thought. The marketplace now was almost deserted. Engrossed by Tor's antics, she had long lost sight of Nance. Exposed on her lonely observation post—the lamppost the pallets were leaning against, no longer protected her tiny frame—she slid from her perch. Innocent little-girl-expression deployed, she sidled into the closest street. The fuzz ignored her.

Chapter 29

AGNES

"Please, Polly. Do come back with us tonight." How pathetic—Agnes hated her own weakness. To forestall a smart-ass comment and to evade any impish grin, she continued to stare at Sera's retreating back.

No answer came from Polly, next to her on the ancient bench in the *Oold Fischhus*.

"I need you." Too late Agnes recognized the ambiguity and stumbled on, "I mean—you know—have to talk—to you…" In complete mortification, she stopped. Her eyes roamed. A door in the back swung closed on Sera in search of the washrooms.

"A girl likes to be needed." The chuckle deep and throaty.

Gratefully, Agnes's mind latched on to the implicit sexism—in vain.

"Well, so does a guy, I imagine.—Hey, no sweat. Sure, I come along. Only… Want to start on a job early tomorrow."

"You work here in town?"

"Nah, just something that needs doing," At her vaguest, Polly, hopped topics. "Say, how *was* the bike tour, then? Hope your eagerness for a heart-to-heart doesn't mean the day trip was a disaster."

"Hmm…let's say it wasn't as successful as I'd hoped." With a grim grin, "My bum certainly won't be the same for ages."

"Tell me about it later." Seeing her face, Polly guffawed, "No, not about your derriere. Don't worry. About whatever went wrong.—Psst—" A sideways jut of her head in the direction of the back of the quaint restaurant to alert Agnes.

Exquisitely poised, yet quite oblivious to the impression she made, Sera strode towards them.

"Mom, Polly's coming back with us to the cottage. You don't mind?"

"Delighted, Polly dear."

"Better go grab Mattie's bike," said the imp. "Meet you at the junction outside of town?"

The waitress, in her mid-sixties and of ample proportions, waddled slowly down the center aisle towards their table. The weariness of the woman's feet transmitted itself to any onlooker. All three scrabbled for their wallets—a contest won by Sera with ease.

"My treat." An apologetic smile to forestall their demurrals.

"Ta, Sera. So sweet of you. Should have been on me, since I invited you." For once—Agnes noted with satisfaction—the elf proved capable of embarrassment.

"Fifteen-minute head start, or so…" A flustered Polly scrambled to her feet.

"Let's say around 10:30—at the intersection leading to the supermarket," clarified Agnes.

"Righto. See ya."

"Why don't we go for a little stroll in the meantime?" asked Sera as she gazed at the retreating back of the server.

The mild evening completed a picture book sunny day—weather-wise. Orange hues of the setting sun suffused the westward sky and spread scarlet fingers onto the water. Not enough time, Agnes realized, to reach the western promenade to witness the sun dipping into the sea. The mellow mood of a perfect summer's eve pervaded the eastern wharf side. So why didn't it penetrate her bilious psyche?

How could she be mad at her mom who'd gone out of her way to be conciliatory? To the point of catering to Agnes's desire for a mid-afternoon cake break. A spectator to her daughter's indulgence—black coffee was all Sera ordered. The rich buttery cream of the outrageous calorie- and cholesterol-laden torte gooey up Agnes's throat in shame for her blatant greed. Reminiscent of the past—whenever her mom reluctantly yielded, she'd remained a detached observer of her child's greedy needs and wants. Or so it felt in retrospect.

As though sensing her mood swing, her parent interrupted before the mental squabble drowned her.

"Lovely night, isn't it?" The gaunt face, now without sunglasses, all genuine serene joy. A regretful glance at her wristwatch, "Time to head home."

Derriere screaming in protest, Agnes obediently mounted the bicycle. Visions of a soothing bath spurned her on while pedaling on autopilot in Sera's wake.

"Watch it!" The warning prevented rear-ending her mother stopped at the junction. No sign of Polly yet. The air, chilly in the dusk on the open road, smelled dank. Metallic bell tinkling in the distance.

The imp waved wildly while steering with her left and caught up with Sera back in motion.

"Sorry it took me so long."

"Perfect timing. A brisk ride will warm us up," said Sera.

In silence, they continued single file as darkness descended. Soft humming reached Agnes following behind Polly, lulling her mind into freewheeling. Sweet voice. An unfamiliar tune—the kind to haunt you.

Clammy vapors wafted low on the tarmac, reeking salty foul of marshy vegetation. Eerie in the twilight, the weak beams of the bike lamps reverberated.

Must be passing the salt marshes toward the northeast.

Means we are almost at the campground, Agnes figured, sore enough now to prefer to pedal standing up. Salt-laden moisture stung her sun wearied eyes.

Gates to the camping place emerged yellowish in the mist, illuminated by lamps on both sides. A momentary relief before murky darkness engulfed them again.

"Sera! Stop!"

The shout made Agnes's head snap up. In reflex, her hands squeezed the brakes. Bike discarded, Polly gesticulated in the direction of the sandhills demarcating the outskirts of the campground. An orange flickering haze illuminated the sky. For a moment Agnes thought irrationally that Polly was pointing to a residue sunset. Not at this hour.

"Fire—in the dunes!"

Too tired to care why her mom's voice quivered with emotion, Agnes resented the delay. "Maybe a bonfire."

"Far too huge."

"You're right, Polly. Dune fires are serious. We need a phone quickly. The café is closest." Back on her bike, Sera didn't wait for them.

Instead of following, the imp sprinted inland, ordering over her shoulder, "Go with your mom. I'll check it out."

"Don't be an idiot!" After all, a grass slash-burn—no reason for such a fuss. Nonetheless, Agnes scrambled to catch up with her friend. No way she could leave her here.

With the agility and speed of a wild rabbit, Polly scampered out of sight. Small chance for Agnes to keep up if Polly had not come to a stop before cautiously proceeding toward the flickering, hazy orange-yellow glow. Smoke tinged the air.

From the crest of a hill, the sky appeared much lighter in the west. At least 200 meters away, the dark silhouette of a larger structure rose above the ground mist. The building sat isolated among the dunes, sheltered by trees and a higher mount in direction of the campground itself. Its upper part the flames now began to devour.

"The guy's private residence."

"You mean Dieken's?"

Eyes on the spectacle, Polly nodded.

Like a pair of ghouls—the insight revolted Agnes. Primeval fear contracted her abdomen.

"We should head back. By now Karl or someone got through to emergency services." No reaction. "Please, Polly. The cops keep us on their radar—don't want to be found near a fire."

"Yeah, you'd better," without turning, Polly agreed. "No worries. Meet you at the cottage."

"Come with me. Nothing we can do to help. Gawking is sick."

A strange look was all—Polly didn't budge. For once follow through on your word, Agnes exhorted herself.

A last "please" and gentle tug at her friend's arm was met by a quick shake of the helmeted head. Defeated, Agnes crept back through the dunes, furtive like a traitor. Reason asserted the folly of tarrying any longer.

Fire mesmerizes, she rationalized, and Polly is curious by nature. Then why did she feel like a street dog retreating, tail between staggering legs?

When Agnes entered the Dune Café after exerting herself for the last stretch of the way, its proprietor welcomed her, emerging open-armed from behind the bar.

Embraced in a bear hug, she heard his reassurance, "Don't fret, fire trucks will be there in a jiffy." A moment later he said, "Mom's gone on to the cottage, love."

As she wriggled free, he soothed, "I know, I know. Tried to prevent her but no use. Refused a ride and asked me to wait up for you guys here." He searched her face. "You okay? Where's Polly? Your mom said you were together."

"Thanks for staying up, Karl." Embarrassed at Polly's ghoulishness, she resorted to a partial truth. "She's to go straight to our place."

"Let me take you home. Castro still needs a run before bed. He'll be glad to see you." With a reassuring pat on her shoulder, he went to fetch the dog.

Later, while he unloaded the bike at the walkway into Road's End, Agnes broke her exhausted silence to say, "It's Dieken's house."

"What! You mean the fire?" Alarmed his voice rose. "Why didn't you say? I thought...a dune fire. Which is bad enough..."

Indeed, how could she forget to mention—

Impatient to leave, Karl said, "Not a particular friend; but neighbors help each other around here. Same as everywhere."

Nevertheless, he and the shepherd accompanied her to the front door. Her apologies for not telling him sooner he dismissed with a wave. Sensitive to despondent moods, Castro licked her hand which hung dejectedly by her side.

Now Karl must take her for a self-centered nitwit. As she stood in the open doorway, hanging her head, two gentle hands cupped its sides and lips brushed her cheek. He'd come back for a last "goodnight."

Chapter 30

POLLY

Shoot, why didn't she bring her camera? Polly rooted through the little backpack, stuffed with a few overnight necessities. The iPhone would suffice. Immobile until Agnes was well out of sight, she now needed to rush and snap pics.

Cautiously she moved closer. Not too close. No sense in leaving footprints right up to the place or in arm's throw of an incendiary device. The cops would be crawling all over the terrain.

No doubt this was arson. The culprits were obvious, too. At least to her.

A careful reconnoiter and she spotted some outbuildings on the outskirts to shelter her from view and the blaze. The crushed brick forecourt won't show prints like sand does, she figured. Better not hang out for too long.

The main building was bound to be old, with a traditional thatched roof. Hard to tell now. Firetraps that burst into flames with little help. Close up, the fire roared like a furnace gone wild. Didn't smell all that different from a wood stove. Mostly natural materials blazing. None of your burned plastic or chemical fumes here. It will reek horribly once hosed down. Poor bastard who owns this. Not much left of his gear, for sure, by the end of the night.

Her mind in a running commentary, Polly kept on shooting photos. The auto-flash was unlikely to alert anyone in such an inferno.

Suddenly, a movement to her right caught her eye. Someone was slinking around the corner of an old stall or something. For a moment, the figure stood erect, outlined against the darker background. A sudden burst of flames cast it into bright light, illuminating a hooded shape.

In reflex, Polly crouched and held her breath. An arm jerked into the air, fist stretched out in a gesture of triumph. A muffled whoopee. Then the other hand went up to remove the hood. A mass of hair escaped. Now the figure pulled down the scarf or whatever covered the face and revealed what had to be a beard.

How bloody foolish—totally obvious who was standing there. Abandoning caution, she snapped pics like mad, hoping some would turn out okay.

Next thing, she saw another shape disengaging itself from the shadows. The general outline brought to mind the huddled figure from the gallery of the hall Sunday night.

Well, well—her hunch proved correct—the boys being up to their usual tricks.

Just in time, she clicked more snaps before the one slunk, and the other lumbered into the background. Must be feeling the heat and getting out of here before being caught red-handed. Escape route via the beach, no doubt. Friggin' pyro-maniacs!

Head raised, she heard sirens of fire trucks and cop cars. No time like the present to bow out. Reluctantly, she retreated—not before taking a couple more shots when an upper story window blew out. Pray to high heaven, no one was in there when this started. The bloody morons hopefully made sure before indulging in their favorite pastime.

Chapter 31

AGNES

Agnes's head snapped up with a start. Her neck muscles screamed with sudden searing pain. Blinding light blurred her vision. Her right arm seemed an oddly foreign object, unconnected to the shoulder. A dim recollection of a clattering noise penetrated the fuzz swaddling her brain. With an agonized moan, she pushed herself into an upright position. Slowly her consciousness took in the moment.

Gingerly, she put her feet on the floor. The cold from the boards made them cramp in the thin cotton socks. Her legs felt stiff like logs when she padded to the front door. Dozing off on the leather sofa in the austere parlor came with a penalty.

Furiously rubbing her limb, she tried to ease its numbness. At the door, a thought struck her. What if it wasn't Polly? Anyone might lurk outside. No chain on the door either.

She crept back and flicked off the lights. Careful not to expose herself, she slid aside the drawn curtains. The yellow outdoor lamp illuminated the nocturnal visitor. Confidence restored, she went to open up.

"Interrupted your beauty sleep?" Well past midnight, the grin retained full wattage.

"Sorry, Polly. Dozed off for a few minutes—"

"Hey, don't apologize. All my fault—keeping you up. Such a long day for—"

"I'm okay now."

"You're shivering, Agnes. Let me make you a hot drink."

"*Ouch!*" As though burned, Agnes withdrew her right hand that Polly had touched. "My whole arm fell asleep and tingles all over now. I'll be alright in a moment."

"Was going to offer to give you a massage. Guess, better not." With a shrug, Polly went to the kitchen cabinets. In self-mockery, she pulled a funny face. "Where's the yummy stuff hiding? A little toddy's quite the thing. Plop yourself down and watch."

The imp climbed a stool and rooted through the upper cabinet and unearthed a can of cocoa and a miniature bottle of rum left thoughtfully by Mathilda or forgotten by a previous tenant.

"Need the bathroom. Be right back."

Anxious not to make any sound, Agnes crossed the corridor upstairs—legs screaming every step of the way. No idea I'm so out of shape, she ruminated. A day of cycling leaves me a wreck. Cold and tepid water run alternating over her arms and hands helped to warm up and to restore circulation. Before going back down, she grabbed a fleece sweater and wool throw from her bedroom. A divine scent greeted her return.

"There you are." Two steaming mugs in hand, Polly used her foot to drag out a chair. Not satisfied, she went back to dig through the cupboard and sat down across from Agnes, placing a packet of cookies between them.

"Feels like stealing Santa's midnight snack." With a deep sigh, she ripped open the wrapper.

"Aaah. Heavenly. You're a brick, Polly." Life returned to body and mind. The potent rum aroma intensified the chocolate flavor. Huddled in her blanket with an extra cushion to pamper her rear end, curiosity awoke. "What happened after I left?"

The answer sounded evasive. "Oh, not much. Lots of fireworks." Prompted by Agnes's incredulous glance, Polly tried to convey some excitement. "A window blew out with a big whoosh. Then fire trucks approached, sirens blaring. Made myself scarce."

"Whatever caused the blaze? One can only hope no one got injured, and the house is salvageable."

"The place's a goner, I'm afraid. Yeah, makes you wanna pray no one was home."

"Did you see anyone?"

Shiftily Polly gazed away. "No one left the house and no inhabitants hung around. If they were in when it started, they'd have run to the campground for help."

Something about this struck Agnes as strange but eluded her like a name one can't recall.

Her nose deep into her mug, Polly was busy drinking for a few moments. Apropos of nothing, she said, "Do you mind if I leave really early in the morning? I'll try not to wake anyone."

Drowsy from the rum Agnes nodded.

"Think I might take the bike again?"

"Mathilda won't miss it. Comes with the cottage. If we brought along a kid to use it, or you do, what's the difference?"

"Thanks, pal."

The sardonic raised eyebrow hastened her to correct, "Didn't imply you're a child."

"No worries. People call me worse at times."

Still flustered, Agnes asked, "Anything interesting planned for tomorrow?" Another faux pas—or Polly's evasiveness was habitual.

"Hard to say," came the cryptic response before a change of topic. "Hey, sleepyhead, let's get you to bed now. In the afternoon we'll chat with our buddy Karl."

Chapter 32
POLLY

"Na, was darf's denn sein, kleines Fräulein?"

Polly turned to the market stall vendor behind her who had asked what the "little lady" might like. Hastily she put back the cauliflower she had aimlessly grabbed as an excuse for her loitering. Before he could repeat his query, she claimed with excessive politeness to need a few minutes to decide.

Impatient not to lose her quarry, she scrutinized the clientele at the adjacent fish truck. No need to worry—the throng this morning was so thick it would take ages to get served.

Meanwhile, the veggie seller—ticked off by her dawdling—grumbled he didn't have all day to wait. Instead of a sarcastic reply, she sweetly asked him to assist other customers first. A gruff warning not to finger stuff she didn't intend to buy, and he switched on his charm for a posh vacationer demanding attention.

Anxious the intended catch might evade the hook, Polly sidled over to the seafood truck. Of the refrigerated type, the broadside was propped up in canopy fashion to reveal a store-front with a glass display counter. By bouncing up and down, Polly glimpsed a multitude of marine creatures, raw fish and fillets resting on ice.

Too bad—much preferable to line up at the fried and baked fish peddler. The delicious smell permeated the entire market-place, only competing with Bratwurst and fries scent. Hard choice what to pick for lunch later on.

For a more panoptic view, she stepped back from the queue. Not a second too early—because her quarry emerged from one end of the counter and made for the outskirts of the market-place, weighted down by an overflowing cloth shopping bag far too big for its owner's size.

At a safe distance, Polly followed cautiously. To mask her pursuit, she scrutinized the wares of other marketers. Last thing she needed was to be taken for a young lout who stalks little old ladies with a view to a convenient purse snatching or mugging opportunity.

Progress resembled Sloth in chase of Tortoise. Eventually, they meandered from the marketplace into a side street. The crowd thinned out. The emptiness of the residential area made trailing rather obvious.

Perhaps chatting up the woman right at the seniors' home after her brief morning visit might've been better. A lucky stroke, Polly thought, to identify her target with such ease. Ready in her previous hiding place opposite the residence well before ten, Polly fretted how to recognize Ellie's neighbor. What if several elderly women came visiting the inmates? The place was bound to be overflowing with seniors.

Redundant doubt in the end—despite the sunny and warm morning, or maybe because of it, only one older dear appeared on the dot at ten. The staff didn't exaggerate Ellie's neighbor's punctuality. Took half an hour for the faithful caller to re-emerge, and no other likely candidate entered or exited in the meantime. Elementary.

The misgivings returned during the lengthy shopping tour around the marketplace—plainly the woman's major entertain-ment and social networking site. Most of the vendors treated her like an old friend, to judge by the drawn-out chats.

Afraid her usual ingenuity might desert her, Polly had no clue when or how to approach her prey casually at this point.

Then the opportunity opened unexpectedly. Visibly tired and exhausted, the ambling gait grew slower and slower, until the small figure finally stopped dead. The heavy canvas tote—put down with a thud unto the pavement—jolted and dislodged a paper bag. Apples rolled merrily down the street.

At lightning speed, Polly sprinted after them to retrieve one and all. Jacket held up as a container, she eagerly brought them back to their dismayed owner, like a well-trained Labrador. A sweet smile replaced the wagging tail.

"*Ach Gott, ach Gott! Besten Dank, Fräulein!*" The poor woman thanked Polly profusely. Not sure God had a hand in it, thought Polly wryly.

To seize luck and ask to be of further assistance carrying the bulky burden home, was a no-brainer. With only a moment's hesitation, sufficient for Polly to muster her most innocent, childlike expression, her help was graciously accepted.

Moments later they had regrouped and—leisurely strolling next to each other at eye-level—they chatted amiably about the warm weather like granny and favorite grandkid.

Chapter 33

AGNES

"Is it working?"

"If by working you mean doing it standing up, yeah, somewhat bearable." For emphasis, Agnes rolled her eyes at Sera who, at present, freewheeled beside her.

"Can I tempt you with a latte, first thing? After, we can walk instead."

"Ah, now you're talking..." The rest left unsaid as her mom pedaled off again. A staunch believer in the theory to 'drive out Lucifer with Beelzebub,' as the Germans say, Sera suggested cycling into town as a remedy to being stiff and aching from their trip to Greetsiel. Well, Agnes's bum begged to differ. Yet, no one said using the saddle was mandatory.

After Polly's departure before breakfast, neither of them wanted to be home in case the police showed up in the wake of the fire. Unlikely for Karl to mention Sera when he raised the alarm, but the cops might still be out there questioning everyone. Sure enough, near the campground, several cruisers and vans lay in wait. They passed unnoticed—the officers too busy sorting drive-by sensation seekers.

Wonderful to be outside, Agnes admitted to herself. The

morning proved glorious—wildflowers and tangy dune grass scented the air. A mild breeze played with strands of her hair pouring forth under the helmet. Several times rabbits criss-crossed their path. Along the saltmarshes, bird calls accompanied them incessantly.

On an impulse, she pedaled like mad to catch up to Sera, calling for her to slow down. When she drew close, her breath came in gasps.

"How about fresh croissants for a breakfast picnic?"

"Delicious," her mom agreed, "The patisserie at the west end of the promenade makes authentic French ones."

A quarter to nine, they reached the beach, loaded with goodies and balancing lattes. Soon they hit a sheltered spot, exposed to the morning sun. Better prepared than any girl guide, Sera whisked out a thin blanket from her rucksack.

First sips of the hot brew and delicious bites from the still-warm flaky almond croissants made both of them sigh and aaah in unison. Heads turned at each other in surprise, they burst out laughing, spattering icing sugar and flakes.

"Like mother like daughter, after all, it seems," said Sera, brushing off crumbs and sugary dust from Agnes's knees.

Agnes couldn't recall her mother laughing so spontaneously and without restraint in ages. She used to often when you were a child, remember? Yeah, and you dissolved in embarrassment whenever she cracked up in public. Not again! To choke off mental jibes, Agnes launched into inane speech, "We certainly got away alright. Did you see all those cop cars?"

"How could I miss them? They virtually blocked the road. Any minute, I expected to be stopped. So, I stepped it up."

"Yup, I noticed. Hope they'll be gone later on."

"We can stay around town all day, as far as I'm concerned.

The press likely will pester everyone out there. This afternoon I intended to do some sketching—do you mind?"

"You needn't ask me." To be considered gave her a warm glow, nonetheless. "In fact, Polly and I plan to meet Karl after he picks up his supplies."

"Glad all works out so well. Would you like dinner at a restaurant again? We should go back before dark, though."

"Mom, are you getting worried about our safety?" A sudden chill induced by the unexpected thought her mother might be afraid made Agnes shiver. The early sun didn't warm her anymore.

"I wouldn't say 'worried.' Prudence demands caution. Thus far we can't tell whether or not the fire was suspicious. Too much is happening on this island in such a short time. After all, the cottage is rather isolated, don't you think?"

"Guess, you are right… Usually, I'm the anxious one."

"All the more reason for me to insist on vigilance."

They drank their lattes in silence for a few minutes, their eyes scanning the sea. The sound of the waves soothed Agnes. Her glance lost its focus. Securing her paper mug in the sand, she leaned back, her eyelids drooping.

A high-pitched screech penetrated her consciousness and brought her upright with a jolt.

"Watch it!" Before Agnes's flaying arm hit it, Sera grabbed her cup.

"What was that?" panted Agnes.

"A gull. No harm done, dear." Still, her mother searched her face. "Would you rather spend the rest of our vacation some-where else? We don't need to stay here for another two weeks. Not if we start to be nervy and uncomfortable."

"But you were so looking forward—" Unsure for whose sake she pleaded, Agnes broke off.

"Oh, I have seen quite enough, I think."

The figure entering the seniors' residence flashed in Agnes's mind. What if the person Sera went to visit was not her mother after all? To remain on Bosum would be redundant. Or, the old granny was beyond profiting from any visits—

"My concern is how it affects you," said Sera. "Your new friends matter to you. Quite endearing ones. I'm fond of them too. Needless to say, ultimately we'll part in any case."

"Well, how about we take Polly along?"

"A sweet thought, darling. Yet, whatever brought her to this island is important to her. We can't expect her to drop everything to join us."

"Sorry, I didn't think…" After a moment's pause, Agnes wondered aloud, "What did she come for… Never speaks of herself or her own life, does she?"

"Some people are sensitive about their privacy." With a brisk change of topics, she asked, "Where would you like to go if we do decide to leave?"

"Would the police let us?—Leave, I mean?"

"We could make a run for it."

"Mom!" Head jerking back, Agnes eyed her mother incredulously. "Are you serious?"

"Just seeing your face was well worth it." The tinkle of Sera's laughter proved contagious.

"Yeah, imagine us hop onto the midnight ferry, hoods pulled low and coats flapping in the wind on the gangway."

"No, no, Agnes, we'll be shrouded in yellow fog, wide-brimmed hats dripping with moisture."

"Pulling our suitcases behind us, their wheels screeching on the empty pavement."

Sera threw back her head in mirth. "Somehow those wheelie things spoil the picture, don't you think? Too utilitarian by far."

"Only if you use 'utilitarian' in the colloquial sense."

"I stand corrected. Honestly, though—What do you think? Bow out?"

"By stealth you mean?"

"No, with their sanction, pet. Why would they stop us? You don't believe they suspect either one of us, do you?"

Upon Agnes's hesitation, Sera glanced at her sideways. To evade the scrutiny, Agnes busied herself collecting their stuff, mumbling an indistinct "of course not." Blood shot into her cheeks and generated uncomfortable heat. Blame it on windburn, she thought. Aloud she suggested, "Let me browse online to check out possible alternatives. On my way to meet Polly, I'll stop by the Internet Café."

"Good idea. Another few days here, and perhaps Mathilda lets us terminate the rental agreement early with a refund. Wouldn't bank on it. No pun intended."

"Any particular area catches your fancy?" asked Agnes.

"Depends on how much we want to spend. Flights to the south, say Mallorca, are cheap from Germany. Rather sweltering down there in July."

The thought of increased costs raised alarm bells for Agnes; her brain's calculator skimmed her bank account. The sessional employment this summer had consisted merely of the condensed May to June term, since she booked off the rest of it.

As if reading her mind, her parent asked, "How about Berlin with its famous museums? Quite inexpensive, as long as we stay at the outskirts. A small apartment and we cook our meals—skip eating out. The parkland, forests, and lakes in the greenbelt surrounding the city are splendid."

Pointless to wonder where she gleaned all this insider knowledge, Agnes thought. Whether or not her mom knew it inside out, Berlin appealed to her own taste. Concerts, if not too expensive, and a raid of the university library. Somewhere in town, they hosted an Aristotle archive...

"Sounds right up my alley," she agreed belatedly. "Accommodations farther out...sure to be easier." Resolutely she pushed back the image of Karl and Polly so determined to intrude.

Their other belongings packed up, Sera folded the throw, while Agnes looked around for a recycle bin for their cups.

"Are you up to more cycling, or would you rather go for a hike?"

"I'm game for just anything on a day like this. You name it, I'll do it," grinned Agnes, amazed at her own daring.

Chapter 34

POLLY

Wait until I tell Agnes. Polly skipped in excitement.

People stared at her. A stocky woman in tight white shorts and neon pink top, fleshy legs crisscrossed with varicose veins, pivoted in her beach flip-flops to ogle Polly. She ejaculated something about 'totally nuts' in broad dialect, stabbing her similarly clad, beanstalk of a companion into the ribs with her elbow to draw his attention. Marine and white striped t-shirt and a sailor's cap—the word 'jaunty' came to Polly's mind—announced holiday spirit. His thin, nylon-socked, hairy legs, stuck in sturdy polished brogues, caused a conflicting work-a-day touch. Her own scrutiny he rewarded with a conspiratorial wink.

To pronounce her totally nuts, Polly supposed, didn't hit the mark. A huge portion of luck contributed to her success in the end. Now for a quiet spot to hunker down with the iPad for an hour to avoid forgetting little details. Far better to record the whole thing, of course. Impossible in the circumstances. The natural flow of memories depended on the illusion of spontaneity.

The Reading Room, originally created to cater to recuperating health spa visitors on Bosum, nowadays also catered to digital nomads in search of Wi-Fi. Its cozy seating, wing chairs, and settees in secluded nooks, still offered privacy for book-worms. Established in a particularly roomy specimen with a high back, Polly relived the earlier hours while her hands flew over the mini keyboard. She wrote:

Approx. 12:00 noon

As we reached Frau Schoemaker's front door, I carried her shopping up to the second floor and into her flat's old-fashioned kitchen. Left me gaping—so awesome and well-preserved. Not substantially redecorated for more than half a century (she told me), it still contained the original wood-burning range with oven and all. The small oak table, flanked by a bench seat under the mullioned window, held a wooden bowl. Emma (her first name) filled in the fresh fruit from the market.

Flowering plants and herbs on the deep sill reminded me of an indoor summer garden. The Delft blue dishware in the antique bleached-oak hutch her mother used daily in Emma's childhood, she said. Neither her parents, nor she ever moved, or in her case, almost never as emerged later. With time her own daughter and family came to live in the downstairs apartment. (On vacation in Spain at present.)

My surprise at the elderly lady ending up with the upstairs flat while the young ones got the ground-floor, showed in my face, I guess. For she explained, children want to run in and out into the garden or play on the sidewalk with other kids. Suited her—she giggled so sweet—to keep the one with the balcony to enjoy the sea view.

While we chatted, I helped her store away her groceries, and she—with a shy smile—asked, would I care to join her for fish soup she intended to make. No question, I jumped at the chance to stay.

Frau Schoemaker is such a dear—told me again and again how happy I made her. A young visitor who really listens and wants to know about old times. Her darling grandkids—at an impatient age now—tend to fidget. (Made me laugh—too aware of my own habits.) I'd adopt her as my granny any time, I said, and meant every word!

What puzzled me no end; how could this sweet woman stand Ellie Schneider as a friend. Granted, the old tartan might have been much nicer earlier in life. Wouldn't be hard to improve on her current miserable self. Still, I couldn't envision the two of them be besties to inspire such lasting loyalty in Emma.

Well, over our delicious soup, and later sitting outside, the whole history came out and made sense. So here's my account of what transpired.

Emma's Story [my trans.]
Ja Lüüntje [she started early on to call me 'sparrow'—googled the meaning now], when a person grows to be my age you never want to ask them about their life or you won't hear the end of it [cackles a bit like a hen].

You asked whether I've always lived here and I can say, almost always. For what are a short four or five years when you get on for ninety? Without Notary Schneider, my family home would be lost forever. The dear good-hearted man!

What happened, you ask? A sad and senselessly tragic story. Nothing compared to all the horrible misery of the Hitler era and the suffering of a world at war, I think now. Nevertheless, when you are only a teen, personal tragedy hits you hard.

A strong student, I enjoyed learning and hoped to follow in my parents' footsteps. My father, the principal of our *Gymnasium* [high school] and my mother, an elementary schoolteacher, encouraged me in my dream to become a music teacher. Every day I practiced piano for hours. The war started and things became tighter and tighter. How bad, I didn't learn until later. Sorry, I'm digressing.

So difficult to talk about the accident—even a lifetime later. They both died motoring to the funeral of my Papa's aunt in Oldenburg on the mainland. Springtime —a sudden cold spell made the roads treacherous. Bereft of all I loved, the generous Notary took on everything and gave me a home with his newly-wed wife. Elenora and I are only a few years apart. Married earlier the same year; she at eighteen and *Herr Notar* already in his early thirties. As her household help I could earn my living while finishing school.

No money left, you see. My Papa lost everything in a stock market crash and still tried to gnaw off a high mortgage and pay debts ever since. Kept me in ignorance. Parents back then didn't discuss such things in front of their children. Social status required a principal to entertain and maintain a certain style of living, well beyond my dad's means.

Notary Schneider bought our house when they died and converted it into two flats. Well, the downstairs is now all modernized, of course. He rented both out, and I lived with them. Left penniless, I could not afford to go to university. Instead, he paid for my training as a typist and upgrading to secretary. Throughout I continued to manage the household for Ellie and gladly helped him in his law practice.

Any children; you ask? *Ach, Lüüntje,* yet another sad story. I think they pined for a child right from the first. Never became blessed. Broke your heart; Ellie forever crocheting pink and blue baby clothes. [Emma wiped her eyes when she spoke of it.]

Near the end of the war, *Herr Notar* travelled to a client on the mainland. Surprised us all when he brought home his brother's little daughter, *Finchen,* just a wee toddler. So much sadness in those years. She lost her parents in the London Blitz, I believe. Or an automobile accident? Sorry, *Lüüntje* I'm getting too old. Notary Schneider's brother went to live there as a young man.

I do remember vividly his return that night. Ellie shouted with anger—I heard her from my bedroom upstairs. Back then I could not understand why. Fond of children; yet she never took to Finchen, poor little mite. The apple of her uncle's eye.

You see, Ellie didn't know of her brother-in-law's daughter. She desperately wanted a child of her own flesh and blood—a boy. Well, sometimes what we want most we never get. Finchen remained without siblings. Mind you, Elenora looked after her well enough. Somehow they never clicked.

The child spent much of her time with me or *Herr Notar.*

Called him *Papa* after a little while. What a melodic little voice and laughter. To Ellie she only said *Mutter* (mother), and reluctantly. The sweetest girl you can imagine, our Finchen, and so talented. Forever drawing and painting, she made her daddy proud, while Elenora scolded her about her messy fingers and clothes.

Actual given name? No, an endearment or diminutive form. Not for Josephine but for Serafine. At eight or nine, she insisted on Fina. Only Ellie never used any short form.

Her Papa spent all his spare time teaching Fina, at home or when they went for long walks. He took me along sometimes too, always eager to improve my education as much as hers. Occasionally, we visited museums or concerts on the mainland. Every year he planned a special vacation for us. No matter how insistently he entreated her—at first, that is—Ellie refused to join us.

How deeply he regretted Elenora's lack of interest in fine arts, music, and literature, one can only guess. Picture pretty, though, when he wed her. Outward appearance swayed him, as many a man before. With time she became a little soured by seeing her dreams unfulfilled. [You can say that again!] A sharp tongue [chuckles]. Not with the Notary, though; he would not have stood for that. A calm and soft-spoken man. Perfectly dignified—*ein feiner Herr* [a real gentleman].

What became of Fina, you say? In the end, she broke the Notary's heart. Of course, his wife later claimed she'd always said, nothing good could come of spoiling the girl. Cast doubt on Fina's provenance! How she dared to question her being the brother's child! Her anger getting the better of her. Ultimately, she blamed her for her husband's early death.

My apologies, dear, for not explaining myself clearly. Old women do ramble, I'm afraid. The trouble came when Fina was about twenty. I worked as secretary at the *Gymnasium* my father had been principal of, and no longer lived with them. Instead, I rented this flat from the Notary. Far under price, I feared. Anyway, I'm digressing again.

When the scandal erupted, *Herr* Schneider felt shocked to the core. Fina, they said, went about with this young lout, Randolph Harmsen, a boy of not quite sixteen. People accused her of seducing him. The shame left the Notary heartbroken.

Some blamed everything on Randy, a loudmouthed brazen youth. Far too forward for his years, he prided himself on his reputation with the girls. Good-looking, dark-haired chap, muscular, though not tall. God's gift to women, in his own view—I'm sure you've met the type. They are more common today, I often think.

By then, he jobbed as manual laborer, mostly in construction. They shared being orphans; and he too hailed from London. Fisherman Harmsen's sister went there to work as a maid. Some English family on their vacation here had hired her and took her home with them. You see, born out-of-wedlock Randolph was. The disgrace and remorse killed her, Jan—the brother— claimed. Nowadays no one would care. Back then it ruined a woman.

From the first, Harmsen treated the boy harshly when he

arrived from England after his mom's death. Neighbors rumored the uncle beat the youngster and made him work long hours on the boat already as a kid. Until the lad grew too much for him. At fourteen Randy finally hit back, they say. Left fishery, quit school, and started as unskilled laborer with a builder. Though he still shared the old man's cottage, they barely spoke, people said.

[Note: Here we retired to the balcony for our coffee. We talked about the amazing view and the island until I saw a chance to return to our earlier topic.]

You are asking what happened to Fina? *Ach, Lüüntje*, if only she had turned to me. Anything in the world I would have done to help her. Without a word to anyone, she left one day. Completely devastated her Papa. Furious and disappointed, he forbade any mention of her.

Later he tried to find her on the mainland. He travelled there again and again. On business allegedly, while in fact searching for his Finchen, I'm convinced. His health deteriorated. After one of these "business trips," he had a stroke and passed away within a few days.

No, *Lüüntje*, our Fina never came back. Too ashamed, I fear. You know, I wondered if he found her on that last trip and didn't like what he discovered. The straw that broke the camel's back.

His widow raved after his death. For what did the dear man do? His will made over this house to me! A sizable nest egg too. All the rental income went into an account in my name for over almost two decades! Never told his wife nor me. In a letter attached to his testament, he charged me with taking care of Ellie if anything happened to him.

Needless to say, I honored his wishes and remained a kind of friend, whether she wanted or not. I still visit her now. No, she no longer lives next door but is in a retirement home. Can't do without nursing these days and is quite senile, poor thing.

You are wondering if Fina married Randolph in the end? Not at all likely. No, he does not live in the area. Eventually he took off. Not right away—many years later. Another bad affair. When? In the late seventies—maybe. The story trickled through by and by. In a small place things make the round. Apparently, one day he just up and left. Terrible and irresponsible thing, everyone agreed; he eloped with a teenage girl.

So many sad stories even on a small island like this. Now, I don't recall her first name. Brave and conscientious, she brought up her two young brothers, since their mother passed away—*aus Kummer* [from sorrow, or trouble], if you ask me. Couldn't stand any longer living with the drunkard of a husband. Elmar Harms—a brutal man. No, not related to the Harmsens.

The girl—Now, it comes back to me—Sandra. By all accounts, smitten with Randolph. Pure puppy love. Double her age. Followed him around like a little lapdog whenever she could, they said.

During her first two years at our *Gymnasium* [Grade 5 and 6, German high school starts early], the teachers thought her brilliant in languages and truly bright. With time, when she minded her alcoholic parent and those poor little brothers, her marks dropped. Sent back to the *Hauptschule* [public school, certificate with grade ten in Germany], since she could no longer cope. Such a pretty girl, too.

What did she look like? Well, I seem to remember her as neither tall nor short—slim with glossy dark hair Later I encountered her in town. The change! Had she not greeted me, I would never have recognized her. Dyed straw-blond and chubby. *Kummerspeck*, I thought at the time. [The expression refers to 'fat put on as result of sorrow or troubles.']

When? Oh, let me think… Yes, shortly before running off with this man. Devastated her little brothers—in the wake of losing their Mama. No other relatives to turn to and coping with a father who rarely kept sober—what a life for them! The dad almost bankrupted his electric supply store. The boys took over in their early teens and managed on their own.

[Didn't they search for the girl, or did she contact her siblings? I asked.]

I imagine, they reported her missing. Scandalous, in the eyes of islander; for a girl of fifteen to let herself be seduced. They blamed the loose morals of the times.

Not to my knowledge—no, I don't believe she ever got in touch with the boys again.

[Frau Shoemaker showed signs of being tired, and I worried about overtaxing her. Soon after, I departed, leaving open the possibility of another visit. A lovely, warm-hearted lady—which makes things easy. In all honesty, I'm not deceiving her about my interest in old lore. As we parted, I mentioned writing stories about the Frisian isles. A valid opening to ask more questions, if needed.]

Too bad we can't pull an identity exchange, Polly's tired mind commented. Agnes would adore her and be thrilled with Frau Shoemaker as grandma. Strange, Sera did not bother dropping in on her childhood ally. After all, Serafine and Sera being identical cannot be doubted. Emma might be right, though. Perhaps shame prevents her from seeking out those who loved her.

Hell, what a relief, the old witch is not Agnes's real granny!

Chapter 35

AGNES

Where the heck are they. Stupid idea—to meet here at this hour.

Frazzled, Agnes jostled her way among the tables of the *Bier-garten*—beer-guzzling lunch crowd as far as the eye reached. The romantic bench hugging the towering willow, where she had sat so undisturbed with Karl and Polly, now seated sweating, noisy, beer-bellied, red-faced tourists gorging on Bratwurst and French fries. Disgusting!

Moisture beaded on her own forehead. Irritated, she ignored the catcalls and waves from various parties, intent on enticing her to join them. Well, her rational self soothed, perhaps they want to help—

"Agnes! Hey! Over here." Swiveling around, she let out a sigh of relief, as Polly entered through the side gate. "Wow, what a zoo!" The imp pivoted on the spot. "Let's beat it."

With her left hand under Agnes's elbow, she propelled her forward. "What are you waiting for?"

"What about Karl?" A shake of her arm freed her from the restraining hand.

"Eh?"

"Aren't we to meet him here?"

"Yup. He called me five minutes ago to say that he won't be able to make it—"

Aware of her face crumbling in disappointment, Agnes glanced away from her friend.

"Not for another hour, he said." The laughter in Polly's voice mocked her. "I'll give him a buzz, once we settle somewhere."

In her relief, Agnes wanted to yell at her tormentor for tricking her, or at herself for being so obvious. Why do they matter so much? Out of your life within a week…

While Agnes sweated to catch up, Polly walked briskly ahead humming a song. Soon she turned into the wooded area with the swans on the tiny lake.

"C'mon, Aggie. Get a move on. Do I need to tow you?"

When Agnes pulled up beside her, Polly threaded her arm through hers. At the touch of Polly's warm dry skin on her own clammy forearm, Agnes withdrew with a jerk. "Too hot—so sweaty," she stuttered and caught a fleeting pained expression in return.

The path around the pond proved blissfully shaded. Sunlight filtered through the dense leafage and intensified the earthy smell of the still damp, peaty ground. Only the middle of the water sparkled in the midday sun. Dragonflies buzzed in lazy pursuit of lunch.

Perspiration now dried; a breeze tickled the down on Agnes's bare arms. She sucked in air greedily through her nose —straightened out her torso and uncramped her diaphragm— and breathed out with a slow, audible sigh. Involuntarily, she glanced down to her left and met the elf's open glance.

"See over there?"

Her friend's outstretched arm pointed to a picturesque, white, thatched cottage, set back in an old-fashioned blooming garden.

"Like ours! I mean, Mathilda's."

"Yeah, kind of the fashion up here—a couple hundred years or so ago," chuckled Polly. "However, its indubitably remarkable affinity did not determine my choice, Watson. Haha, no, the place hosts a tea room, bound to be quiet this time of day. Make mini sandwiches and pastries, if you're famished."

Through an arbored break in the white picket fence, they entered a garden studded with elderly, somewhat rickety bistro tables. Umbrellas weren't necessary with heavily shaded trees and a high hedge on three sides. They plunked themselves down at one of the more remote tables on the far side.

"Aaah, this feels so good," groaned Agnes and stretched out her feet. A moment later she winced as the slats of the chair worked their way through to her aching bum.

"Too hard for the princess?" With a merciless grin, Polly studied her.

"Easy for you to laugh. You didn't do all that cycling!"

"Hey, okay—Here, take my hoodie. Softens the pain."

To the thick fleece sweater folded up, Agnes added her own from her backpack before she eased her behind onto the seat.

From an adjacent table, Polly grabbed a menu with limited offerings. "Take your pick, and I'll go order,"

"The currant buns with clotted cream and homemade strawberry jam. Plus, Earl Grey tea, please."

"A brilliantly healthy lunch," commented the imp and made for the backdoor.

Time to de-stress—Agnes closed her eyes and gave herself up to releasing all tension. Easier thought than done. The folding chair refused to serve as a recliner. After a few minutes, the quiet did the trick. Faint bird chirping and rustling of leaves penetrated her consciousness.

Something interfered. First indefinable. Then a persistent sense of being watched. With a start, she snapped back upright. The chair crunched in the gravel when its front legs hit the ground. Saved her. A moment later she might have toppled over backward. Wide-eyed now, she scanned her surroundings with suspicion.

The shimmery gloom among the trees confused her eyesight. Then she spotted them. Nodding at her—like elderly puppets of uncertain gender—under a willow tree off to the side. One ruddy round-faced, the other pallidly gaunt, both close-cropped gray-headed.

Hey, relax. They aren't likely to be spies. Innocently entertained by the prospect of you crashing backward. Ha hah, how very funny. She raised a lame hand in a half-hearted salute and busied herself with her backpack.

"Tea will be served momentarily, Milady," announced the imp in her penetrating baritone imitation.

"Psst, we are not alone," whispered Agnes and jabbed her chin in direction of the odd couple.

Half-rising, Polly turned ostentatiously and called out a bright, "*Moin.*"

More vigorous nodding in response, a mouthed reply, and the puppets renewed the silent contemplation of their teacups.

"So, what's up, Watson?" Before Agnes could respond, she went on, "Oh, our fellow sleuth will be here in half an hour or so."

A burning sensation worked its way up from Agnes's chest into her cheeks.

"Still feel the heat? A real scorcher today," commented Polly sympathetically. "Cool down soon under these trees—"

A punk-style, androgynous, black-clad person set down a laden tray on the little table, to be whisked away again with tattooed arms and deposited instead on an adjacent table. With dainty movements, the server placed their order bit by bit in front of them. Each time the head bent over their table, silver rings from the heavily pierced immobile porcelain face swung forth and back. Multiple rings, studding the eyebrows, tinkled. The androgyny retired without having spoken a word.

As Polly didn't seem to find anything unusual in this performance, Agnes held back any observation. With a shrug, she poured her tea and loaded the bun with cream and jam. Mouth lowered over her plate, she took a bite too huge to fit without major drippage. No napkins. One hand rooting in her backpack, while red-and-white streaked rivulets made their way down her chin, she must be quite a sight. A wad of tissues proffered by an amused Polly saved her from further disgrace.

"Say, Agnes, I've got something to tell you."

"So? Why do you stop and play chase with your crumbs? Spill."

Rather than comply, Polly toyed with her teaspoon until it clattered against the brittle china cup.

"Watch it! You'll get us evicted if you smash dishes." To Agnes's amazement, the imp flushed dark pink. Realization dawned. "Polly?—You did more snooping! Out with it. What did you do?" Indignation rose and straightened her posture.

Oddly, her outrage calmed Polly. Her face regained its natural unblemished tone.

"Come off it, Agnes. You agreed to let me go on investigating. So don't—"

"I did no such thing!"

"Yah, well, you didn't stop me either. So, I felt licensed to—"

"Stop you? You are unstoppable! Like a bloodhound on the trail—"

"Nay—the imagery hardly fits a little—"

"Quit this BS and tell—"

"Shh—Aggie—the people." Eyes rolled up, she jabbed her chin in direction of the table under the willow.

The obvious mockery made Agnes fume, yet furtively glance over her shoulder. Sure enough, the puppets nodded, broad smiles splitting their faces. Her brows puckered into a frown, Agnes glared at them before spinning back to face Polly, only to see her waving at the spies in Elizabethan fashion. Just her winking spoiled the queen's act.

Annoyed, Agnes hissed at her, "Stop this and get on with it."

"A contradictory command—Okay, never mind—Sorry, Aggie, you don't want to listen now… You're all upset."

"Upse—et?" A placating raised hand and shushing made her drop her volume a notch. "You bet; I'm upset if you stall like this. Why—"

"Alright, alright—"

Chapter 36

AGNES

"Hel—lohhh, ladies. Having a bit of a spat?"

Agnes spun around to encounter a broad grin on Karl's face. A white shirt—hung casually and haphazardly over his navy shorts—accentuated his tan. Before she could say anything, he bent over her and brushed her cheek with his full lips. Pulled close in a sideways bear hug, Agnes shivered, aware of a pleasant masculine smell.

With his other arm, he drew in a reluctant Polly. "C'mon, girls. We're in this together. No infighting," he said as he ankle-hooked a chair and straddled it with one fluid motion. "So, what's up? Why the commotion? Could hear you all the way to the street."

"Come off it, man." The imp pushed her chair back to glare at him. "I'll go for more tea. Don't expect the Gothic will honor us with his presence."

"The Gothic?" "His?" Karl and Agnes spoke in unison.

"Yup, he's a 'he' alright." An enigmatic smile and she retreated to the back door.

"So, what's up with the He-Gothic-Man?"

"The server—thought he was a she—an unwarranted

assumption. Dressed in black, tip to toe, beringed and tattooed wherever bare—"

"Clear as mud. Forget Gothics. Why the chick war?"

"Nothing of—"

"Gimme a break. Never seen you so hot under the collar."

"A veritable study in phraseology you are."

"Ignore my linguistic idiosyncrasies and spill the beans," laughed Karl then sobered. "Unless…you don't trust me with…"

Awkward and sensible of making him uncomfortable, she rushed into speech, "Okay, Polly did some 'investigating' and—"

"So? Why do you stop? She's supposed to go sleuthing. We all are—"

"Yeah well. This is different. Digs into my mother's past."

"Why? What's wrong with your mom?"

"How do I know? She hemmed and hawed, which pissed me off—and you came."

"Sorry, my bad. Shouldn't interrupt revelations. Want me to leave so you girls can finish?"

"No!" For a moment, Agnes studied him and made her decision. "On the whole, I prefer you to be here."

"I'm flattered. Honestly. Sweet of you. Nudge me if you change your mind, and I'll split. Promise?"

The way he took it, Agnes grew uneasy. Yet, better off with someone else there to keep her from emotional fission. Yeah, right—

The timely reappearance of the imp—a tray precariously balanced at arm's length—cut off her mental contortions.

"No Gothic?" Disappointed, Karl glanced from Polly to the door.

"Curb your curiosity—he'll come for a curtain call later."

To make more room, Karl dragged over a second small table and removed some of their used dishes. With a flourish, he relieved Polly of her load. "Here. Let the pro be of service to you, ladies."

"Do quit the antiquated 'ladies,'" commented Polly.

Legs stretched out in Agnes's direction, Karl leaned back as far as the rickety chair allowed. Her glance traveled up from his muscular calves dappled in an errant ray of sunlight to make their peachy down stand out against the bronzed skin.

"Now, let's call this meeting to order. Anything to report, Agnes?" inquired Karl.

Snapped out of her contemplation, Agnes's cheeks burned. How she hated her body for its betrayal! Both hands cradling her cup, she addressed the tea instead. "No. Only cycled the island with my mom." Head jerking up to point her chin at Polly, she said, "Ask her what she did?"

The sarcastic and accusatory tone snuck in without any intention and made Karl sit up straight. With forced calmness, she faced Polly. "Please, do tell us."

For a moment, the elf eyed her. A slight shrug, she grabbed her messenger bag and fished around in its depth without speaking. Under their expectant gaze, she moved things out of the way to make room for an iPad. To subdue her impatience, Agnes clenched her hands into fists.

"There—if you're sure—read this."

"Why? What—" Uncertain now, hoping to procrastinate, Agnes stared at the open screen pushed in front of her.

"Stuff I discovered today. About your mom—plus other interesting items."

"Should we leave you in peace?" asked Karl.

For no reason, Agnes thought of the elderly couple under the willow tree. "No—don't go."

Bent over the iPad, she began to scan the text. The title "*Emma's Story*" only served to puzzle. Who the heck is Emma? Head lowered, hair curtaining her face, gave an illusion of privacy. After a paragraph or so, however, engrossed in the writing, she lost consciousness of everything around her.

At the final words, her breath escaped in a violent puff. Without lifting her eyes, she spoke to make sure of her own voice, "The interpolations in square brackets, I take it, are your comments?" With a sudden decision, she slid the device over to Karl. "Go ahead, read."

"Sure?" Karl hesitated. "Here, I wouldn't want to butt into your private sphere or whatever."

"Don't worry. Since she dug up the past—" Aware of the small person across from her—hunched like a beaten pup certain of its own innocence and goodwill—compassion won. "Thanks, Holmes. Of course, you meant well." Moved by Polly's oddly shy glance, she added after a moment's thought, "At least, it throws some light on things. Though I still don't quite understand."

To grasp the implications, she closed her eyes. Yet her mind only jumped from one confusing image to another. Why would an unconventional person like her mom not speak of her childhood and youth? The old woman—thank heavens!—no blood relation at all. How she'd have loved Notary Schneider as her *Opa*... No—a great-uncle—

———

"Appreciate your trust, Agnes," said Karl as he handed the iPad back to Polly. "Unsure, though, what to make of it. No connection to our current case—Sorry, Agnes, interesting as a reminder of your family history—"

"My mother never mentioned her past. All this is news to me. Except about Ellie—found out yesterday—"

"*Gosh*—must be so tough for you. Nothing in this woman's story puts your mom in a bad light. Makes her only more likable. An awesome person." The way he beamed at her. As if playing cheerleader for Sera should make her particularly happy. "Otherwise, nothing much remarkable, or did I miss something? How the heck you tracked down your darling Emma is the real mystery to me."

"Oh, have my ways." To deflect Karl's attention, as Agnes thought, Polly rushed on, "Do you believe in coincidence? Strange how Sera's history links with the girl Sandra. The teeny who ran away with your mom's old beau, Aggie."

"Can't say I do," replied Karl, hiding a yawn as he sat back. "No idea who the Sandra person or the guy are."

The last bit of the old lady's account Agnes had skimmed over as digression. Now she wondered. Could the man be her father? To make sure she asked to reread the passage.

Intrigued, Karl leaned over, his face close to hers—the scent of his skin, sweet, like suntan lotion or something.

Involuntarily, she shook her head, and he pulled back.

"Sorry, didn't mean to butt in."

"No, you're welcome to read. I reacted to my own thoughts."

In a time-lapse response to her mental musing, Polly remarked, "Don't think he'd be your dad. Occurred to me too, and I asked Emma, what happened to Randolph Harmsen. A gap of many years until he left with that fifteen-year-old. The time frame and circumstances don't fit."

Unless he dumped the girl and made up with Sera—too convoluted, Agnes judged.

Finger tapping the iPad, the imp lectured them, "Don't you guys realize who this girl is? Two brothers? Dad owned an electric supply store? Harms? Eh?"

"Holy sh—" shouted Karl, making both of his companions shush him. Their heads craned to the willow tree. No one there —the puppets dissolved into thin air.

"Aren't you two getting a wee bit paranoid? Anyhow, got the message. The Harms. You reckon she's Kai's and Udo's sister, don't you?"

"Full marks, dude." Eyebrow raised with a sardonic expression, "Curious, eh?"

"Yah well. So what? Where does the tidbit lead us?"

"Precisely what I intend to find out."

Confused, Agnes lost interest in the matter and leaned back, her hand twirling the teaspoon.

As if to grab her attention, Karl changed the subject. "Talked to Hinrich earlier. The man has something on Rosso, I'd be willing to bet." His listeners waited expectantly. "Right now, he's too flippin' mad about those arsonists. Screams blue murder and offers a reward for information on the arson attack. He suspects the environmentalists, of course."

"Why 'of course?'" asked Agnes.

"Because they refuse to leave his campground. Most booked until Thursday and are still there now. Brought in more and more of their buddies yesterday intend on squatting long term, he fears. Like the old Occupy movement or so."

"Well, he can call in the police," said Agnes, bored with Dieken's plight. "Aren't they investigating the blaze?"

"Yes, but—"

"If they've paid, they don't squat," interrupted Polly. "More to the point; how sure are you Dieken got something useful on Ponytail?"

"A mere hunch. Holds back and becomes evasive when I start to probe…" One hand scratching his brow, Karl sounded pensive. "Puzzles me. Usually, you can't shut him up.— Remember Erika saying Hinrich threatened Ronny with letting the cat out of the bag, or something, if he backed off their deal?"

Bewildered, Agnes searched for a trace of memory. Too much happened in the meantime. Or senility setting in…

A stranger to mental data loss, Polly sniffed like a terrier scenting a trail. "I wonder… Think he'd do an info trade—dirt on Rosso for a lead on the arsonists?"

"Hey? What do you mean?" Bolt upright now, Karl's full attention focused on the imp. The reason for her interest in the fire, Agnes thought uneasily.

"Just answer. Would he spill, and can you arrange for us to meet?"

"Yeah, sure. He's not going anywhere far right now." A satisfied nod from Polly prompted a change of topics. "Another tidbit for our records. Listen."

Grins lopsided like a dog offering his cherished ball, tail wagging, Agnes diagnosed complacently.

"You recall Eibo owes me some?" In reaction to Agnes's wide-eyed frown, he explained, "The cop you met first on the fateful day."

"Oh." Agnes's voice went flat. "What about him?"

"Cornered him this morning, and he caved in. Hey, for your ears only though." A conspiratorial glance from one to the other, and motioning them closer, he leaned his head forward. When Agnes automatically followed suit, he winked at her, before his face grew stern. "It's murder." His voice reminiscent of a hushed shout. "Well, homicide, to be more precise," he amended.

"So? Didn't we assume that all along?"

"Indeed, Polly." One finger shot up in triumph as he pointed out smugly, "Assumptions are not knowledge, are they? Forensics say he didn't pass out and drown—he suffocated. In the sand— under duress, not merely accidentally."

"How did they establish—"

"No idea, pal. You don't think Eibo lets me read the forensic report or something? He claims they premise the investigation on willful homicide. He took a chance telling me."

"Helpful of him," admitted Polly. "What's your hold over this cop?"

Uncomfortable, Karl wriggled in his chair as he brushed off the question with a wave of his hand. Arms stretched up, he brought them down with a resounding slap on his thighs. "Gotta head back with the booze. How about I give Hinrich a buzz now? Never averse to free beer, my dear neighbor. We could chat with him at my place in half an hour or so."

"Alright with me. What about you, Aggie?"

"Yes, only planned dinner with Mom tonight. In town, though. Takes me too long to cycle forth and back."

"Guy can drive you, or you can take my motor. We'll pop your bike in the back."

"Let's get cracking." Polly jumped up.

"We need to pay," said Agnes.

"Hey—My promise." Two fingers in her mouth, Polly issued a piercing whistle that made Agnes's hands shoot up to cover her ears. "Demian!" The shout further shattered the peaceful afternoon daze of the garden.

On command, the goth appeared from the back door, met by Polly halfway. With a flourish, she took him by the hand. Both bowed to Karl and Agnes. Like a courtier, the elf intoned, "May I present to you, His Highness, Demian, the Gorgeous Gothic." The two of them smiled at each other and winked.

"Hey, man. That pleased to meet ya," the server uttered. A royal wave and he turned on his heels to march back.

"Wait," called out Agnes. "Our bill!"

A salute and he vanished gracefully.

"Don't fret. All taken care of." One hand reaching for Agnes, Polly skipped ahead to the gate. Cell phone to his ear, Karl trailed after them.

Chapter 37
POLLY

"Can I buy these charming young ladies a drink?" Man-of-the-world charm laid on thick, his voice all syrupy, Dieken reached out and pawed Agnes's arm.

"*Lass man, Hinrich.* Never mind. All on the house. What can I get you?"

Way to go, Karl! Polly cheered silently as he insinuated his body in between, elegantly forcing the old sod to take his paw back. On cue, Agnes slid away to the bar to help with the drinks.

Strategically choosing a rectangular table, Karl deposited Hinrich's beer at the head and, catching Polly's eye indicated for her to sit opposite him towards the middle, to shield Agnes at the foot end.

Oblivious to the maneuver, Dieken eyed Karl for a moment. Arm stretched along the back of his chair, his other hand tilted back his seaman's cap. "So, where's your maid of all trades today? Sent her for a decent haircut and manicure, did you?"

At his guttural "hohoho," Polly's stomach churned. Nails digging into her thighs, she prevented a bilious outburst. No use antagonizing the geezer, or he'll never spit out any info.

"As much as I like a chummy chat, we're here for a reason. Confidential," said Karl.

No longer jocular, the campground proprietor narrowed his eyes in a hard expression. "What's up? On the phone, you said you had something for me. Seeing you with these two beautiful women here, I thought—"

"Not likely, Hinrich. Some information of interest to you—about the fire—"

"The fire!" Purple spots appeared on his jowls. Both hands grabbed the corners of the table. "What could you—or these good ladies—possibly know of it?"

"Something she's got a hold of might help identify the culprits." A jerk of his chin at Polly, he avoided using names.

The dude's steel-blue eyes boring into hers disconcerted her. With forced calm, she said, "We want some info you can give and are willing to trade. To make it fair, I show you a bit and after you come across, you receive the rest."

The purple intensified and a gurgling sound escaped before the man shrieked at Karl, "What kind of crap is this? A slip of a chick tell me about arson?" Half-raising himself, he stared from Polly to Agnes. "Who the hell are they?"

"Calm down, Hinrich. The way you raved like mad about catching the arsonist bastards—we thought—I—want to help you." Head stretched forward to regard the older man closely, he asked, "A schnapps? Steady your nerves?"

Amazed how the old dude allowed Karl to lead him like a lamb to the bar, Polly went and crouched on her haunches beside Agnes. "You okay? All pale and jittery you are. Let Karl and me handle this." Head bent now over her knees, hands clasped so tightly the knuckles and veins sticking out, Agnes's hair shrouded her face. At the sight, Polly's throat constricted. On their own accord, her fingers stroked Agnes's to ease the tension. "So sorry I didn't stop to think. Should never have let you come along."

At this, Agnes faced her. "No, Polly, if anyone, it's you who shouldn't be involved. Since we decided the three of us are in this together, we need to live with the fallout." A mischievous grin split her mouth wide. "Besides, who are you, sister, to let or not let me?"

An artificial cough announced Karl's return as he crossed the room, balancing a tray perched on his right hand. In his wake followed Dieken, a half-empty shot glass in hand. When the women shook their heads at the raised schnapps bottle, Karl poured a finger's width for himself, yet put it down untouched.

"Told Hinrich here what we want, and he's agreed to tell us if our info proves worth his while, he says."

"No point shielding the dead. What business of yours it is beats me." A vicious glare at Agnes, he breathed schnapps fumes enough to make her push her chair back. "You're the daughter of the Canadian woman. Could've realized right away. You found poor Ronny. Easy to find out your name. If I cared." Disgusted he switched his attention to Polly. "What's this stuff you got for me?"

Instead of answering, Polly extracted her iPhone with extra slow deliberation from her pocket and busied herself pulling up a file with a blurred image of Torch she had prepared on their ride back from town.

"You dare tape this or shoot photos of me, and I'll have your garters—"

"Don't get your knickers in a twist, Hinrich. Here, you need a refill."

Wordlessly Polly held the iPhone in front of Dieken's face. With a short 'ah,' she sat back when he made a grab for it. "Keep your hands off. Better ones come your way when you've told us what we want."

"Hold it still then, dame. Not gonna buy any damn cat in a bag."

The picture she offered for inspection showed the house in flames with Tor only in silhouette.

"How in hell did you get this?" fumed Dieken in renewed wrath.

Glad no one else is home here, Polly thought. The man clamors enough to wake the dead.

"Were you there? Are you a bleeding arsonist?" Whipping around, he yelled at Karl, "What is this? *Die ist eine von denen!*"

No, I'm not one of them, Polly wanted to shout back. Fascinated she watched him splutter and spew oaths, his face crimson, blue veins popping up on his temples.

"Wow, man. Take a hold of yourself and pipe down. People can hear you all the way down the street." One-handed he grabbed Dieken—who had jumped up, clenched fists holding onto the table—and pulled him back down into the seat. "Two witnesses can vouch for her at the time of the fire. What makes you think she took the pics herself?"—Smart thinking, Karl; Polly gave him silent kudos.—"Seems you're satisfied they are of value to you."

"Another two or three are far clearer. They should help trace whoever did this to you." Her voice all little-girl-innocent, Polly aimed for a shy expression to soothe the man into compliance.

Deflated after his outburst, Dieken slumped speechless in his chair.

"You need a strong coffee, my friend. The espresso machine is already on. Anyone else for a short?"

"No thanks, Karl. We use the Ladies in the meantime," said Polly. A breather to regroup would serve better than caffeine, she reckoned.

When they got back, Karl had cleared the earlier debris and placed mugs and a glass teapot within reach. Glad for a hot drink, they both nodded assent when Karl offered to pour. The patio door opened, and Dieken returned from a smoke break, to judge by the stench, Polly noted. Nose deep in a mug, he ignored them.

In a leisurely tone, Karl eased him into conversation. "Got a feeling you and Ronny go back a long way, don't you?" Stirring sugar into his tiny cup, he continued, "Never met the man to speak to. Quite a guy, eh? Did you like him?"

The more questions Karl heaped on, the deeper Dieken's frown grew. Now he shook his head impatiently. "Liked him? Where does that come in? *Gott, ja*, been kind of buddies forever. Never thought about liking him or not."

At least he warms to his topic and will relax his guard, Polly figured.

Mug balanced on his chubby thigh, he reminisced almost dreamily. "Takes you right back, doesn't it? Played together as kids. Two, three years younger than most of us in the gang. Chaps older than him couldn't keep up the way he scored *mit den Weibern*—broads, I mean," he added with a leer.

"The gang?" interrupted Agnes. Annoyed, Polly kicked her shin under the table and rolled her eyes to shut her up. Let the man talk.

Eyes unfocused as though tuned in to visions of the past, Dieken stared at the wall. His inattention enabled Polly to fumble with her iPhone in her lap to activate a recording app.

"Figure of speech. The local lads, if you wish." A throaty chuckle. "Our Randy was mostly into skirts—*Weiber*—Bragged he lost his virginity at twelve." Fleshy lips pursed, his tongue glided over them in slow motion. "Swarmed around him *wie die Motten um's Licht*—like moths around the light—the hussies did." Hooded eyes strayed once more to Agnes.

Across from her, Karl's jaw muscles contracted. His right hand, balled into a fist, swiped under his chin. A gentle nudge with her toes, Polly tried to head him off. Fingers spreading, he visibly forced himself to relax.

With a soft chuckle, he mimicked Dieken's mood. "Randy, eh? Got the name from his conquests—"

"*Nee, nee. So hiess der.* Did you take Ronny Rosso for his real name?" An amused rasp at their ignorance. "Plain Randolph Harmsen he used to be. Randy for short. Hahaha—went after the chicks to prove he earned it. Quite a legend around here in the days of yore."

Holy mackerel—the plot thickens. To avoid her glance straying to her conspirators, Polly stared at the ceiling.

"Strange. Why the heck use a pseudonym here if he's a local?" Trust Karl to keep his cool.

"Just the point. They'd forgot all about randy Randolph. No one recognized him. Or so he thought."

"Well, you did. Didn't he realize?"

At Agnes's quiet question, he waved dismissively. "Completely different case, young lady. Of course, he did. After all, we kept in touch over the years. Off and on. Never doubted he could trust me."

Yeah, right. Not if what Karl's Erika says is true, Polly silently sneered.

"Still… I don't understand," persisted Agnes. "Why the false name? Surely, being a Bosumer benefited his sale's pitch for the wind farm?"

A snort and headshake showed what he thought of her point. "Bound to kill his scheme. People still bear a grudge for how he left." Voice lowered, he leaned forward. "Made off with some floozy. Underage."

Winks at Agnes, the sod! Polly gritted her teeth.

"A few claimed he'd abducted her." Artful pause calculated to increase their outrage, before he complaisantly demolished any belief in teenage innocence. "Fat chance! Flung herself at him. Another of the moths caught in his light." The witticism bowled him over in mirth. "Couldn't shake her off, poor guy."

"C'mon, man! A bit much—"

"*Nee,* Karl. For real. Said so himself when he finally dumped her." Still gasping, Dieken wiped his face with his sleeve.

Here comes our clue, thought Polly. Yet the ancient mariner

made no move to continue. Instead, he consulted his wristwatch. Toe-nudging Karl once more prompted his inane remark, "So hard on a dude being chased by a minor—"

"Ha, hah! Hard on him—hahaha—exact—" Raucous laughter and knee-slapping choked off his words. "You always pick the perfect word, my friend." Tears build in the creases of the wrinkly, now puffy, eyes.

To calm him, Karl poured him a mug of now tepid tea. "What a yarn," he said. "So, how did he manage to be shot of her?"

Sobered sufficiently, the tattletale adopted a hushed tone. "Tell you the truth—left her behind in India, he did.—Or Goa? Kathmandu?"

Why search us for the answer? Fed up with his narration style, Polly wriggled in her seat.

"Stupid bitch got herself pregnant. When she took sick on top of that, Randy lost patience. Mind you, made sure a native midwife or someone cared for her. Cost him almost all the money they'd scrounged from nitwit tourists. The trip back turned into a nightmare. Beaten up a couple of times and hitch-hiked for weeks in their horrible rain season."

Are we to feel sorry for the bastard? Nails dug into her palms, Polly suppressed an urge to shout. The creaking of their raconteur's chair, as he rocked to and fro on its hint legs, ground on her nerves. Now he scrutinized the ceiling for further inspiration, or to refresh his memory.

A crash landing stimulated his mental faculties. For he ended, "A real mess he looked when I ran into him in Italy. Rich lonely widow paid for his last passage by boat. No idea how he managed to pay her back in her cabin. Or the merry widow took the wind out of his sail."

Sick to her stomach of the guy, Polly groaned, while Karl chuckled dutifully. "What a lad. How long ago are we talking?"

"*Och*, '70s or '80s, maybe?" As if the past retreated farther as he attempted to pinpoint it, the elderly face grew vague.

"Who was the girl?"

The censorious undertone of Agnes's question raised alarm bells in Polly. Shoot, he'll clam right up.

"Young woman, don't expect me to reveal names. The family still lives here.—Or some of them," he said in an aside. Brought to his senses, he recalled their trade deal and confronted Polly. "I did my share. Now hand over the pictures."

"Okeydokey—I'll email them tonight."

"Send them to me? You out of your mind, bitch? Karl, I'm not leaving until you deliver on your promise!"

"*Immer mit der Ruhe*, Hinrich. Easy does it, man." Calm and soothing in words and tone, Karl sought to reassure his neighbor. "Don't you worry; the pics are yours. Won't keep them all on her cell phone, will she? What's your email? Here, write it down."

From a table behind him, he fished a coaster and whipped a pen from his shirt pocket. Address jotted down, Dieken threw it in front of Polly but spoke to Karl, "Those photos are in my inbox by seven tonight, or you'll regret crossing me."

A full body turn, and he loomed over Polly. "Show me again."

With a shrug, she dug out the iPhone she'd slipped into her pocket again a minute ago, leaving the file open. Without delay, she offered a view of Torch in his element, illuminated by the flames, hair streaming out, and fist raised against the sky.

The sight caught Dieken's breath in his throat, he rasped and grunted. Blood shot into his face, hands grabbed the edge of the table to steady himself. Easy to imagine what it must cost him not to lunge for the phone.

To speed things up before he could burst a vessel, she swiped to a close-up of Tor's arm holding up a canister, followed by a third image, a skinny hooded figure slinking away from the blaze. A rear shot; unclear whether male or female.—Unless, she thought, you'd caught him crouched down in the hall gallery and recognized him as Flipper. End of show—she pressed the side button and pocketed the mobile.

"Who are these bastards?"

The no-nonsense sternness made her glance at him. "How should I know? Came across some pics. No idea of anything else."

"*Die will mich wohl verarschen,*" protested Dieken and grabbed Karl's shoulder.

"No, she isn't effing—or otherwise—kidding you. Listen—"

"You just wait," Dieken hissed at Polly. "German police make you squeal soon—"

"Hinrich! No threats, please. Listen, as far as we are concerned, this conversation never took place."

"What do you mean, man? I sure as hell plan to pass them on to the cops."

"By all means, feel free to forward the email. Come to think of it, better still, they'll be on a stick drive delivered to your mailbox," said Karl.

Hey, clever idea, grinned Polly, giving him a discreet thumbs-up. Don't want this to be traceable.

The unexpected change provoked the man's wrath and made him splutter, "*Du wirst noch von mir hören!*"

Unimpressed, Karl echoed, "Yes, I'm sure I'll hear from you again, Hinrich. As long as you remember: we never saw you today."

Close to apoplexy, Dieken stormed to the door. The dramatic exit was somewhat mucked up when his haste propelled him right against its glass. In vain, he'd tried to yank it open. Apparently, Karl had locked up for privacy.

Chapter 38

AGNES

"Are you alright?"

Lost in her resentment, Agnes hadn't noticed Karl coming back from opening the door for the odious campground person. What a slimy creature! A shudder brought Karl to her side. The nearness of his masculine body infuriated her. Men! Far from stopping the disgusting foul comments about the poor girl, he egged him on. Joined in this shyster's laughter!

"Hey, what's wrong, Agnes? Why are you staring at me like that?"

How dare he play innocent ignorance now—

"Whoa! What's eating you?" Now the imp chimed in—looming over her too.

The touch of Polly's hand on her arm brought her anger to the boiling point—shaking it off, she jumped up and faced them.

"I don't understand how you two can sit there listening to this horrible jerk spouting awful things. Cackle at his innuendos! Yes, Karl, don't dare deny it. For Christ's sake, he applauds seducing a minor and dumping her thousands of miles from home when she is pregnant. The way he himself ogles and harasses women. Patronizing bastard!"

Exhausted, Agnes stopped and collapsed onto her chair—hating herself for the uncontrollable outburst, yet sure of being self-righteously right.

The calm male voice penetrated through the fog of her mind in turmoil. "C'mon, I merely indulged his mood to keep him talking. Don't think he'd continue if I tell him his opinions of women suck, or do you?"

To this, Polly nodded like a cheerleader, saying, "Only pretended to go along—"

"*Nee*, Polly. To claim to be holier than thou would be quite disingenuous of me. Make no mistake; in the '70s, we were sexually liberated and carefree. Pre-AIDS, remember. Not terribly unusual for a fifteen or sixteen-year-old to get herself pregnant."

"Get *herself* pregnant?" The screech jarred her own ears. More controlled Agnes said, "A woman hardly achieves that by herself."

"Yeah, takes a man. For sure." Arms waving to placate her, he explained, "All I mean—both guys and gals indulged in free love. Especially hippies bound for India, the *Kamasutra* wrapped in their sleeping roll. Heck, tons of chicks and dudes over the years I've hung out with shared a loose attitude to sex and subscribe to a—by your standards—lousy moral. Women no less than men. Majorca ain't no convent."

Supposed to endear him to her, was it? In disdain, Agnes shook her tresses.

A faint murmur, "Been a changed man since—"

Before he could go further, she burst out, against her better judgment—after all, what was he to her to care one way or another. "Aah, the roaring '70s justify leaving a pregnant and sick girl stranded? Penniless, without friends, and no one to turn to. For God's sake. How could a teenager communicate with anyone there? The man made her elope with him and got her pregnant. So, she was his responsibility."

"Aren't you jumping to conclusions?" All reasonableness, Karl crossed his arms.

"Sounds downright Victorian, Aggie."

The betrayal of the two whom she regarded as friends robbed her of speech—wishing to clasp her palms over her ears to shut out their treasonous opinions. Instead, her fists grabbed masses of hair and pulled to divert the pain.

The reasonable voice droned on. "First off, you can't be sure Randy—Ronny, whatever—put her in the club. Make love not war times—"

"Slander her, why—"

"Listen before you judge me. Secondly, Hinrich mentioned the guy left her all his money. Yeah," hand raised at her glare of protest, "not much, most likely. Can assume they lived off petty theft and begging. Back in the day, Goa and Kathmandu were flooded by foreigners. Everyone drifted east—a veritable Babel. Plenty of people she could ask for help and—"

"In short, you agree with this despicable jerk. Perfectly okay to abandon a pregnant and sick teen?" In shouting, her hands grabbed the edges of the table to jump up and leave.

"Calm down, Agnes. Didn't say anything of the kind. For the record, even in my wildest days, or now—no matter whether I had fathered the child or not—I would never turn my back on anyone in need, ill or pregnant, male or female. Pray to God, I never will."

As if regretting his pathos, he shook his head mockingly. "Listen to me…and me not even believing in one. At least not the one the churches sell."

"Guys, please stop." The imp rose and waved like an umpire. "None of this is about our own beliefs or opinions, I thought. Though, personally, I deny anyone the right to expect others to be saints." Her childlike fingers stretched towards Agnes without touching. "We need to move." To set the tone, she whipped out her iPhone. "What do we do—"

"Could you show me that photo again? You know, of the skinny one sidling off?"

Surprised, she fiddled with the mobile. "Here. Take it."

Bent down to peer closely at the screen, Karl frowned at the image. A slight, impatient head shake, he handed the phone back. "Thought it reminded me of—Nah, can't recall."

"Might come back later," she soothed him.

"Yeah, maybe…" Unconvinced, his glance drifted around the room.

"Well. Shall we?" No-nonsense brisk, Polly reverted to her usual energetic self. "I suggest we list all information gathered thus far. After sifting through, we draw inferences and connections and figure out where we dig in next. All onboard?"

Still stewing in resentment, Agnes refused to respond. Arms crossed, she observed Polly digging into her messenger bag to pull out an iPad and a mini keyboard. God, she came all equipped. High-tech Polly, we should call her. Despite her desire to hang on to her wrath, Agnes's analytic training kicked in and tickled her curiosity.

Amazed, she followed the elfin fingers flying over the keys, typing at lightning speed. To read along, she positioned herself close to Polly. With the same idea, Karl moved in on the other side.

"Let's use bullet point form," said Polly, and proceeded to give a running commentary as the text appeared.

Ronny Rosso [RR]

- Ronny Rosso identified as Randolph (Randy) Harmsen;
- Local; born in London; raised on Bosum by his uncle;
- Mother: single mom, died when RR was a kid; uncle mistreated him;

- RR sexually active as teen (popular with females);
  prone to assault;

"Hey, Polly. Don't exaggerate. No evidence for being prone to violence. Hit his uncle in self-defense, by Emma's account. What would you do if someone beat you up for years?"

An odd glance at Karl, before Polly revised the wording to his nodding approval.

- RR sexually active as teen (popular with females)—
  allegedly hit his uncle after years of provocation;
- In his late 20s, left Bosom accompanied by a 15-year-old girl;
- Went to India (or Goa?)
- RR returned alone via Italy ('70s or '80s—Dieken claims)

At this point, Agnes cleared her throat. Wouldn't do to suppress facts merely to spare her feelings. "Kind of you to leave it out, Polly. Yet for consistency's sake you need to insert his affair—or whatever—with Sera."

"Well, 'sexually active' covers this and similar ones. Can always add details later, if you like." While speaking, she typed the next line.

- Abandoned the pregnant and ill teenager (at 15 or 16) in India (Kathmandu or Goa?) [Source: Dieken]
- Girl: Sandra (Sandy) Harms; Kai & Udo Harms' sister [Source: Emma Shoemaker]
- At some point, Randy changed his name to Ronny Rosso;
- Dieken kept contact and was aware of name change & history;
- On recent return to Bosum, RR failed to disclose his identity;

- Acted as *WKA* agent for Niederwinder & Co;
- Feared local repercussions [source: Dieken] (e.g. from Sandra's family, i.e. Kai & Udo?)
- RR and Dieken struck a deal about *WKA* site search —RR tried to rescind [implied by Erika's testimony]

A loud slap interrupted—Karl hitting his forehead with the palm of his hand. "Got it! Reminds me of the guy Erika saw slinking off to the beach."

"Who?" "What?" The women spoke in unison.

"The pic—the one you showed Hinrich." When they still regarded him uncomprehendingly, he said, "Erika said someone entered the dune path Sunday night. The photo fused with the mental image."

"Hold on—didn't you say she couldn't tell whether male or female? Where does 'guy' come in?"

Leave it to Polly to spot vital details, Agnes admitted grudgingly.

The imp's mind jumped onto another track. "Let's add her to the list."

"Hey, she didn't do it," protested Karl. Rather weakly, Agnes thought.

Enmities:

- Erika's grounds for grudge against RR—he harassed her the night before he died;
- Dieken has a hold over RR he intended to leverage in case of deal breaking [source: Erika overheard Dieken threaten RR]
- Dieken's aware of RR's true identity & history;
- Animosity between RR and Daniel Dregger (DD)— RR threatened DD with revelation akin to the Guttenberg [plagiarism] scandal;

The typing ceased. Vigorously, Polly rubbed her fingers and stretched them. "Apropos—did you tell Karl about DD? You doing coffee with him?"

The questioning glance their male conspirator leveled at her made Agnes self-conscious. Silly, she scolded herself, he doesn't give a hoot who you chat with. Nor do you care if he cares.

Nonetheless, she stumbled and blundered through an abridged, choppy account of the bookstore encounter. "Plan to google further," she ended lamely. "The father's academic track record—"

Not giving Karl a chance to respond, Polly cut in, "Our RR sure made a lot of enemies, didn't he?"

Fingers hacking away at her keypad, she typed:

- Various environmentalist groups and individuals;
- *Wattwächter*, especially spokesperson Hermann;

"What's his last name?" asked Polly. "Or Mattie's? Any idea?"

"Not off-hand—should be in her emails."

"No worries. Although—" Rather than finish her thought, she wrote,

- Local property owners, e.g. Hermann and Mathilda
  —RR died close to their cottage;

The image of her landlady floated unbidden into Agnes's mind. "She dyes her hair blond...on the heavy side too..."

"What are you mumbling to yourself?"

Unlike their pal, the elf followed effortlessly. "Sure—could be. Didn't hubby mention she's from around here?"

"Who the heck are you talking about?"

"Mathilda—duh." No patience with anyone so dense, Polly rolled her eyes. "Being almost neighbors, you must be acquainted."

"Yeah, sure I am. Männi and her come by once in a blue moon. Don't mix with the likes of me. Or he doesn't. A trifle bossy, isn't she?"

"Well, yah." Uninterested in the tangent, Polly zeroed in on what mattered. "Facts: she's an artificial blond and a local. Question: Is she the right age?"

"For what?" Still confused, he threw up his hands.

"Being Sandra! Man, are you ever—"

"Rubbish! Why she'd been recognized by her brothers ages ago. How likely for her not to go running to them on her return? A load of bull, I say."

"No idea," Polly retorted. "Worth looking into, don't you reckon?"

The force of Karl's objection struck Agnes. Highly unlikely to remain incognito in a small place. Yet, what if they were in it together? What maelstrom of emotions would Randy's home-coming unleash?

On the same wavelength, Karl mused, "Must admit, the brothers do seem to pop up too often. Makes you wonder… What if they cottoned on to Rosso?" Lost in thought, he scratched his forehead. "Didn't Hinrich hint at something…" A slap on his thigh. "No use. Was thinking just now, I'll try them again tomorrow morning. Chances are they'll clam up. Taciturn pair."

"Why don't I chat them up?"

On the verge of a smartass rejoinder, to judge by his smirk, he refrained. "Yeah, a light touch might work. Come over at seven, if not too early for you. Bring back the van; I'll need it first thing."

In disbelief, Agnes stared at them. "Are you crazy! You can't let Polly talk to them on her own. What if they did murder him?"

Before she could call her too tiny to defend herself, Polly burst in, "Who's he to let me or not?"

"Whoa, pipe down you two. It'll be the three of us. I'll not put anyone in harm's way. Hey, that's a pun." Childishly happy with his linguistic achievement, he grinned at them. "While we prepare breakfast, we take turns standing on guard at the window. Never doubted your capability to look after yourself, Polly. Still, real friends help each other."

"What else do we need to do?" Back to business, Polly answered her own question, "Your job, Agnes, find out Mathilda's provenance without raising suspicion. At least her maiden name, can you?"

For a moment Agnes stalled before she awkwardly plunged headlong. "As a matter of fact—I intended to drop by anyway to ask about terminating the rental agreement early." Neither one of them spoke. Yet, they observed her intently. So, she rattled on, "Perfect opportunity to—" Still no reaction. "I'm sorry, Mom and I consider spending the rest of our vacation somewhere else."

Both of them jumped into speech now simultaneously. "Makes sense. Can't expect you to stay after—" "No sweat, Aggie. Do what's best for you and Sera."

Deflated, Agnes bit her lips. Shoulders hunched, her mind spun on. They just don't care. What did you expect? Them clutching the hem of your skirt in tears? I don't wear skirts. Throw themselves into your path? Dream on. You've barely known them for a few days. Eyes tearing up, she hung her head to hide behind the curtain of her hair.

Delicate fingers enfolded hers in a brief squeeze. Two big hands warmly closed around her shoulders.

The spell broke when the imp bounced into action. Her paraphernalia collected and stowed, she allotted Karl's task. "Try to pump Dieken. What did the deal with Ronny amount to? How did they stay in touch over the years? Etc. etc."

"Aye, aye, Sir!" A click of his heels—more a thud—he saluted. "Save the photos on a USB stick and drop them off here. I'll pop them in his mailbox. The fuzz is used to me and Castro out for a midnight stroll."

"What if the odious man calls the cops if he does not receive them by seven?"

"No worries, Agnes. Stay calm. Once you leave, I'll give him a buzz and tell him to expect delivery after closing time." A glance at the ceiling brought inspiration. "In case he acts up, I hint at a certain conversation he had about a deal the other night. Vague enough but clear to him."

"All set, are we?" Bag slung over her shoulder, Polly chafed to leave.

In response, Karl dug car keys out of his pocket and dropped them gently into Agnes's lap. "Here, treat her well— prone to be a little temperamental."

"Wow, how's that for sexism? Karl, me dear, you've got a long way to go, baby." With a roll of her eyes, the imp strode to the door.

Chapter 39

AGNES

The wood of the window frame pressed into Agnes's arm. To ease the discomfort, she bent forward. All peaceful for the moment—yet nervous anxiety fluttered below her ribs. Behind her, she sensed his warm body again. Close enough for transmission of heat, without touching. Heartbeat, accelerated despite her inactivity, throbbed in her ears—embarrassingly loud, she feared.

One hand cupping the window frame above her head, he leaned in, his chin brushing her hair. "Anything happening yet?"

"No—still unloading. She's helping fetch and carry."

The touch of his chest on her shoulder burned through the light cotton sweater. Unable to move, she stared out. When Karl withdrew to continue breakfast preparations, she felt strangely bereft.

A potent aroma of strong coffee, mixed with baking scent, permeated the kitchen. Croissants, her nose deduced.

"Eggs okay with you?"

In answer, she nodded without facing him.

"Whoa, Agnes, relax. You are as tense as..." The analogy remained unfinished, as she startled when his breath tickled her ear. Willing complete immobility, she managed to suppress another shiver.

"Must ache for a massage." Without waiting for a response, his fingers gently kneaded her upper back and neck. "Didn't realize your observation post might be so nerve-racking for you."

Something in her wanted to shout at him to stop. The traitor in her gave way and offered her up to his ministrations. Almost forgotten sensations flooded her body.

A sudden image brought her to herself. "Where is Erika?"

"Upstairs making the beds, I suppose." All casual, Karl's voice floated over her head.

Offense crimsoning her face, she spun around. Here he is coming on to me, while—

Mischievous, Karl's eyes lit up as they locked on to hers. "Nah, not what you think." Flat palms brushing one last time along the curve of her shoulders, he moved back a step. "Erika cleans and tidies the apartment for me. Supposed to once a week. Every few days, if things are quiet, I catch her sneaking up armed with a broom or something."

In reaction to a buzzing timer, he crossed to the oven. "Thinks two bachelors like Guy and me can't cope on their own. Me! Who's done his own cleaning and cooking for years. Important for her to be needed, I guess." As if reading her thoughts, he hastened on, "Never intrudes if us guys are up there. We respect each other's privacy." A slow wink and he devoted himself to stirring a pot.

To her embarrassment, she realized how mesmerized she was listening—to the point of neglecting her vigil. To compound the distraction, a heavenly smell now suffused the air, wafting from a baking tray of steaming croissants. More relaxing even than his words. A male who can bake, cook, and housekeep. What a treat. Satisfied, she took up her task, a crooked smirk at the reversed sexism.

The sight she beheld made her stiffen. Both hands gripping

the windowsill, she abandoned all caution, nose almost touching the glass. The brothers—who had appeared laid back earlier—now jumped up, their faces distorted by emotion.

"Scrambled okay by you?"

"Karl, quickly!" Not turning around, when he leaned over her to catch a glimpse, she urged him, panic in her voice, "There! You've got to do something." Yeah, superman to the rescue, her calmer self mocked.

"We got to help," she corrected herself, craning her neck to confront him. "She's done it! What if they are dangerous?"

Outside the men stood motionless and evidently speechless.

"Nah, don't fret. Our Polly manages fine. Shocked them a little, no doubt."

Indeed, the taller one clutched at his face, hand covering his mouth, and then turned away. The morning sun bathed the other brother's features in a soft light, wide-eyed expression of disbelief. Stunned rather than warped by rage. Across from him, Polly continued talking as if nothing was amiss, oblivious to their reactions. The first one hung his head and softly kicked at the gravel of the parking lot.

"Time to step in, so she can make her exit," said Karl. "A strong brew and fresh croissants should do the trick."

Next minute, he hollered from the door, "Hey, pal, brekkie's ready."

The two men straightened up as if caught slacking on the job.

"*Kaffee Pause! Hallo, Udo!*"

Hailed for a 'coffee break,' the shorter of the two moved towards the door. Must be Udo, Agnes deduced, as Karl handed him a heaping plate of pastries and a thermos. With a start, she realized how rude it was to be staring out at the man still shaken and disoriented. How distasteful the whole thing was. Determined to speak to the imp alone, she crossed the kitchen.

In the hallway, Polly rushed by, raised fingers spread. "Need the loo. Be right back."

"Hey, Agnes, grab that batch of croissants from the counter, and let's eat. I'm going to run late otherwise." Without stopping, Karl brushed past her and proffered the fragrant goodies. "We'll use the table on the right of the patio doors." A gentle shove with one hand on her back, he stirred her into action.

In the dining room, Polly materialized next to her, calling out to Karl, "Can't we have breakfast outside? It's such a glorious morning." How flippant and carefree after ruining those guys' day! Day? Crushed them, period.

"Let's better stay where we are." From close behind, Karl cut into Agnes's mental outrage. "Afraid you're in for a lashing, Polly, and we don't want the neighbors—and hired labor—to listen in." A teasing jut of his chin at Agnes, "Storm clouds are gathering."

"Me? What did I do wrong now?" The imp threw herself into a chair.

"Make it quick, Agnes, so that we can eat in peace. Aggro is hazardous for my digestion," said Karl, reaching for the thermos carafe of coffee.

Clenched fists, Agnes took a deep breath to let fly.

Two little palms jerked up as if threatened by a gun, Polly beat her to it. "I know; I know—shock therapy. You disapprove. Yeah, you've said so before. With due respect, I beg to differ." For emphasis, she waved her croissant and bit into it. In response to Karl's proffering the coffee pot, she held out her mug. Flakes spewing, she mumbled, "No alternative. How else would we determine they don't put on an act? Should have seen their faces. Man, if ever guys were bowled over, it's them."

"Here, take a sip of water, Sherlock, before you choke your-self to death," their host remarked unperturbed.

Instead, Polly added hot milk from a steaming stainless steel pitcher. Still stirring, she asked him, "The dudes are not members of the local theatrics outfit or something?"

Head crocked sideways, Karl considered the question. "Not to my knowledge. Don't look the type either."

"Ah—and what's the type like? Gay, with dainty, fake accents?"

"Polly! He meant no such thing!"

"No, she's right, Agnes. I stand corrected. Not my mental image of actors at all—your point's well-taken, though. Countless kinds of people are drawn to the profession, never mind to amateur theater."

"Fatuous of me—forget it. Still, no other way to be sure they weren't lying. Or they might clam up. Not your most chatty blokes, are they?"

"To blurt it out point-blank was totally brutal. Plus, now they wonder how you knew Rosso's identity in the first place."

"What do you take me for, Watson?" The imp sat bolt upright, arms akimbo. "First off, brutality is not my style. Second, I don't blunder." A sip of her *café au lait* steadied her. "Promise to eat your breakfast, and I'll tell you all about it."

"Yeah, Agnes, dig in. Eggs gonna be shoe leather on the warming plate." The lid of the serving dish dripped condensation water as Karl lifted it.

Not to offend him, Agnes took a generous helping and forked up a bit. Mmm—oh God, how delicious. "What did you put in there? Downright fabulous."

"Basil, fresh from the garden, and a touch of smoked salmon. Pinch of very special cheese." The delight in her approval set his face aglow.

"Okay, Polly, out with your story." Her mouth full of delectable food, Agnes's anger evaporated.

"Here goes. First, we chatted about sweet nothing. Soon, the conversation turned to the fire—talk of the town, of course. Allowed me to mention rumors. Stuck with what was in the local rag—mildly embroidered. Speaking of rumors, I said, did you come across this strange gossip? As insiders, you must know if it's true. Garnered their full attention—local pride." An elfin little hand reached for Agnes.

"Gentle, wasn't I, Aggie? Broke it slowly. Bloke found dead

on the beach, people say, hailed from Bosum. To give them time to chew on it, I declared it seemed highly unlikely. Only when they got used to the idea did I spring it on them: dude's name is not Ronny Rosso but Randy Harms, or Harmsen, or something. They jumped—"

"Yes, I saw them," admitted Agnes. "The very reason it worried me so." A pseudo-apology for her temper tantrum.

A nod from Polly as she tore off a huge piece of croissant with her teeth, chewing noisily. Wiping flakes and butter from her chin with the back of one hand, she took a deep swig of coffee and held out her mug for a refill. Only after she'd thanked Karl and added more milk, did she continue.

"Truth be told; I felt rotten. Shocked, almost devastated by the blow, their faces crumbled. And me—pretending not to notice—spouting inanities. Don't think they took in a word after." With a grateful glance at Karl, "Perfect timing to butt in just then. Couldn't think how to extricate myself." Eyeing them in turn, she concluded, "Don't you agree, they were clueless before?"

"Absolutely. Proven beyond doubt," said Karl. To Agnes, he added, "Told you Polly's on the ball."

Rather than pacifying, it gave new cause for worry. "What if they go around telling everyone?" When neither reacted, she went on, "What if that awful man from the campground finds out we leaked the information? He's nasty enough to take revenge."

"Leave Hinrich to me, Agnes. I can handle him." Calm and unconcerned, Karl sat stroking his chin. "Besides, I don't expect he'd give a hoot if it became front-page news."

"But the police." *Why do you have to whine like that? Can't you stay rational and detached? They'll think you're hysterical,* Agnes's better self chided. *What do I care! I'm upset. I want to whine!*

A quietly assured voice penetrated her mental turmoil. "Precisely what I intended." When Agnes stared at her, uncomprehending, Polly elucidated, "I want the police to catch on."

Stunned, Agnes cried out, "Are you out of your mind?"

"How else would we pass the message to the cops? Call them ourselves saying 'Look what we've found, nah nah nah nahna.'"

"But—" Agnes could only stutter, "but—"

"Aggie, do you want the killer caught, or not? I thought our intention was to help them out—speed up the process, and all?"

Face on fire, Agnes murmured a dejected, "I guess so."

A noisy throat-clearing from Karl, "Girls, ahem, ladies, or should I say, women, in this day and age of emancipation? Let me call this meeting to order." Tension eased, he explained, "I've got to pick up supplies. It's already past eight. Could we make some plans? First off, can I drop you at the cottage?"

An embarrassed demurral from Agnes not to bother since he must be ridiculously busy on a summer weekend, he brushed aside.

"Secondly, can we recapitulate? Where does this leave us now? The brothers are out of the frame, or what? You agree?" They both nodded. "From what you said this morning; so is your Mathilda, *née* Foster."

"What luck Mattie had regaled your mom with her life history," cut in the imp. "Kudos to you for ferreting it out so causally last night."

"Which leaves the mysterious figure Erika spotted entering the beach path." As if he feared his factotum might be listening, Karl's eyes swerved apprehensively to the ceiling. In answer, the silence magnified a faint droning of a vacuum. His brow uncreased.

To Agnes, their entire plotting and sleuthing suddenly appeared ridiculous and futile. Tired and deflated, she wondered, what on earth are we trying to do? We've no clue about anything. Out loud, she said, "Not to mention, countless activists and God knows how many others we've never even touched on. You can't just make up lists and think whoever killed the man must be on them."

"On second thought," interjected Polly, "Mattie and hubby are still in. Your man was hopping mad at Rosso for ruining paradise single-handedly."

"Don't be silly. Someone of his caliber is not going to risk his career and whole future for that," snorted Agnes. "Caught, he'd lose everything—including his chance to enjoy paradise."

"Killers rarely anticipate being nabbed," mused Karl. "Always assume everyone except them is too stupid to figure things out. Otherwise, no one would commit murder, would they?"

"You've got a point," admitted Agnes grudgingly. "Hermann certainly is hubristic enough to believe himself inviolable."

"Well, I'd love to stay and chat; but as they say, a man gotta do—"

"Could I hitch a ride into town, Karl?" Preoccupied, Polly avoided Agnes's astonished glance.

"Tell you what." Palms slapping the table, Karl got up. "How about we all go for a walk on the beach this afternoon. The wind is quite cool. Ideal for a hike. I'll bring Polly back with me around lunchtime. Works for you, Polly?"

"The beach?" Agnes gaped. "I don't think—"

In a gentle tone, Karl coaxed, "Look, Agnes, we've got to exorcise the ghosts. We can't have you and your mom leave next week with this haunting you."

"I don't think my mom—"

"He's right, Aggie. Never good to run away from a bad memory. Nasty habit of sneaking up on you later, memories have. Don't you worry; Sera is strong. I'm sure, she's already decided to go back on her own before leaving. Wouldn't it be better we'd all be there together?"

A sudden vision of her mother alone on the beach this very

moment suffused Agnes with anxiety and shame at her own weakness. Polly was right. So was Karl. Determined, she agreed, "Yes, let's do it."

Chapter 40

POLLY

Polly watched her approach. An ineffable mien suffused the woman's still smooth features. Good bones, plenty of outdoor exercise, and still on a low-carb diet. Or high protein now. Or both. Not a gram of extra fat anywhere on the slim-line frame. Can't remember her ever not watching her weight. Total phobia about it. Curious—not anorexic, though.

As she came closer, the impression of stillness dominated. An indefinable elusive aura of transcendence instilled by a life-long yoga and meditation addiction. The vision of a naked body contorted into impossible knots floated back and overlaid that of the living woman. Taught by a real master, she'd once said.

Doesn't care for this joint, to judge by the disdainful twitch of the nostrils. At least, thought Polly, it's devoid of cake-gobbling matrons at this hour.

"Did you have to pick a dump if you need to talk to me?" Right on, Polly congratulated herself with a grin but chose to keep mum. "You're lucky your message reached me. Why such a roundabout way to begin with? If Mark hadn't found Shady, you'd be waiting for nothing in this godforsaken place."

"Not sure he forsook it," muttered Polly, eyes on the small cross over the entrance. "My messenger was a cert. Always knows where Shady hangs out." He tries so hard to avoid her. "And, where there's a Shady shadow, you're not far off."

"Leave her alone. If more people were of her sincere and loyal sort, the world would be a better place. She never let me down."

'Yet,' added Polly to herself. Grasping her cue, she said, "Speaking of let-downs, any idea where Flipper is?" Bad move. At the mentioning of his name, Nancy threw uneasy glances in all directions as though spies lurked under the abandoned tables. No waiting staff, never mind anyone else, in sight.

Poise regained in a tick, Nancy countered offhandedly, "Why ask me? What is it to you?" Nervous fingers picking at the edge of the table betrayed her.

"*Sind Sie jetzt soweit?*"

Whoa—where did she come from? The gruff waitress materialized next to them like an evil genie from a bottle. Paranoia proved contagious.

"No, we are not ready yet. Give us another minute." The mirrored impatience in Nancy's reflex response annoyed the server into tapping her pencil on her order pad.

To ward off further assault, Polly requested mugs of tea, which heaped insult on injury, if she caught the drift of the dragon's mumbled, 'well worth waiting for,' correctly.

This starts to be entertaining, Polly smirked to herself, watching the waitress retreat through a door behind them. The bow of a white, frilly apron tied on an ample, black-clad behind lent a crowning professional flair and gave the curt manner authoritative license.

Attention recalled by her companion's drumming fingertips, Polly refocused. Wordlessly, she reached into her bag and threw a few photo printouts on the table right in front of Nancy's fingers. Fortunately, the drugstore down the street boasted an instant developing self-serve machine. Saved her from repeating the mistake of showing the originals on her own iPhone. In silence, she observed the older woman across from her.

At first, Nancy made no move to touch the photos, letting her eyes roam. The awesome knack to make her face go blank at will must be useful in police interrogations, Polly speculated. The silence settled in before slender fingertips reached out and —as if afraid to be scorched—pecked at the pics to separate them for a clearer view. Three showed Flipper and one a triumphant Torch. In slow motion the head came up, and devoid of expression she asked, "Where did you get these?"

"Never mind whence and wherefore. Were you in on what these lunatics got up to?"

Instead of responding, Nancy scrutinized the images. Indifferent expression reassembled, she pushed the prints across and rose to leave.

"Wait!" Annoyed at her own outburst, Polly thrust the shot of Flipper furtively leaving the scene right in front of the pacifist's nose.

The sound of the door behind them—clanked open by means of a metal tray—made them both jump. In one sweep, Polly turned the photos face down.

The tray rattled as the waitress banged it onto the table and unloaded two mugs. Armed once more with the salver close to her ample bosom, she unbent to leave two creamers and a couple of tiny lemon slivers on a saucer. Automatically, they thanked her.

Why do we display gratitude for lousy service? If I were German, Polly grumbled to herself, I'd give her a piece of my mind. Won't change her grumpy self. No wonder, when you serve bloody tourists all day—

"What do you want from me?" Crossed arms and stiff back, Nancy refused to comprehend. Neither of them touched their teas.

With slow deliberation, Polly proffered the hooded figure once more. "A person closely resembling this image was observed slinking down the dune path at the café the night Ronny Rosso died."

Wow—bull's eye! Shakes her out of her blasé superiority. Sure enough, blankness shutters her face again like blinds concealing a window. No comment either. Got to up the ante, or I'll lose my audience.

"It was around one AM or so."

Head bent over the picture now, her opponent challenged, "How do you know? Were you there?"

"Me? Are you kidding? Not remotely."

"Then, who told you?"

"Nance, you recall the drill; can't reveal sources." Let's stay professional here. "What I'm saying, did the friggin' nutcase go berserk and off the geezer?"

For a moment, the older woman gazed at her intensely. Slowly she got to her feet. Made no move to depart—maybe needed to be on higher grounds.

When she finally spoke, her voice reminded Polly of a severe, yet well-meaning, old-fashioned schoolmistress. "Flipper might be psychologically challenged and may seem odd to you or others. It does not make him a killer. He—"

"C'mon, Nance! We both know the kind of things Flipper gets up to. To put other people's lives on the line is not far off from taking their lives."

"Where's your evidence of this, and how much is mere hearsay? Everyone's bias against him rests on his appearance and quirks."

"All I can say, he gives me the creeps," muttered Polly.

"Polly! I would have thought you of all people used better, less emotional, judgment," To put the offender severely into her place, the pacifist sat down again. "Only because someone suffers from mental health issues, or is different from the masses, does not make him weird or creepy. In any event, I can assure you: Flipper did not kill Ronny Rosso."

"How do you know?" No reaction. So, she hastened on, "Someone did—kill him. Might as well tell you—" God, I start to sound like the Dieken sod. Can't be helped. Dramatic pause,

Polly. Whisper for stage effect. "His real name is not Ronny Rosso."

Press 'pause' again. Do I get her full attention, or what? "Randolph Harmsen." Let's be formal about this. "A local man. Or, at least, his mother hailed from the island, and he was raised here."

Too late. The pacifist had run out of patience. Rising, she hissed, "Up to your usual tricks, Ms. Holt? Keep your nose out of this." The intensity of her glare was intimidating.

Awesome woman when aroused. Polly shivered. With a little laugh—pitifully uncertain to her own ears—she sought to justify herself.

"Preferable to get involved rather than let innocent people suffer. Talked earlier today to a couple of guys who might happily have broken the man's neck in an honest way. If they'd recognized him as their sister's seducer. When the cops realize Rosso is the Randy sod who made off with and then abandoned their sister, the two of them become everyone's favorite suspects Number One. For God's sake, a girl of fifteen, and he left her pregnant to fend for herself in India or something!"

Carried away by her own outrage, she only now noticed the other woman's vacant stare. Jeez! Not even listening. Does the fate of young girls bore her to death?

"For pity's sake, what the hell is wrong with you? I thought you cared!" Yah well, about the environment and its creatures. Never laid claim to concern about people, did she?

Blank mask in place, slender hands gripped the table. Bent forward, she said, "Don't worry your head about what I care about or not. More to the point, how did you discover such things? About—about these brothers? How come you were talking to them about such private matters?"

"Oh, a long story," drawled Polly, to avoid further questions. "Hey, you've actually seen them yourself." Argh—idiot me. Never reveal a source's identity, Polly! Of course, Nance pounced.

"What are you talking about?"

In for the whole hog. "Saw me talking to them the other night. Remember, you did dinner with Shady at *Die Krone*. The guys I sat with. Don't expect you paid any attention to—" Well, stop right here.

From far away, Nancy's gaze returned. "I only saw the back of a man and someone else hidden by the partition. Yes, I did see you, but never—" With a headshake, she ceased to speak and made to leave.

Phew, close call. Irresponsible of her to jeopardize the identity of the Harms—mentioning their names would have been unpardonable. Was it the need to still score with this woman...? At the thought of Nancy simply walking out on her, anger and exasperation rose. Why shield an asshole like Flipper? And her a pacifist who disavowed violence—effect change by peaceful means. Nice slogan. What's the use of reminding her of her vows? If you can't evoke her emotions, nothing will work.

Let's play our last card. "Nancy," her voice now pitiful little girl mode, "please." No reaction. "Friends of mine who are totally innocent are under suspicion. I warn you; I rather see Flipper burn in hell than sacrifice those dear to me." C'mon Polly, don't overdo the dramatics. It'll turn her right off.

Vain hope. Not even a semblance of listening. Back turned, the gaunt woman mumbled something like, "Got to go." After a couple of strangely awkward steps, she stopped abruptly. "Polly, stay out of this. One day you'll get burned."

Hell, does she mean, literally? Surely, not her!

Not heeding the shocked silence, Nancy scanned the far counter, ostensibly searching for someone to take money.

"Don't bother. My treat." The sarcastic tone didn't hit home either.

The front door gaped wide behind the retreating back. A sea breeze wafted in and lightened the stifling stale air of the place. No longer the self-assured woman who entered, Polly pondered. The haste gave the impression of guilt at doing a runner.

Rightly so, for shielding madhatter Flipper! Whatever she claims —her actions shout, "he did it."

Better be off. Where the heck is Mrs. Gruff? No matter how little you order, they do let you stay forever around here. Her mind idly went back to the image of Nancy's departure. Something eluded her. Staring at the entrance didn't bring it back.

A clinking sound next to her made her gaze focus sharply. The frilly white apron had materialized again *ex nihilo*. Gosh, I wish I could master that trick. One hand in the money pouch strapped below the bulging midriff, tinkling a steady stream of coins said more than words. Time's up.

Chapter 41

AGNES

Snatches of song competed with gull clamor and frantic deep barking. The famous Bob Seger tune fit the headwind perfectly. Not a bad voice he's got, thought Agnes, contemplating Karl's back a few steps ahead.

Farther down at the water's edge her mom jogged along throwing sticks for a wildly wound-up Castro. How can she be so energetic—at her age. Ouch! In mid-swipe, Agnes's fingers dropped from her face, abandoning the painful attempt to wipe off blowing sand. Like scrubbing grit paper over your—

"Aren't you enjoying our stiff north-westerly?" The amusement died in Karl's eyes. "Sorry. Are you okay?"

Dismayed at tears welling up, she nodded without convincing him.

"Let's go the other direction. Rear wind won't hurt." Helloing, he waved both arms pointing like an air traffic controller to prompt Sera to follow suit.

Relieved, Agnes's attention wandered to Polly at her side. The imp appeared morose, chin tugged in as if scrutinizing her navel. What's wrong with her today? Not three words since they picked us up. About to say so out loud, Agnes somehow was reluctant to break into such quiet reverie. Instead, she fell into companionable step with Karl, his body heat sheltering her other side. Only her tresses beat a painful staccato on her cheeks. Hands reaching up, she threaded them into a rough braid at the nape of her neck. A sideways glance caught Karl watching as if fascinated. To escape his gaze, Agnes fixed her eyes on the horizon. And stopped dead.

"Karl! We can't go—Where we found—" Lost for words, she stabbed the air at the promontory. How stupid not to have realized where they were heading.

"There, there now…" With gentle pressure, he placed his hand on her arm. "Believe me, Agnes; far better to face it on a nice sunny afternoon than to bury these awful images in your memory forever after."

"But—she—" stammered Agnes.

"Mom's alright. Doesn't miss a beat in playing with Castro."

Their sudden stop alerted Sera who, moving towards them, whistled for the dog.

"She assumes we're turning back now. Exactly what we should do, Karl." Why do I sound so pleading? Just tell him you don't want to go on, Agnes chided herself.

"Castro and I plan to elope to Nova Scotia," joked Sera and patted the shepherd's crown.

"To judge by his adoration, I'll need to lock him up to prevent it. Faithless brute, you!" He ruffled the scruff of the canine's neck. Before Agnes could say anything, he continued, "Thought we'd walk towards my place along the beach. Alright with you, Sera?" A mute exchange passed for a few seconds.

"Sound idea. Unless Agnes minds." More softly to Agnes, "Do you, dear?"

Can't chicken out now. Her mind raced. Mom beats me at everything; bravery, sensibility, tact, you name it, she's got it. Say something, you moron! Why do you act like a clot? She shook her hair; or tried to. It failed to curtain her burning face. Tied it back, didn't you?

A brief sideways hug from their male companion saved her and propelled her along. "Let's mosey on, shall we?"

Determined, Sera led the way, the pooch at heal. After a few steps, they broke into a sprint. High spirits and boundless vitality united them.

And not a single word from Polly who trotted beside them, self-contained. Odd.

Not giving her a chance to brood, Karl launched into a series of amusing anecdotes about his first year on the island. To believe him, he'd stumbled from one blunder into the next. Some locals proved helpful from the moment go, while others gleefully recorded his every misstep.

"Don't blame them. A close-knit community putting up with the tourists is tough at times, let me tell you." Headshaking, he chuckled. "An outsider who tries to prop up a rundown business is a recipe for disaster and a source of mirth. Mind you, my uncle was sort of an oddball. What could they expect of the nephew?" With a mischievous grin at her, he added, "Back in the day, yours truly was quite a sight—an unpromising wreck just like the café. Still amazes me how I managed to pull us both back from the brink." Arm stretched out, he flexed his bicep in self-mocking conceit.

After rounding the promontory, they were blissfully sheltered from the wind. Startled, Agnes found herself relaxed. The self-deprecating irony of Karl's reminiscence effectively lulled her. Only his, "Polly, all okay over there?" recalled her to the silent third. A guilty peek revealed the elf's unease; oddly, furtive glances to all sides as if expecting something to spring at her. Now she stabbed the damp cold sand with her toes. Must be freezing her feet off in the chill, Agnes realized, glad herself to be wearing trainers.

"Nay, I'm fine," murmured Polly, sounding far from well. "Only...like...don't dig them nudist..." A sullen frown at him. "I know, I know. You people over here think that's anal—"

"Literally," he guffawed.

"See," the imp said accusingly, "you're laughing at me."

"Sorry, Poll." Contrite, he mussed up her already wind-blown hair. "No worries. Need to keep Castro close now anyway. Here they come." Indeed, dog lover and best friend ran up at a trot. "Them nudes are too concerned about losing their vital parts when big brutes roam free. Keeps them at bay. The bare asses, I mean." The witticism brought on a grin from Polly. "Besides, far too chilly today. They'll be hiding behind wind-screens or are all covered up."

A sandy wet canine shook himself and rubbed his nose against his owner's leg, vigorous tail-wagging swerved his whole body. Eager to rejoin Sera who'd slung an arm around Polly's shoulder, the sound of Karl slapping his jeans-clad thigh brought him back. "Hey, buster stay close." A last regretful keening for Sera, to say "sorry, can't play with you now," and Castro fell in step with his bread- or kibble-winner. Needn't have worried, since his new friend joined them, no doubt to exchange dog-talk.

With a smile, Agnes steered the elf by the elbow to follow close behind. This way, their vision was restricted to the front. In fact, Agnes admitted to herself, encountering bare bottoms while walking with Karl would have made her terribly self-conscious. Grateful, she slipped Polly's arm through her own, squeezing it lightly. "Glad you spoke up. To think we might have blundered into this area unprepared—Bad enough on Saturday when I meandered along the fringes. Remember when we first met?" The ruse worked because Polly finally cracked her trade-mark grin.

"Yup, I sure do. What luck we connected." The elfin face illuminated by pure affection, she looked up.

Encouraged Agnes asked, "Say, Polly, did anything happen? I mean, in town? You seem so different from this morning." No answer but also no rebuff. "You seem…preoccupied."

Still, Polly stared at Karl's back. A minute or two ticked away, before she responded hesitantly, "Aggie, do you ever have the feeling there's something in the back of your mind, but it eludes you? Like…you're forgetting something but know you're forgetting it?" Impatient, she shook her head. "I'm not explaining this well."

She gazed at Agnes searchingly. "You see, this morning I talked to someone." When Agnes made to interrupt, she clarified, "No, I don't mean Kai and Udo." Her gaze strayed to the sea and became unfocused. After a moment, she continued, "Since then I've got this really intense knot in my gut—something vital escapes me."

To break the little person out of her odd mood, Agnes said with forced briskness, "No use worrying about it. Off and on it happens to me too. Say, when I'm writing a paper, it hits me—a strong conviction I'm missing something. For the life of me, I cannot pinpoint what. If I try hard to recapture it, it recedes farther. If I let it go, it usually comes back. In the middle of the night, say, or under the shower, more often than not."

Unconvinced, the elf scrutinized her. Yet she agreed, "You're probably right. Pointless to worry." As though to herself, "No idea why I'm so antsy—Doomsday looming kind of—"

"Hey, gals," a booming voice broke the spell. "Hate to interrupt girls' talk," he said in a quiet tone. "The older generation has just decided for you to head home with the hound and later come with my van for dinner at my place. Cook you something real special."

With a start, Agnes realized they had walked the lowest part of the beach well beyond the trail to the Dune Café. Way up she spotted the bench-lined platform at the mouth of the path. Furtively she glanced over to its left—where they'd found him. Horrified, she recognized it must have been exactly where now a bunch of families had pitched beach tents. Kids chased each other, throwing balls.

Interpreting her expression correctly, Karl said in level tones, "Life goes on… Sands are silent. They don't tell tales."

Chapter 42

POLLY

Hell, what a racket! Can't understand a word… So much the better. Don't wanna talk… Sera's frazzled. Too bad. He tried so hard.

The grub had been awesome. Polly stared down at her plate. Half-eaten fries swimming in fishy butter sauce. Crisp garden veggies now limp in congealed fat. Made her stomach heave. A paper napkin draped quickly over the dish committed the detritus of absent appetite to oblivion.

"May I take this?"

Cheeks on fire, she raised her eyes. "Sorry, Karl. You've done a brilliant job. No idea what's wrong with my tummy…" Need to shout for him to hear over this din.

Her eyes strayed to her companions, mother's and daughter's heads almost touching sideways over the edge of the table. Lip reading didn't work. Now Sera unobtrusively pointed to something behind Polly, a worried frown creasing her brow. When Karl bent down to remove Sera's plate, she drew his attention to whatever it was.

With a jerk, Karl straightened up and glared over Polly's head. "I'll fix him." His strong voice easily penetrated the din.

Sidling over to Agnes, Polly asked, "What's up?"

"Don't look now—the nasty cop's here—Mom says he's been staring at us."

Unable to resist the urge, Polly wriggled around for a peek. Couldn't make out anything because Karl's broad back blocked her view. To judge by his stance, he was laying down the law. Renewed laughter erupting at the bar drowned other sounds.

A moment later Karl came to pick up the tray stacked with their used dishes. "Told Eibo to stop bothering my guests. Claims they tried to reach you at the cottage several times since yesterday. Even so—none of his business now he's off duty."

Tray balanced on his right, high over his shoulder with just two fingers of his left to steady it, he yelled. "Hey, Guy, *komm mal her*!" His shout made not only his bartending buddy jump.

Without hesitation Guy abandoned whatever he was doing and came over, smiling. "Can I get you anything?"

"Nay, I'll fetch coffees. You take a break and join the ladies."

"Thought you'd never ask." Mock-sighing, he hunkered down next to Polly, while Karl bent close to instruct him quietly. With a nod, Guy slid his chair to face the Eibo person's table. How that prevents the asshole from ogling us, beats me, Polly thought.

"Cappuccino, tea, decaf?" Dishtowel whipped from Guy's shoulder to drape it over his own arm, Karl played waiter. "How about yummy ice cream for dessert for Mesdames?" He beamed at them hopefully. "Or rather cake? The daily special: brandied fruit with cream?"

"Sounds tempting. Thanks, Karl. Another time? Your delicious fries made me over-indulge tonight," said Sera, smiling her regret. "Were they home-cut?"

"You bet. Erika does them. Fish straight from the boat." His eyes swiveled to Agnes. "Surely, you don't say no to a tiny dessert?"

"Do I look such a greedy little piggy?" Before he could lodge his protest, she laughingly agreed to try the fruit. Delighted, their host withdrew.

"I hear you plan to leave us soon," his pal turned to Sera. "Did you decide where to go?"

"My daughter googled some options. Berlin tops our list."

"Yes, I saw a vacancy near *Grunewald* and one place close to *Tiergarten*," chimed in Agnes, while Guy nodded, his grin growing broader.

A sense of intense desolation welled up as Polly listened. Such eagerness to depart etched like acid drips on a fragile spirit.

"Hold on—I might have the right thing for you." Guy's excitement oddly drew her out of her misery.

"Somewhere to rent?"

"I can do far better, Sera. You can borrow mine." When the women made to demur, he raised both hands in supplication. "No, please. You'd be doing me a favor. The flat sits empty. Though, you might not like to be away from the city," he qualified apologetically. "Out in Potsdam, I mean. The *S-Bahn* connection—a surface type of subway—makes for fast commute, I find." Like an eager schoolboy, he piled on the merits.

"Ah, I love the area," an enthusiastic Sera assured him. To Agnes, she explained, "Scenic lakes and extensive parks for our relaxation, and Berlin close by for cultural stimulation—"

"There you are, then," interrupted their returning host. "Decaf for the ladies. Guy, brought you a blond," he said and unloaded a small draft. "Now the highlight," he lifted a glass dish with a high stem up in the air and offered it with a flourish for Agnes's approval. "Voila. For Mademoiselle."

"Fantastic!" A wide grin split Agnes's face.

Berries in several shades of red and blue sprinkled the whipped cream crowning a generous helping of ice cream. Potent brandy sauce or something drizzled over it, to judge by the delicious scent. Well, perhaps another day, thought Polly. If things work out okay—

"Put in a word, Karl, to convince our friends to take my place off my hands for a couple of weeks," implored Guy.

"Hey, a marvelous idea." A sound slap on Guy's back marked approval. "Terrific, man. Just the ticket. You two will adore it. A restored *Datscha* in an old-fashioned garden shared by a Villa. Huge, with trees several hundred years old, I swear." A squeeze of his buddy's shoulder, "Hope you did your laundry." Still chuckling at his own joke, he departed.

While Agnes savored every spoonful of her dessert, the three of them chatted animatedly about Berlin's must-sees. No one, it seemed to Polly, remembered her silent presence. Anxiety mounting, revved up by the cacophony of a bantering crowd—

"*Stell mich der Kleinen doch mal vor.*" The loud request to be introduced to 'the little one' cut into her mental turmoil.

Despite the casual summer outfit—checkered open-neck shirt under a beige blouson and dark chinos—the intruder's attitude screamed 'Cop!' A few schnapps too many, Polly guessed, as wafts of booze hit her nostrils. Demanding and belligerent yet slightly slurred—he'd spoken to Guy. The unfocused stare meant to intimidate only her.

At the first words, their protector had jumped up. Now he interposed his giant frame to shield her and told the obnoxious Eibo person to get lost. Towering over the cop, he pressured him through sheer physical presence to retreat out of Polly's vision. Though he tottered, the copper refused to budge.

Out of nowhere, Karl appeared at Eibo's elbow. Whatever he hissed into the man's ear made the jerk eye Karl in drunken defiance. An unintelligible growl and a menacing glare at her, and the aggressor melted into the background, lambasted by an angry proprietor. The encounter left her trembling.

"So sorry, Polly. Unforgivable to let him pester you like this." Contrite, Guy knelt to soothe her at eye level.

"Maybe we should go home," suggested Sera, her voice unsteady. "You are far from well, dear."

From her other side, Agnes leaned over and squeezed Polly's

hand that aimlessly toyed with the coffee spoon. All this solicitude made her want to bawl.

"My apologies, ladies. He won't bother you again." Returned from his knight's errand, Karl draped a gentle arm around Polly's shoulder. "You OK, pal?" Her nod did not fool him. "Bedtime, I take it. My buddy here will chauffeur you, and tomorrow you can talk housesitting arrangements with him."

"Sounds like a plan," chimed in the driver. "Whenever you're ready. I'll just go and grab the keys."

The two males had barely left when a smallish young woman with tousled multi-tone hair and a tight leather jacket over skinny jeans manifested like a specter before their table. Without a word, she pointed a very small digital camera straight at Polly's face, shooting pics like mad.

Palms covering her face in reflex, Polly yelled, "Stop it! What the heck are you doing?"

"Michy Meltau," the woman informed her in staccato, "*Abendblatt*—"

A roar drowned out the rest, "Stop! *Mach dass du raus kommst.*" More than a foot taller, Karl loomed over the reporter as he told her to get out.

Instead, she swerved the camera one-handedly at his face, not reckoning with the speed of his reaction. His right arm shot up under hers as if to grab Guy's abandoned beer glass that tottered on the table, upset in the kerfuffle. An elegant flowing move knocked the device out of her hand. With a satisfying plunk, it landed right in Polly's cold coffee.

"*Verdammte Kacke!*" The woman's surprisingly strong voice swore unladylike. "*Meine Kamera!*" As she made to rescue her camera that was half-immersed in the stale black brew, Karl beat her to it.

Apologizing profusely—which enraged her all the more—he fished it out with two fingers and holding the dripping thing high in front of him, he backed away. The reporter ignored his promises to dry it and made grabs for it by jumping up like a well-trained poodle. A number of pub regulars cheered. The noise became deafening.

"Let's leave quick," said Guy, who came hurrying back. None of them needed further prompting. A last furtive peek before ducking out of the door, Polly spotted Eibo back at the bar, his hand casually on the woman's bum. Both of them were yelling at Karl, who loudly insisted the camera had only accidentally slipped into the sink.

Chapter 43

AGNES

"So sweet of you to chauffeur us yet again this morning, Guy," Agnes heard her mom say.

"Not at all," replied their driver. "We go into town most mornings anyway. Always some—"

"Let me out here." A 'please' straggled behind in afterthought as if to apologize for interrupting. The van rolled to a stop. A mumbled thanks and Polly made to clamber out without a goodbye to anyone.

"Meet us at the Internet Café around noon," Agnes called out.

A nod like a marionette and hunched shoulders, Polly slouched off in direction of the Youth Hostel.

"What's eating her all of a sudden?" inquired Agnes of no one in particular.

In the front passenger seat, her mother's concerned eyes followed the retreating figure.

"Maybe not your morning person," volunteered Guy. "So, you want me to drop you off at the *Kurgebiet?*" he asked Sera, who nodded agreement.

Shortly after, they were strolling in the cool morning air through the park-like spa area. Quite a number of people milled about headed no doubt for massages, aqua therapy, beauty treatments, and whatnot.

"Do you want to walk on the promenade?" asked Agnes. "The sun might come—" Silly, she thought. Of course, brazing sea air in any weather marked her mom's daily reality.

Instead of the expected sarcastic rejoinder, Sera said, "I'd like to show you something, if you feel up to it."

The gentle tone filled Agnes with vague apprehension. This turned into acute cramping of her gut once Sera led them into the street of the seniors' residence. Heat rose up her neck and prickled her face. Under cover of her hair—simultaneously preparing to deny and admit—she stole a glance at her mom's immobile features.

Neither of them said a word as they passed through the rose arbor. Frenetic turmoil sparked up in Agnes's brain. Say something! Stop her! Run! Like a delinquent in chains, she moved on, step by step. This is bizarre. You revert to acting like a toddler with no control over your destiny.

Before she could muster her feeble resources to utter any refusal, they were inside. A nurse in a traditional white uniform rushed to greet them. Her face beamed goodwill and sunshine as she enthused that Ellie would be so thrilled. Visitors. And two of them, how nice!

Worst fears come true, Agnes resigned herself to her lot and determined to grin and bear. Knees shaking, or not. What's there to be afraid of? Old Mrs. Schneider is not your granny. So she's nothing to you.—The mental pep talk did nothing to ease her trepidation.

Meanwhile, their guide prattled on. A veritable living info reel. Earlier, Ellie had attended church, wheeled by a volunteer. Cheery she'd been.

Stopping to let a cleaner pass with a cart, the nurse laid her hand on Sera's arm and said confidently (in German), "You're coming at the right time. She seems unusually lucid today. Not at all like you've seen her before. Now, she's napping in the morning room," the woman added as they walked on.

Reluctantly, Agnes trailed behind, sweat breaking out on her forehead. Only dimly conscious of the corridor they traversed— eyes trained on the shiny institutional mustard green flooring to avoid catching glimpses into any open doors—the bright airiness of the room they now entered came unexpectedly.

Wide patio doors for easy wheelchair access opened onto a beautiful garden, presently cast into shade by a cloudy sky. The bumblebee yellow curtains pushed to both sides, gave the illusion of eternal sunshine. Scandinavian furniture with blue-white cushions added to the summery flair.

In stark contrast, a sour indefinable smell emanated from the shrunken, shriveled woman in front of them. What held the deteriorated frame upright in the wheelchair was anyone's guess. Dry wrinkled, bumpy turtle eyelids, tightly shut. In horrified fascination, Agnes watched a thin line of drool making its way from the sunken mouth through a dark furrow onto a hairy chin.

The nurse's cheerful voice shocked her out of her voyeurism. It took three attempts before the turtle lids rose in slow motion to reveal almost colorless, opaque eyes. Not daring to breathe, Agnes waited, stock-still. A friendly pat on Sera's arm and a reassuring "call if you need me," the matron playfully reminded Ellie to be good and left them to the quasi silence of the room.

Turtle eyes shut, the only sound issued from the labored breathing of the ancient chest. After a moment, an echo from behind penetrated Agnes's ears. Startled she whipped around to perceive two very elderly men asleep in wingchairs in the opposite corner, side by side as if in stereo-breathing colloquium. Newspapers strewn on their laps and the floor, they appeared oblivious to visitors and to the world.

A movement close at hand made Agnes turn to see her mother pull up a straight-backed chair. As if in need for protection, Agnes angled for another chair and slid in close, her view of the shrunken figure mercifully obscured. To break the tension, her mom said in a soft conversational tone, "She's always been fond of church. Not only on Sundays—I recall her going a few times a week to prayer service."

Curious, Agnes bent forward. The creaking of the chair raised the relict out of her stupor. With startling suddenness, the eyes opened to muster them intensely—drool dripping in large drops onto a bib-covered chest.

"*Hallo Ellie. Ich bin's. Fina.*"

The stare zeroed in on Sera. At first, it seemed to look right through her with no recognition of the words, 'it's me, Fina' or the name itself.

From the resignation on her mom's face, Agnes guessed that she'd given up hope that the old woman's failing mind might recall the girl who had once shared her home.

Suddenly, the cavernous face twisted into a venomous mask. In a spray of saliva, she cursed, "*Zur Hölle wirst du fahren! Sünderin!*"

Both Sera and Agnes involuntarily ducked under the force of the hate issuing from ancient lips that had screeched, 'You will go to hell! Sinner!'

With an almost inhuman effort, the shriveled body heaved to inflate itself. The feeble voice mounted to a shriek, "*Nicht mein Kind!*"

As if physically battered by the rejection implied in, 'not my child,' Sera winced. Mesmerized, she seemed unable to take her eyes from the attacker. Stunned, she slid her chair back in retreat. Agnes half-jumped up to intercede between her mom and the spewing fiend. In the background, the centenarians stirred. A strangled snore indicated one at least was sputtering back to life.

"Now, now then, Ellie," came the nurse's voice in German. She breezed in and—two capable hands pushing Ellie's chair around to face the wall—scolded mildly, "My, are we ever cross today. If we can't be nice, we can't have visitors."

Relieved, yet horrified, Agnes stifled hysterical laughter. To treat the elderly like naughty children would have outraged her at any other time.

Meanwhile, matron tut-tutted dear Ellie's behavior and insisted the elderly often lost control over what they said. Simultaneously, she hastened them to the exit, hoping they would return another time.

Neither of them spoke until they were out on the pavement, gulping crisp clean morning air.

"You know who this is, of course?" Sera asked rhetorically.

First Agnes merely nodded but then admitted, "Polly told me."

"Yes, the staff mentioned a niece came shortly after I left the other day." Garbled excuses cut short, her mother moved on.

As if in silent agreement, they walked towards the promenade. Visibly shaken, Sera did not resist when Agnes hooked an arm through hers. Once they reached the waterfront, she took a deep breath and launched into an apology for the ordeal.

"Please, Mom. None of this is your fault. You meant well. After I've bombarded you with questions about the past... So, here's one answer: There's an evil witch in our closet."

"Strictly speaking, she's not in ours," her mom matched the lighter tone. "Were you afraid she might be your grandmother?" A quizzical glance before she explained, "To set your mind at rest—Ellie was my stepmother, or more precisely, foster mother."

A pause, while Agnes scrutinized the pavement in silence.

"The sad irony is…I've come here to talk to her…before it's too late. Each visit now my hope was she might recognize me after all. But her mind is too far gone, the staff told me." Ruefully, Sera smiled at Agnes. "You know what they say, be careful what you wish for." She shuddered.

Agnes touched her hand shyly. "Mom, don't let it get to you. You heard the matron."

"Nurse was mistaken. Ellie meant every word she said. In fact, she repeated what she yelled at me when I left the island. Sometimes in my dreams, I still hear her shout that I'm a sinner —that the devil's going to take me, and I'm bound for hell."

Slowly wiping slender fingers along her brow as if to remove the cobwebs shrouding the past, she said, "I was only six or so the first time I overheard her. The image haunts me. She was chatting to a neighbor on the sidewalk outside our front door. They stopped for her to scold me for drawing with chalk on the pavement. In an aside, she said how glad she felt I wasn't her child. The neighbor cackled."

"But why did you want to come back here to see her, if she was such an awful witch already then?"

"To find closure?" As if puzzled at her own words, Sera shook her head. "When you come to my age, you like to be at peace with yourself. I wanted to ask her about Papa...how he... So, I made inquiries through the internet. A local lawyer found her for me."

After a moment, she added, "I'm so sorry to drag you into all this... Somehow, asking you on this trip into the past gave me...strength, I think."

For a while, they walked on in brooding silence. In a flash, Agnes realized her mother's constant need for movement, underscored by the rolling sounds of the waves below, helped her to come to terms with memories ebbing and flowing forth.

"To give her credit, she really loved Papa, no matter how cold and hard-hearted she appeared to me. I was the proverbial intruder. Not the lovechild she craved."

Then, a few moments later, "I called him Papa—her only Mother when he insisted—never Mama." Pausing to scan the sea, Sera's voice softened. "In secret, I fantasized. My real mother was a princess. Typical romantic notion of a little girl. Papa, I imagined, remarried after losing his beautiful bride. Evil stepmother syndrome. Too many trite fairy tales, no doubt." A wry shake of her head. "Only much later, I discovered to be a kind of foster child."

Lost in thought, they walked on at a faster pace.

A hundred yards later, she said, "One day, older children at my school teased me. They jeered Papa was not my father. He was only my uncle, they laughed. The usual cruel children thing chanting I had no father." In the cool breeze, Sera shivered.

When Agnes tried to wrap her own fleece around her mom's shoulders, she smiled in gratitude but declined. "A bit of wind will blow the sadness away."

"That day, I ran home crying and hid in the darkest corner of the garden. Papa found me. He rocked me in his arms and by and by consoled me. I would always be his Finchen, he said, and he my Papa, no matter what." Blissful joy momentarily suffused Sera's features.

The painful stab in her own gut brought a blush of shame to Agnes's cheeks. How can you begrudge her the memory of a father figure? That's rotten and mean!

Unaware of Agnes's turmoil, her mother went on, "Months later, he told me his brother and wife had died in London. I refused to listen to more. They were intruders in my life, best kept in oblivion. He never mentioned them again."

Tired or purged from unwanted memories, Sera came to a halt at one of the sheltered benches. "Let's sit for a while. The sun's indeed peeking out." Chin lifted upward to catch the wayward rays, she closed her eyes and leaned back.

For several minutes, Agnes did her best to suppress a restless urge to move or fiddle. Her mind returned to Emma's story. Why would Sera seek out Ellie who hated her instead of Emma who'd been fond of her? Maybe it's much harder to face someone we were close to than those we dislike when we left them under a cloud, she mused. Mom must have felt rotten to leave back then with people bad-mouthing her. Probably never knew whether Emma condemned her. Didn't consult her at all…

Following her own train of thought, she asked, "Did you ever see him again after you left Bosum?"

No need to say whom she meant. Beside her, Sera stiffened.

"He died when I was in my twenties." Almost too quiet, she added, "I had already killed him when I left." Now she really shuddered with cold. Rubbing her arms vigorously, she sat erect. "Time to move on."

Chapter 44
POLLY

"*Pass doch auf!! Du Trottel!*"

Frigg off! Moron yourself. Watch your own bloody step!

Tears welled up and spilled over. For a moment, the pain from the collision masked the agony hurting her head. Drowned thought.

Of their own account, Polly's feet started running again. The guy swore after her. She took to the street. Avoid the throng of bored tourists browsing storefronts. What are they all doing here anyway? Kept from the beach by the biting wind. At least they occupied her mind. Hungrily, she sucked in random images to keep others at bay.

But failed. Stills insinuated themselves stealthily. Disheveled hair falling over a bowed face. Hiding tortured desolation.

A small child, diapers showing under ladybug balloon knickers, tottered into her path. Sidestepping without breaking her run, she avoided another collision. They'd lynch me if I trampled on innocent toddlers.

She'd always avoided kids. Said they made her feel queasy. Thought she didn't like them.—A vision of walking along a beach floated back. Somewhere near Victoria in BC? Not the west coast of Vancouver Island, for sure.—They'd left again within minutes. I wanted to stay…watch them play… She was frantic to leave…

A side street opened up. Much quieter. No distractions. Run faster! If only they'll be waiting. As if they'd be her salvation— Nothing could ease the pain. Add more pain. They'll be leaving too.

Her mind's eye replayed the scene. Over and over.

Police cars—sirens blaring—surrounding the house. You'd think the noise would drum up the whole island. Only a few queued the curb when she'd got there. Not daring to go near, she'd hovered in the background.

An officer leading a woman to an unmarked car. Her hair wild. Flowing garments, an incongruously brightly flowered dress messily hanging to her feet trailed the ground. Leather thongs slapped the pavement. Reeled back when the cop woman opened the car door. Evidently disputing. Wildly shaking her head, the woman broke loose and strode away. The cop raised her hands in mute defeat. A gesture meant for onlookers. She'd done her best, it said.

The disheveled figure came towards her. Tears streaming down streaked cheeks. It was Shady alright.

Keep running. Just a little longer. And then what—

Chapter 45

AGNES

"Wow—this is amazing. You can stroll right through. Don't even need to go there."

In excitement, Agnes tilted forward in her seat.

A gurgly laugh close to her ear sounded musical. "Didn't you realize? And you a researcher."

Intent on maneuvering a narrow hallway inside the *Alte National Galerie* on the Museums Island in Berlin Center, Agnes followed the google street view arrows into the next room and zoomed in nose-close-up to a painting. "Try that in reality and alarms blare all around you," she said.

"Hope you still want to view the original."

"You bet! Simply brilliant." Cheeks aglow she twisted to grin at her mother. "I'm so glad you made me check this out."

Strolling along *Am Kupfergraben* for a panoramic view of the *Museumsinsel* across a side arm of the river *Spree,* she stopped dead. A white and green van faced her—*Polizei* blazing in prominent letters. "Can't avoid them anywhere, can you?"

"Dear, Google Street View isn't like a live webcam. No one's out to spy on you." Her mom's hand gently brushed back a strand of hair from Agnes's forehead. "Which reminds me—we need to pop by the detachment first thing tomorrow to inform them of our planned departure."

"Hope they'll let us go," grumbled Agnes.

"I'm sure they have no reason to prevent us. Shall we check out Potsdam now or leave a surprise element? As a kid you hated sur—"

"No worries, Mom. I did grow up a little—in some respects."

For a brief moment, Sera's arm rested around her shoulder as she asked, "Will you mind terribly leaving so soon? To part with new friends is never easy." Wistfully, she continued, "Remember in senior kindergarten—the time Rachel went away for half a year when Michael was on sabbatical in Athens, and—"

"Mo—om! That's—what—thirty-some-odd years ago. I—" A stab of anticipated loss burned into her guts.

"Darling—there's no shame in our emotional attachments and in missing friends. Our Polly is a sweet person—I'll truly miss her." As if expecting the imp to materialize, her glance strayed to the window of the Internet Café. "Karl and Castro too." With a mischievous smile, she teased. "One senses a certain fondness for you."

The last thing Agnes wanted to contemplate—so she plunged recklessly into yet more dangerous territory. "You're not angry with Polly?"

"You mean for checking up on me?" Trust Sera to use diplomacy. "No, one can't blame her for being naturally inquisitive."

"Curiosity is not only her middle name by nature but also professionally," responded Agnes without thinking. "Never told you what I discovered on the Web the other day. Our Polly happens to be a freelance writer. Mostly publishes on environmental and social issues. Want me to show you?"

"No thanks. I prefer to take her at face value."

"Well, no personal info popped up anyway—zillions of Polly Holts and no Google image—"

"*Heh, mach mal langsam!*" As if in defiance of the injunction to slow down, a door slammed, followed by clattering of cans. The stack of coke at the entrance, Agnes surmised and reluctantly dragged her eyes from the screen.

Both arms extended, her mother hastened to the storefront. In disbelief, Agnes witnessed a panting and tear-stained Polly hurl herself into Sera's embrace, like a wounded puppy seeking refuge in her owner's lap. What the hell ailed the imp?

With soothing murmurs, Sera tried to calm both a distraught Polly and the guy who ran the café. After realizing how upset the culprit was, he quietly began to restack the pile.

Unsure and timidly, Agnes approached. Such situations tended to render her helpless and useless. Like students who failed a course breaking down in tears in her office. Beyond the inane "are you okay?"—obviously she wasn't—not much came to her benumbed mind.

Practical as always, her mother took the reins. "Settle the bill please and meet us across the street behind the church." Not waiting for a reply, she guided the sniffling elf, holding her close and mouthing apologies to the guy who said not to worry.

In haste, Agnes logged out of the computer and grabbed their backpacks. The twenty Euro bill she proffered to the store attendant, still on his knees chasing errant cans, caused him to throw up both hands and wriggle them in tune to his protestations of 'too much.' The money dropped on the counter, she tried to rush out.

"*Hier, nimm die,*" he held out three Coke cans.

Instead, her eyes fell on a glass teapot stewing away on the counter. Visions of strong black tea with tons of sugar as a shock remedy surfaced. "*Einen Tee, bitte.*" For once the German came unbidden.

A minute later she crossed the road, cradling a large paper cup, glad to escape his profuse concern for her friend.

A black wrought-iron gate almost hidden by ivy and overhanging trees appeared a likely means to access the area behind the church. As she pushed through, she found herself in an overgrown, timeworn churchyard. Well, what a perfect place to bring someone who's upset and crying, she thought. Then the utter calm and silence of the cemetery—broken only by a startled bird who resented the midday intrusion—engulfed her. Not such a bad place after all.

There they were, on a bench—under a weeping willow tree, of all things, appropriate for the occasion. With an uncomfortable sense of breaking a sacred peace, she went to join them. Polly's agonized cry, "I killed her," brought her to a dead halt.

Chapter 46

Muffled, as if issuing from the chest to which she clung like bindweed, Sera's voice—thanking Aggie—reached her. Polly burrowed into the arms cradling her.

Gentle fingers raised her reluctant chin. "Take a sip, Polly dear. Careful. Quite hot."

Super sweet black tea eased her throat, making her unbearably greedy for more. Tears trickled down her nose onto her lips, adding salt to the sweetness. Tiny sips demanded all her concentration—preempting a need to face anyone or anything. When she came up for a breath, a tissue gently dabbed her burning cheeks. Of its own accord, her body straightened, shedding the urge to be propped up.

No one spoke. Blissful, leafy silence smelled earthy dank of decaying vegetation.

A desire to share. Pass on the burden. Impossible. Vocalize to turn memory into objective reality. The voice, flat like a mechanical recording, gained breathless momentum once unfettered.

"Nancy McLennon is dead. Found by Shady. Nine-thirty this morning in a bathtub filled with bloodied water. Wrists slashed. Pills too. The bottle empty on the tiled floor. Uncertain how many she took. On medication for years—suffered from anxiety attacks. I'd forgotten. Called 110, Shady did."

"Polly, who is Shady? Who are these people?" Only now Polly became aware of Agnes's restlessness.

"Don't rush her, Agnes," said Sera, soothing like around an invalid. "She'll explain all in good time."

Stung, Polly tried to pull herself together.

"Remember the leader of the pacifist environmentalists? Spoke at the demo. When you arrived here. She's called Nancy. Shady's her sidekick. Nance and me go back a long time." Her expression hardened into a mask of defiance; she said, "A brief affair. I was eighteen." Searching for signs of disgust, she met confusion in Agnes's eyes. "Didn't work out. We stayed kind of uneasy—well, really long-distance—friends."

Boundless support and tranquility emanated from Sera.

Wearily, she continued, "Anyway. Shady had a key to the apartment Nancy rented. The two arranged to meet at the Youth Hostel at eight-thirty this morning. When Nancy didn't show, Shady figured she'd overslept and went to rouse her. They'd tons to do, like coordinating further action."

A shudder shook Polly's whole body. One arm hugging her tightly, Sera's other hand brought the cup with a remnant of tepid tea to her lips.

After a couple of sips, she managed to say, "Told you already what she found." Several gulps of air steadied sufficiently to weave her tale.

"Police swarmed the place. I stayed in the background. My gut sensed it involved Nancy. First thought they meant to arrest her. Only when Shady came out—" Again she choked up. Sera rightened the cup gliding from her grip. Surprised, Polly's mind registered its presence in her own hand. A few last drops did nothing to open up her cramped throat. Silently, Agnes offered a water bottle.

"Unforgivable," she forced herself to go on, "not to realize much sooner. Anxious and fretful I've been since I talked to

Nancy. Something bothered me. An image lurked at the back of my mind yet refused to take shape. Like a dunce, I got it all wrong, Aggie." Eager for her friend to recognize the magnitude of her folly, she clutched at her hand. "Suspected Flipper and read all the evidence through a distorted lens. All at once, last night in the dark, up there stargazing, everything fell into place—"

"Polly, please." In frustration, Agnes's voice vibrated. "I don't understand. Please! What are you talking about? Who's Flipper?"

With a sense of resurfacing from a dream, Polly sought to bring Agnes into focus. Leaden fatigue numbed her body. Exhausted, her brain stuttered to a halt. "Never mind. Not important." All her remaining strength barely sufficed to raise the water bottle once more to her lips—to find it drained.

"Not important? How can you stop—"

"Agnes, please, don't shout. Let's stay calm." To placate, Sera raised herself up between them.

In a final effort to pull herself together, Polly gulped for breath.

"You're right, Aggie. After all you've been through, you deserve an explanation. Last night, I realized several things. First off, remember the photo I showed Dieken? The guy sneaking away from the fire? Everyone calls him Flipper."

While she spoke, Sera shifted, only to suppress the restiveness when Polly hastened on, "An animal rights activist on the FBI's 'wanted' list, because of some crazy stunts with tons of property damage. The pic reminded Karl of what Erika claimed about a person going down to the beach. The night Rosso was murdered."

Another sharp intake of breath from Agnes's patient mom. As much to express her regret as to seek comfort, Polly leaned into the older woman's side, mumbling, "Didn't mean to hold out on you. Too complicated to untangle now... I promise, one day..."

A surprisingly strong arm hugged her close in response and encouraged her to pick up the thread. "In the scene, people view Flipper as an unpredictable loose cannon. To confirm my suspicions, I confronted Nancy with the shots of him as arsonist. Pretty well said he murdered Rosso. Reacted oddly the whole time, she did. Then insisted flatly, she could tell me for certain, Flipper did not kill him. Alarm bells should have gone off—"

Shivers ran through Polly. To stifle them, she stared into the green canopy above. Their shelter, she only now perceived, was a weeping willow. How bloody ironic... The incongruous surrounding penetrated her awareness—lichen-covered gravestones, some crumbling with the onslaught of centuries of salt air. Let's bury the dead, once and for all; she sighed.

"A mental snapshot of Nance leaving the café yesterday morning flashed back last night—fusing with the images of Flipper and Erika's mysterious dune prowler. Yet—Nancy kill Rosso? Unthinkable."

"Why? Totally opposed to his scheme—she might want him out of the way—permanently," said Agnes.

"Because she is adamant about non-violent activism. Split publicly from the ELFs to disassociate her own organization from the wild cards using violent means." To Sera, she explained, "The Earth Liberation Front."

"Yes, I read about them."

"I'm so confused. Did this Flipper person murder Rosso, after all?"

"No, Agnes, Nancy did." Over her listeners' frustration, she hastened on, "She left a note, amounting to a confession."

"Why didn't you say so right away," exploded Agnes, "instead of claiming as a pacifist she wouldn't—"

"Because she did not kill him as a pacifistic activist—"

"You're splitting hair!" interrupted Agnes.

"No—she killed because she's Sandy Harms." Into Agnes's stunned silence, she said, "The girl Rosso took off with from this island—"

"Yeah, give me some credit. I'm not totally senile." Under her mother's restraining gesture, she calmed enough to ask, "How come you think she's Nancy. Or Nancy is her, or whatever?"

A worried glance at their silent onlooker before committing any more blunders brought no help. Sera merely observed, serious yet detached. How much to reveal in front of her? Avoid Rosso's real name, for sure. Don't want to open up old wounds, Polly fretted. Coward, she accused herself. Inevitable—If I'm right...

Aloud, Polly said, "Here's what I figure, Aggie. Mind you, only in retrospect. Last night, my brain spit out jumbled bits and pieces. After a while, they crystallized into the better hypothesis. First off, she's the right age. She speaks German. You heard her speech on Friday at the rally. Didn't strike me at the time as unusual, because I knew she loves languages. Yesterday at the café, she responded to the waitress who spoke German—"

"At the demo," interrupted Agnes, "she fumbled for words a few times and talked with a heavy American accent. Besides, the brothers described the Harms girl as blond and overweight. Basically, even if—your reasoning doesn't add up to anything. Fits countless people."

"Not the point, Aggie. Don't forget—she admits to killing him. The motive matters to me."

The catch in her voice prompted Sera to pass another bottle of water from her knapsack. Unscrewing the lid, Polly took several gulps—glad for the break.

"Way back when, Nance drove me nuts about gaining weight. Never touched fast food or high-calorie stuff—total health freak. What if she'd been obese at some point and shunned revisiting fat street? Kai said Sandy dyed her hair blond to please Rosso and used to be slim before she took up with him. Why would Nancy be so passionate about this island? Lobbied and mobilized like crazy for this cause. Little Bosum's kind of out of the way for a BC-based activist, don't you think?

Plus, I recalled she's not a native of Canada's West Coast either —migrated up from California."

As she piled on more, she went into overdrive. Not heeding signs of hyperventilation, she raced on, intent only on spilling all her mind had conjured up in the deep of the night.

"No stranger to India, I figure. Yoga and meditation day in day out tied herself up in knots, I tell you. Trained with a true guru when young—the real thing, she said. Always assumed she meant in California—quite the fashion back then. Now I think she hinted at Goa more likely, or wherever Rosso took Sandy. I knew she'd traveled when young and lived on her own forever. One of the things that didn't work out for us. Neither of us excelled at cohabitation. Nor at steady relationships—"

Memories welled up like tears, choking her vocal cords.

Chapter 47

AGNES

The agony in Polly's face sent shivers along Agnes's skin. Trust Sera to take charge and fold the elf into an embrace. This way, we never reach the end of the story, she thought in impatience and shifted uncomfortably on the bench. A noisy intake of breath and a sigh escaped her. At least it made the imp rally and pick up her tale in mid-stream.

"Avoided little kids like the plague, Nance did. Just assumed she loathed them. Now I believe she couldn't bear the sight of them happily at play or coming up to her. All would make sense if she'd lost her own. Remember, the bastard left Sandy when pregnant? Dieken said so."

The reasoning appeared still too sloppy for her liking. Yet, Agnes nodded as Polly took another swig from the water bottle.

"What hurts the most, you see, I pushed her. Told her, shielding Flipper harmed innocent people. Like a moron, I went on about Sandy and her brothers and claimed the brothers would be prime suspects once the cops figured out Rosso's real name. Can you imagine how she felt? Her kid brothers taking the rap? Again? It unhinged her. Drove her to slash her wrists. To protect Kai and Udo. After what she did to them—abandoning them—"

"That doesn't mean you killed her!" broke in Agnes. The way Polly regarded her, brought a burning flush of realization to her cheeks. The automatic inference served as an accusation in disguise.

"I mean—I caught your words when I came with the tea," Agnes stumbled in irrelevant explanation. "The woman's sense of guilt drove her to—to suicide." The harsh word hung in the still air. Almost superstitiously, Agnes eyed the dank graves around them.

"A religious person might say it's between me and my maker. Since I lack faith, my conscience insists I might have saved her if I'd been faster."

"No, Polly." With quiet authority, Sera went on, "No one can save another. The trite truism holds; we all make our own mistakes and pay for them eventually." The fingers interlinked in her lap absorbed her attention. Despite the lack of visible clues, Agnes sensed she must be thinking of her Papa.

After several moments, her mother's gaze rose to seek Polly's who'd started to fidget. "One thing I would like to know. What was the man's real name?"

The imp hesitated, and Agnes cut in, "Mom, we better—"

"Let me simplify matters." Panic in their expressions, they both followed her words as if hypnotized. "Yes, I do appreciate your concern for me. Rosso was Randy Harmsen, wasn't he?"

Dejectedly, they nodded, not meeting each other's glance.

"At the event on Friday, his general bearing reminded me of the past. Too absurd, too farfetched to be true, I thought. Yet, something about him—the swagger—the brazenness and big-mouthed confidence, triggered memories. Later at the Tea House, the conviction grew. One never does forget a first love, they say, no matter how ill-advised and doomed to cause pain to others—"

The voice sounded so forlorn, Agnes's throat constricted. The elf just enveloped Sera in her skinny arms.

"No need to talk about me, though," said Sera, recovering her poise. Gently, she stroked Polly's hair.

"But, Mom, if you recognized him, wouldn't you recognize Sandra Harms too?"

"I don't recall a girl—"

"Not likely, you should," interrupted Polly. "Sandy was far younger than your mom, Aggie. A mere kid when Sera left—" She broke off and covered her mouth.

"I am not going to ask how you discovered so much about me. Back then, some Harms lived on the island. Not an uncommon name along the coast. First names I do not recall offhand. In any event, can we continue this conversation another time? The bench makes my back act up—sitting so long—"

Both Polly and Agnes broke out simultaneously, "I'm sorry, careless of—" "*Jeez*, didn't think—" until Sera's raised hand stopped them in mid-profession.

"Not to worry. A little exercise will set me straight. Literally." She smiled and tousled Polly's wispy hair. "The main thing; are you feeling better, dear? Can you manage now?"

For her part, Agnes considered another question more pressing. "Are you going to share all this with the police, Polly?"

A shifty glance from one to the other, before the imp muttered, "Nay, I don't do police. Besides—" She paused, then appeared to come to a decision. "Need to wait and see what happens. My gut tells me Nancy won't leave unfinished business behind. Wouldn't want the cause to suffer through her personal actions."

By now, Agnes's head felt like mush. Something deeply incoherent about Polly's reasoning nagged her. Not being quite conscious of speaking out loud, she tried to pinpoint the flaw.

"How can she be nonviolent and shun killing qua environmental activist, yet kill qua shunned teenager? Decades after—"

"Could we not postpone this discussion?" Sera got up. "Clearly we are not likely to ever understand what prompted the woman to kill against her convictions." Abruptly, she changed the subject. "What is next then for you, Polly?"

"Me? I'll hop on the four o'clock ferry," said the elf carelessly. "In fact, got to run to grab my gear, don't I?"

"What? You are leaving us today?" Stunned, Agnes became breathless in outrage. Desolate—abandoned—anguished.

"Aren't you leaving as well?" Her eyes challenged Agnes as she threw out, "Never like to be the one left behind."

"But—but—" Lost for words, Agnes faltered. With renewed effort, she groped for reasons. "What about the police? What if they ask us about the fire? What about those guys you saw? If Dieken tells the cops—You can't just leave us so sudden like…" Her mental engine running out of fuel, she petered off. A desperate sense of acting ridiculous pervaded her. She swiped viciously at the tears that refused to be held back.

Making it all worse, the elfin body hugged close—like a little child trying to appease an angry parent. Through a roaring in her ears, Agnes thought she heard a soft murmur, "Love you even more when you're passionate…"

Briskly stepping back, Polly said aloud, "If need be, give the cops my number. I'm not on the run but got work to do."

"Will we meet again?" asked Sera and clasped both Polly's hands into her own.

"If you still want to after all this blows over… Yes, somewhere where nothing much happens." A lopsided impish grin. "Here, got a scrap of paper?"

From her knapsack, Sera withdrew a sketchbook and pencil. The pad against her knee, Polly scribbled in a corner of the last page. "My email address. In a few weeks, if you feel sure, email me." Both hands free, she clung to Sera who kissed the top of her head.

"Take good care of yourself, Polly."

"You bet." Uncertain, the imp faced Agnes.

Conflicting emotions churning her insides; Agnes was torn.

Against her will, her arms reached out and pulled Polly close. Wordlessly.

A murmured 'forgive me,' and the next second Polly ran off. Stopped, however, immediately to call back, "Thank Karl for me and buy a huge bone for Castro."

The gate—now bathed in an errant ray of late midday sunshine—swung shut behind her.

A stabbing sense of loss, infused with impotent anger, made Agnes want to stamp her foot like a toddler on the verge of a gigantic tantrum.

Epilogue
AGNES

The phone intoned a discreet old-fashioned purr.

"Could you get that please, Agnes?" her mom called out from the kitchen. Serene and mellow from a long shower, Agnes grabbed the heavy black receiver with her left while clutching the bath towel closed with her right hand. For a breathed 'hallo,' she mustered her best German pronunciation.

"Hey. Instant service." The masculine voice intensified the glow on her cheeks. "Were you waiting for a poor working guy to give you a buzz?"

"Oh, I hate to rob you of any illusions, Karl—just happened to cross the hallway." With a satisfied grin, she pulled up the three-legged milking stool next to the plain rustic oak stand holding the ancient black rotary phone. Though Guy's bedside commode held a portable, she loved the solid heaviness of this Bakelite relic. It certainly made you sit down to enjoy a chat. The intricate colorful piece of contemporary art on the opposite wall contrasted effectively and invited contemplation.

"What's up?" After their conversation the night before, she didn't expect him to ring again so soon. In fact, he and Guy checked in on them every other day. Not that she minded in the least. Bare feet tucked under to escape the cold creeping up from the Mexican tiles, she wondered whether to ask him to wait for her to put on some clothes. Too ambiguous—

"Won't keep you long. Today, I mean." A chuckle echoed down the line. "Log in to Guy's computer and check your email. Sent you a link to an article you want to read."

"Thanks, Karl. Much appreciated." The hollow phrase conveyed disappointment rather than gratitude and prompted him to laugh.

"Yeah—reading articles during your well-deserved vacation might not thrill you. Trust me, this one you'll find worth your immediate attention."

"Stop beating around the bush or whatever." Still, he hesitated. "Tell me what—"

"An exclusive on the murder. Gotta run now. Talk to you Monday morning." In a rush to hang up, he hastened on, "Am curious what you think of the piece—and the author."

"Wait!" Reluctant to revisit what she believed to be a closed chapter safely left behind on Bosum, she didn't want to end the call on this note. "What about—"

"Right you are. Almost forgot—all set for your last weekend. Our Erika's ready to pet sit the brute. Expect me and Guy on the Friday. If you guys—pardon me—you ladies share the larger bedroom for a couple of nights, buddy and I can crash in the spare."

"Mom and I better take the smaller one with the twin beds, Karl."

"Are you kidding! Us males in the French bed together? Not on your life!"

The mock outrage made her laugh. "Okay, no worries. I'll tell Sera."

"Perfect. Give my love to your mom and happy holidaying!"

After cradling the receiver, she realized how effectively he had diverted her from what they'd been talking about.

From the kitchen door, salad spin in hand, her mother smiled. "Our friend Karl?"

"Yes, he sends his love."

"You sound preoccupied. Is anything wrong?"

"Not sure—wants me to read something… On the murder."

"Oh," was the only response. Her mom's tone said the rest. An intake of breath and straightening her upper body, she turned back to the counter. "Lunch in fifteen minutes. Afterward, we can take the subway to Berlin Center—unless you change your mind."

"Yes, of course. Well, first my dish duty," said Agnes bewildered and decided to dress before heading for Guy's desk in the living room.

Logged in shortly after, the email instructed, "Check this out (they also publish a German version on their main site)—talk soon—Karl," and provided a link to a page of one of the major weeklies' English edition. Legs crossed and hunched over, she read:

Much Wind About Nothing, By Maggie Vendetta

[Must be a direct translation of '*viel Wind um nichts*' with a Shakespearean twist…, Agnes mused in passing. The author's name didn't mean anything to her.]

It's been a stormy time on Bosum, an East-Friesian island usually known for its sedate ambiance. A proposed wind farm project is tearing the sleepy island asunder.

Tensions climaxed Monday of last week when Canadian tourists stumbled upon a dead body on the *FKK* (nudist) beach. Police identified the gruesome early morning discovery as the body of Ronny Rosso, a representative of the wind energy company, *Niederwinder & Co*.

Rosso's death put a sudden temporary stop to his company's application to erect a *WKA* (wind power installation) on Bosum. Police soon suspected foul play. Suspicion fell on the various groups of environmental activists that had joined anti-wind protests on the island. Many of them saw Rosso as the driving force behind the *WKA* project and became his vocal opponents. Yet local authorities released no names of anyone helping police with their inquiries.

This Sunday, news began to circulate that Nancy McLennon had admitted to the crime in a suicide note. The well-known activist took her own life Saturday night by slashing her wrists.

Her assistant Shawndra Fitzpatrick discovered the body —gruesomely immersed in bloodied water—Sunday morning in the bathtub of a rental apartment on Bosum.

Justice was meted out, many said. McLennon's death ended the hunt for the killer of Ronny Rosso. Thus, the killer, as expected, was an environmental activist, one of Rosso's fierce opponents. Case closed.

Yet many questions remained unanswered. A note—
pinned to a sweater found neatly folded on a bath stool
—puzzled not only police. For it read:

"More sorry than words can tell. Not for his death.
Don't think I betrayed you all in killing Rosso. I'll
explain."

Who was it addressed to? Who is the 'you?' What was
the betrayal? Most of all, where is the explanation?
None showed on the note—a slip of paper far too small
to provide any elucidation.

Her own circle felt even more puzzled than the police.
Friends and activist comrades esteemed Nancy
McLennon as the co-founder of the pacifistic environ-
mental group PPS (Pacifist Planet Savers).

Was the note addressed to them? What is more, why
would a pacifist environmentalist kill a foe over an environmental issue? Thus far, no information on how the
deed was committed leaked to the public. Much is left to
speculation.

Many of us recall the headline in one of our most
popular daily tabloids. "WIND KILLS AGAIN,' it
screamed. The article insinuated that Rosso died for his
belief in wind power. By citing a number of turbine
accidents, its author sought to show that wind energy
kills.

At the end of the day, all this proves to be much wind
about nothing. Rosso's death had nothing to do with the
much-protested wind turbine project. Nancy McLennon

did not betray her environmental beliefs. Nor did she betray her environmental pacifism.

As many pacifists before her, she ultimately discovered that she was human, all too human. For a few moments in her life, she was overcome by a primeval urge. An urge for retaliation. A Hobbesian moment, perhaps, where the right of nature is unfettered from the bounds of any rational law of nature that enjoins humans to seek peace.

What happened at the foot of the dunes on this lonely stretch of beach that fateful Sunday night?

Soon, Nancy herself will tell all in her final posthumous public appearance. Her *apologia*, we might call it, a defense speech in a Socratic vein.

Sources able to preview the YouTube video—set to be released at 2:00 AM Monday night, exactly two weeks after Rosso's death—reveal that McLennon lays no claim to any lofty rationale for her deed.

In part, it was self-defense. Rosso, completely intoxicated, tried to sexually assault her on a lonely beach in the middle of the night. Admittedly, she could have defended herself against the drunken aggressor and fled to the nearby Dune Café.

In part, it was retaliation. McLennon and Rosso shared a past history. They were both raised on the island. Born in London, Rosso came to live with a relative on Bosum as a young child. A native of Bosum, many years his junior, Nancy fell in love with Rosso. She was only a teenager.

They call it puppy love. Infatuated, she ran away with him. Still a minor, she followed him to India. There he left her. Five months pregnant. Sick and almost destitute.

She survived. The baby didn't. The life-threatening illness caused a miscarriage. A kind Indian woman nursed her with the help of two compassionate Americans. They eventually enabled her to get to the States and to a new identity.

Perhaps it was Rosso's undoing that he forgot her. She certainly never forgot him. Did she meet him with revenge in mind? She believes she didn't. She hoped to persuade him—out there in nature under the starry sky —that his scheme would destroy this serene island refuge for countless creatures.

Drunk and lecherous to the end, Rosso never recognized her—until perhaps in the final moments when she pressed his face into the sand. Unable to let go, she told him then.

Did he hear her? Or did he die in a drunken stupor without ever knowing who and what killed him?

Nancy McLennon did not regret the death of an irresponsible lecher. But she deeply regretted killing. It violated her innermost principles. She never betrayed her environmental beliefs or her comrades. Much worse than a betrayal of pacifist convictions, it was the final self-betrayal. Only her own death might atone for that.

Editor's Comments:
We will publish the link to the YouTube video, announced by Nancy

McLennon, on our website as soon as it becomes available to the public.

Watch for more sensational revelations in the sequel to Maggie Vendetta's article in next week's edition.

Also Interesting:
"Application for Controversial Wind Farm Withdrawn"
"Police fail to nab arsonists after tip-off"

Stunned, Agnes sat back. Any sense of time in abeyance while immersed in the tale, she felt disoriented. The closing of the fridge door penetrated the silence. Then clattering of dishes. To dislodge the fuzz clouding her brain, she shook her head vigorously, only to induce dizziness. One hand pressed against the desktop, she rose, heavy as if suddenly twice her age. For a moment she stood still to let the wooziness pass. A cold drink should help. Or a stiff one. Not her thing at all. At least one vice she ran no danger of falling prey to.

In slow steps, she joined her mother, who arranged freshly sliced bread in a basket. One glance at her and her parent proffered a glass of cold water.

"Should I make a strong tea? You appear in need of sustenance."

After the first long gulps, Agnes nodded. "Let me brew some while you go and read it too."

"Honestly dear, I don't think I'm—Not right now. Before lunch—" Unlike her usual self, her mother groped for excuses.

"Please, Mom. Do it for me." A dirty trick.

Without another word Sera gave her one last doubtful look and reaching for her glasses on the counter, she went into the living room.

Drained, Agnes plopped down at the scrubbed pine table, set for lunch for two. A beautiful vista through the uncurtained patio door opened onto a flagstone terrace and old-fashioned garden fully abloom. The glass door—tilted open at the top—transmitted the twitter of an insistent bird in the ancient chestnut tree. The weather today proved too cool to eat outside. On the morning after their arrival, they had breakfasted in the sun, amazed at the peaceful atmosphere. One might completely forget being close to a huge city.

Her eyes swept the minimalist kitchen. Its contemporary style utterly soothed. If only life would be thus in order. The restored *Datscha* as a whole appeared to her a most relaxing place. Every piece carefully selected, its interior breathed comfort and ease. You just wanted to curl up on a rainy day and watch the world go by. Absentmindedly, Agnes started to nibble from the large salad bowl placed at the center of the table.

"Not with your fingers. We do have forks." She might have sworn her parent spoke. No sound from the living room yet. As she'd grabbed a fork to attack in earnest, the computer played its shutdown tune. Fork in hand, she waited.

Unconcerned Sera entered and strode to the counter to fetch a tray loaded with bread, butter, and fresh herb cheese. Without speaking, she went back to turn on the electric kettle, all forgotten by Agnes in her reverie. Mugs pulled out from an upper cabinet, she said, "Grab a carton of milk from the fridge, please. Earl Grey alright, or do you prefer Orange Pekoe, or—"

"Mo—om!" Aware of drawing out the vowel like a petulant child, Agnes tried to moderate her tone to ask, "What did you make of it? Who's behind this article?"

Teapot raised, Sera stopped. "Surely, Agnes, that's a rhetorical question." Teabags from a red box plopped in—choice made—she added boiling water. "The real question is: Can you forgive her?"

Somehow her words came as a relief. Buoyed, Agnes rose to root out the milk. Her glance fell on a *Guide to Berlin* on the counter next to the fridge. The open page showed a heading, *Pergamon Museum*. A photo of the famous Pergamum altar with its impressive stairs and friezes greeted her. The image fueled joyous anticipation. And Karl and Guy would be coming soon too.

Loads lighter, she returned to her seat and selected a thick slice of rustic bread. As she smothered it in creamy fresh herbal cheese, Sera placed a steaming mug in front of her. Biting into her bread while whitening her tea with her other hand, Agnes considered. Only after her first long sip did she answer.

"Ask me again in a few weeks. More to the point; can we please start all over now and enjoy our holidays?"

Get your next Agnes Taylor Mystery today
amazon.com/dp/B099436TY2?

Follow me on
amazon.com/author/evabernhard

EB Press Release

BREAKING NEWS

LOUISE PENFOLD MYSTERIES

DEATH AT ROSEWOOD MANOR

CASCADE GAZETTE — SPECIAL REPORT

A condolence card delivered before its time has unsettled new resident Louise Penfold. Locals say the freelance editor, recently moved from the city, has uncovered troubling circumstances around the recent death of a well-known Cascade resident.

Authorities remain tight-lipped, but whispers suggest secrets at Rosewood Manor may prove darker than its fresh paint.

DEATH AT EAGLE ROOST

HURON DAILY CHRONICLE

Thanksgiving festivities at the lakeside estate Eagle Roost turned tense when visiting editor Louise Penfold and companion Nora Norton encountered a household rife with quarrels.

Sources describe strained relations among guests and hosts. Penfold, already linked to past investigations, is said to be watching closely as unease grows by the hour.

MORE INFORMATION AT AMAZON.COM/DP/B0FR9TDN2T?

Fictional press release prepared by EB Press. Events described are from the Louise Penfold Mysteries series.

Louise Penfold Mysteries are available as
eBooks and in standard font editions at
amazon.com/dp/B0FR6M4CTL?
For Large Print editions go to
amazon.com/dp/B0FR9TDN2T?

The Perfect Gift...

Treat yourself and Loved Ones and tell your Friends about the Agnes Taylor Mystery series

Standard Font and eBook Editions
amazon.com/dp/B099436TY2?
amazon.co.uk/dp/B099436TY2?
amazon.ca/dp/B099436TY2?

LARGE PRINT – AGNES TAYLOR MYSTERIES

amazon.com/dp/B0D8K71ZMM
amazon.ca/dp/B0D8K71ZMM
amazon.co.uk/dp/B0D8K71ZMM

My sincere thanks for your support!
Stay in Touch
amazon.com/author/evabernhard

Acknowledgments

A writer rarely works in isolation. There are so many kind people who directly or indirectly help in our creative pursuits. I thank you all from the bottom of my heart!

Foremost, I would like to thank you, my reader, for choosing my books. I hope you enjoy our creative ride into the fictitious world of mystery.

The support of friends, neighborly friends, and beta and ARC readers means so much to me. My awesome editor, Pam Clinton, keeps me on my toes. (Of course, any remaining stylistic choices and editorial idiosyncrasies are mine.)

A big hug to my son, who is always only a text message away when I want to toss around some ideas. His support means the world to me.

Last and not least, what would a writer do without a furry friend? My trusty canine is right by my side, patiently watching me plotting and writing away.

A hearty thanks to all of you!

Eva Bernhard is a member of Crime Writers of Canada.